THE

FIERY BOYS

Sage Ardman

Fame series #1

R.L. Ranch Press

Portola Valley, California

Books by Sage Ardman

The Westerley Series:

#1: *Executive Sweet*

#2: *I'll Get You My Pretty*

#3: *Seductive Synchronicity*

The Fame Series:

#1: *The Fiery Boys*

#2: *Rock Con Roll*

The Fiery Boys

Acknowledgments

This book was shaped significantly by Amy Lansky, my publisher, editor, collaborator, close friend, and so much more.

My other editor, Jena Roach, continues to push me to do better. She takes my unpolished ideas and makes them sparkle. Thanks also to Mark Manasse and Izaak Rubin who gave the book a final cleanup.

Diogo Landô did a great job on the cover art.

Finally, thanks go to the Fiery Boys for writing some memorable tunes. Those of you who were around back when the band was hot will surely remember their hit single, "Fiery Life." If you missed it and can't find it on any of the oldies channels, you can still find the song on this book's website: sageardman.com/FieryBoys.html. Thanks go to Gregory Jones for sending me a copy of this wonderful old song.

Table of Contents

Fiery Life

by Fiery Boys

The engine's rumble, the speed,
The drive to break out, the need,
The push to prove it, your creed.

    Living by a precipice,
    Dancing on the blade of a knife,
    Liberty means so much more,
    The promise, the promise of a fiery life.

The winding road draws your prowls,
It grabs for your heart, and growls,
With blood on its bed, it howls.

    Living by a precipice,
    Dancing on the blade of a knife,
    Liberty means so much more,
    The sorrow, the sorrow of a fiery life.

Honor the fallen with depth,
Live and remember each death,
Burn the life bright with new breath.

    Living by a precipice,
    Dancing on the blade of a knife,
    Liberty means so much more,
    You owe it, you owe yourself a fiery life.

The Fiery Boys

One

I never found out what happened on Kira's tragic date last night. We were about to hear the grisly details when she stopped, mid-sentence, staring across the room at the television over the bar. Jo and I traded looks of confusion as we waited for her to go on, but Kira was elsewhere. As she sat there, transfixed, her face lit up, brighter and brighter.

I turned to look at the television behind me, but it was just the same basketball game that the other screens were showing. I looked all around the bar, trying to figure out what would explain this sudden delay of gossip. Then I turned back to Kira and examined her more closely. I wondered if I'd find a tranquilizer dart sticking out of her neck, or rays of light streaming down from an alien spaceship. Anything that could explain why last night's dismal date was now forgotten. To paraphrase the announcers at the end of Elvis's concerts, Kira had left the building.

Jo waved a hand in front of our friend's blank eyes. "Hello! What's going on?"

That snapped her out of it, and she turned to us with a hard gasp. "Oh my God! This is too good to be true." She yanked out her phone and started to work it like a video game. This only made her more excited. Did Kira just win the lottery? Maybe she'd just been awarded a Nobel prize.

Whatever this was, Kira was definitely taking it seriously. You'd think her world had just been turned upside down. She tapped her phone one last time and looked up. "You're not going to believe this. Guess which band is back and making a reunion tour? They're playing here at the end of June!" She sucked in her breath and jumped a little.

I started to work on her riddle but was impeded by two and a half pints of beer. What can I say? It was a Thursday, girls' night out. And we'd been at it for a while. Also, I hadn't been paying complete attention up to that point because, honestly, this had started off as just another one of Kira's breakup stories, and I'd heard them all since, well, forever. So I had to recalibrate my brain to focus on whatever it was that Kira was now talking about.

Neither Jo nor I actually had a chance to answer Kira's question—she was way too excited to let anyone guess. She waited a tenth of a second, then blurted out the band's name, loud and fast like a popped balloon.

"Fiery Boys!"

Whoa, had I just heard her right? I sat up straight, knocked my hand against my beer glass, then miraculously caught it before anything spilled. See? I *can* hold my liquor.

But between the close call with my beer and the thought of seeing the Fiery Boys in concert again, half my buzz was gone. I was on high alert. I swear, they're my favorite band.

Now I knew what most people thought about the Fiery Boys. Just a manufactured band of sixteen-year-olds who burst onto the scene ten years ago, hit the top of the charts for a while, then slipped off into obscurity. And all that was true.

But if you'd gone to high school with Kira and me, you'd know how incredible that band once was. These weren't some mellow kids harmonizing in squeaky prepubescent voices. The Fiery Boys were hard rockers, with a lead singer who howled like an angry lion. Their drummer was probably the most gorgeous man on planet Earth. In fact, all of them were pretty hot—they'd been selected for their appeal as well as their ability to rock. They were magnificent.

The Fiery Boys ruled during my last two years of high school. There wasn't a kid in my class that didn't love their pounding beat and intense lyrics. One of their theme songs, "Fiery Life," got me through some really tough times. So no matter what others might have said, I knew that the Fiery Boys were the most important band in the known universe.

Well, *my* known universe, anyway. And interestingly, the band broke up at the same time as my life did. Because of that, I never really had a chance to mourn them. Suddenly, I had more pressing issues to deal with. Besides, when you're dead, you're dead—and the Fiery Boys were dead. Or so I thought.

I hopped up and down and latched onto Kira's arm with both hands. "Really? The Fiery Boys are back? I'm in!" I turned to Jo. "Kira and I were totally in love with them."

Kira looked up from her phone, now much less manic but still far from calm. "Remember how we'd play their videos and dance all night?" She gave a nostalgic sigh. "Too bad they broke up so quickly. What was it? Two years, three albums, then they were done." She shook her head. "Not enough. I blame Danielle for breaking up the band. Buck really blew it when he married her."

I laughed. "You always liked Chuck best. But Buck was on my short list, along with River."

I had posters of River and Buck in my bedroom. The bigger poster was my absolute favorite Fiery Boy: River Sticks, the drummer. Shaved head and sexy as hell, his poster hung above my desk where I could see him when I studied and at night from my bed. Anytime I needed a boost, all I had to do was take one look at his ripped body, deep dark eyes, and breathtakingly chiseled features. Pure animal energy seemed to shine from him, spilling out over his drum kit and right into my heart. When I was really in the zone, I could hear him grunt as he pounded those skins. God, how I wanted him.

My second favorite Fiery Boy was Buck Morris, the bass player. The one who Kira hated for marrying Danielle. Buck was classically handsome, with a sculpted face and straight black hair that draped over sapphire blue eyes. And talk about built! His body was ripped. I guess I wanted him, too.

Buck's poster was at the head of my bed, which had the disadvantage that I couldn't see him as well when I was lying there. In the poster, he was working the bass while giving the camera a lidded stare and the barest sliver of a smile. I used to wonder about that smile. Whereas the first thing I wanted to do to River was tear his clothes off, the first thing I wanted to do to Buck was ask him what he was smiling at. Then I'd tear his clothes off. Face it: he was seriously sexy, too.

Jo squinted at me. "River? Sorry. And Buck? Why bother when he had someone else? I'm with Kira on this one. Give me Chuck any day. When he howled into the microphone, I used to break out in a sweat." She nibbled at her lower lip for a few seconds of fantasy desire. "And what about Gabe? I could watch his fingers fly over that guitar for hours. I wonder if he's still the horny one." She grinned and wagged her eyebrows.

Yeah, yeah. Chuck and Gabe, Chuck and Gabe. Everyone wanted Chuck and Gabe. And I had to agree that Chuck had some appeal. He was the tallest in the band, handsome, wiry, and muscular. When he sang and danced with his flirtatious smile, nobody looked away. And the way he growled on "Fiery Life" made me forget everything that was wrong with the world. For sure, I'd do him, too.

But Gabe. . . no. I couldn't deny that his guitar solos were things of beauty, but he simply didn't do it for me in the looks department. That's okay. I had three other guys to drool over.

I laid it all out for Jo. "Sorry, girl. You can have Gabe. And as far as Chuck goes, I guess I wouldn't kick him out of bed. Still, I'm sticking with my two favorites. Buck is pretty damn hot, and River. . ." I clutched my hands together and stared heavenward. "He's a god. So incredibly studly. I used to dream about marrying him."

I suddenly needed to see River again, eight years after the breakup. Was he still fabulously good looking? Did he still have a muscular build that I longed to have wrapped around me? I took out my phone and found a recent picture. Oh yes, my racing heart told me, I definitely needed to see this concert.

Kira kept working her phone and muttering encouraging words to urge it on, as if her exhortations would make it respond faster. I laid a hand on her arm. "Relax, girl." She flashed a smile then returned to her phone.

I scooted closer to look over her shoulder. "Are you getting tickets to the show?"

"You bet. I'm nearly there." She cocked her head toward Jo. "I assume you want a ticket. Want one for Larry?"

Jo rolled her eyes. "Sure, why not? Two tickets." I hadn't heard many good things about her latest boyfriend, but at least she had one. Kira rarely bothered with the notion. And although I currently had one, I knew he wouldn't last.

"You want a ticket for Palmer?" Kira asked, as though reading my mind.

Did I want a ticket for Palmer? I doubted it. I didn't even know if he liked the Fiery Boys. We'd only been together a half-dozen times over the past two months, so I didn't know much about him at all. If I had to guess, I'd say that his opinion of the Fiery Boys would be the same as his opinion of everything else: he'd be critical and dismissive. Yeah, he'd hate them. The more I thought about it, the more I knew I didn't want a ticket for Palmer.

Now Palmer wasn't a complete fail. He was good looking and decent in bed. But he was dull. Whereas I was always looking for new adventures, he was always looking for a steady routine. All my enthusiasm for life meant nothing to him.

Still, I understood Palmer's point of view. After working long hours as a plumber's assistant all week, the only thing he wanted to do on the weekend was stay home and watch videos. I couldn't blame him for being a homebody, but I wished he wasn't clingy and testy, too.

So although I wanted an extra ticket, I wasn't sure it would be for Palmer. But since this was a Fiery Boys concert, tickets would certainly be good to have. "Sure, get me two."

Kira grinned and returned to her phone. After a few final taps, she finished the purchase and smiled at the screen. "Yes!" she whooped as her arms punched the air. "We're gonna see the Fiery Boys!" She chanted it loudly in a sing-song voice.

Kira's little display of happiness got noticed all over the bar. Not that there was a man there who hadn't already noticed her. Long blonde hair, a great figure, and the face of a model, it didn't hurt that she wore black shorts and a white lace midriff-baring top over a black bra. Half the men in the bar looked her way as soon as she walked in the door. Now the rest of them were staring, too.

One man at the next table raised his glass toward her. "I'll drink to that," he slurred. The others at his table laughed.

Ignoring them, Kira lowered her head and motioned us to lean in. She still had that manic glow on her face, and I could tell she had more news. I mean, look at her! She was actually shaking with excitement. I scooted closer to find out why.

"Here's the special part," Kira whispered. "The news ticker on the TV mentioned a contest. It said that the winner gets a week on the Fiery Boys tour bus. I looked it up —it's a real contest. All you need to do is send in a photo." She sat up straight and smiled, then spoke with cool confidence. "I'm going to win that contest."

I forced myself not to laugh at the absurdity of her statement. Kira often got grand ideas like this, and I understood why. After all, no man had ever refused her. They couldn't—probably some law of physical attraction. If Kira said she was going on tour with the Fiery Boys, it might actually happen.

I patted her arm. "Sure you are. And you're going to marry Chuck. You've been telling me that since high school."

"But I'm serious this time. Look." She held out her phone. "Here's the entry form where you submit your picture. See? Winner gets a week on tour with the band." She sat up straight and flashed a sultry smile. "That'll be me."

Jo, a psychologist, had been watching this interchange with what seemed like professional detachment. "Excuse me. . ." Her voice was serious, but her smirk warned us that things wouldn't stay that way. "Is there a casting couch to help them choose?"

Typical. Jo took the same approach to this contest that she did toward so many things: she made it be all about sex. And since she specialized in relationship counseling, she might well have been right. Jo had heard many strange things from her sexually challenged clients.

Kira ignored Jo's sarcasm and pointed to her phone. "It says here, 'We want to see what you look like, but we also want a picture that tells us something about you. If a picture is worth a thousand words, then make sure we can read some of them.' I've got great shots from when I was modeling. So my photo will tell them that this model can rock it with the Fiery Boys."

Jo and I snuck sympathetic looks at each other. We knew all about Kira's so-called modeling career, which had lasted for one entire photo session. The agency wasn't really looking for models. They just suckered naïve girls into paying for a photographer and some worthless lectures about the amazing life of a model. It never translated into any real work.

Now don't get me wrong—Kira was beautiful and could rock any outfit. But life doesn't always give you everything you want. I understood that by the time I was done with high school. Kira learned it a few months after that photo session, when no modeling opportunities actually materialized. To her credit, she moved on once she understood this. She found a job selling electronics and recently got promoted to be a branch manager. So even if she was delusional about this contest, Kira had real drive.

"Hey, you've got your beauty shots." Jo wagged a finger. "But what about Annalisa and me?" She flashed a sarcastic grin. "Looks like we have some work to do."

I snorted. "As if we can compete with Kira." We all knew that if they were choosing based on a photo, then Kira would beat us easily. And to be honest, Jo would be number two. She might not be as classically stunning as Kira, but she had a short, slender body and a bob of red hair over a fairly pretty face. Tonight she was wearing a jean jacket, a frilly black miniskirt, and yellow leggings. No doubt about it, I'd be the last one they'd choose.

It's not like I'm a dog or anything. Honestly, I'd describe myself as "average." Average weight, not very thin but not too heavy, either. Average breasts, neither tiny nor busty. An average face, rather plain in my opinion, with what I always thought of as simple features. Even average length black hair, straight and hanging lifelessly. The only thing that was more than average was my height; at 5'10" tall, I had both Kira and Jo beat.

But I wasn't doing much with my height tonight. Unlike my girlfriends who were drawing looks from all over the bar, I'd dressed down in jeans and a light blue sweater. The outfit didn't garner much attention around here, especially sitting next to my girlfriends. But after dressing up all day at the car dealership, I preferred something casual for drinking night.

I might have seemed like a lonely woman who didn't dress up and whose only boyfriend options were boring, angry, and clingy losers. But I could do better if I wanted. I knew how to work what I had—I'd learned it from the Fiery Boys in high school. Back then, I would dance in my room while their music played in my ears and their posters watched over me. In my full-length mirror, I practiced moves I'd seen in videos, and I got pretty good. So I knew how to do all those things that make guys pay attention. And when I threw in my natural enthusiasm, I had everything I needed to attract a man. Yeah, I could do better than Palmer, I just hadn't bothered lately.

Not since Zedediah Turner.

Zed, as everyone called him, was my first lover back in high school and still ranked as my best. He was also the only man I'd ever actually fallen in love with. We were magical during our two years together, and he was anything but boring. But then he died, a month before the Fiery Boys broke up, and the pain of lost love still stung.

One day I'd find a lover like Zed—I knew it would happen. Hey, maybe I'd win this contest and turn my charms on River Sticks. My mind wandered back to those youthful fantasies in which River and I shared a make-believe life together. We were a great couple.

Okay, I admit it—I could be as delusional as Kira. My brain liked to take me on wild rides, thrilling me with spectacular outcomes or scaring me with horrifying possibilities. One little thought, and I'd be off to fantasyland. I couldn't help it; we all get that way some days.

But when I was done fantasizing, I knew that my chance of winning this contest was the same as Kira and Jo's. Zero. However, by this point in the evening, with my beer and adrenaline-fueled bloodstream fully operational, reality was irrelevant. I was definitely going to enter that contest. So what if I didn't win?

I grabbed my glass and got to my feet. "You're right. Let's take some pictures. Right here." The enthusiastic, try-anything-once part of me actually thought that this bar would be the perfect setting for my Fiery Boys spotlight.

Jo got up and started scouting for a good location. "We could pose over by the bar." She shot a playful smile. "No, wait! How about in the bathroom, posing by the sinks?"

I could play that game. "Or in the toilet stall. That would be a winning shot." Even Kira laughed at that.

"Let's do this." Jo ran to the bar and laid back against it in a lusty pose, her arms stretched out past other people's drinks. "Out of the way! This is a photo shoot." The men on either side of her laughed and obliged her while I took some pictures. We also posed by the exit sign and the jukebox.

We horsed around and took pictures for the next fifteen minutes. The bartender knew us and let us come behind the bar. I posed with my head under a beer tap, my mouth open. He obligingly poured a squirt while Jo snapped away.

Not willing to be outdone, Jo got up on the counter behind the bar and posed in front of the mirrored shelving, two bottles in each hand. Then she stretched out on the bar and pretended to be asleep while the bartender decorated the scene with empty bottles. Pretty soon, everyone was throwing out suggestions. We even made it to the bathroom for a few unusual poses.

Finally, we stumbled back to the table, giggling like school girls. "Okay!" I pounded the table. "We're ready to do this contest." Kira laughed and shook her head.

Two

I sat in my Creative Writing class and stared at the paper. An A! Underneath the grade, the professor had written, "Good passion." That was a first. I had been struggling with this class all semester.

I wasn't sure I liked Professor Norbert's concept of Creative Writing. His suggested reading list had way too many dense books, with wordy sentences, thick layers of abstraction, and ambiguous conclusions. Hadn't I read enough of that in high school and college? These night-school classes were supposed to be light and easy—an opportunity to do something fun. So why did I have to read such tedious books?

But I put up with the class because I wanted to be a writer. And we've all heard the advice: if you want to be a good writer, you have to read. So that's exactly what I did. I spent much of my free time plowing through book after book, finishing another one every few days. But *I* was the one who picked those books, not Professor Norbert.

If I could have created my own reading list, I'd have chosen the sort of articles and books that I someday hoped to write: stories about rock and roll. That was my goal: to be a famous reporter who covered the music scene, followed bands, and interviewed musicians. I dreamed of being like Ivory Doe of *No Moss* magazine, one of the most famous music journalists out there.

Now some would think I was a hopeless dreamer, and they'd probably be right. But I knew that only one person could make my dream come true: me. So I kept reading, and I signed up for a literary masters program at the local college. A master's degree would be a nice ticket-punch that would establish my cred as a writer. And it would improve my writing, too. Along the way, I'd get to read even more books, which seemed like a good thing. Too bad Norbert's reading list was so tiresome.

A woman sitting next to me leaned over and noticed my grade. "Wow! How did you get an A out of Norbert? He's such a hard ass." She had a good point—the guy had been beating me up all semester.

I shrugged. "I just got tired of writing stories based on his reading list. Every time I did that, I got a C. So I figured, the hell with it. Since I can't get a good grade out of him, I'll write about something I really love. A song lyric." I pointed out the title on the first page of my paper. "Fiery Life," of course. My song.

The woman saw where I was pointing, and her mouth fell open. "You're kidding. He let you write about a Fiery Boys song? Since when is he allowing rock-and-roll lyrics in this class?"

"Beats me. But since the Fiery Boys announced their reunion tour, I can't think about much else. So I went for it." I didn't bother telling her that the Fiery Boys were playing here in San Jose, seventy-six days from now. She might think I was obsessed.

To be honest, there was another reason why I wrote about "Fiery Life"—Jo made me do it. She knew all about my lame boyfriends and my issues with Zed. When I signed up for this class, she suggested that I work his story into one of the assignments as a way of processing his death. And Zed's death was intimately linked with that song.

At first, I pointed out that I was already beyond it. I didn't cry for Zed anymore—hadn't in years. But she told me I still had some work to do. I had to stop holding every man up to my idealized memories, because nobody—not even the real Zed—could measure up to the way I remembered him. She was right about that.

Zed had become something of a legend in my mind. The thing I remembered most about him was that he loved to push the boundaries. He was always on the lookout for the next car race, rock concert, or page from the Kama Sutra. Each day with him was like a trip to someplace new.

After he died, I sought out challenging activities that would remind me of him, things outside of my comfort zone. And whenever I did those things, I'd think of Zed and how he'd loved to have all those crazy adventures. I started renting race cars at the local track so I could pretend we were still racing together. I even rode my motorcycle everywhere, shunning my car so I could more acutely feel his presence.

I went to punk and metal concerts, the louder the better, and I danced in the mosh pit, bouncing off other people like human bumper cars. I even went parachuting a few times because Zed and I had talked about it. I didn't worry about jumping because I knew he was proudly watching over me. He wouldn't let anything bad happen.

Yeah, maybe I was a little hung up on the guy. But I couldn't deny that Zed's posthumous encouragement helped me to do all sorts of amazing things. The most recent example was this paper, where I'd ignored the class reading list and used a rock lyric to tell my story. Zed would have approved.

And Jo approved, too. But she was worried about me. She wanted me to stop using him as my silent advisor, living for his imagined good graces. And she wanted me to open up to love. I couldn't keep pushing men away just because the best one had died and the others couldn't compare.

She even pointed out that I had issues with abandonment. Besides Zed dying at the end of senior year, my parents had also abandoned me, at the start of that year. They moved, like they always did, but for the first time in my life, I didn't follow them. Jo claimed that this abandonment by key people in my life was what kept driving me to choose bad boyfriends. If I could let go of these issues, she was certain I'd find love again.

But so far, that hadn't happened. So I stuck to my main priorities, like my writing. And the good news was that I'd just aced this assignment. Maybe all of my reading *was* paying off.

The class ended, and we started to file out of the room. My new admirer stopped at the professor's desk and pointed to me. "How come you let her write about a rock song? Can we all do that?" Curious, I stopped to hear the answer.

Norbert grunted and leaned back in his chair. "I hate pop music, and I hate song lyrics. They're certainly not what I would call creative writing. But Ms. Ricci did much more than analyze a mediocre poem. She wrote a compelling story that tied in with the lyrics and gave them depth." He nodded at me. "I was moved by your tale. A very inventive story."

My *tale?* Did he think I'd made it up? I'd be much happier if my paper really *was* creative writing. But things weren't that way, and I let the professor know it. "I didn't make that story up, sir. It's really about me."

The professor gave me an astonished look. "Very interesting. I'm sorry about your boyfriend."

I returned a weak smile. "That was eight years ago. I'm over it."

But obviously, I wasn't. I was far from over it. Palmer was a typical example of the uninspiring men who filled my life these days. Pale shades of Zed, I tolerated these men but never loved them. Besides, I had better things to do. My job kept me going all day and even on occasional evenings and weekends; I went to writing class two nights a week, did kickboxing on another, and still took time to unwind with my friends on Thursdays. That didn't leave much time for boyfriends.

Palmer was busy, too. He and I both knew that our relationship was going nowhere, and I even asked him about it last week. But he told me he didn't care any more than I did, and then he asked me out again. So at least he knew what he was getting.

And in the meantime, I kept my sights on the things that mattered to me the most—my work, my plans to become a writer, and now a Fiery Boys concert.

Three

Jo and Kira came over to my place on Friday, buzzing with excitement. It had been over a month since the Fiery Boys tour contest had been announced, and tonight they were revealing the winner. Some gorgeous groupie would soon be chosen to ride on their bus, and then the three of us could return to our regular lives.

Palmer was there, too, belittling us for caring so much. Yeah, he and I were still going out, but barely. I ignored his teasing and turned on the television.

Kira poured herself a glass of wine and took a sip. "I'm trying to think positively here." She started to repeat her contest-winning mantra. "I am going to win. I am going to win. I am going to win."

Jo smiled and picked up her glass of whiskey. "I'll show you positive thinking." She shot the drink and dropped the glass on the table. "I am going to get drunk. I am going to get drunk. I am going to get drunk." We laughed, and even Palmer agreed with that sentiment.

Jo turned to me on the sofa. "What about you, Annalisa? Are you going to win or get drunk?"

I wondered if I might just throw up. Even though I was still working on my first beer, my stomach shook like a jumping bean. I mean, how silly was it to be nervous over this, especially when I knew I wouldn't be picked? Neither would Jo—the photographs we'd submitted were jokes. Only Kira had a chance. Maybe I was nervous for her.

We plodded through a few commercials, then an announcer told us what we already knew: it was time for the contest results. And to make the announcement, they introduced the man himself, the lead singer of the Fiery Boys, Chuck Van Dorn. The three of us held our collective breaths.

Chuck wasn't a kid anymore, and he looked great. Even better than he had ten years ago, if that was possible. He wasn't as rail thin and gangly—now he exuded real sexuality, with a come-hither grin and those perfect features. He had his usual beard shadow, long dark hair, and green eyes. Although not my favorite Fiery Boy, I couldn't deny his appeal.

Chuck stood in front of a custom press wall that had the Fiery Boys logo emblazoned all over it. Flashes went off every few seconds, and the camera panned back to show that he was addressing a crowded room of reporters. After a minute of this, he raised his hand to get everyone's attention. Kira crawled to the screen to give him a remote kiss.

As much as I loved the Fiery Boys, I had to admit that I hadn't followed their individual careers since the band broke up. Kira and Jo had to fill me in on the past eight years. They told me that Chuck was the only member of the band who continued to perform. He lived in Las Vegas and played a solo act that he called the Fiery Boy, a one-man tribute band. Although I'd never seen his show—that's how little I cared about him—Jo had seen him three or four times, and even Kira had seen his act. Their rock-and-roll crushes still ran strong.

The one I longed to see, of course, was River, the drumming hottie. Like Gabe and Buck, he'd pretty much dropped into obscurity after the band broke up. But I remained faithful. In my fantasies, he was still the same as in that poster, sitting on his drum throne with his arms in the air and his sticks blurred on their way to strike a cymbal. His bald head still glistened with sweat, and he still had a sparkle in his eye, just for me.

Back in high school, I knew everything about River and read every piece of gossip I could find. Six feet tall, solid and built, he was a Native American who grew up in Minnesota. His last name was Locklear, but he didn't use that in the band. Instead, he made a joke of his name and called himself River Sticks. Back then, I even imagined marrying him, and I would doodle my new name during boring classes. Annalisa Locklear.

In the past month, I'd learned some new things about River, including the fact that he had a girlfriend who he'd been with for years. River didn't want another fiasco like what Buck and Danielle went through, so he kept his relationship quiet—nobody knew anything about this woman. Some reports suggested that he was with Talia Dare, a famous rocker. But other reports denied that rumor. In any case, the fact that he protected this woman so well made me like him even more. I couldn't wait to see him again.

But River wasn't on the television today, only Chuck. The crowd in the audience quieted down and we knew something was coming. "Oh my God!" Kira squealed as she flapped her hands in the air.

Chuck warmed up the audience like a true entertainer, owning the space as if this was a concert. "Let's see, are there any Fiery Boys fans here?" The crowd cheered and whistled while Chuck bathed himself in their love.

After a few seconds of this, he held up his hands to quiet them. "Okay. So the good news is, we're back." As expected, the reporters erupted again, and more flashes sparkled Chuck's dazzling face. He stepped from the podium to hug a female reporter who hugged him back with a little scream. The lead singer of the Fiery Boys knew how to work a crowd.

Chuck got back to the podium and went on with his pitch. "We have some new songs, some new videos, and we're going on tour next month. Gabe, Buck, River, and I are totally stoked. We're coming to *your* town, and we're *burning it!*" He couldn't resist the usual fire-related expressions—a band theme. Almost all of their songs had something to do with fire, especially my special song, "Fiery Life," which Chuck had written. So although he wasn't my favorite band member, I wouldn't complain if the author of "Fiery Life" wanted me to go on tour with him. I wouldn't complain if he wanted to do anything else with me, either!

Chuck finally got down to the matter at hand. "Now some of you may know that we've been running a little contest here. One lucky girl is going to be picked to tour with us for a week. We got fifteen *thousand* pictures from all of you, and it was hard to decide. River and I loved all of the pretty faces. Gabe was particularly fond of the X-rated pictures you girls sent us." He pointed at the camera and winked. "He'll be writing to you later for more."

Chuck paused, and I knew what was coming: a Buck joke. He always teased Buck, calling him dumb, mocking him about his girlfriend, or suggesting that he was so stupid, he couldn't even remember his own name. And the name issue wasn't as far-fetched as it seemed, because Buck's real name was Charles. Before he'd joined the Fiery Boys, people had called *him* Chuck. But the band couldn't have two Chucks, so the bass player became Buck. Of course, this only gave Chuck more openings to mock him.

The zinger arrived on schedule. "And Buck?" Chuck grinned for an extra beat before delivering the punchline. "He can't even remember which end of the bass to pluck." The audience laughed.

This was the standard Fiery Boys story. Chuck was the lady killer singer, Gabe was the Zen-yet-horny guitarist, River was the hard-drinking drummer, and Buck was the dumb bass player. I didn't mind this much because I was willing to drink hard with River. All he had to do was say the word. And I seriously doubted Buck was dumb.

Chuck continued to ride the media frenzy. "Okay, so here's the big announcement. Believe it or not, none of the entries got unanimous approval from us, but the winner was definitely the first choice for three of us. So without delay, let's have a drum roll for the lucky girl." He turned around as if looking for his backup drummer, but the other band members were obviously not there. He turned back to the camera and laughed lightly. "Oops, no drums. Okay, the winner is. . ."

Chuck paused and gave the camera a sly grin. Kira screamed a little. Jo shouted at the television, "Do it, already!" Palmer was so bored that he was on his phone, ignoring us. And I just sat there perfectly relaxed, calmly gripping my beer with enough force to shatter the glass.

Chuck reached into his pocket, pulled out a piece of paper, and stared at it for a few seconds. Then he faced the camera with a smile and said the most outrageous thing I'd ever heard in my life.

He said my name.

"The winner is Annalisa Ricci from San Jose, California."

I froze and stared at the television, too stunned to even let the news register. A dreamlike cloud wrapped itself around me, challenging me to accept the fact that the lead singer of the Fiery Boys had just invited me to tour with him. Kira and Jo were screaming, but I could barely hear them next to the dizzying vortex that was swirling around my head. Something was wrong here. My friends must have slipped something into my drink.

The crowd in front of Chuck kept applauding for what seemed like an hour. It went on and on and on in druggy slow motion while my name actually flashed at the bottom of the screen. I still didn't believe it—someone was punking me. They were just waiting for me to buy it, then the truth would be revealed and everyone would laugh.

So I sat there and let their joke play out, waiting for the inevitable resolution. Perhaps Chuck would say "LOL, just kidding," and then read the *real* contest results. Or this might be a fake video that Palmer had made to tease me. He enjoyed doing things like that. I scrutinized the screen to see if I could detect signs of a cheap video editing job, but the picture looked good, so this probably wasn't a prank. Besides, Palmer seemed just as surprised as I was. He even yelled at the television and warned the Fiery Boys not to mess with his girl. How quaint! He thought he had to defend me from them. As if I'd choose Palmer over anyone in the band. And it was starting to occur to me that I might actually get such a choice.

Jo slapped me on the back, which brought me back to reality. "Congrats, girl! I told you that picture would be a winner."

A winner? Impossible! It didn't make sense. After we'd taken those pictures at the bar last month, we sat at our table and reviewed them. All of them were so ridiculous that we simply couldn't choose. So we decided that each of us would choose the other's best shot. I picked the first picture of Jo, lounging against the bar. She looked good—

sexy and desirable. The Fiery Boys would appreciate the fire in her eyes.

Then Jo chose the worst possible shot for me—the dumbest, most embarrassing, and most awkward picture that anyone had ever taken of me. Contest suicide. I remember pointing this out to her, but she refused to reconsider her choice. She reminded me that our photos needed to tell a story, and this one said all sorts of things about me. In her opinion, it was a winning picture. I guess she was right.

But back then, I didn't protest the picture selection because it didn't really matter. There wasn't a single picture of me in the batch that I thought could win this contest. I was not supposed to be the winner. Someone else was.

The excitement finally died down, so Chuck went on. "And for all you other girls who didn't win, I'm going to show you why. Take a look at Annalisa!"

I cringed and tried to sink deeper into my chair as the screen filled with my contest submission. Jo had caught me laughing and spraying my drink, beer erupting from my mouth in a fine mist. If it hadn't been for the drink spray, it might have been a decent shot. A wisp of black hair swept across my face, my dark eyes sparkled, and my laughter was so infectious that the reporters joined right in. But I was no beauty, so I couldn't understand how I got picked.

Palmer hadn't seen this picture, and he wasn't very happy to see it now. "You look like a drunk whore." Wow, thanks for taking it to the next level. I get that I was drunk, but couldn't he have stopped there? As if I needed more reasons to break up with him.

Chuck spoke again, which saved me from having to defend my photo. "Now that's the kind of girl we want on tour with us. I bet she could drink us under the table." The reporters laughed harder, which didn't seem to help Palmer's mood at all.

Kira scowled at the television. "I can drink, too, Chuck!" Right now, I wished she had won.

My new buddy, Chuck, took me aside for a moment. He faced the camera and spoke quietly. "Hey, Annalisa girl. You'll be getting a call soon from the band manager. If you don't hear in the next hour, get in touch with us and we'll get you on the bus."

Chuck's voice returned to normal. "And for everyone else, come on down and see us. You can check the tour schedule and get tickets online."

Finally, Chuck gave everyone his famous exit line. "Bye for now. And remember. . ." He wound up for the big delivery and roared it into the microphone, "Keep on burning!" He raised his arms in the now-famous Fiery Boys hand sign, the backs of his hands to the camera with his fingers wiggling straight up like licks of fire.

I stared numbly at the screen until Jo turned off the television. That helped return my breathing to normal. But then my phone rang and the sensation of weirdness returned. I reached for the phone but it slipped through my fingers. Good thing Jo understood my temporary inability to function normally—she picked it up and handed it to me.

Wow. Either this was an incredibly elaborate prank, or I was about to go on tour with the Fiery Boys.

Four

By Monday, I was over the shock. I'd finally accepted that I—*yes I*—was going to live with the Fiery Boys on their tour bus. For a whole week! I had moved past the disbelief, the spontaneous eruptions of excitement, and the attempts to pinch myself awake.

I spent most of the weekend immersed in the Fiery Boys, listening to their music on endless loop, especially the new album they'd recorded to accompany this reunion tour. I danced myself into a daze, like I used to ten years earlier. But now, I imagined them playing live, right in front of me. Yeah, I was getting pretty fixated on the Fiery Boys.

Unfortunately, the rest of the world didn't spend the weekend fixated on the Fiery Boys. Instead, they focused on me, giving me something I never thought I'd have. Fame.

As soon as Chuck spoke my name on Friday, the world went certifiably insane. I had thousands of friend requests from total strangers, and I had to close all my social media accounts. New websites popped up, filled entirely with lies about me. I really should have stopped using the web altogether, but I couldn't resist checking myself out. It was just so bizarre to see my name on every fan site I visited.

Some of the sites were silly and made me laugh. Others were not so nice. One site gave out my cell phone number, and dozens of strangers started to call and text me. Now I couldn't even use my phone and had to get a new number. Quite a few sites were filled with haters making angry diatribes against me, calling for my death and disembowelment. One of them even sported a cheap photo edit of my head on a spike. I mean, seriously? These hate sites had hundreds of nasty comments about me, and I admit I read quite a few of them before I stopped looking.

Strange as it sounded, I was trending.

This new attention made me—shall we say—concerned. But the Fiery Boys had it under control. When the band manager, Jason Bartholomew, called me on Friday, he told me not to worry about any death threats that might appear on the Internet. And just in case, he sent a bodyguard to watch over me. Of course, this only made me worry more.

Half an hour later, my hired muscle arrived. And I do mean muscle. Dressed in a classic henchman's black suit, Vaughan was medium height but super built. And cute. He had a smile lurking under that solid exterior, and he exuded an enthusiasm that I liked right away.

Vaughan gave me a few pointers about dealing with the media and also gave me his cell number, assuring me he'd answer at any hour. Then he went outside to camp on my street, promising to always be near.

Kira and Jo were still caught up in the excitement of my victory, so they stopped Vaughan and plied him with questions about the Fiery Boys. Kira even came back over the weekend, ostensibly to see me, but primarily to talk to my bodyguard about his amazing rock-and-roll bosses. She was starstruck.

On Saturday morning, Vaughan took me outside, wrapped in a hoodie to hide my face. He'd been wandering among the paparazzi who had quickly gathered around my home, so he gave me a tour, pointing out where each of them was hiding. To put it mildly, I was shocked. All these people were here for me?

That afternoon, I tried out the fame game, just for fun. I went out to a grocery store without concealing my face, and the cameras flashed nonstop. Then I looked around the web and found the pictures, hideous photos that made me seem ugly and misshapen. It was as if they'd intentionally chosen the worst ones. Lesson one was simple: stay covered.

But even with my face hidden, the reporters shouted questions as I moved quickly to my car. Each question was more absurd than the last.

"What do you think of the theory that they projected all the pictures on a wall and threw a dart?" I thought the theory was great—it explained so much. Of course I didn't tell them that. Vaughan insisted that I resist the urge to talk to them.

Besides, the next question got fired at me before I could have answered the first. "Can you confirm that you've been River Sticks' secret lover for years?" Ahh, don't I wish.

Then came the question that stopped me for a few seconds, no doubt with a look of shock that the paparazzi loved to shoot. "Are you going to have sex with all four of them?"

Oh, come on! In my more reasonable moments, I knew that I wasn't going to have sex with any of them. But my life was suddenly steeped in nonsense, and I became less and less reasonable every day. I couldn't deny that I'd gladly jump River or even Buck—two gorgeous men who I hoped I'd be able to meet without losing total bodily control. Even Chuck was a fine-looking hunk of man who I'd never turn down. But all four of them in one week? Not happening.

With Vaughan at my place, protecting me, I was able to deal with another aspect of my newly skewed life: Palmer. As expected, he was majorly upset by all the attention I was getting and instantly became jealous that I was going on vacation with four famous, handsome, and desirable men. He was also envious that I was being talked about everywhere. And yes, he was even uncomfortable that I had a muscular bodyguard. I couldn't deny that he had plenty of reasons to be jealous.

Palmer insisted on staying with me Friday night, claiming he needed to protect me. I knew better, and I could have done without his issues, but I let him stay because he was part of my former life, when nobody knew who I was. I found some small comfort there. Too bad he spent the entire time online, cursing at the screen and announcing each new website about me with increased irritation. I ignored him and eventually went to bed.

When I woke up Saturday morning, he was asleep next to me. Relieved that he wasn't venting anymore, I got up quietly and went to the kitchen. Then I sat and thought about my life, grateful for some alone time.

Unfortunately, Palmer soon got up and decided to confront the reporters directly, even though Vaughan had already advised us not to do that. Armed with his need to protect me and his lack of common sense, he stormed outside and exploded at the reporters who descended upon him. He even punched a photographer and trashed the man's camera.

Good thing Vaughan was there to help me out. He dragged my raging, purple-faced boyfriend inside and made him sit down. I stepped back to take a long look at this man, and I didn't like what I saw.

Vaughan tried to explain things once again, but that only made Palmer more angry. He railed at my bodyguard and accused him of trying to steal me away. But when Vaughan wouldn't respond to that, Palmer got even angrier.

And with nobody else left to attack, he turned his anger on me. This—he raged—was all my fault.

That did it. I'd finally had enough. I was through with this angry man who thought his smothering devotion was more important than a week with the Fiery Boys. Did he actually think he could save me by fighting the paparazzi?

So I told him about his new status as my ex-boyfriend. Vaughan glared at him the entire time, then threatened him with assorted bodily harm if he talked about me to the press. Stunned and speechless, Palmer grabbed the various personal effects he kept at my place and left. It was one of the easiest break ups I've ever had to do. Yeah, the next time I needed to end a difficult relationship, I'd definitely get another bodyguard.

So with all this screwy stuff going on, I was very happy when Monday rolled around and I got to go to work. The house had become my prison—a change of scenery was essential. I drove to the car dealership and went directly to my supervisor's office. "Ed, I'm taking off a week in June. Vacation."

He looked up from his desk and smiled. "Yeah, I heard about your vacation. Partying with a rock band. Nice."

Was there anyone who didn't know? I squinted at him. "Are you a Fiery Boys fan?"

"Nah. But my wife loves them. She recognized your name when they announced the contest winner. Got real excited. I knew you'd be taking some time off."

I nodded toward the showroom, which already starting to fill up with suspicious-looking, camera-wielding men. "Then you don't mind the photographers who are taking pictures out there?"

"Are you kidding? This is great publicity! I've got a famous saleswoman now." Ed laughed. "But the gents are totally annoyed."

Ugh, the gents. I worked at a high-end auto dealership and was a pretty good salesperson. The other three people doing sales were "the gents," a group of men who thought women didn't know anything about cars and couldn't sell one to save their lives. But thanks to my dad and Zed, I knew plenty. I could tune an engine so it purred, knew all the automotive jargon, and had good people skills. But as far as the gents were concerned, there was no place for me on the showroom floor.

All during my first week of work, the gents did their best to make me fail. They insisted on "helping" me with every deal, and corrected each thing I told the customers. From financing to warranty issues to the forms needed for custom orders, they would interrupt me and do their best to make me look foolish. Sometimes they would actually steal my customer away. I was ready to dig three shallow graves.

But instead, their challenges only drove me harder. I paid careful attention and soon had all of the details right. In the middle of my third week, I confronted them and demanded that they stop sabotaging me. With smug condescension, they agreed to leave me alone if I could outsell them for just one day.

That was their big mistake. I went home that night and made a list of their offenses, vowing to use every one of those tactics against them. The next day, I made sure to interrupt every customer they had, using the same lame excuses they had used on me. Where they had once pointed out, "You're new, so let me help you with this," I commented, "You're a bit rusty, so let me help you with this." Where one of them had said, "I know you kids like to write with a flourish, but you have to stay inside the boxes or the machine won't read it," I told him "I know you old people have shaky hands, but you have to stay inside the boxes or the machine won't read it."

I even matched the nasty comments they'd made to me. One of them had attempted to steal a customer by pointing out that it takes more than a skirt to sell a car. So on payback day, I interrupted him and pointed out to his customer that it takes more than a cheap suit to be a car salesman. This started a round of ribbing that quickly escalated. I stayed calm, but the gent totally lost it. And after a few insult volleys, the customer walked away. Of course, I followed him, apologized for the outburst, and offered him an extra discount. The man agreed, and bought the car from me.

The gents kept up the fight all day long, using every tired trick that I'd seen for weeks. But I was beyond their games, and I already knew how to play. Their attempts to steal my customers backfired royally.

Did I really need to go that far and be that nasty? Probably not. I could compete fairly with any of those losers. But they were the ones who had declared war, so I rolled out the heavy artillery. I sold quite a few cars, and by the end of the day, had outsold the three gents, combined. They were supremely annoyed.

I made them honor the bet, and I never let them give me grief again. We agreed to stop sabotaging each other's sales and to talk to each other only when there weren't any customers around. This was exactly what I wanted: to be left alone to do my job. Good thing Ed was on my side.

Back on the sales floor, I wondered how many customers would be Fiery Boys fans. Would my job still be normal? The Fiery Boys had a young audience, and the people who could afford these cars were usually older. With any luck, I'd be able to escape my life as a Fiery Boys contest winner for a few hours each day.

Soon, a nice-looking family came into the dealership, Mom and Dad strutted proudly while their children played hide-and-seek. Dad pointed to some of the cars, and Mom nodded. A serious couple—I could tell they were ready to buy. I watched them carefully, noting which models each of them favored while I leaned against a car, waiting for Dad to notice me. When he finally did, he smiled, but thankfully didn't recognize me. I smiled back, sauntered over, and sold another luxury vehicle.

The guy barely bargained with me, and I scored a hefty commission. Hell, I could have made that sale in my sleep. I wondered if I had. After my crazy weekend, I still wasn't sure I was fully awake. But it was nice to know that I didn't need to be the famous contest winner all the time. I could be my old self when I went to work. Life could be normal.

But in the back of my mind, I knew that nothing was normal anymore. The sooner I was on the road with the Fiery Boys, the better. And even though River had a girlfriend, the chance to ply my charms on him still ranked as my most cherished fantasy.

Day One

Five

As the plane took off from San Jose, I was bursting with excitement. Soon I would meet my teenage idols. I would live with them, go to their concerts, and watch from the wings. Yes, I would have the coveted all-access backstage pass. The dream vacation of fifteen thousand women, and I was living it.

By the time the plane landed in Chicago, my overactive mind was at it again. I worried about being able to get along with these four unknown men. How would I fit in to this all-male environment? I also fretted about my reputation, already shredded on the Internet and about to get significantly worse. The haters had gotten vitriolic over the past month, all of them certain I was going to have legendary sex that would kill the band. And although I knew I wouldn't be that much of a groupie, I couldn't deny my nervousness over being so close to Chuck, Buck, River, and Gabe. This was going to be a wild adventure.

Vaughan, my invisible bodyguard, had come with me all the way. In the airport lounge, he stayed on the other side of the room, watching everyone. Whenever people recognized me and gathered around, he was there, pretending to be one of the fans but secretly making sure nobody got out of line. After I finished chatting with them, they would disburse, and he would walk away like the rest of them. On the flight, he sat a few rows back.

When I got off the plane, I suddenly felt light-headed to be in the same city as the Fiery Boys, about to move in. I blindly followed the other passengers toward baggage claim.

Just past security, a cluster of limousine drivers stood holding out cards with passenger's names on them. I spotted my name, and I nearly laughed when I saw who was holding the card. This guy had "roadie" written all over him. Whereas the other drivers wore black suits, white shirts, and ties, my driver had a well-worn T-shirt and threadbare jeans. And I'm not talking about those stylishly distressed jeans you see people wear. His were seriously torn, with large pieces missing around the knees. His T-shirt was for Alejandro, a popular rocker whose music I also liked. And rather than standing at attention like the other limo drivers, he was dancing in place, rocking to the music in his ears, having a grand old time. I stopped in front of him and watched.

He was obviously enjoying himself, smiling wide with his eyes closed. I didn't want to disturb him. Besides, he was doing a wonderful little dance there, throwing his head back and shaking his hands while he clutched the card with my name on it. It made me happy to be there.

Vaughan gave him a whack on the shoulder as he walked by, forcing him to stop moving and open his eyes. The two men exchanged brief grunts of recognition, then Vaughan wandered off and left me to introduce myself.

"Hi, I'm Annalisa."

The man nodded and gave me a thumbs up. "Hey, contest girl. Welcome to Chicago. I'm Big Tim." He didn't seem that big to me. We shook hands and headed for the baggage area.

"Are you a roadie, Tim?"

"I'm a driver. Actually, I'm *your* driver, if you're riding on the band bus. And also, call me *Big Tim* so everyone knows who you're talking about."

I laughed. "You got a Tiny Tim, too?"

"Nah, but we got a *Bigger* Tim. You gotta use the full name because nobody knows who you're talking about when you just say Tim."

I was having fun now. Big Tim was 100 percent rock and roll, a classic. Tattoos on one arm, long unkempt hair, and dark sunglasses. I was definitely with the band.

Okay, maybe I wasn't with the band yet, but I was *with* someone who was with the band. That ought to count for something. While I waited for my bag to arrive, Big Tim plugged his headphones back in and bobbed his head to the beat.

When we got to his car, it didn't surprise me to see Vaughan sitting in the back seat. We drove into town while the car's impressive sound system pounded us with music. I had a million questions I wanted to ask, but it was hard to speak with the volume cranked. So I sat and watched the road go by.

In the silence between songs, I worked in a question. "Are we going to meet the band now?"

Big Tim turned down the volume. "I'm supposed to take you to see Mr. Bartholomew. He's the manager."

"Right. Jason Bartholomew. This contest was his idea, right?"

Big Tim shook his head. "Not likely. He hates this contest."

"He does? Then whose idea was it?"

"Beats me. Whoever it was must have been out of his fucking mind."

I understood completely. Lots of people seemed to be out of their fucking minds. Like the people who chose me as the contest winner. And the people who hated that I was the contest winner. And perhaps even Big Tim. Maybe they all were—I was about to find out.

I started by asking about the band manager's mind. "Why does Mr. Bartholomew hate this contest? Is he upset about having a girl on the bus?"

"Hey, we get lots of girls on the bus. But they usually only stay until they've gotten a piece of ass, then they're gone. That's why we don't think you'll survive a week. We even got a pool going on you."

"A pool? You're betting on how long it'll be before I run?"

Big Tim grinned. "Yep. I got you down for two days."

"I got you down for five," Vaughan chimed in from the back seat.

I sat there stunned. Everyone on the crew thought I'd wash out. I hadn't considered that I wouldn't last a week.

My litany of fears started to play again, loud and insistent. But I forced them away, refusing to worry about how long I'd last. After all, I was here now, on my way to meet the Fiery Boys. And even if it lasted only fifteen minutes, I could handle it.

The truth was, meeting new, potentially hostile people didn't scare me—I'd endured plenty of that when I was younger. My dad was in the military, and we moved every year or two, from city to city and from country to country. Each time we moved, I'd have to make new friends, break into new cliques, and get accepted. I learned to stay quiet at first and observe people, then dive in when I was ready.

Most of all, I learned the importance of having a good attitude when meeting new people. And since I was about to meet the Fiery Boys, my attitude was at an all-time high. So I told myself that I was once again making new friends, and we'd soon be having the best of times together. Just another first day at a new school.

I gave Big Tim a defiant grin. "Two days, huh? Am I expected to just quit, or will they find me by the side of the road, drooling and babbling?"

Big Tim laughed. "I was thinking drool and babble, but now that I've met you, I'm upgrading you to just quit."

"Thanks, Big Tim. I appreciate that. But you might want to revise your bet. I'm not afraid of any crap the band might throw my way. This is a huge dream of mine, so I doubt they can scare me off."

"Oh, they're plenty scary. But it's not just the boys who are going to drive you away. It's the fans. That's the reason we all think this is a bad idea."

"Yeah, nobody's happy about me winning this contest. Have you seen what they're saying on the Internet?"

Big Tim sputtered. "Hey! Rule number one: don't read about yourself on the Internet. None of the band members do, except maybe Chuck."

"Oh, well, too late. I know women are jealous all over the world. Some of them get really nasty. And men are either calling me an ugly dog or a CWILF."

"A CWILF?"

I didn't know why, but I was fond of this acronym, even though it was crude and rude. With perverse pride, I explained it. "Contest Winner I'd Like to Fuck." I waited while he chuckled. "Pretty cool, huh? I've got my own Internet meme."

Big Tim tilted his head. "This doesn't bother you?"

"Maybe a little, but I'm not sure what I expected. This whole deal has been strange from the start. The night

Chuck spoke my name on television, I became an instant celebrity."

And it never let up. Eventually, I got used to the fact that every story about the Fiery Boys had to mention me. I'd seen myself on television and even on the front page of a supermarket tabloid. After a month of this abuse, I longed for the safety of the band bus where I'd be surrounded by four much more famous people. Another reason why I didn't think I'd be running home anytime soon.

I blew out my breath. "I don't have a normal life anymore, Big Tim. The Fiery Boys took care of that. So even if the bus is a living hell, I'm staying on board, safe from the paparazzi, while you drive me around. I hope you don't mind."

Big Tim stared at me. "I think I'll revise my bet to six days."

I laughed. "Not going for all seven?"

He shrugged. "Don't need to. Nobody's betting on any more than five." He smirked as he nodded toward the back seat.

Six

We pulled into a motel and parked, kicking my heart into a thumping Fiery Boys beat. I knew it was just a meeting with the band manager, but that put me one step closer to the band. Tonight I'd be sleeping on the bus with my rock-and-roll heroes. Alone—I understood that part—but still *on the bus*. I fanned myself with my hand.

As we walked to the room, Big Tim explained. "The band members get their own bus, and the lowlifes crowd onto the second one. But Mr. Bartholomew is so important that he has his own car and stays in motels." He grinned. "Personally, I think he hates us. Don't know why he's managing this band." Big Tim stopped and knocked on a door.

Given that Jason Bartholomew didn't like this contest, I doubted he'd be happy to see me. Regardless, I was going to do my best to make friends with him. He could love me or he could hate me—it would be up to him. I knew there was no in-between with me anymore; peoples' opinions always fell to one extreme or the other.

The door was opened by a balding, medium-height man, wearing a button-down shirt and dark slacks. He squinted at me. "You must be Annalisa." Oozing propriety, he crisply shook my hand and escorted me into the room. I'd guess he was in his forties, going on sixty. And awkward. Either he disliked me, or this was simply his way with everyone.

I made sure my opening salvo was full-bore friendly. "I'm really excited to be here, Mr. Bartholomew."

"I'll bet you are." He gave me a smile that was half real and half plastic. I didn't mind—at least he was smiling. "Have a seat." He waved stiffly toward a chair. "And call me Jason."

We sat down at a table that was scattered with papers, many sporting the Fiery Boys logo. I noticed equipment manifests, song lists, security schedules, and motel reservations. Everything about the Fiery Boys was right there.

Seeing all this back office activity for my favorite band made me even more excited. I realized where I was, at the hub of Fiery Boys central, talking to the faceless man who pulled the levers. And he was preparing to admit me into the inner workings of the machine—the fabled Fiery Boys engine. I started to breathe a little faster.

Jason looked at me, and his smile grew slightly. "I assume you're a big fan."

He had me there. I fluttered my hands. "Oh, God! Huge. I hope I can keep it together when I meet them." I was barely doing that already, and this guy was just the manager.

Jason laughed derisively. "Well, let me give you a tip. The Fiery Boys are nothing more than four stupid kids who made it big. And I'm not just talking about Buck, the so-called dumb one."

There was that idea again that Buck was dumb. Sure, he didn't say much and was somewhat slow when he spoke, but he never said anything truly stupid. Back in high school, I decided he was cautious. It seemed to me that the people who called him stupid were just annoyed that he had a steady girlfriend and a famous father. And as I now understood, haters gonna hate.

I cocked my head and stared at Jason. "So-called?"

He allowed a half grin. "You know that the Fiery Boys are a manufactured band, don't you? I handpicked them over ten years ago." He leaned toward me and thumped the papers on his desk. "I *created* them."

Okay, that was disturbing. I leaned away from the table. "Are you saying that you scripted their personalities? You told Buck to act dumb?"

He nodded, his smile gone. I wanted to tell him how appalled I was, but I knew better.

"Impressive," I lied.

Jason smiled and leaned back in his chair. "In truth, it was more of a group effort. I had to work with these four kids. So I adjusted them here and there, crafted them into the perfect product." Wow. The Fiery Boys weren't people; they were product. Very creepy.

"So Buck's not really dumb?"

"It would have been more accurate to call him deliberate. And certainly horny. He and Danielle couldn't keep their hands off each other. The dumbest thing he did was to marry that woman, for which he's still paying."

"Everyone says Danielle destroyed the band." This was a test, of course. I was floating the most popular story just to see how Jason would react.

"Everyone is wrong." Good—he passed the test. Perhaps we'd get along, after all.

He sat back up and knit his brows. "Listen, the boys are together again, but it's a fragile truce. And I intend to keep it that way through this tour." He leaned closer. "*That means you, too.*" He glared at me.

This seemed like the true Jason Bartholomew. Nasty and controlling, but direct. "What about me?" I gave him a fake smile to show I could do that, too.

He blew out a long breath. "I'm not terribly crazy about this contest idea—our public relations people insisted. But you're here now, so I'm not going to complain. Still, I don't want you screwing the Fiery Boys like some horny groupie. It'll really anger the fans. Your job is to smile, be friendly with the boys, and *don't get too close*. Especially with Chuck. He's a whore who fucks four groupies at once." He wagged a finger at me. "Just don't do it."

Don't have sex with the Fiery Boys? Well, first of all, I didn't really believe that would ever be an option. But I had dreams, and if any of them came true, I was certainly not going to refuse. I wasn't sixteen years old anymore, and I didn't need daddy's permission to stay out all night.

I pushed back lightly. "Or if I do have sex with any of them, I should keep it a secret, right?"

Jason shook his head. "It's no secret that the contest winner is riding on the bus, and every fan expects the boys to screw your brains out. Even if you never go near them, we'll have a hard time convincing the fans of that. But if you show up at Chuck's orgies, the fans will get even nastier." He lowered his gaze at me. "Don't think they can't get nastier."

"Jeez, all right. I'll be good." Maybe. Unless River smiled at me—then I'd be bad. Real bad.

Jason nodded. "There's something you need to know about how you got chosen. Truth is, this was *not* a beauty contest."

I raised a curious eyebrow. Jason might not like me, but he was offering all sorts of useful information. Good thing I was meeting him first. "Okay, why did you pick me?"

"First of all, it wasn't me. The boys chose you. But I wouldn't allow anyone too pretty or sexy because it would anger the fans, so I culled them out. You see, by choosing someone plain, someone who looks like an average fan, the other contestants would think it could have been them. They wouldn't feel like they were ineligible because of their looks, just unlucky. So if you thought there were four horny boys on that bus who couldn't wait to jump your bones, you're wrong."

All right, hold on a second. Did he just tell me I was ugly? Did he say I was chosen because I'm no better looking than the average Fiery Boys fan? Wow, talk about a punch to the ego.

Look, I get it. I'm not a breathtaking beauty. Kira and Jo are both prettier than I am. But couldn't Jason let me hold onto the delusion that my smiling, beer-spraying countenance had somehow charmed the Fiery Boys? I didn't need to hear that I was an unappealing dog right before meeting them.

"Ugh. I'm sorry I asked."

"Hey, don't get all paranoid here. Besides, I have to say you're better looking than I expected." He sat back in his chair and studied me. "You only sent a head shot, so I assumed you had an unattractive body. But you're really not bad at all. Tall, too."

Nice attempt at a compliment. He was willing to admit that I wasn't a complete mongrel. But Jason's honesty was starting to wear thin, and my good mood was shot. I couldn't resist poking back at him. "Screw you for wishing I was fugly."

He shrugged, apparently unperturbed by this kind of abuse. "It only means you'll have to fight off Chuck even harder. Other than that, I don't care. You won the contest, so go enjoy yourself."

Fine, I could adapt. As the woman who won the title of homeliest fan, I was still the winner. And I'd play it for the incredible victory that it appeared to be. So what if River wouldn't hunger for me? So what if nobody would want to party with me? I'd still be on the bus and behind the scenes during shows, watching the Fiery Boys up close. And who knows? Perhaps someone in the band would be nice to me.

I nodded at Jason. "I guess it's good to hear the truth, every once in a while. But I still love the Fiery Boys, and I can't wait to meet them."

Jason smirked. "You like to hear the truth? Then let me give you a little background about the boys. Stuff we don't usually release to the press. It'll help deflate your overblown love of those four clowns."

Jason held up one finger. "First, let's talk about Chuck. I know all you fan girls love the boy, but trust me, he's an insecure and egotistical rocker. If you sleep with him, you'll end up like a thousand other groupies." He grunted a warning. "Don't. Fuck. Chuck." I could tell he said that a lot.

Jason raised two fingers. "Gabe. Horny lead guitarist. Don't get any ideas with him, either. He's a zombie."

Like Chuck, Gabe was a lady-killer, always seen with different women. But he was also the peaceful one who closed his eyes when he played. This gave him the unusual reputation of being horny and Zen. "I thought he was the meditative one. How did he get to be a zombie? Drugs?"

Jason twisted his mouth and nodded. "Fucking pothead. The guy is totally checked out. I used to rely on him to take care of things, but he's much less invested this time around. You're going to have to reevaluate your ten-year-old crushes on him and Chuck."

"I didn't have a crush on Chuck or Gabe. It was the other two I always liked."

Jason stared at me. "Really? You preferred Buck?"

"Well, River was actually my favorite. Buck was a close second."

"Hmm. Maybe they picked the right girl, after all. Still, River isn't happy to be back on tour. I made him shave his head again and now he just sits and stews. You'll be lucky if you get one sentence out of him. And as for Buck, these days he's just plain angry. Something about his divorce. I'm sorry to tell you that the two Fiery Boys you liked the most are the two most unpleasant members of the band. I hope you're good at making friends."

I laughed because I was a pro at making friends. "I'll do what I can."

"Well, if it gets too weird, you can stay in motels. It's up to you. Personally, I think it's much better than that bus."

"Rolling pigsty?"

"Absolutely. And you never know when some groupies will storm it to get a piece of band ass. Some of them can be mean and crazy."

"Gee, this sounds better all the time." I still wasn't worried. If some groupie wanted a piece of band ass, they were welcome to it.

"So you'll take the motel?"

A motel room sounded much nicer than the bus, which was certainly the belly of the beast. But I'd come here for that beast and I wouldn't be denied. Adventures like this were the things I lived for, so motel rooms would be my last refuge. For now, I wanted them to bring on the circus. Horny groupies? Who cares? Surly band members? No surprise there. An abrasive band manager and roadies who think I'll wash out? What did I expect?

"No. I'll take the bus. Like the song says, I owe myself a fiery life. If I'm going to do this, then I'm going all the way."

"'Fiery Life,' huh? You like that song?"

"It's my favorite. The melody always makes me weepy, and the lyrics were custom written for me. Chuck is a genius. I might be more attracted to River and Buck, but I wouldn't refuse an offer from Chuck simply because of that song."

Jason darkened. "Chuck is *not* a genius. Song or no song, if you screw him, I'll throw you off the bus myself."

"Jeez! Don't worry, Jason. I won't have sex with Chuck. Okay?"

Jason sputtered a laugh. "We'll see."

Seven

The Fiery Boys had been on tour for the past week, but their first Chicago show was coming up that night. As we approached the back lot of the arena, the band's tour bus was instantly recognizable. Mostly black, with bold red flames licking upward, the artwork from their first album filled all four sides of the bus. The band name was spelled out in fat red letters that hovered in the blackness, just out of reach of the flames. Either I was a little too excited to be here, or that hot red bus carried a phallic message that was hard to miss.

Next to this rolling billboard for the Fiery Boys sat a more average-looking bus with the band name written in appropriate-size letters. And over by the arena, two tractor-trailers were parked at a loading dock. The band name on the trucks was also reasonably sedate. A part of me wished I wasn't riding in that advertisement-on-wheels, but another part of me was thrilled with the idea.

As we got closer, I saw a small crowd, desperate to see a rock star but thwarted by a makeshift fence that protected the busses and trucks. I couldn't blame the fans—I wanted to see these rock stars, too. But unlike them, I was about to do just that. I tried to suppress the feeling of superiority that I knew I didn't deserve.

We pulled up to the fence, and the fans gathered. Mostly female, they squinted into the car to find out who had arrived. Even though the windows were tinted, I shrank down, afraid of their reaction to me.

Quite a few women gathered, and I was surprised by what I saw. If I didn't know there was a famous rock band close by, I'd have wondered if these women were hookers. They were dressed in some incredibly revealing outfits, not all of which were street legal. Clearly, they were hoping to seduce a Fiery Boy or two.

On the other side of the fence, people ran back and forth, consulted clipboards, yelled instructions, and hauled equipment. Big Tim rolled down the window as a larger man approached the car. This guy was tall and solid, like two Marines squeezed into one body. He leaned in and squinted at me. "You're Annalisa?"

I nodded, and the man leaned farther down. "I'm Bigger Tim." He certainly was. "Fiery Boys head of security." He punctuated his job title with a curt nod, then grumbled as he stood back up. "Didn't expect you this soon."

Bigger Tim seemed upset to see me, so I did my best to placate him. "I'm willing to wait, if you're not ready for me."

He leaned back down. "Yeah. Now's not the best time. . ." He tightened his mouth and looked away.

I tried to lighten the mood. "Room's not made up yet?"

My joke cracked Bigger Tim's facade and he blew out a half-laugh. "Okay, what the fuck? Go on in. You won't last long, anyway." With a smirk, he pulled away a section of the fence.

Why did everyone think I'd wash out? Were the Fiery Boys the most evil band ever, or did the crew have me pegged as a timid wallflower? Even Bigger Tim seemed to dislike me, more than the others. I wondered if his bet was measured in hours instead of days.

As we pulled up to the Fiery Boys bus, I realized that I didn't care what the crew thought. I was here now, and nothing could take that away. Big Tim already liked me and

Jason didn't hate me too much. I'd simply have to work on Bigger Tim, too.

I got out of the car and stared at my new home for the next week. The tour bus loomed over me, tall and black with flaming red highlights. And inside it were my rock heroes. The big red band name screamed to me in bold letters that were as tall as I was. "Fiery Boys!" it yelled. "Door's open; step right up."

I should have raced up the steps—I'd imagined doing it hundreds of times. But something held me back. Maybe I wanted to soak in this moment. I needed to remember, for the rest of my life, the day I first climbed on board. Or maybe I was worried that I *would* wash out. Bigger Tim's reticence certainly didn't help.

Whatever it was, I stood by the huge bus, unable to move. My heart pounded so hard that I thought everyone could see it beating, stretching away from my chest then snapping back like a cartoon character in love.

I had to admit the truth: I simply wasn't ready to meet them. Not that I'd ever be. My busy mind also wondered if I was even worthy. But I quickly told that part of me that I was at least as worthy as those groupies by the fence who, by the way, were now shouting derisive comments at me.

"Cheater! She doesn't deserve this."

"Why does she get a free pass?"

"Look! She's dressed like my mom."

That last one hurt. It was true, though. I had on modest light-green shorts, white sneakers, and a long gray blouse with a blue scarf. Sadly, I realized that I *was* dressed like that groupie's mother.

Kira had given me lectures about how to dress like a rock goddess. She had even given me some of her outfits, just in case the right opportunity came along. But I didn't want to show up like that. And I certainly couldn't compete with the women at the fence for slut supremacy.

This moment of contemplation needed to end before the fans started to throw rotten food. So I stepped onto the bus, ready to meet my high school idols.

I had barely climbed the first step when I felt the difference. The interior of the bus was painted black. The afternoon sun might be bright outside, but in here, it was always night. The hidden cave of the Fiery Boys. Excellent!

I took another step and had to downgrade my "excellent" rating. The bus smelled bad. I could detect stale beer and male sweat, with a hint of marijuana. It reminded me of the boys' wing of my freshman year dormitory. Nothing I couldn't handle, of course, but my fantasies had imagined the Fiery Boys in a more elegant setting.

This shouldn't have come as a surprise. Did I think that any bus with four men living on it would be pleasant? Men are slobs. If it seemed like a dormitory, then perhaps it was. I certainly wasn't going to get bothered by that. And I couldn't let Big Tim down by making him lose the roadie pool. I'd had some fine times in dormitory rooms, and I was about to have some fine times here.

As if to confirm that fine times were indeed on their way, the first one suddenly materialized. I glanced up to see a bald head looking down at me. River! My heart jumped into my throat at this first encounter with a Fiery Boy, my favorite one, too. I felt a sense of kismet, a vision that we were destined to be together. And damn! He looked exceptionally hot in person. Hotter than that recent photo I'd seen. Mature, solid, and just plain perfect. A sharp frisson of excitement ran through my body.

River quickly turned and retreated into the bus, shouting, "It's Annalisa!" His footsteps pattered into the distance, and he was gone. That's okay, we'd get to know each other later.

I finished my ascent onto the bus and looked around. My eyes were already adjusted to the dark, crypt-like space. What I didn't expect to see was a continuation of the jarring color palette from the outside. Only a man would have decided to decorate the interior of a bus in black and fiery red. Only a man would want to live in there. The bus oozed sex and drugs and rock and roll.

Standing at the top of the steps, I found myself in a living room, with a sofa, table and chairs, and a wall-sized television tuned to a sports channel. Guitars sat by the wall along with cables and boxes of gear. The table was cluttered with beer and liquor bottles, a mostly empty bowl of snack food, and an ashtray with quite a few hand-rolled cigarette butts. Yeah, yeah, I knew they weren't cigarettes. So what?

River was gone, probably busy farther back, but Chuck was standing there, watching the screen, and Gabe was sitting at the table, buried in his phone. I took a moment to check them out. Even in the dim light, they looked so amazing that I wanted to jump like a teenager. In person, Chuck was even more handsome than he'd appeared on television. He wore tattered jeans and a T-shirt, with an unbuttoned long-sleeved black shirt over it.

And Gabe Ashford, my least favorite Fiery Boy, also looked better than I'd expected. He was actually rather cute, with a thin face, brown eyes, and spiky blond hair. His outfit was all black, including his jeans, his T-shirt, and even his leather biker's jacket. I'd never really paid much attention to him, but now I could see that I might have been wrong. Wow! It was a good thing River and Buck weren't there or I probably would have made inhuman noises and wet myself.

Eight

It took me a few seconds to adjust to the reality of the situation. I was there! I was actually on the Fiery Boys tour bus, standing in front of them. Chuck and Gabe were right here. And River! I'd seen River already! Swoon! Somebody needed to pour a bucket of water on me.

Gabe cracked a smile, and the tension lifted. I could do this—it was new friend time. I stepped forward and offered my hand. "It's nice to meet you."

Gabe broadened his smile and shook my hand. Then he leaned back and closed his eyes, peeking every few seconds at his phone. He never said a word. Jason wasn't wrong there—the boy *was* a zombie. I wondered if he'd smoked all those joints.

Chuck came over to give me a hug. A hug! I was hugging one of the Fiery Boys! It didn't get any better than that. Or so I thought.

But when he opened his mouth, he ruined it all. "Welcome to the house of Chuck, now offering hot sex with the lead singer of the Fiery Boys." He grabbed his crotch and leered at me in a childlike way, as if a pre-teen was still in control of this man's body.

Jason had called that one, too. I mentally thanked him for warning me about this, otherwise I might have responded to Chuck's offer. Instead, I pulled out of his grip and smiled. "How about a tour of the bus?"

Chuck's eyes widened, clearly surprised at my response. "Of course. I'll show you the bedroom." Yeah, *that* was the reason I didn't agree to instantly spread my legs for him. I'm one of those sensible women who need to make sure the bedroom's properly appointed before I let someone seduce me there. But I didn't want to get sarcastic with Chuck, so I let his understanding of the situation stand. As long as I got to see the tour bus I'd be happy. Baby steps.

Chuck snaked his arm around my shoulder and led me farther back. Just past the living room was the kitchen with a refrigerator, a stove, a sink full of dirty dishes, and an overflowing box of empty bottles on the floor.

Beyond the kitchen were the sleeping quarters with six cubicles stacked two high. Each had a bed and a few shelves for personal effects. The front part of the sleeping area had four cubicles, two on each side. Beyond that were two more on the left and the bathroom on the right. And at the very back sat the aforementioned bedroom.

Chuck pointed out which cubicles were for which band members. The two in back, across from the bathroom, had Buck on top and nobody in the bottom. The front four had River and Gabe on the right side, leaving Chuck and me on the left side. He gave me the upper cubicle and I wondered if he intentionally put my bed near his. Did he plan to visit me at night?

Chuck wrapped up the tour at the back of the bus. "And now the bedroom. I'm sure you'll like it." I felt like Chuck's new sex toy. And here I'd thought that none of them would want me. It was comforting to discover I'd been wrong, and yet a little disconcerting. I didn't want to shut the door completely on this man, but I simply couldn't bring myself to go there yet.

"Can we not do this right now?"

True to form, Chuck was unperturbed. "Some other time, then." I heard Jason's warning echo in my head, "Don't. Fuck. Chuck."

Then I reminded myself that this man was the lead singer of the Fiery Boys. That had to count for something. I wondered if I should go for it and make Kira proud. But Chuck's oversized ego was making it hard for me to feel any kind of special. I'd be just another conquest, along with thousands of other fan girls. And what would the rest of my week be like if I jumped him in the first ten minutes? Awkward. It didn't seem like the right thing to do.

So I gave him a friendly-but-not-too-friendly smile. "I'm guessing you were one of the three who *did* vote for me."

He stepped closer and ran his fingers through my hair. "Trust me, I want you on the bus. You're kinda cute." His hands slipped down to my shoulders then ran down my arms, thumbs extended to "accidentally" swipe my breasts as he made his way down to my hips. Jeez, what a lecher.

But honestly, did I think I would be treated differently than all the other groupies? As far as the Fiery Boys were concerned, I was no different than them. Just another woman who couldn't wait to have sex with a rocker. But I was here for a full week, not a half hour, and that should have meant something.

If Chuck had treated me as anything more than an easy lay, had shown even the tiniest morsel of respect for me as a person, I might have ripped my clothes off by now. And if River had come on to me, we'd both be naked. I'm only human, you know.

But Chuck simply wasn't motivating me. And it only got worse.

"Tell you what. . ." I could see by the glint in his eye that another attempt at my body was imminent. "Any time I'm in the bedroom with my groupies, you're welcome to come join us. Three-way, four-way, I don't care. I'll make room for you, too."

This was offensive in so many ways that I couldn't even focus my reaction. Why did he think I'd group-fuck him after I'd just refused his attempt for some one-on-one action? Should I sarcastically thank him for inviting me to take part in sloppy thirds or fourths? I silently begged whatever deity was available to make Chuck stop talking about sex.

Too bad none of the gods were listening. Chuck wrapped his arms around me and crushed my body against his. Pressed up like this, I couldn't deny that he was a fine specimen. His tall, solid, muscular body felt wonderful. No wonder he didn't know how to talk to women—he didn't have to.

I hated to disappoint him, but I needed to. And besides, Jason would throw me off the bus if I let Chuck have his way. I pulled back and shook my head. "No, thanks." Before Chuck could continue his attack, I steered the conversation away from his penis. "So where did River go? And where's Buck? Is he sleeping in the bedroom?" Seriously, where were my two favorite Fiery Boys?

Chuck laughed. "Sleeping? No. Nobody sleeps in the bedroom. We do *other* things there. Things we can't do in our cubicles unless we want to end up in traction." He wiggled his eyebrows at me as if his meaning wasn't already glaringly obvious. Subtlety was not Chuck's forte.

"Nobody's in the bedroom. Yet. Here, I'll show you." He opened the door at the back of the bus and led me in. I stood there, amazed.

Besides being spacious, this room was like a portal to a different world. In direct contrast to the heavy black-and-red motif on every surface of the bus, the bedroom was a welcome relief. The walls were a gentle off-white, the carpet light blue. Even the furniture was tastefully simple: plain nightstands and a solid wood headboard on a huge bed. I nodded my appreciation then headed out to the safety of the hallway.

In an effort to escape Chuck's horniness, I went to my cubicle to unpack. But he wasn't done with me yet. He pulled me to his side. "You want to see Buck? Check this out." He knocked on the bathroom door and shouted into it. "You ready?"

Ready? What was Buck doing in the bathroom? Another setup from the oversexed Fiery Boys? But this time, the man in question was Buck, my number two heartthrob. If he came out of the bathroom and propositioned me, I wasn't sure I'd be able to refuse.

The door opened and instead of the handsome Buck Morris, a naked woman stepped out. I was so surprised to see her that my whole body snapped to attention. There I was, mentally prepared to meet a rock icon only to come face-to-face with a naked groupie. This bus was full of surprises.

But the woman was far from surprised. She seemed to be completely at ease with her lack of clothing, and given her shapely body, I could see why. She fell easily into Chuck's arms, then she noticed me. "Contest girl." She laughed and kissed Chuck hard. Then she turned back to me with a smirk. "You lose."

As if. She could have him. I took a step back, ready to return to the living room.

But Chuck had a surprise in store for both of us. He peeled the woman away from himself and pointed to Buck's cubicle, whispering, "He's in there, and he wants you."

One rock star was clearly as good as another to this woman. And I couldn't completely disagree with that sentiment at this point in my new role as a band-sanctioned groupie. So it didn't surprise me when she scampered up the ladder.

There was a rustling sound followed by the woman's cooing. "Hi, Buck. Let me help you out of those pants."

From inside the cubicle, Buck shouted, "What? Stop that! Get out!" The rustling turned into jostling and the woman reemerged, pushed out by a strong arm.

She managed to grab the edge and lowered herself safely to the floor. Then she turned to Chuck without the slightest indication that it bothered her to have been thrown out of a man's bed. "I don't think he wants me," she giggled.

Chuck patted her naked backside. "Don't you worry about a thing. *I* want you. Go back to the bedroom, and I'll be there soon." She eagerly bounced through the door and disappeared.

Instead of following her, Chuck turned to me with one last attempt at what he seemed to call romance. "Join us, contest girl. The beast between my legs wants you." God, what a dick. And I didn't mean the beast between his legs.

My answer was still "no." As much as I wanted to pursue a fiery life, I definitely didn't want a fiery crotch. "Maybe another time. Go ahead and have fun."

Chuck gave me a mock salute and headed toward the bedroom. As he passed Buck's cubicle, a fist shot out, hitting his shoulder and knocking him against the bathroom door. Then the curtains flew open, and Buck leapt out, wearing boxer briefs and a black T-shirt. I stood in awe.

Buck had always seemed like a gorgeous man to me, but that was back when I was looking through teenage goggles. Now that we were older, Buck looked even better than he had ten years ago. According to their bios, he was an inch shorter than Chuck, but I could hardly tell the difference. He was certainly much more solidly built and more muscular—I could see his entire body primed and flexed as he held Chuck against the wall. So handsome, so sexy. What a delightful first impression of the man: his pants off, his muscles toned.

Unfortunately, Buck didn't seem delighted at all. He didn't even notice me—he was focused entirely on Chuck. "Could you be any more of an asshole?" He glared with hard, venomous eyes.

Chuck laughed. "Why sure. Find a few more groupies and send them back here. And make sure they bring some tequila." He grinned at Buck then shook free of his bandmate's grip. "Chip!" he shouted toward the front of the bus. "Little help, please." I didn't know who Chip was: the only one up front was Gabe. Before I could inquire, Chuck disappeared into the bedroom.

"Fucker," Buck muttered and flipped a finger in Chuck's direction. He stood with his back to me, facing the bedroom, seething. Jason had called this one, too. Anger and hatred poured from Buck, and it touched a sensitive spot in me. Just like Palmer, who easily got angry, Buck was disturbingly touchy. Sure, Chuck had just played a prank on him, but most guys I knew laughed off that sort of thing.

After a few seconds, Buck started to climb back into his cubicle. Then he noticed me and stopped. After staring for a second, he shot out a short laugh. "Welcome to hell." With a shake of his head, he finished climbing into his cubicle and closed the curtain.

Nine

I stood alone in the back of the bus, relieved to be free of that scene but concerned about what might come next. I had now met all four Fiery Boys, and they were certainly a letdown. Chuck and Gabe were, if anything, even more worthless than Jason had warned. River was obviously hiding from me, and Buck had emerged long enough to fight with Chuck then go back to into hiding as well. I might have once dreamed about Buck, but his anger doused that flame. He could stay in his cubicle for all I cared.

I noticed muffled giggles of delight coming from the bedroom door. That groupie might not have any shame about running around the tour bus naked and jumping into multiple band members' beds, but I felt a little embarrassed listening to her. I went back to the living room.

Gabe was still there, now working both a phone and a tablet. He didn't look up when I sat down across from him, and I felt alone again, even sitting with the famous guitarist. Sure, they had better things to do than talk to me all day—I could handle that. But the band had barely acknowledged me. Only Chuck seemed pleased to see me, and his pleasure extended only as far as his groin.

After a few more seconds of silent treatment, I decided to regroup. I muttered at Gabe, not expecting him to hear me. "Well this sucks." Then I stood up and got off the bus.

I was about to call Kira and tell her what a bunch of jerks these boys were, when Gabe came bounding out. I watched carefully, wondering what had motivated the zombie to move his body. Probably hungry for some brains.

Gabe walked up to me with a tiny smile. He seemed about to speak when he noticed the women standing by the fence and stopped with an exasperated look. He raised a finger at me and leaned closer. "Don't go anywhere."

He walked to the fence, slowly pacing the line. I couldn't blame him, really. These women had everything on display. And Gabe, the reputedly horny member of the band, was definitely shopping. After a few seconds, he pointed to two tall women standing next to each other. "You two. Come on in." He nodded to Bigger Tim.

The security chief flashed him a grin. "Sure thing, Chip." Gabe darkened and folded his arms, apparently unhappy with this nickname. Bigger Tim just shrugged. When he opened the fence, the two women came screaming in, surrounding Gabe with a well-rehearsed coordinated grope.

Being this close to the Fiery Boys was eye-opening—they were jerks *and* whores. Did Gabe want me to stick around for an even more epic sexual encounter? Besides, where would the four of us go, now that the bedroom was in use? I felt slightly sick when I considered that the Fiery Boys might pile in there with as many hot bodies as the room could hold. No wonder Bigger Tim was reluctant to let me get on the bus right now: it was orgy hour.

I took a few steps back, hoping to avoid a messy situation. But then Gabe did something I didn't expect. He pushed the two women away. "Not me, girls. Chuck's looking for some fun. He's in the back of the bus with someone already. If you're interested in a four-way, go on in. If not, back to the fence." He pointed out the only two directions they could take. Both of the women instantly ran for the bus.

As much as I was relieved to be free of a six-way with two band members, I was still disappointed and needed some space. I turned and escaped through the fence, moving it aside without Bigger Tim's help. Then I stepped through the crowd of waiting groupies. One or two of them probably yelled something derisive at me, but by that point, I'd heard it all and was tired of listening.

Big Tim should have left his bet at two days, because I might not last a week at this rate. I shuddered at the thought of even *one* day watching zombie-Gabe wake up long enough to arrange sexual liaisons for Chuck before returning to his coffin. At least he didn't try to get me to join in Chuck's orgy. I reached for my phone again, ready to disappoint Kira with the sordid news.

Behind my back, screams started up. "Gabe! Here! We love you!" Was he pimping again, choosing mates for the others? Or did Chuck need more than three? I wondered if the zombie guitarist had any libido of his own.

As much as I didn't want to watch any more of this, I couldn't resist turning to look. After all, my girlfriends needed to hear the full story of fiery depravity. Also, the sound of the fans screaming seemed to be growing louder.

What I saw behind me forced me to a stop. Gabe had also left the fenced enclosure and was headed straight for me, pushing women away as he approached. When he saw that I'd stopped, he jogged and quickly made it to my side. "Annalisa, wait. Let's talk." Fans surrounded us and pushed pieces of paper at him.

After signing a few autographs, he took my arm. "Let's get inside the fence."

Now my least favorite Fiery Boy was chasing me. What unseemly sexual role did he have in mind? I nearly laughed when I thought of all the erotic fantasies I'd envisioned over the past month, and how they'd all been dashed in such a short amount of time. See? I knew I wasn't going to end up with any of them.

He led me back through the fence where we could talk in private. "How come everyone calls you Chip?" I gave him a light smile.

Gabe let out a laugh. "I just picked up that stupid nickname yesterday, and already everyone's using it. Please call me Gabe."

"Okay, Gabe." I paused before asking, but I couldn't resist, so I let it out. "Do you often choose partners for the other band members?" Like—I hoped—River? I still held on to some erotic fantasies, but they were fading fast.

Gabe gave me a mildly self-deprecating smile. "Not too often, and only for Chuck." He shrugged. "A happy lead singer makes a happy band."

"That's disgusting." The time for discretion and politeness was gone. "I definitely liked you boys better before I stepped onto that bus." Someone needed to hear this, and although Gabe might not remember anything I said, I still had to say it before his deadened nervous system stopped comprehending language completely.

Once again, he surprised me. "You've got it wrong, Annalisa. I'm not trying to convince you to go with Chuck. In fact, I was impressed with how you kept your distance from him just now. I only want to apologize. And try to explain. Come on, let's talk."

I stood with my mouth wide open, unsure I'd heard him right. I mean, that was an awful lot of words, and nice ones,

too. I didn't think he could do that. A sensitive Fiery Boy—
he had my complete attention.

"Okay, sure."

"Let's go backstage." He pointed to the massive arena,
sitting innocently like a citadel that had admitted the
Trojan horse and had no idea what would happen when the
sun went down. Backstage with Gabe sounded like fun. It
had all the promise of rock and roll with the added
attraction of a Fiery Boy who was willing to pay attention to
me. Chuck needed to take lessons from this man.

I followed him, unable to resist further inquiry into the
way I'd been treated. "Do you guys hate me or something?
Am I ruining your all-guy bus experience? Because I can get
a motel, you know—Jason said so. Just say the word and I'll
go." At this point, I wouldn't mind.

Gabe held up a hand to stop me. "No, don't go. Not the
best way to meet the band, though." He led me to a side
door, and a guard let us in. "Come on."

I followed him to the stage, which was getting piled
high with speakers and other band equipment. Gabe was
about to head backstage when he muttered, "Oh, no," and
ran up to a roadie. "I told you not to change the battery in
my pedals." He knelt down with a groan and started to play
with some equipment. After a few seconds, he looked up
and explained it to me. "My programming got lost. I have to
reload it—hang on." He worked for a minute to restore
order, using two phones and assorted hardware that
magically appeared from his pockets. Then he got up, and
we started to walk away. "Okay, sorry about that."

I looked back at the guitar pedals on the floor, now
flashing little green lights to tell the world that all was well.
"High-tech band toys?"

He grinned. "Yeah, I'm a sucker for the stuff." He led the way back to a dressing room, sat down, and motioned for me to take another seat.

Gabe leaned close. "As I was starting to say before, nobody's mad at you. It's us. Not all of us are happy to be back on the road, and some of us don't even want to see each other. We're a pretty dysfunctional band."

"Then why are you touring?"

He grinned. "For fame and money, of course. I've got a high-tech toy habit that I'd like to feed. River wants to buy more fancy Japanese drums. And Chuck wants to give his Vegas act a boost. So when Jason suggested a ten-year reunion tour, we mostly agreed."

"Mostly? You didn't mention why Buck's back on tour."

"Yeah, he's the only one who didn't want this. We had to talk him into it." Gabe took a long breath. "Anyway, it hasn't been the smoothest ride, so I doubt we'll do anything else after this tour."

Oh no! Their reunion was a sham, and the band would soon be dead again. "I guess I'm sorry to hear that. I imagined the Fiery Boys would stay together and make lots more music." A laugh escaped from me. "Nothing's what I expected. I didn't expect to see orgies, either. Didn't that go out with the sixties?"

Gabe rolled his eyes. "Chuck's the only one who likes to have his groupies in groups."

"So why do you enable him? Can't Chuck find his own women? Maybe he needs a take-a-number dispenser." I pretended I was Chuck, selecting my next faceless female. "Number eighty-seven? Come on back and spread your legs."

Gabe laughed. "Just let it go."

"I can't, Gabe. You're like a predatory fraternity. It's offensive, sickening."

"I told you. It's only Chuck."

"Fine. So why am I getting the silent treatment from everyone else?"

"River hasn't got much to say to you—give him time. And I'm here, aren't I? Talking to you." He reached out and took my hands in his. "Don't leave. We want you on the bus. Well, I do at least. And I know River wants you there, too."

River wanted me? That was good news. But why did he run away as soon as I showed up? I pulled my hands back and sunk into the chair. "He certainly has a strange way of showing it. And what about Buck?"

"Buck wants you there, too. Although he also has a strange way of showing it. Besides not wanting to be on tour, he's going through some evil shit because of his divorce from Danielle. So don't take it personally."

"There's a lot of sexual pressure on that bus." I wondered why this would surprise me. It really shouldn't have.

"Again, that's Chuck—ignore him. I promise that the rest of us will treat you with respect." He stood up with his hand outstretched. "Come on. Let me help you get settled on the bus. In a few hours, we're doing a sound check, then we'll all have dinner and do a show. This is the first concert where you're with us, so it's going to be special."

I doubted the concert would be special for them. But I couldn't deny my own enthusiasm about standing in the wings while the Fiery Boys played to a huge Chicago crowd. And I did feel special when Gabe escorted me back to the bus, past vitriolic groupies who screamed their love for him and their hate for me with equal volume. Some of them needed to get a life, and all of them needed to put on more clothes.

Back on the bus, River and Buck were still hiding in their cubicles. Gabe walked me back there and demanded that they act nicely. Which, to my surprise, they did. They opened their curtains and welcomed me to the tour.

With the two most drool-worthy Fiery Boys smiling at me and acting nice, I gushed like a groupie. "Oh my God! I can't tell you how excited I am to meet you. I've been in love with you guys since high school." I bounced on the balls of my feet.

River gave me a light smile. "Well, I hope you enjoy this week."

Buck was a different story. He rolled his eyes and shook his head, then, without another word, he pulled back into his cubicle and closed the curtain.

Gabe smirked at Buck's reaction, then he led me back to the living room table. "You have to forgive Buck. He hates groupies, so when you went all fan girl on him just now, it annoyed him."

That made sense. Buck's father, Wyatt Morris, was also a famous rocker. So I could understand Buck's dislike of desperate fans. I respected his desire to be treated like a human being, and I promised myself I'd act normally to all of them from now on. It wouldn't be hard with Buck: I'd just pretend that he was another one of my angry boyfriends.

Gabe and I sat in the living room and maintained a steady conversation. It helped drown out the sound of three women screaming for Chuck's rosy ass. Swear to God, I actually heard one of them say that.

Ten

"So are you getting any?" Jo wanted a body count.

I was standing in the wings of the stage, talking to her on my phone while trying to keep out of the way of roadies, techies, suits, and other symbiotic creatures from the world of rock-and-roll. Tonight I wore something more appropriate for the Fiery Boys: a black blouse with swirling magenta and blue leggings and a slate blue hoodie. I purposely kept it band-moderate so Chuck wouldn't get going again.

Fans were filing into the arena, and the show would be starting soon. The boys buzzed around with an extra level of energy, clearly ready to rock.

I retreated into a quiet corner of the wing so I could talk. "I'm lucky to still be on the bus. The Fiery Boys are not what I expected."

"No naked flesh?" Jo sounded disappointed.

"There was a naked groupie in the bathroom when I arrived. Does that count?"

"Not unless you had sex with her." She paused, then went on in a provocative pout. "*Did you* have sex with her?"

"Sorry, no." I was doing a poor job of delivering vicarious Fiery Boys thrills. Jo and Kira were two horny women who needed details.

She pressed on. "So you didn't have sex with anyone, but there was a naked groupie on the bus. Did *she* have sex with anyone?"

"Yep. Guess who with? Your favorite Fiery Boy, Chuck! He seems to enjoy group sex." I couldn't resist teasing her. "Maybe you and Kira could do him as a team."

Jo gasped. "Seriously? That'd be hella hot! Can you set this up for us?"

Okay, I didn't see that coming. I thought Jo would go prudish and proper. After all, she was a professional woman —a psychologist with an office and a receptionist and clients who paid for her good sense. Sure, she talked about sex all the time, but I didn't think she'd instantly be willing to team fuck Chuck. Was I the only woman in the world who didn't offer up her body as soon as he came close? Sheesh!

But before I promised any arrangements with the lead singer of the Fiery Boys, I felt like I needed permission from someone else. "Shouldn't we ask Kira first?"

Jo laughed. "No need. She's down with it. We've done it before. Remember that time the three of us went to Los Angeles for the weekend and you caught a cold? Well, Kira and I. . ."

"Stop!" I'd heard only vague moans of satisfaction from them that weekend, but they never admitted they'd been with the same man. In any case, I didn't need to hear about it now. Perhaps I *was* the only woman in the world who wouldn't fuck Chuck. I was also—let me point out—the only woman in the world who'd been warned not to. It was good to have an excuse for avoiding those things your gut tells you are wrong.

A tech wandered by with a clipboard. As he came close, the radio on his hip squawked that the show was all set up. "Hey, Jo. The show's starting soon, so I'm going to go. I'm really stoked!"

"Go get 'em, you lucky dog. Talk to you later." She hung up.

I noticed the band gathered together over by the side, so I approached with caution. The boys were all dressed up and looked quite fine. Chuck still wore tattered jeans and an unbuttoned long-sleeve shirt, but now he didn't have a T-shirt under it, and his bare chest flashed all kinds of desire. River was down to jeans and a sleeveless white T-shirt with a black leather vest over it. His shoulder muscles alone made my knees weak.

Buck and Gabe were much more dressed up. Buck wore black slacks and a black jacket over an untucked white shirt with the top button open and a loose white tie. The sleeves of his shirt and jacket were rolled up like a businessman on the Wall Street trading floor. And Gabe was looking the most impressive, with black pants, black calf-boots, and a black Nehru jacket with two rows of gold buttons marching down the front. The boys looked hot and ready to rock.

Gabe nodded at me and they all turned to look, so I smiled bashfully and gave them a thumbs up. Regardless of their personal issues, they were still my favorite band of all time, and I wanted to show them that I was good. If it made a difference to anyone, that is.

Nobody said a word, but Chuck blew me a kiss by way of reply. Gabe and Buck fidgeted with their guitars while River casually tossed drumsticks from hand to hand. I took a step back to give them space.

Jason paced back and forth by the edge of the stage, peeking out every minute to check on the audience. Each time he looked, Chuck would ask if it was time to start the show. He really *was* a child, complete with are-we-there-yet nagging. Like a patient parent, Jason set his hand on Chuck's shoulder. "Wait for it. I figure ten more minutes."

Jason might not like having me there, but he had at least been civil to me, so I felt like I could talk to him. "How do you know when it's time to start the show?"

He grinned. "I like to wait for it to get restless and loud. Right now, it's a bit too quiet for my boys."

"*Your* boys?" There was that swagger again, his I-am-God attitude.

Gabe laughed. "We're back under contract, so he owns us until the tour ends."

River nodded. "Chip's right, you know." Gabe puffed out a breath at River's use of the nickname. Of course, he wasn't the only one whose identity was fluid. River had a fake last name, and Buck used to be called Chuck. Nobody was who they seemed.

River continued, oozing sarcasm. "We're Jason's indentured servants now, forced to play for our lord and master."

Buck joined right in, bowing to Jason. "My lord and master."

"You're making nice money, Buck."

"I *have* money." He growled. "Can't stand this fucking tour." He stomped away. I let my shoulders slump and backed away in the other direction. No need to make them any more testy before the show.

Ten minutes later, as predicted, Jason took a quick peek and then spoke into his phone. He turned to the band with a nod. Like puppets on a string, the boys became animated by their manager's signal. They straightened up, excited and ready.

A voice boomed through the hall. "Ladies and gentlemen, welcome." The announcer gave a lecture about recording, smoking, throwing things, and all the other uncivilized activities that they hoped they could count on the audience not to do. Then, with the fans whipped into a delirium, he wrapped up his introduction. "Let's give a big Chicago welcome to *the Fiery Boys!*"

The house lights went down, the stage lights went wild, and the crowd went wilder. The boys marched onto the stage.

Chuck grabbed the microphone and did his best to own the crowd. "Hello Chicago! Are you ready to rock?" River clicked his sticks together, and the band seamlessly launched into their first song, an old chestnut called "Sizzling Love."

I had always liked this song, with its powerful beat and soulful lyrics. It had been rerecorded recently and popularized by Alejandro, the rocker whose T-shirt Big Tim was wearing when he picked me up. There was definitely some crossover between the two bands. I'd even heard a rumor that they were planning on trading guest appearances when their tours intersected in Seattle. Too bad I'd be gone by then.

I felt woozy, standing in the wings and watching them play. No fan could get any closer. Gabe stood nearest to me in his power-zombie stance, legs apart, head thrown back, eyes closed. River thrashed the drums like a mad man, a smile on his face that left little doubt he was enjoying every second. Chuck howled and growled as he postured for his fans, clearly happy to be the center of attention. Even Buck seemed pleased, standing near the drum kit and bobbing his head. He and River occasionally traded hand signals and nods, keeping the rhythm section solid.

And me? I let it all go and rocked out. This decade-old song brought back so many memories—I was transported. My body moved without thinking about it. I wanted to let go completely and dance with abandon. Unfortunately, there was too much activity going on back stage, and I didn't want to get in anyone's way. But down on the dance floor, everyone was having a blast. I realized that I needed to join the rest of the fans out there. Then I wouldn't have to worry about anyone else.

I hid my backstage pass and went down to the floor. The music was thumping even louder as I made my way in from the wings. I found a nice spot and started to dance, blending with pumped fans who were totally into this song. Gabe improvised a little, and each deviation from the overplayed studio version elicited a cheer. I took a few seconds to appreciate that I was at my first Fiery Boys concert in years. The energy was overwhelming.

After the song ended, I checked out the crowd. One woman was instantly noticeable because she was tall and had long, bright red hair that spilled over bare shoulders. She stood by the edge of the stage, as close as possible to Chuck. All around her were other women who also had artificially red hair, but this fan distinguished herself with her height and the furious energy she brought to her dancing when the next song started. Curious, I worked my way toward her.

As I approached, I could see more of her outfit. She wore some sort of red corset that had flame-shaped pieces of leather rising up all around her body. Two of the flames conveniently managed to provide minimum legal coverage of her breasts while revealing most of their obviously enhanced ginormousness. I gasped and stared.

Now I knew what it meant to be a serious Fiery Boys fan. Compared to this woman, I was nothing, a mere poser. She was completely out there, living the life. I *was* impressed. I inched my way closer, fascinated with the scene.

As I got nearer, I could see more of this fan girl's true dedication to her obvious goal of seducing the Fiery Boys. The bottom of her tight red corset had inverted flames, hanging down below her waist. The thin leather tendrils didn't even pretend to cover anything and left her backside completely exposed. Once again, she remained minimally covered thanks to one particularly long lick of leather flame that snaked down between her legs and reappeared as a thong string in back. She topped this incredibly erotic getup with some thigh-high fuck-me boots, red of course, with towering heels. That explained her height. Her outfit was so powerfully kinky that I doubted she could be more alluring, even if she was naked. This was finely tuned slutwear. Chuck really needed to invite her back to the bus.

"Hey! It's the contest girl. That bitch!" I wondered when someone would recognize me. Too bad it was one of the red-headed friends of the corseted queen. Their leather leader turned, noticed me, and waved a hand. Then, like a bacteria absorbing nutrients, the perimeter of women surrounding her opened up, and I was brought in. I stood face to face with the kinkiest groupie I'd ever seen.

Whoever she was, she didn't seem happy. "Well, if it isn't the contest whore. How's the bus, bitch? Fucked Chuck yet?" She had to yell to be heard over the pounding music.

I shouted back a reply. "No, I think he's more your speed." I wanted to suggest that we just ask him. After all, he was standing right in front of us on the stage. I glanced up and saw his eyes on the two of us, watching us carefully. Of course, when I looked again I realized that he was watching *her* carefully, not me. I couldn't blame him.

The song ended and in the relative silence, the queen bee lashed out at me. "I hope you die!"

It's always nice to know where you stand when meeting new people. And in the case of this woman, I stood in a very difficult place. I needed to say something in response to her death threat, so I tossed back a light quip. "Why? Are you second in line?" I gave her a little grin.

She didn't even crack a smile. In fact, her frown only deepened. Okay, fine. Humor wasn't going to work here, so I went for flattery, something that she seemed to desperately want. I stepped back and gave her an approving nod. "Honestly, you look super hot! I've got to tell you how impressed I am with your outfit. Chuck will love it—I'm sure he'll fuck you."

She practically snarled at me. "You stupid cunt! I've fucked him plenty of times." Why was I not surprised?

"Well then, you're way ahead of me. Look, don't let me stop you from doing him here in Chicago or anytime I'm on the bus. I promise I won't get in your way." I can be quite accommodating when I try.

But it didn't work. She clenched her fists and seemed to tighten every muscle in her body. I couldn't win with this one, so I decided it was time to make myself scarce. But before I could move, she hauled off and slapped me across the face. Really hard! Then, just in case I had forgotten her earlier death threat or had otherwise thought we were becoming fast friends, she screamed, "Die!"

I got the message. Loud and clear and ringing in my head from that slap. I turned and charged the queen's guard, ducking between two of them to get out into the crowd. Keeping low, I pushed people aside, my head down, my arms in front of me.

I made it to the edge of the dance floor and followed signs for the bathroom. When I got there, I examined myself and could see a red area where my cheek felt warm.

No broken skin. I was also pleased to note that she hadn't injected any toxic biochemicals into me with micro needles implanted in her fingernails. Hey, it's a sick world out there, and my overactive brain likes to drift.

I took a slow breath and calmed myself down. Disappointed, I realized that I now had to watch the shows from the wings, not the audience. I was the famous contest winner, and the other fans were not my friends. I headed backstage.

It took me a few minutes of wandering around the wings until I found a place where I could dance without bothering anyone. From there, I had a great side view and nobody yelled at me. Thirty feet away, my rock heroes were pounding out a more recent song, one that Buck wrote. I swayed, entranced by this so, so pretty song, enjoying the thrill of seeing the Fiery Boys play it. They were right there, so close, and I felt like they were playing only for me. I had to admit this was better than being on the dance floor.

After another few songs, they finally played "Fiery Life," and I nearly lost control. I danced much more intensely, flailing my arms in the air and singing along at the top of my lungs.

A pair of panties flew onto the stage, landing at Chuck's feet. He scooped them up and turned to hook them over the end of Buck's bass guitar. Although the fans cheered at the gesture, Buck was not amused. He kicked Chuck and knocked him off balance.

The next verse was up, and Chuck was already singing the lyrics. Ever the professional, he kept going while he stumbled, which elicited applause from the audience. Then he straightened himself at the front of the stage and finished the song as if nothing had happened.

Angry Buck again. He didn't need to react so strongly to what seemed to me like classic playfulness. Women must throw their undergarments at these four men all the time—what part of that was bothersome? And it's not like Chuck had laid the panties over the strings or otherwise affected Buck's playing. Interestingly, I noticed River give Buck an approving smirk. Was he angry with Chuck, too? Jeez, they were as bad as Palmer.

I was so tired of angry men. All that mattered was their petty grievances. I wondered if they were this childish ten years ago, when they really were children.

Eleven

After the show, the boys made their way to the bus. I followed at a distance, unwilling to get caught in their band hell or the backwash of stage door groupies. I waited for the four of them to climb on board before I came out of hiding and ran to the bus.

The locker-room odor now overpowered the smell of beer and pot. The bus simply stank. I saw River duck into the bathroom, a towel around his narrow waist. Buck and Gabe were collapsed at the living room table, while Chuck could be heard from the bedroom along with some number of women.

I sat at the living room table and tried to make conversation. "You were wonderful tonight."

"Thanks." Gabe smiled and lit a joint. He took a deep drag, then held it out to Buck. I noticed a moment of hesitation before Buck took the joint and puffed on it. Then he handed it back to Gabe and wandered to his cubicle. Gabe watched him leave the living room and laughed. "Lightweight." He held the joint out to me.

I considered his offer. It's not like I'd never gotten high before, and Gabe was really my only friend in the band. But I was still high from my first night with the Fiery Boys, so I didn't need to get any higher. I waved my hands to decline.

But before he sank into total oblivion, I decided to ask about the scantily clad leather fan girl, screaming for my blood. "Hey, Gabe, this may be a stupid question, but did you notice that woman in the front wearing a skimpy red corset?"

Gabe laughed. "You're right, that *is* a stupid question." He took another drag and held it for a few seconds before exhaling. "She's a Vegas showgirl. Her real name is Mary, but she calls herself 'Inferna.' Nice Fiery Boys name, huh? She runs a popular website and claims to be our biggest fan."

"So that's Inferna." I'd heard her name before, and I'd read her blog. One of my biggest haters, as far as I could remember. And I understood why, too. I was a major threat to her reputation as the best Fiery Boys fan ever.

Gabe nodded. "She drives from city to city, gathers a crew, and monopolizes the front of the dance floor." He frowned. "I saw what happened tonight. Are you okay?"

"Yeah, I'm fine." I laughed. "She claims to have bedded Chuck lots of times."

"Yep. They go way back. Chuck lives in Vegas, too, so they're fuck buddies. And she *has* visited the bus a few times since we started this tour. Chuck thinks she's a fine piece of ass."

"What about the rest of you? Have you had a tumble with the hot Inferna?"

Gabe shook his head. "Not me. I'm eternally amused by her outfits, but I'd never drop my pants anywhere near her." Aha! A rocker who was concerned about sexually transmitted diseases. How downright sensible.

Buck emerged from the back with a six-pack of beer and some bottles of soda. He set some of the drinks on the table while he dealt out the rest: beer for himself, another for me, and a soda for Gabe.

I took a sip. "What about you, Buck? Have you jumped the angry Inferna?" I wondered whether two angry people would make a good couple, or just a recipe for pain.

He winced and shook his head. "Not a chance." Make that two sensible rockers. Buck focused his attention on the bottle of beer and quickly finished it off.

As he opened his next bottle, I tried another approach. "I loved your music for 'Seattle Summer.'" That movie had been quite popular a few years ago, and I was surprised when I realized that he had written the music.

Buck raised an expressionless face at me and stared for a few seconds. Finally, he dropped his head and muttered, "Thanks." Still too much fan girl? This guy really hated praise.

Soon, River came out of the shower with a towel wrapped around his waist. I felt a sliver of excitement seeing my favorite musician nearly naked and standing so close. I wanted to give him a hug and maybe something else. Instead, I held back and tried to treat him normally. "You really love those drums, River." I didn't want to hear what he thought of Inferna.

River pulled up a chair and sat at the table, giving me a nod. "Yep." This rocker really didn't have much to say.

Buck handed him a bottle of soda water and started to work on his third beer. Gabe got up and headed for the shower.

I decided to venture back into conversation with the silent member of the band. "Soda water, River? I thought you were a beer drinker." Years ago, he did a series of beer ads. One particularly memorable picture showed him with a bottle in each hand, eyeing them thirstily. That's why they called him the hard-drinking drummer.

River shook his head with a partial grin. "I'm trying to cut back." He picked up the water bottle and swallowed a huge gulp.

I turned back to Buck. "When do you get to take a shower?" I may have wiggled an eyebrow at the notion of Buck in a shower. But as soon as I'd done it, I realized it was exactly the sort of groupie-level thing he hated.

And I was right. Without saying a word, he got up from the table, wandered down the hall, and climbed into his cubicle. Buck and I were definitely not making any progress here.

River was the only one left at the table, which was fine by me. "I'm surprised Chuck doesn't want a shower before letting those groupies have his body."

River grinned. "Doesn't need to. Those girls will lick him clean."

My gut churned involuntarily, and I realized I was nowhere near the level of these groupies, blindly willing to engage in Chuck's twisted kink. I almost retched at the thought of licking whatever it was that was stinking up the bus.

And then things got worse. The bedroom door flew open, and Chuck stepped out, completely naked. From my seat in the living room, I could see more than I wanted to. I could see his excited state, which like the rest of him was tall and well built. I could also see two naked women hanging on his shoulders, and behind him, two more laying on the bed. These were not things I wanted to see.

Chuck bellowed out across the bus. "Annalisa! Join us. I've saved my thighs for you, girl! Lick me and then I'll lick you." And here I thought River was joking.

Any interest I may have had in Chuck's physique was instantly obliterated. How was it possible for any woman to be so desperate for this man that she would overlook his smelly body and smellier attitude? River must have noticed my reaction because he burst out laughing. I needed to escape Chuck's pandering, so I got off the bus.

Standing outside in the fresh air, I took a few long breaths to purge my lungs. It didn't help. I flopped against the side of the bus with my head down and my hands on my knees.

"How did you like the show?" Jason was standing there, smoking a cigarette. He was talking about the music, of course, but I was thinking about a different show that I'd just seen.

"You were right about them. Chuck has got to be the biggest pig on the planet, River doesn't say much, and Buck gets upset by everything I do. Only Gabe is nice to me. Not what I expected."

"I warned you. But you said you wanted a fiery life, right? So get back in there and burn. Fifteen thousand women would trade their ovaries to be you right now."

"That's an unpleasant image. You actually think I can get along with these guys? How? By watching them screw and get drunk?"

He nodded at the beer in my hand. "You're already on your way. Have a few more with them, and they'll loosen up. Don't forget you won the contest because your photo screamed 'party girl.'"

"Don't give me that crap, Jason. You picked me because I'm ugly."

He held up his hands to ward off my anger. "I didn't pick you. Whine to your precious Fiery Boys."

"Yeah, like any of them cares about me." I shook my head in disgust. "It stinks in there. I needed some air."

"Want a motel room?"

Motel rooms would be more pleasant, but they wouldn't solve the problem of getting along with these irascible band members. "That's okay, I'll ride on the bus. I just need some space right now. I don't know if I can listen to Chuck have sex for hours."

"Oh, don't worry. He'll be done soon."

"Seriously? I think he's got four women in there."

"Four tonight? Then he should be done *very* soon."

I winced. "You're not making this any easier, Jason."

"I told you Chuck was a train wreck. You seem to be able to resist his charm, so just get back in there. He'll probably stop bothering you if you say 'no' enough."

"Oh? Has any woman ever gotten away with saying 'no' to him?"

He laughed. "If so, I haven't heard about it." He draped an arm across my shoulder and pulled me close. "Why not come with me, and we'll get a drink somewhere?"

Oh, great! Now I had to worry about Jason, too. I could feel the veiled sexual heat coming from him, which made me tense. At least with the Fiery Boys, the sexuality was honest: either totally in my face or completely absent. But Jason was pretending to be friendly, and I knew better.

Interestingly, his leering was exactly what I needed to face the Fiery Boys again. It reminded me why I was there, which wasn't because of the band manager. I made my excuses and returned to the bus.

As I approached my cubicle, I was surprised to see Gabe standing in the hallway, completely naked. My first reaction was to be annoyed with another Fiery Boy who was using inappropriate seduction techniques. But Gabe was not Chuck—he had already established that. Instead, I realized that the tour bus was simply a boy's locker room. And since the bathroom and bedroom were often in use, the hallways were the only place to get changed. Gabe rummaged through his clothes and started to get dressed without even noticing me. Although not my favorite band member, I couldn't deny that the boy was in good shape. Still, I waited until he was decent before I ventured down the hall.

After a long day, a strange introduction to the band, and an exciting show, I needed to relax. I unpacked my suitcase and headed to the bathroom to get washed up. While I was in there, I heard Chuck's party breaking up, with footsteps and women's voices. By the time I came out, the bedroom door was open and the only one left was Chuck, wrapped in a towel and waiting for his turn in the bathroom. I had to hand it to Jason—he certainly knew the Fiery Boys well.

The band was playing in Chicago again tomorrow night, so the boys stayed up late and partied. I sat with them for a while, but after too many come-ons from Chuck and too few words from nearly everyone else, I hid in my cubicle. I wasn't really tired, just tired of them. Eventually I fell asleep.

Day Two

Twelve

I woke up with a thrill at the realization that I had just spent the night on the Fiery Boys tour bus. Regardless of their personal issues, this was still the best vacation I'd ever taken. Also, the bus seemed to smell much better in the morning, but my nose was probably just numb. I got dressed and stepped outside for a breath of real air.

My girlfriends needed an update, so I called Kira. "Well?" She started right off. "Who did you sleep with last night?"

I couldn't resist the urge to tease her. "All five of us slept together."

"Yeah, bullshit. Jo gave me the dirt. I know you're not getting any from those boys."

"Hey! You should have won the contest. You'd have nailed Chuck by now."

"You mean Jo and I would have, right? You said he does groupies like potato chips, never satisfied with just one. She wants us to fly out there and jump him."

I laughed. "You guys are too much."

"No, it's Chuck who's too much. I saw pictures of him from last night's show. God, what a stud. Did you get to watch him up close?"

"Yep. I started in the audience, but the fans weren't too happy to see me."

"Uh huh. I read about that."

She did? I doubted that my visit to the audience last night was news. "You read about what?"

"Let's just say that there's a website out there that's not too sympathetic to you."

I knew exactly what she was talking about. "Inferna, right?"

"Yeah. And wow, does she ever hate you. The woman's nuts."

"I know. I met her last night. She slapped me and told me to die. So I get it. . . she's not my closest friend."

"She's obviously jealous. I'd avoid her if I were you. And don't read her website, please!"

Oh, now she tells me. I'd seen plenty of hate sites, including Inferna's. "I looked at her site once. Just the usual hate."

"It's not the usual hate anymore. Today she edited a picture of you so that you had nails through your eyes and blood running down your face. The girl's certifiable."

That stopped me. I mean, there are haters and then there are honest-to-God crazy people. Inferna might actually be mentally ill. "Wow."

Kira offered to help. "Tell you what. I'll watch her site and let you know if there's anything you need to see."

I took a long breath to purge Inferna's hate. "Okay, thanks."

"Hey, I've got an early meeting so I have to get going. But keep me posted. I'm totally proud of you for winning this contest."

I knew she was jealous, but it was nice to hear encouraging words occasionally. "Thanks, Kira." We hung up.

When I returned to the bus, Buck was in the kitchen, and Chuck was sitting at the living room table. I sat down at the table and he wiggled closer. "Good morning, cutie pie."

Cutie pie? Was he still trying to get me into the bedroom, or was this simply how he talked to all women? Either way, I wished he'd stop. "Save it for the groupies, Chuck. Inferna would kill for a piece of your ass."

"Inferna's already had a piece of my ass. What she'd kill for is week on the bus."

"Don't I know it. How long have you two been together?"

"We're not what you'd call 'together.' But I've known her —let's see—six years. Things only got weird recently when this reunion tour came through."

I wasn't feeling very generous, so I threw out a zinger. "I guess it was easier when you were a second-rate Vegas performer like her."

Buck's laughter filled the bus, and I could see him looking at me with what seemed like admiration. He kept laughing as he wandered back to his cubicle. It wasn't hard to please Buck—just help him bash Chuck.

And apparently, I'd done a good job of it. Chuck touched his finger to my hand and pulled it back quickly, making a hissing sound as if he'd been burned. "You've got a nasty little mouth there, contest girl." He frowned.

I suddenly felt bad for him, and I resolved to be nicer. "Sorry." I slumped my shoulders.

"Don't be sorry. You're right. She's bitter. I thought she was mad because she didn't win the contest, but I'm not so sure."

"Oh, I'm sure that's part of the reason. Maybe not the whole story. So tell me, did she just dye her hair red, or was it always that way?"

Chuck smirked. "Pretty obvious, huh? She dyed her hair and started her website when this whole reunion tour idea got going. The hair's kind of creepy, if you ask me."

"But not creepy enough to keep you away from her."

He shrugged. "Hey! She still has a great body. Why should I care if her hair looks like a circus clown?" Chuck turned in his seat to face me directly. "What I can't figure out is why you keep running away from me. Wasn't I your favorite Fiery Boy?"

"No, sorry."

"Let me guess. You were in love with Gabe."

"River."

"River? That guy's butt ugly."

So he hated Buck *and* River. Probably Gabe, too. "Why are you so nasty to your bandmates? You've already got nearly every fan girl in your camp. What more do you want?"

"I want you."

"Well, believe me, I'm honored. But you're kind of making me uncomfortable. Besides, you could have held onto those four groupies from last night."

Chuck shook his head. "I had them—last night. Now I want you." He squinted at me. "Is there nothing about me that appeals to you?"

What a fragile ego. I had to give him something. Chuck was, after all, the lead singer of the Fiery Boys—he deserved more than my disdain. And I'd gotten to the point where I wasn't bothered by his sexual advances anymore. I could talk to this man, perhaps even be his friend.

"I'm sorry for being rude. There *are* things about you that appeal to me. You're certainly good looking. You used to be too skinny for my taste, but ten years have filled you out nicely. I couldn't help but notice a fine physique when you were standing in the bedroom door naked last night." I grinned at him, and he shot it right back.

Before he could react to my statement with another sexual advance, I went on. "And second, I like the songs you wrote. Well, one of them, anyway."

Chuck brightened. "Which one?"

Before I could answer, River stumbled out to the living room wearing a bathrobe. "I know which one she likes." He plopped down at the table and gave me a smile that warmed me from the inside out. "'Fiery Life,' right?"

Little parts of me were already starting to liquefy, and now I felt like I could melt into a puddle on the floor. River, my rock idol, was paying attention to me. I thought he was ignoring me, but now I knew that he wasn't. Maybe this week would bring us closer, after all. "Did Jason tell you?" I managed to ask in an almost normal voice.

"Nobody told me. I saw you dancing to it last night. Obviously your favorite." He noticed me? Now I was buzzing all over.

Chuck gave a little shrug. "Yeah, that song's okay."

River laughed. "Okay? It's one of our signature songs." He leaned closer to me. "Why do you like it?"

I was in heaven. River actually wanted to know about me. I felt so lightheaded that I gripped the table to keep from floating up into the air.

"That's my life Chuck wrote about." Thinking about my life back then took me down a little, but I couldn't keep any secrets from River. I smiled guiltily. "All of that actually happened to me."

Before anyone could ask *what* had happened to me, I explained it with the song's lyrics, growling it out the way Chuck did.

"The engine's rumble, the speed.
The drive to break out, the need.
The push to prove it, your creed."

River drummed the table with me. When we finished, Chuck smiled. "You can almost sing good."

I nearly laughed at the way he could make a compliment sound like an insult. Sure, I could carry a tune, but I was no Chuck. I ignored his dig and sang the song's chorus. Chuck joined in.

"*Living by a precipice,*
Dancing on the blade of a knife,
Liberty means so much more,
The promise, the promise of a fiery life."

We whooped together and gave each other a smile. "Anyway, that was Zed and me in high school." I sighed. "He liked fast cars and motorcycles. We rode them, souped them up, and even raced them. My dad had taught me a few basic car concepts like how to change the oil, but Zed taught me to get in there and really work the engines. I'm telling you, we lived a fiery life. We were totally in love."

Chuck nodded. "Did you get married?"

River rolled his eyes and swatted Chuck on the shoulder. "Moron. It's a sad song." He looked at me. "I'm guessing something happened to him. Did he die?"

I swallowed and nodded. "Two months before we graduated. Motorcycle accident on a windy road—just like in the song. Not only that, but when they found his music player, he'd been listening to 'Fiery Life' on endless repeat." I sang the second verse.

"*The winding road draws your prowls,*
It grabs for your heart, and growls,
With blood on its bed, it howls."

I pushed away the pain that always hit me when I heard those words. Not only did I lose Zed back then, so close to graduation, but my parents had already moved away. Zed's death left me even more alone.

I pulled myself together and dove into the second chorus. Each chorus was the same except for the last line, which followed the mood of the verse. So rather than repeat all of it, I sang only the last line.

"*The* sorrow *of a fiery life.*"

River took my hand. "I'm sorry to hear that, Annalisa." I gasped silently—his comfort was so warm and perfect. Chuck may have written a beautifully poetic song, but River understood it. He understood me.

I smiled and looked at him. "It's all right. That song gave me the strength to put my life back together and move on."

The third verse was exactly what I'd needed to recover. Chuck sang it for me.

"*Honor the fallen with depth,*
Live and remember each death,
Burn the life bright with new breath."

I recited the final line of the third chorus, the line that got repeated a few times before the song ended.

"*You* owe yourself *a fiery life.*"

I swallowed to push back a tear. "If it hadn't been for that song, I wouldn't have survived. 'Fiery Life' saved me."

Chuck beamed. "So if my song saved you, why don't you want to have sex with me?"

I gave him a doleful smile. He was right, of course: I would have let him seduce me because of that song. But I wasn't so sure anymore.

Before I could say anything, River reached across the table and punched him. Chuck glowered. "Hey! What was that for?"

"That's for being a pig." He punched Chuck again, harder. "And that's for calling me ugly."

Oops. River must have been listening for a while if he'd heard Chuck call him ugly. And that meant he'd heard me when I'd admitted that he was my favorite Fiery Boy. Would he find that awkward?

Apparently not. River stood up and offered his hand to me. "I'm making breakfast. What would you like?"

Most excellent! I wanted one smoking Fiery Boy, hold the clothes. But I didn't want to come across like Chuck, drooling with every word. So I jumped to my feet and took River's hand. "I'll have whatever you're having." I managed to restrain myself from adding, "For the rest of my life."

Thirteen

The second Chicago concert was hours away, and the boys had little to do. So they spent the afternoon in their usual pursuits: drinking, smoking, grumbling, staring into space, barely talking, and—in Chuck's case—chasing groupies. He found three women who were willing to share their favorite singer's naked body.

Later, I stood in the wings, nearly as excited as I'd been at the first concert. Feeling a little bolder than last night, I had on red leggings with a fitted black tank top and black ankle boots. Leggings worked well for me since I was so tall.

I took a minute to soak in my surroundings. Honestly, how amazing was it to be backstage at a Fiery Boys show every night? *Mega* amazing. Regardless of the way the band and the fans treated me, this was something I would never forget.

From the wings, I could see Inferna and her minions near the front of the audience again. I peeked at her but tried not to let her see me. Yep. Same skimpy corset tonight. Now here was someone who needed a pair of leggings.

The Fiery Boys did a great show. Already, the song list and Chuck's banter with the crowd were becoming familiar. He made the same jokes with the fans, and they loved it. I could see what a showman he was.

Everything was going well until they got to "Fiery Life." I had a copy of the set list tonight, so I knew it was up next. Even River gave me a wink, and we smiled at each other. But then Chuck went rogue.

"Hey there, Chicago. I'm sure you know about the contest where one lucky girl got to go on tour with us. Well she's here tonight, so I want you all to put your hands together and give a big Chicago welcome to Annalisa Ricci." He turned toward the wing and held out his arms. "Come on out here, Annalisa."

Before I could take a step toward the stage—or away from it, as my instinct suggested—a nasty jeering rose up from the audience. Women were booing me. Inferna and her besties were engaging in their usual mantra, shouting for my death, over and over. I felt like my boots had been superglued to the floor.

Chuck dropped his arms and laughed at the crowd. "Aw, now. Is that any way to show her how you feel? I'm hearing from a lot of girls, but what about you guys? Don't you want to see Annalisa?" The deeper bellow of male voices was more encouraging, although it still had a threatening ring to it. And the louder voices that could be heard above the clamor were all demanding pieces of my underwear or parts of my body.

Chuck tried to appeal to the men. "Hey, you saw that picture. This is a girl who can drink you under the table and spray you with beer while she does it. Be nice to her, or I'll have her come out and hose you all down."

Oh great! Did he really think that would help the audience's attitude? Because if he did, he was wrong. They just got louder.

But apparently Chuck wasn't done humiliating me. "And you girls out there don't have to worry about Annalisa. She's the first woman I've met who *doesn't* want to have sex with me."

The man had no sense in his head. Once again, his attempt to make the audience like me backfired. Now the women's booing was louder than the male voices. I turned and ran.

I made it back to the bus as fast as I could and climbed into my cubicle. Safe behind the closed curtains, I let my tears fall.

What was wrong with Chuck? Why was he so dedicated to abusing me all the time? He'd seemed like he wanted to honor me at the show, but the way he went about it left me wondering. How could he be such a showman and yet be so clueless? And if he really was a fool, then how had he written "Fiery Life" and those other sensitive songs? That left me with only one conclusion: he hated me. Probably *because* I wouldn't have sex with him. I pulled the blanket tightly over myself and somehow fell asleep.

When the show was over, the band piled onto the bus. I awoke to the sound of groupies screaming for Chuck, the clacking of their heels mixing with the heavier stomping of male shoes. One woman's voice was familiar and aggressively unfriendly. "Where's the contest bitch?" Inferna was on the bus.

I shrank back in my cubicle and prayed she wouldn't find me. Of course, there was no chance of that—Inferna knew this bus as well as anyone. She drew back my curtain and glared at me. Two other women stood by her side. "Fucking-A, Chuck! You put her right above you?" She snarled at me. "You little whore."

Inferna had me at a distinct disadvantage, so I flattened myself against the back of my cubicle, as far from her as I could get. If we'd been standing in an open space, I might have said something, engaged her in some way. But I was trapped in there, vulnerable, afraid, and no doubt showing it. All the power was hers.

She hissed at me through clenched teeth. When she reached toward me, I grabbed my backpack to use as a shield. If necessary, I'd swing it at her, although I knew it wouldn't be very effective—my purse and a change of clothes were the only things in it. After last night, I'd decided to stay lightly packed at all times in case of trouble. Trouble like this.

Before Inferna and I could come to blows, Chuck intervened. Chuck! The last person I expected to help me was suddenly my savior. "Leave her alone." He pulled my nemesis away and motioned toward the bedroom. "Go on, now. I'll be right there." Inferna sent the other women back. Then, still standing in the hallway next to my cubicle, she pulled Chuck in for a kiss. He responded as expected, groping her enhanced breasts and completely exposed backside. I closed my cubicle curtain, but Inferna quickly slapped it open again, forcing me to watch them grind their bodies together. Her mouth was on his neck, teeth bared like a slutty vampire. I was tempted to shout, "Get a room," but I knew they had one.

Inferna finally lost interest in making out with Chuck when I pulled out a book and started to read. She turned and walked to the bedroom, where the other women cheered her arrival. It sounded vaguely like the gobbling of prize turkeys waiting for Thanksgiving. Mercifully, she closed the door behind her, which muffled the sounds.

I was about to thank Chuck when heavy footsteps thudded down the aisle. "I'm going to kill you!" Buck grabbed Chuck and slammed him hard against the wall. Chuck fought back, which caused the bus to shake from the tectonic stress of their fight.

If the adrenaline from my close call with Inferna hadn't already primed me for action, watching Chuck and Buck lay into each other finished the job. Before I could think coherently, I'd jumped out and landed between them. Only then did it occur to me that I might get hit trying to break up a fight between two big, strong men. Too late now.

"Stop it! Both of you."

Chuck backed away, but Buck advanced toward him, his quivering fist pulled back. He tried to get past me, but I shook my head. "You too, buster. Back off." I was in no mood for this band's petty crap, so I gave him a shove.

Buck's a big guy, so I figured I needed to put a little muscle into it if I expected to budge him at all. But I must have pushed him harder than either of us expected because he lost his balance and crashed against the wall, a look of surprise on his face. "Damn, woman!" He straightened himself with a partial smile.

Chuck had a bloody nose, but otherwise seemed fine. He grinned hugely at Buck. As he was about to stir up more trouble, the door to the bedroom opened and Inferna stepped out, completely naked. The woman really did have an incredible body. Too bad she was such a monster. She flipped me the bird then sneered at Buck and Chuck. "I don't know how you boys ended up with *her* on your bus."

"She's okay," Chuck snapped. "I told you, leave her alone." He turned to me and spoke softly. "I'm sorry about what I said tonight. It didn't go over too well, did it?" Wow, actual sensitivity. Who would have guessed? Perhaps Chuck didn't hate me after all. There was obviously more to him than I'd realized.

Regardless of his mental state, I didn't need to discuss it in front of Inferna. And I could tell she didn't need it, either. "Forget it, Chuck. Your fan club awaits you." I pushed him toward the bedroom, and he followed Inferna into some level of hell that Dante never envisioned.

That left Buck and me. Handsome Buck, for whom I once harbored a dreamy teenage crush. Angry Buck, who barely talked to me. Bruised Buck, with a cut on his lip and a dark spot forming on his cheek. I didn't know if I loved him or hated him—I just wished I understood him. "Why are you so angry?"

"It's him!" Buck snapped. He pointed toward the bedroom door. "He's the reason I'm so angry—I've hated his guts for ten years."

I propped my fists on my hips. "Well, you don't have to take it out on me!"

His face fell while his anger deflated. Finally, much more calm, he let out a long breath. "You're right—you've done nothing wrong. It's my crap—I'm dealing with too much right now. Touring with Chuck, annoying groupies, divorce lawyers." He dropped his head. "I'm a mess. You really should stay away from me."

A particularly loud orgasmic scream pierced the thin bedroom walls, which elicited a groan from Buck. "I have to get out of here." With that, he walked to the front of the bus and left.

I took a few seconds to collect myself, then I walked to the living room table. River was in the shower, as usual, and Gabe was sitting there with a joint in his hand, as usual. He handed me a beer. "Here, you need this." My only friend.

"Thanks, Gabe." I dropped down, took a long pull from the bottle, then collapsed against him.

He wrapped his arm around me and pulled me close. "Buck's right, you know. Chuck *is* a huge jerk. Anyway, the good news is that we're leaving this town. I've had enough of Chicago, and I bet you have, too."

He took one last drag from the joint and stubbed it out. "Let's take a stroll and get some air before we're all back on the bus again. Besides. . ." He glanced down the hall toward the bedroom. "You don't want to be here when those women come out." He was so right.

We wandered around the busses and trucks. In two hours, we'd be leaving for Minneapolis. Just enough time for the roadies to load up the trucks and for those who wanted a shower to take one. Also enough time for Chuck to get licked clean and sucked dry, or whatever it was he did behind the closed bedroom door.

Day Three

Fourteen

The bus rode through the night, silently across the prairie. River and Gabe crashed out early. Buck hid in his cubicle with his guitar, playing soulful acoustic songs reminiscent of the band's earlier works. I would have approached him about it, but he seemed so remote that I kept my distance. Buck wanted me to stay away, which was fine with me.

Chuck and I sat in the living room for a few hours. He apologized once again and promised to be good all night. And he was.

We watched television and played some video games. He told me stories about rock and roll. We even snuggled together while watching a movie, his solid body next to mine. Thankfully, I didn't have to fend off a single sexual advance. Before I went to bed, we exchanged chaste kisses on the cheek and a light hug.

Chuck's behavior made me happy. Perhaps his failed attempt to be nice to me on stage had taught him something. In any case, we had made it to the friend zone, which was better than the love-em-and-leave-em zone those groupies all fell into. Chuck and I were good, and I curled up in my cubicle with a smile.

I awoke in the predawn and made my way to the front of the bus, past the living room. Big Tim was at the wheel, guiding us down the road. "Morning, Big Tim." I stood next to him as we stared at the scenery. "Don't you ever get tired?"

He shrugged. "I sleep when I can and drive when I must. We're roadies—the band's punching bags." He chuckled at his lowly status. "Anyway, congrats on lasting this long. You've eliminated half the bets. Most of the guys thought you'd bail after that first concert, and all of us thought you'd bail after last night."

"I can't bail, Big Tim. I'm a punching bag, too."

"Yeah, I can tell."

"So were the boys like this before I got here, or did they get worse in Chicago?"

"I'd say they're about the same. Although I haven't seen Buck and Chuck fight like that before. Still, it's been coming for a while—they really hate each other."

"I noticed." I gave him a pat on the shoulder and went back to the living room. For the next hour, while the Fiery Boys slept, I actually enjoyed riding on the tour bus, watching the road roll by.

The busses and trucks gathered outside of the Minneapolis arena and huddled together for safety. The first thing they did was to set up the fence, a secure encampment to protect them from overeager fans. After that, the roadies got seriously busy preparing for the show.

River had arranged to get a car, and he left within minutes, gone for the day. Gabe needed to do some shopping, so he tagged along.

I wished I could have gone with River to see his home. He lived nearby, so he was probably going there. The delusional part of my mind still dreamed of spending my life with him, so I was curious to see where I'd be living. But the sensible part of me pointed out that he was really going to visit his secret girlfriend.

Buck and Chuck sat around the living room table and glared at each other. Chuck was in his usual tattered jeans and a white T-shirt. Buck's jeans and T-shirt were both black. I took in the situation with numb resignation. Here I was, witness to a full Fiery Boys feud between two incredibly good-looking band members.

I stood by the table for a few minutes, waiting to see which of them would break the silence. Finally, I gave up and took matters into my own hands. I fetched three bottles of beer in an effort to make peace. It was early, not even lunchtime for normal people and way before that for us. But these boys definitely needed a drink.

"You two have got to stop acting like children. Buck, you're too sensitive, and Chuck, you're too *insensitive*." I held my bottle out. "To the two of you. May you survive the next month together."

My gesture seemed to work. Chuck had the cold bottle against his still-injured nose, so he pulled it away to join my toast. Buck looked up at me for a few seconds, then tapped my bottle with a partial smile as he nodded his thanks. We drank in silence.

The Minneapolis concert was just like the Chicago ones. Standing in the wing with Jason, I felt awash in déjà vu. Even the song list was the same.

When it was time for them to play "Fiery Life," I turned to leave the wing. I did *not* want to see what Chuck would do tonight. It saddened me to think that the band was quickly turning my favorite song into a dreaded event. As I walked away, I heard Chuck start up his usual inter-song banter.

Suddenly there was a clattering sound, and Buck's voice rang through the hall. "Wait a minute. This is important." Even I stopped to listen.

With the microphone in his hand, Buck took center stage, his bass guitar hanging in front of him. "Listen up,

Minneapolis. We were in Chicago last night. Those people think they're the best Fiery Boys fans in the world." The crowd booed and Buck held his hands out to silence them, grinning at the expected reaction. "You may be right. Minneapolis seems like it *is* better." The city roared its agreement.

"So here's the thing. If Minneapolis really is better, then you gotta prove it to me." They roared even louder, but Buck waved a finger back and forth, shaking his head with disapproval. "No, no. I don't mean by cheering. I mean by being the nicest fans on this entire tour."

Buck started to pace along the edge of the stage, the microphone in his hand, scanning the audience. "You all know about Annalisa Ricci, the contest winner who's touring with us." The crowd started to respond, but he raised his hands in a sign for them to stop. "Wait for it, Minneapolis. Hear me out. Last night in Chicago, they booed her! I mean, the nerve of that city! So let me hear what you think of Chicago for doing that to Annalisa." The audience erupted in angry shouts. He waved them on, encouraging them to be louder and angrier. Mr. Angry certainly knew how to push the crowd's rage button.

Buck waited for their wrath to pass, a tight grin that made it clear just how much he was enjoying this. "Now— and here is where you can prove to me that you're better than them—let me hear what you think of Annalisa." The audience actually cheered. I stood in the wings, frozen in shock.

When the fans had settled down again, he went on. "I love you, Minneapolis!" He let them cheer for themselves some more before he continued. "We're about to play Annalisa's favorite song, but first, I want to introduce you to her." He turned toward the wing and beckoned to me. "Come on out here, Annalisa." The crowd cheered again.

I couldn't decide whether this was a good thing or not. The fans were being very nice, but I knew it was because Buck had manipulated them carefully. I worried that they could sour in an instant, and for no reason. Chuck might say something to ruin it—that seemed to be his specialty. Or Inferna might start a riot, although I had to admit she wasn't front and center tonight, so perhaps she wasn't there. But to be safe, I stayed where I was with folded arms, letting Buck know that I wasn't going to move.

Of course, Buck was unperturbed. He turned back to the audience. "You know, she's kind of shy. So let's hear it for Annalisa. Come on, Minneapolis." He started to chant, "Annalisa. Annalisa. Annalisa." He waved his hands, and the fans joined in. Suddenly, everyone was shouting, "Annalisa."

A trancelike state enveloped me, and I tingled all over. Being on tour with the Fiery Boys was strange enough, but having thousands of fans call my name was positively surreal. Immobilized, I stood in the wings and held my breath.

Jason snapped me out of it. "Go on out there!" He gave me a little push, and I took my first step. Then, to the accompaniment of their insistent call, I kept walking right out onto the stage.

As I crossed from the darkness of the wing into the bright stage lights, the audience switched from chant to cheer. Their applause stopped me again, and I looked around nervously. Buck ran over and took my hand, leading me to the front of the stage. He held me tightly, one hand holding mine, the other around my waist. I felt strangely safe in his embrace, even in front of this unpredictable crowd. And since I still found Buck to be stunningly handsome, having him escort me onto the stage was pure fantasy gold.

Chuck came over to stand on the other side of me, his arm wrapped around my shoulder. To my delight, the crowd only cheered harder.

"Crazy, isn't it? Say 'hi' to Minneapolis." Buck pointed the microphone at my mouth and gave my waist a little squeeze.

Oh my God! A huge crowd of Fiery Boys fans was waiting for me to speak, so I kept it simple. "Hey there, Minneapolis. You rock!" The city howled its agreement.

"Very nice." Buck smiled and released me from these suspiciously happy people. "Go on back there, and we'll play your favorite song." I turned to walk back offstage. It seemed to take ten times as long as it had to walk out there. Why wouldn't the lights go away? Why wouldn't the crowd stop clapping for me? Forget the longest mile—this was the longest fifty feet.

As soon as I made it back to the wing, the band broke into "Fiery Life." Jason gave me a big hug and we stood together while we watched them play. Still buzzing from my first positive brush with Fiery Boys fans, I thought the song was more beautiful and meaningful than ever before.

Fifteen

I made it to the wing and exhaled, glad to be in the shadows after the bright stage lights. Safe, and giddy with excitement from all the positive energy, I turned to face the boys as they launched into "Fiery Life." It nearly blew me over.

The blast from the song filled me up, supercharged me, then lit my fuse. I danced so hard that I practically skyrocketed off the walls. When the song ended, I took it down a notch, but my dancing continued to be turbocharged for the rest of the show.

On his way off stage, Chuck raised his hand up for a high-five slap. "You're beautiful, babe." I gave him five, and he continued to the bus, leaving a smile on both of our faces. Gabe wandered by, mimicking the cheer. "Annalisa. Annalisa. Annalisa." Even Buck gave me a thumbs up before running off to the bus.

Then something wonderful happened. River stopped to talk to me. "I'm really glad Buck did that. This is the sort of welcome you deserve."

His attention took my breath away. He was dripping sweat and breathing hard from the intensity of that last song, but I still wanted to throw myself onto his phenomenal body. I took a second to calm myself before answering. "Thanks, River. That really means a lot, especially coming from you."

He grinned proudly. "Yeah, I heard you tell Chuck that I was your favorite. So I think we should show up in some photos together, just for fun." He held out his hand. "Come on, let me escort you back to the bus." I took his hand, and my head spun wildly back in time to the days when I would stare at his poster and let my desire roam. We headed toward the bus hand in hand, like lovers strolling in the park, like newlyweds walking down the aisle. In my fertile imagination, I was the envy of every woman on earth.

After the two Chicago concerts, I had either waited for the band to get to the bus, or fled there before anyone else had arrived. Now, for the first time, I was leaving with the band. That meant exiting the stage door while fans pressed in for a glimpse. The wall of camera-wielding groupies descended on us like iron particles to a magnet. Gabe and Buck stopped to sign autographs. Chuck groped any woman who got close to him. I heard Buck shout, "Back off!" as he peeled some woman's arms from his shoulders. He really hated groupies, and I understood why.

Thankfully, River protected me from desperate hands. He pushed away every fan girl who tried to trade places with his date tonight. I wanted to kiss him, but didn't want to start a riot. And Jason would not be happy. So I let him lead me safely to the bus.

By the time we got there, Gabe and Chuck were somewhere else, probably in the shower and the bedroom, if I had to guess. The only one in the living room was Buck, with two beers in his hands and an empty bottle on the table in front of him. River sat down at the table and swatted him on the shoulder. "Go easy there, buddy. It's a long way to Kansas City."

"Just keeping my strength up." Buck blew out a single laugh and tilted the second bottle upward, finishing it.

I sat down next to him. "Thank you for doing that, Buck. You really know how to work an audience." His smile was tight as he handed me a beer and started on his third. I took a sip, then dove back into an attempt at conversation. "By the way, how did you know that was my favorite song?"

"River told me." Buck nodded at his bandmate. I must have looked shocked, because he laughed a little. "Just because I hate Chuck, doesn't mean the rest of us don't get along." He tilted his head back to pour more beer down his throat.

Gabe came out of the shower, and River got up. He looked down at me. "I'm going to clean up, then I've got something I want to ask you." He walked away before I could begin to figure out what he meant, leaving me sitting at the table, stunned.

River wanted to ask me something, and my meandering brain spun dozens of happily-ever-after scenarios. What if he was planning on leaving his girlfriend and taking me as his lover? Okay, I knew that wasn't going to happen. But we were getting along so well, and he was going out of his way to be nice. So it might. Reality slipped into the background as fantasy wedding bells chimed in my head.

Gabe sat down in River's seat wearing only a towel. His body was quite fine looking, wiry and muscular. He lit up a joint and took a deep drag. "To a great gig and a wonderful crowd." He tapped the joint against my beer bottle in a mixed-intoxicant toast. Then, before taking a drink, I tapped my bottle with Buck's, too.

A beer with the band and my future lover in the shower. Everything was looking up. Finally, I was experiencing the Fiery Boys tour as I'd dreamed it would happen. I was sitting on the tour bus with friendly faces, having a drink with my new buddies and longtime imaginary lovers. Those roadies who expected me to run away were going to be sorely disappointed. I was busy living a fiery life.

By the time I'd started my second beer, Buck had finished his fourth. River came out of the shower, so Buck stumbled back for his turn. Gabe was off getting dressed, which left just me and River at the table. Exactly how I liked it.

Yes, the most gorgeous man on Earth was sitting next to me wearing nothing but a towel and a grin. I leaned away from him and feasted my eyes for a few seconds. River Sticks was as phenomenally sexy as ever. "I had such a crush on you when I was sixteen."

River chuckled. "Seems like you still do." He had me there.

I decided to find out where I stood with him. "Is it true that you have a secret lover?"

"Afraid so. And I don't wander when I'm out on the road. As I said, we were just playing out there."

"Oh." I straightened up. "So what was it you wanted to tell me earlier?" Maybe wedding plans weren't as likely as I'd hoped.

"Right!" He got up. "I was going to offer to let you play drums on 'Fiery Life.'"

"What! I can't play drums."

"Not all of them, of course. I was going to teach you the cymbal part and let you play it in the chorus. It's easy. Want to give it a try?"

"Absolutely!" I didn't need a marriage proposal anymore. River's offer, combined with the way Buck had the audience chanting my name, made this a day I'd never forget.

"Then let me get dressed, and we'll go backstage and play with some drums." He wandered back to his cubicle and soon returned in jeans, a brown shirt, and a tan hoodie, his usual casual attire. We went back to the stage.

His drums were still assembled, but most of the other gear had already been hauled off by busy roadies. He pointed to one of the cymbals, a big one at the edge of the kit. "When we play 'Fiery Life,' this one only gets used during the chorus. It's easy—just keep beating along with the song. Watch. . ." He pounded out the turnaround between the verse and the chorus, then started to sing the chorus while he played the drum part.

"Living by a precipice,
Dancing on the blade of a knife,
Liberty means so much more,
You owe it, you owe yourself a fiery life."

As he played it, I watched him rhythmically pound the cymbal. Then he handed the drumstick to me. "You try it."

I could keep a beat as well as most people, so I did a fine job with my tiny part of the song. We rehearsed it a few times before retreating to the bus. The Fiery Boys tour was turning out to be everything I wanted it to be.

Sixteen

When River and I got back to the bus, Buck seemed thoroughly drunk. He grinned at me and slurred, "How 'bowdda brew?" I could smell quite a few of them on his breath.

"I'm good, and you've had enough."

"Wuzza madder? Can't hold yer liquor? Gonna spray me wid it?"

"You didn't like that picture, did you?" Now I knew which Fiery Boy had voted against me: Buck.

"Hey!" He laughed. "Watch me do my imitation of Annnnaliiiisa." He took a swig of beer, threw his head back, and blew it into the air. Unfortunately, instead of spraying in a mist, the beer launched in an arc and landed on my blouse. I liked that blouse. Sleeveless and knotted at the waist, I thought I looked good in it. Now it was soaked with beer and spit.

I scowled at him and walked away to clean myself. Behind me, Buck called out, "Sorrrreeee."

I had to wonder why things like this happened to me. Was there a sign on my forehead that said, "Give me shit"? That would explain my boyfriends. And Buck. And Inferna. And every hater on the Internet, for that matter.

When I got back to the table, Buck had collapsed forward, asleep with his head on his arms. River looked over at him and shook his head. "I've never seen him like this."

He looked peaceful, released from his demons. "Should we try to get him to bed?"

River nodded and stood up. "I got him." He hauled Buck to his feet and dragged him down the hall, helping him into his cubicle.

Buck roused when he landed there. "I'm okay."

I peered at him. "You don't seem okay. How about some vitamins to help you deal with that hangover?" I reached over to my cubicle and dug around.

Buck tried to refuse my offer. "Don't do vitamins." He groaned. "Feeling sick."

I got the pills and climbed up to sit next to him, shoving them into his hand. "Take these, Buck."

He started to protest. "Told ja. I don't. . ."

I silenced him with a raised finger. "Doesn't matter. When you puke, they'll come right back up." I grinned and even Buck gave a light laugh.

He covered his eyes with his hand and turned away. Then he slapped the hand with the vitamins up to his mouth and threw his head back. I gave him a glass of water to wash them down. "Good. Now rest." I got down from his bunk.

Before I'd made it two steps toward the living room, River stopped me. "Stay with him." He spoke softly, but his deep voice was impossible to resist.

I was confused. Why was he pushing me to Buck? Angry and drunk Buck, who grumbled all the time and spat beer at me. I'd vastly prefer to sit up front with River. "But. . ."

He cut me off with a wave of his hand. "Just climb up there and sit for a few minutes until he falls asleep." He kissed me on the cheek and whispered, "Do it for me." For River? How could I refuse? Too bad I hadn't met him before he'd found his lover. A man this kind and devoted and powerfully attractive was a rarity.

I climbed back into Buck's cubicle and sat with my feet dangling out. Laying on his back, he looked up at me and groaned. He might be drunk and he was certainly annoying, but I couldn't deny the fact that he was a fine-looking man, someone I'd idolized for a decade. And tonight he had talked the audience into liking me. So I reached out to give him a pat on the shoulder.

Before my hand made it to his shoulder, he snagged it and pulled it to his stomach. Then he rolled away from me and curled up in a ball, forcing me down to the bed, spooning him. I was simultaneously alarmed and delighted. I sighed and gave him a little squeeze, which thrilled me more than I expected. He felt so solid and warm, that I even entertained a few naughty fantasies. Ridiculous, of course.

Buck's breathing soon grew regular. I considered pulling away and leaving his side but thought better of it. This was Buck Morris, the bass player of the Fiery Boys and my second favorite rocker of all time. So why was I objecting to lying next to him in his bed with my arm wrapped around him? Besides, if I left now, I'd never hear the end of it from Kira and Jo. So I relaxed and continued to spoon him.

The bus squealed to a stop, waking both Buck and me. Somehow in the night, we had changed positions so that he was now spooning me. He grunted and pulled his hand from my breast. "Sorry."

I rolled over to face him. "Feel better?"

"Yeah, much. But I gotta return that beer. Move." I hopped out of the cubicle so Buck could run for the bathroom.

From across the aisle, River peeked up at me with a smile. "Did you sleep?"

I blushed. "Yes, thanks. Are we in Kansas City?"

"Probably." He walked forward so he could peer out the front window. "Yep. Another day, another arena." He shook his head with a smirk. "What a life."

I smiled at the spectacular drummer. "A fiery one."

"Sometimes I wonder." He crawled back into his cubicle and closed the curtain.

Day Four

Seventeen

Although I was leading a fiery life, the rest of the people on tour with me seemed to be having more of a monotonous life. I watched the roadies set up for another concert like they were robots. Even the boys were merely going through the motions, showing up for the sound check hung over and lethargic.

River made them play "Fiery Life" twice so I could practice my part on the cymbal. He applauded after the second time, and Gabe gave me a hug. Buck bowed to me in silent approval, and Chuck gave me a kiss on the cheek. I was on top of the world.

We went back to the bus before the show, and Chuck challenged me to another video game. He'd been much more considerate lately, sitting up all night without a single sexual come-on. It made me like him more than I ever had. I could almost see adding benefits to this friendship. Almost.

We flopped down on the sofa to look through the choices. After considering a few titles, he lost interest and started to kiss my neck. Clearly his way of saying that the choice of a game was unimportant. His kisses felt nice, a warm sensation from a gorgeous rocker. I kept browsing for games, but my attention wasn't on the selection, either.

Chuck's kisses started to feel even better, and crazy ideas filled my head. The thought of making out with this handsome and talented man suddenly had powerful appeal. I certainly wasn't afraid of his advances anymore. So I discretely turned to find his mouth, transforming his innocent pecks into a fully-realized kiss. His lips were warm and firm and lightly parted, offering a taste that I instantly wanted more of. We reached out our tongues at the same time, which sent a flush of excitement coursing through me. Who needed video games?

I could see that Chuck was going to make it past the friend zone, which worked for me. Face it, the week was half-way done, and there weren't any other offers. River was in a committed relationship. Buck was wound-up so tight you needed extra insurance just to go near him. And Gabe was my friend. So Chuck, who'd professed his desire from the moment I boarded the bus, might just get his wish. He'd be the perfect Fiery Boys fling.

Just as our kiss was getting serious, the mood was shattered by the sound of rattling glass. I pulled away as Buck came into the living room with the box of recycled bottles from the kitchen. "Box is full, gotta move it out." He swayed comically when he got near us, grinning and pretending to lose control of the box as it teetered in his hands. The bottles crashed against each other and one of them actually fell onto the coffee table. "Oops," he let out a laugh. The bottle had sunk into a day-old bowl of mystery snack food that nobody wanted to finish. Buck pulled it out and tossed it loudly onto the top of the pile. "Sorry to disturb you." He laughed some more as he slowly made his way across the living room, dancing with the noisy box of glass until he was off the bus and heading towards the recycling bins.

Chuck and I laughed at the interruption. The moment had passed, so he gave me one brief kiss, then he pulled away and actually did choose a video game to play. But now the game was filled with a new kind of tension.

The show that night had an exciting edge to it. Not only was I feeling Chuck's heat, but I was also nervous about playing with the band. In fact, I was so keyed up that I didn't even notice when Jason appeared by my side. "What's eating you tonight?"

I jumped at the sound of his voice, but acted nonchalant and kept facing the stage. "River's letting me play drums on 'Fiery Life.'"

Jason stepped around to face me. "He's *what*?" Definitely unhappy—I wondered if he'd try to stop me. Should River have cleared this with him first?

In an effort to placate him, I pointed out how small my part was. "I'm only playing during the chorus, and all I get is one cymbal. I'll dance during the verses."

I couldn't wait to dance next to River. And playing drums with him would be an unforgettable experience. "It wasn't my idea—River offered. He wants my week on tour to be special. Hey!" I grinned. "How could I refuse?"

Jason stiffened. "Don't expect him to fall in love with you. You'll be gone soon, and he has his own life." As if I didn't already know that. I ignored Jason so I could focus on the band. At least *they* weren't counting the days until my week was over.

Jason shifted to get back in my face. "And another thing. This is *not* how you dress for the stage."

"What's wrong with the way I'm dressed?" I admit that I'd toned it down a little tonight because I was going out there. I didn't want to be flashing mile-long leggings or a short skirt to an entire crowd. So I had on a nice pair of blue jeans, calf-high boots, and a tan top, loose fitting with open sleeves.

Jason grumbled. "It's not sexy enough. I can't stop you tonight, but in the future, when you're on stage with the

Fiery Boys, you have to dress for it. Tight and colorful, with lots of skin showing. Not some stupid jeans and a baggy blouse." Wow, what a micromanager. I wondered if he had makeup tips for me, too.

I was used to Jason's irascibility by now, and I'd had enough of it. With a nod, I stepped away from him to watch the show.

When it was time to play "Fiery Life," Chuck introduced me without saying anything embarrassing at all. Instead, he teased River. "We have a special guest drummer tonight who's going to help River make it through the next song." He waved to the wing. "Come on out, Annalisa."

I ran onto the stage to light applause and stood by the side of River's drum kit. He handed me a drumstick, then he clapped his sticks together to start the song.

I felt woozy but forced myself to stand straight. I also had to force myself to stop grinning so much while I waited under the bright stage lights. The song got going, and I started to move. At first, I felt a little self-conscious being on stage. Was I dressed wrong? Was my dancing wrong? Were the fans annoyed?

Then I decided to let it all go. After all, I was there with the Fiery Boys, helping them play the most important song of my life. How could I not rock out?

The song seemed to progress much more slowly than ever before. I heard the notes distinctly, as if they were being played in isolation. When it was time for the chorus, an autonomic muscle response moved my arm and I crashed my stick to the cymbal. Then, without thinking about it, I started to pound with the beat.

Whoa! I was drumming with the Fiery Boys. I felt as if I'd passed through the looking glass of my high school poster and had emerged on the other side, jamming next to the incredibly sexy River Sticks.

The chorus ended much too quickly, and I caught myself just in time, stopping my rhythmic crashing at the right moment. River gave me a huge grin then turned back to thrash the drums like a madman.

I fell back into my dance easily, proud to be part of the song. As the guest groupie, playing with the band under the approving gaze of the world's hottest drummer, my life had never burned as brightly.

The song ended and I stood there, basking in the applause. Then, as if my fairy godmother had waved her magic wand over the audience, the applause transformed into the Annalisa chant from Minneapolis. Suddenly, thousands of fans were yelling, "Annalisa. Annalisa. Annalisa." Even the Fiery Boys joined the chant, pumping their fists in the air.

I stood by the drums with a huge grin on my face. Chuck came over so he could lead me to the front of the stage. He hugged me and gave me a kiss on the cheek while the audience continued to chant.

I tried to take all of this in, but I still couldn't believe it —my life was more than bizarre. In mere months, I had gone from a nobody who rarely got noticed to a well-known rock personality who stood at the front of the stage while thousands of people shouted my name.

Eighteen

The show ended, and the band ran from the stage. Chuck stopped to pull me into a hug. "I've got to get cleaned up, then I'm dealing with the press. Come along—it'll be fun."

I liked this new Chuck, a vast improvement over the desperately horny rocker I'd first met. He was considerate and pleasant and respectful. And when I factored in his kisses and his crazy good looks, he was almost irresistible. We went to a dressing room where he peeled off his sweaty shirt. I stared at him for a few seconds. Tall and trim, his chest glistened lightly. For the first time, I could see how running my tongue over his body might not be as repulsive as I'd imagined. He started to dry himself with a towel.

"You do have a fine body, Chuck."

"As do you, my dear. You have no idea how badly I crave it."

"I think I'm beginning to feel that craving, too."

Chuck's grin ran clear across his face. "Let's see what we can do about these cravings after the press meet." He gave me a firm kiss, then he put on a clean shirt and led me out of the dressing room.

As we headed down the hall, Chuck held my hand. "You know, Annalisa, next time you play, come to the front of the stage and dance with me during the verses. Then you can go back to River when you play the chorus. More showy that way. We can even dance together." That sounded like an excellent idea.

Chuck led me to a Fiery Boys press wall in a room full of reporters and photographers. I couldn't help but notice that they showed the same level of enthusiasm for him as a gaggle of groupies did, except that they didn't fling their bodies at him. Instead, they flung a barrage of questions. And to my surprise, many of the questions were for me.

"How are you enjoying the tour, Annalisa?"

"Are the Fiery Boys as fiery as ever?"

"Who's your favorite Fiery Boy?"

Chuck leaned close to me and whispered, "Don't bother answering them. Just kiss me."

When he dropped his lips onto mine, the reporters let out a howl. I'd been thinking about his kisses for the past few hours, wondering if we'd get a chance to do more. Although this didn't seem like the right place for it, the waves of heat running through my body made it hard to complain. Solid and so seductive, Chuck's gorgeous eyes locked onto mine.

Oh my God! I was kissing the lead singer of the Fiery Boys in front of the whole world. Flashes went off constantly. Kira would explode when she saw this. Jason would be supremely annoyed. And Inferna. . . well, she could kiss my ass.

It didn't matter what anyone thought. I'd kiss Chuck if I wanted to. Something burned in me, and I threw my arms around his neck to kiss him back, hard and willing. His tall, muscular body felt great.

Jason stepped up close to us. "You're here for a reason, Chuck, and it's not about Annalisa. Focus!" He pointed to one of the reporters and moderated a question. To my surprise, I was still the most interesting person in the room. They wanted to know where I stood with the band, how I liked the bus, and what I thought of the fans. I gave brief, evasive answers to avoid any controversy.

Chuck stood there tapping his foot. Finally past his ability to endure being ignored, he cut in after one of my answers and took my hand. "We're done here. Let's go." Feeling proud of myself and too charged up to resist, I let him lead me to the bus, our arms around each other, stumbling and laughing.

On the bus, he took my hands and walked backward down the aisle, pulling me along with a huge smile. I followed along happily. Gabe narrowed his eyes as we walked past. "Want any more to join the party?"

"Yes," Chuck said at the same time that I said, "No." We stopped and stared at each other. "It's better with more girls." His eyes flashed a few times in an attempt to convince me.

Disappointed, I shook my head and groaned. We continued to stare at each other, at an impasse by the living room table.

He really wanted to invite other women, but I simply couldn't go there. Sex with the handsome lead-singer of the Fiery Boys? Sure. Sex with some strange, unfriendly woman? No.

But Chuck wasn't yielding, so I had to think about this a little harder. Was I being too proud to share this man, this buff rock god who wrote my favorite song and had a voice that could shred my soul? So what if another groupie joined the fun? Would that be so terrible?

I already knew that Kira and Jo would do a three-way with Chuck. And they'd tell stories about it for years. So if I was willing to encourage my friends' wild sex parties, why wasn't I allowing Chuck to throw one for me? Dazed and already lightly aroused from Chuck's kisses, I caved in and decided I could handle it.

I said "Okay, yes," at exactly the same time that he said, "Okay, no." We grinned at each other.

"So can we get two more girls?"

I shrugged and exhaled my discomfort. "Oh, all right."

But Chuck did have a sensitive side, after all. He gave me a concerned look. "You don't seem happy."

"It's okay," I slumped my shoulders. "I'll do it your way if you like, but I'd prefer it if we were alone. I guess I'm just a romantic."

"Um, well. . . oh, okay." Chuck looked down for a few seconds before he raised his face with a smile. "None tonight, Chip." Then he pulled me into the bedroom and shut the door.

This was it. My moment with a rock star. I was about to have a tabloid-scale sexual experience in the back of the tour bus, and I was ready. I knew I'd be just another groupie, but I still wanted that Girl Scout badge. Why not?

Jason's rules meant nothing anymore. Nor did I care what the fans would say about me for doing this. Besides, the press already had enough pictures of us kissing to draw their own conclusions. As the contest winner, I had some serious opportunities, here. I *would* fuck Chuck. So there, Jason.

Chuck's hands and lips and ripped body were doing a fine job on me—I was totally stoked. It didn't even bother me that he usually bedded a harem. So what if he had a lead-singer-sized ego and only thought about sex? Right now, that was all I could think about, too. Our mouths collided and stayed firmly locked in place.

After a few minutes, Chuck pulled away and leaped onto the bed, his arms spread out. "Let me look at you." His sparkling eyes drilled right through me, even across the room. Mesmerized, I started to approach the bed but he raised a hand. "No. Stay there. Undress for me, slowly."

Yes, I would. I was completely under his spell. A slow strip-tease for Chuck sounded perfect.

I removed my blouse, one button at a time, tugging it gently from my jeans, and letting it slide off my shoulders, inch-by-inch. My boots and jeans went next, leaving me in my underwear. I made a huge show of removing my bra while Chuck cheered me on. Then for my finale, I worked my panties down then up again, left then right, teasing and flashing until I finally slid them down my legs. Chuck applauded.

I approached the bed but Chuck stopped me again and insisted that I continue the show. So I continued to tease him with my best moves, a pole dance without the pole. The sexy green-eyed singer was very appreciative of my act, which made me enjoy it even more.

I soon found myself growing surprisingly excited. I'd been so busy working to please Chuck that I'd forgotten about my own pleasure. But my body hadn't forgotten. It knew that I was naked and putting on an autoerotic show. By this point, it wanted more—no, it *needed* more.

I approached the bed. "Now it's your turn. I'm going to undress *you*, slowly."

He paused with a shrug. "Okay." He didn't seem convinced, but he wasn't stopping me, so I got to it.

I made him sit up and tugged on his shirt, slowly inching it up his body and over his head. His approving grunts told me how much he enjoyed that. I needed to get Chuck naked already, so I pulled him to his feet and unzipped his pants. I got them down his legs as slowly as possible, the two of us grinning the entire way. Chuck stood there in his briefs, with one hand resting over his crotch. I'd seen what he had down there and knew I was in for a treat.

I couldn't wait another second. Given how quickly I'd watched gangs of women pass through the bedroom with Chuck, I was surprised at how patient he was being. But patience was no longer a virtue, so instead of a slow tease with his underwear, I grabbed the sides and yanked them straight down his legs. He let them go, but his hand still covered the good stuff. That wouldn't do. So I pulled his arm away to get at the only thing that could satisfy me.

But something was wrong.

He was limp, completely not turned on. I stood up and looked into his clearly embarrassed eyes. "What's wrong, Chuck?"

"I. . . I don't know if I can do this."

"Why not? Am I doing something wrong?"

"It's not you. I just need more than one girl, more than one thing happening at a time. That gets me going."

What could I say? We were done before we began. I could never be enough for Chuck unless I shared him. After staring for a minute, I stepped away from the bed, defeated. "Okay, never mind."

"We could find some more groupies. . ."

I blew out a long breath. "I don't think so." Even though I was pretty turned on by this point, I knew it was time to give up. If some sexy woman waltzed in here and immediately got him hard I'd be devastated. Reluctantly, I dressed and wandered to the living room in a daze.

Gabe and River were gone. Buck looked up from the living room table, shook his head darkly, then marched right by me and into his cubicle. Before climbing up, he turned to the bedroom door and glared at Chuck. "I hope you're happy, fucker."

Chuck got dressed and managed to make it past Buck without starting a fight. Then he collapsed on the sofa with a whispered, "Sorry."

What I was doing here? The two band members who were nice to me were gone. I was left with Chuck the sexually challenged, and Buck the angry. When they weren't trying to kill each other, each of them could occasionally show moments of kindness to me. But I was tired of digging so deep, and my arousal called to me. At the very least, I needed a private place to attend to myself.

I turned to face Chuck. "I've got to get out of here for the night. I'll be back tomorrow."

He nodded like a little kid who had just broken an expensive vase. "Okay."

I grabbed my backpack, left the bus, and found a cab. "Take me to the nearest decent motel."

Nineteen

I sat in a cab, upset and horny. After Chuck's failure to launch, I needed a warm bath and my hand between my legs, pronto. Four days with the Fiery Boys certainly hadn't gotten me anything better.

My phone rang, and mercifully, it was Jo. I wasn't sure what I would say to her, but I was glad for a friendly voice. I took the call. "Hi. What's happening?"

Jo laughed. "Uh, no. That's supposed to be my line. After seeing pictures of you and Chuck kissing, *I'm* the one who gets to ask what's happening."

"Don't." She'd love to hear what just went on, but I couldn't tell her.

"That doesn't sound like a woman who's had a toss with the lead singer of the Fiery Boys."

"That's because I didn't. I'm in a cab right now, heading to a motel for the night. Alone."

"That little prick! So all he did was kiss you for the cameras then kick you off the bus?"

"I kicked myself off the bus."

"Oh no! Are you coming home?"

I sighed. "I'll be back on the bus tomorrow. I just wanted someplace else for the night."

"Sounds like the tour bus is a huge fail."

Frustrated, humiliated, and up to my ears with arousal, I let it all go in an outpouring of tears. The cab driver looked at me in the rearview mirror but was decent enough not to say anything. Jo also let me sob for a while. Finally, I got it under control. "I'm sorry. I can handle this, but I need a little alone time first."

"Do you want to talk about it?"

"I do, but not right now." The cab pulled to a stop, and I looked around. "I'm at the motel now, so I'm going to go. I promise I'll tell you all about it someday."

"That's okay. Take care of yourself, Annalisa. Call me any time." She hung up.

The motel looked pretty nice—one of those places with suites for businesspeople. I took a deep breath and walked over to the desk clerk, who seemed like he was just a high school kid. He wouldn't even look up from whatever game he was playing. Great, nobody was on my side tonight.

I waited a few seconds, then rattled things on the counter to get his attention. The clerk finally looked up at me and burst into a big smile. "I know you! You're the girl who's touring with the Fiery Boys." He started to chant, "Annalisa, Annalisa, Annalisa."

I couldn't escape. As much as I wanted to scream at him, my problems weren't his fault. I forced a smile. "I didn't realize I was that famous."

"Well, I'm a big Fiery Boys fan. I was even at the show tonight. I can't wait to tell my friends I met you." He turned to look at his computer. "And by the way, I have a room waiting for you." He worked for a few seconds and then handed me a key card.

I frowned. "Don't I have to register first? Give you a credit card?"

"Special deal for you. It's all set up." He gave me a wink.

I worried about what he had in mind. Sure, I was horny, but not for this kid. I held up the key. "I don't want any visitors, understand?"

He slapped a hand to his chest. "Of course! I promise you'll be alone." He seemed sincere, and I was anxious to get to the room, so I thanked him and wandered down the hall.

As I walked to my room, I wondered if there would be something unusual about it. Did the desk clerk really give me a free room, or was there a catch? I usually got treated worse because of this contest, not better.

I slipped the key card in the door and it unlocked, already a good sign. When I stepped in, I was even more pleased. On the right was a living room, with a sofa and chairs facing a big television. On the left was a small kitchen. And straight ahead was a hallway which led to a bathroom and a bedroom.

Alone at last, in my very own suite, it felt nice. I had to admit that I'd been feeling cramped on the bus. Now I could relax in my own room, spacious and luxurious, even if for just one night.

I double-locked the door and got right down to the business of my arousal, still raging through me from whatever it was that Chuck and I had done. I pulled off my blouse much more quickly than I had for him, and shucked my boots and jeans in short order. Feeling playful, I danced around for a few seconds while I unhooked my bra. Then I pulled it off and flung it at a lamp, just like in the movies where clothing gets strewn everywhere. Yeah, I was getting into it.

Unfortunately, I threw my bra too hard and the lamp fell over on the table.

Then things got weird.

A man's voice called out from the bedroom. "That's fast room service!" The bedroom door opened a crack and the man spoke again. "Leave it on the table. Tip's there." Then he closed the door.

Oh great! I was right about that desk clerk—he had given me someone else's room. Now I'd have to go back to the office and deal with it. I simply couldn't get a break.

I was about to get dressed when something dawned on me. That voice was familiar—it sounded like River. Could it be? The desk clerk had recognized me, and would certainly know if River had previously checked in. Did he give me this key because he thought we were hooking up?

I noticed that the bedroom door had drifted open a little, allowing the barest slice of light to emerge. Was River Sticks in the next room with his secret lover? I needed to know.

Since I was wearing nothing but panties, I picked up my open-sleeved blouse and slipped it on, not sparing the time to button it. I couldn't wait to find out if River was here, and if so, who he was with.

Besides, a coarser part of me, which still hadn't been satisfied tonight, wondered if I could get in on the action. Why get completely dressed when there might be a hot lover waiting for me? Yes, I know I'd been refusing three-ways with Chuck all week, but this was River. For him, I'd do just about anything. Don't judge me!

I disguised my voice in a deep grunt, pretending to be the room service waiter. "Thanks." I even opened the suite door, made foot-shuffling sounds, and closed it again. Then, I tiptoed toward the bedroom to see who was in there. Oh, I was being very bad.

Through the crack in the door, I could see a few inches of the room, and as I shifted from side to side, more of it came into view. I slowed my search when I found a mirror, which reflected directly onto a bed. And on the bed I saw a man's feet and legs. I continued to scan upward so I could see more of his body, which definitely looked like River's. When I got to his head, I knew I was right.

My heart started to pound, and my mouth went dry. River's naked body entwined with his lover's, moving like liquid heat. Back in high school, I used to masturbate to his poster, but watching the real man was so much better. My hyper-aroused state shot into overdrive and I dipped a hand into my panties. I knew it was wrong to watch, but my hormonally agitated brain wouldn't be denied.

River rolled on the bed and his lover came into view. As she turned her face to me, I watched carefully, ready to learn the truth.

That's when everything screeched to a halt.

I knew this person. River's secret lover was very familiar. And even more shocking, River's secret lover was a man. Gabe.

I stood like a statue as I digested this new information. River and Gabe were gay—I did not see that coming. Of course, my concern wasn't that they were gay, I had no issues with that. What upset me was that River was supposed to be *my* lover. I had to admit it hurt to find out this would never happen. Sure he had told me that he was committed, but I still fantasized that I had a chance. Not anymore.

I should have turned away from this shameless lurking. But a depraved and Fiery Boys-deprived part of me kept watching. And whoa! Talk about hot. These two didn't have any arousal problems, and my own arousal no longer seemed like a problem, either. Suddenly, I was back in high school, masturbating to River's poster. I pushed down my panties so I could get serious.

Lost in a carnal daze, I was mesmerized by the splendor of River's body. Naked, buff, and aroused, he was an incredibly sexy man. And Gabe's body looked pretty damn good right now, especially when moving against River's. When I thought about it a little more, I realized I was glad they were lovers. I would have been much more upset if I had to watch River with some strange woman.

These two naked men reminded me of young Greek gods. Their muscles flexed as they glided in erotic dance. Their faces showed both sexual excitement and a deep longing for each other, the exquisite joy of being in a lover's embrace. I was incredibly happy for them.

Their cries of passion started to grow louder, and I circled my hand faster. Something powerful began to build for all three of us. Suddenly, they cried out, which triggered an orgasm that blew through me like an explosion at a fireworks factory. I remember thinking that I should keep quiet, just as a scream burst from my lungs. But nothing mattered right then.

I definitely needed this. Given Chuck's inability, River and Gabe's removal from the mating pool, and Buck's overall bad attitude, I suspected that this was the best I was going to get from the Fiery Boys. So I took a moment to enjoy a shattering climax.

Unfortunately, when I opened my eyes I saw River and Gabe staring at me from the bedroom door. And all three of us were naked. Even my blouse had slipped off my shoulders when I wasn't paying attention. Awkward!

I spoke quickly. "Don't be mad—I can explain. I wasn't following you. Honest!"

River held up his hands. "Whoa. Slow down." He took a motel bathrobe from the closet and tossed it to me. Then, safely wrapped in towels, he and Gabe joined me at the living room table.

"So, Annalisa." River grinned. "How did you end up sneaking into our suite and beating off while we made love?" An unusual but entirely reasonable question.

I blew out a loud breath. "Chuck's been much nicer to me lately, so I let him take me to the bedroom." I looked over at Gabe. "You were there, you saw what happened."

Gabe nodded. "I wondered what would happen between just the two of you. Did you actually get any?"

My eyes widened. "So you know that Chuck can't get it up unless he has multiple women with him?"

Gabe practically giggled. "Of course I know that. Why do you think I keep fetching groupies for him? Like so many lead singers, he's always on stage, even in the bedroom. And it's simple enough to find fans who'll share him. Also, I love it when the paps take pictures of me with those women. Makes people think I'm straight." He shot me a big smile. "Fooled you."

"Lots of things fooled me. My naked romp with Chuck certainly did. It left me frustrated and seriously turned on." I let out a pathetic laugh. "I couldn't sit around on the bus with a sorry-eyed Chuck, so I came here to get a motel room. Unfortunately, the clerk recognized me and gave me your room key."

I apologized for my shameless activity in the suite, but also pointed out that they were thrilling to watch. To my relief, they weren't upset. River even told me about a masquerade party they'd once attended that turned into an orgy. The costumes were pretty good, and you couldn't always tell who any two people having sex really were. So River and Gabe found a quiet corner and made love right there, while all across the room a dozen other straight and gay couples did the same.

River tilted his head. "What we want to know is, can you keep this a secret?"

Tonight definitely seemed to be band-secret night. I felt bad for these two closeted Fiery Boys, and I needed to apologize for intruding on them. I let my smile grow in warmth. "Yes, of course I can. Do Chuck and Buck know?"

River relaxed some more. "Yeah, they know. So does Jason. But that's about it. Oh, except now you know."

I was truly happy for them and wanted them to feel comfortable, so I gave them my warmest smile. "Did you come here to hide from me, or do you always go to motels?"

"We always leave the bus. Too many strangers show up when you least expect it."

It all made sense, and much of my confusion about the band evaporated like the morning fog. Knowing their secret brought me closer to them in a different way. A way that made me happy. These were the two band members who had been the nicest to me, and I understood that it was because they felt no sexual tension. Now that I knew their secret, I felt none, either. We were friends.

There was a knock at the door, this time the real room service. Gabe and I hid while River opened the door. As the cart got wheeled in, a half-dozen flashes went off in his face. The hallway was crawling with paparazzi.

River slammed the door. "Fuck. Someone leaked our whereabouts, probably that desk clerk. Now we're stuck in here."

I got a crazy idea and gave him a devilish smile. "You know, I could leave with you. Give them what they want. Then Gabe could sneak out later."

Gabe shook his head. "I can't sneak out now. Someone would see me. If you're willing to be photographed with River, would you be willing to do it with both of us?"

"Certainly," I laughed. "Let them think we had a three-way. In fact, why don't we put on a show. Let's act lewd and horny. In the morning, we can make a big scene when we check out together."

River bolted out a laugh, and Gabe hugged me. "You sure? You're going to get a lot of hate for it."

"I can handle haters. Besides, when this week is up, they'll forget all about me." At least I hoped that would be true.

I got dressed, leaving a few buttons from my blouse unbuttoned. River and Gabe put on pants but left their shirts off. Then we stumbled to the office, giggling and grabbing each other as flashes went off all around us. Standing by the front desk, I got more than a little turned on again as the bald and bad River Sticks held me to his side and kissed me. I squeezed him tight and let me tell you, he felt great. So what if he was gay? He still had a sizzling hot body. Gabe wasn't too bad, either, now that I'd seen more of him. I was having the best time in the world groping them.

Prying myself from River like a sated lover, I gave the desk clerk my most vampy look. "Say, honey. Where can we get some booze?"

The kid grinned at us and pointed out the door. "There's a liquor store a few blocks from here."

I couldn't resist pushing it too far, so I let out a growl and ran my hand over River's scalp. "Hey." I was speaking to River and Gabe, but made sure the clerk and the paparazzi could hear, too. "Let's do that thing with the whipped cream and chocolate sauce." I giggled and turned back to the clerk. "What about a grocery store?"

The kid swallowed. "Uh yeah, there's one next to the liquor store."

"Mmm. Can't wait." I dragged my two favorite Fiery Boys back to the room where we collapsed onto the sofa, laughing uncontrollably. Then we finished dressing and talked.

Suddenly free from secrets, River and Gabe became downright voluble, and we talked for hours. I heard how the two of them were instantly attracted to each other when the band was formed. They were only fifteen at the time and hadn't fully realized their homosexuality. But because of their attraction and the close working conditions, they figured it out together and lost their virginity soon after. The relationship stuck.

I was surprised at the steps they had taken to keep their love secret all these years. They worked hard to act straight, guarding both their speech patterns and their body language. They made up fake girlfriends and extensive lies that they told when anyone asked about them. Gabe even went so far as to keep a decoy house in his hometown of Detroit. The two of them actually lived together on a remote farm, an hour southwest of Minneapolis.

At one point, River gave me a friendly kiss. "You're the best, Annalisa. I'm glad you're on tour with us." I was glad, too—very much so.

Day Five

Twenty

River and Gabe let me sleep on the sofa that night, although we talked so much that we hardly slept. By the time we got back to the bus, it was nearly noon. Another incredible night with the Fiery Boys.

Gabe found a number of articles about our phantom threesome, and he showed them to us on the bus's living room screen. Because of my earlier public display with Chuck, most articles threw him into the mix too, declaring that the contest winner had scored with three Fiery Boys in a single night. The fans seemed quite proud of me. We didn't bother to look up Inferna's reaction.

In addition to now being an established Fiery Boys tramp, I was also getting some attention for my stage presence during "Fiery Life." A viral fan video had captured one of my wilder dance moves, and everyone was citing this little act as the siren song of a horny groupie. Male fans called it my CWILF dance, referring to their earlier acronym about my desirability. And everyone was declaring me the winner of much more than a simple contest.

Jason climbed onto the bus and stepped in front of the screen. His scowl reminded me that all was not well in bandville. "You!" He pointed at me, his hand shaking angrily. I knew what was coming, and it wasn't about River and Gabe. "Pack your shit and get *off* my bus."

Given that I hadn't done any of the things he thought I had, I figured I might have a chance at redemption. "It's not what you think, Jason. I didn't do anything with Chuck."

"Bullshit. You and Chuck were all over each other at that press meet. And everyone saw you two run back to the bus like naughty school children. I warned you not to fuck him, but you didn't listen. Now everyone's talking about it." He stepped closer to where I sat on the sofa. "Out!"

"It's not my fault he kissed me. You know how horny he is. But we did *not* have sex. Ask him yourself if you don't believe me."

Chuck chose this moment to come into the living room. "She's right, Jason. Didn't happen. As much as I wanted it, Annalisa is still a Chuck-virgin."

That stopped Jason. He squinted at Chuck for a second. "You're defending her? Why?"

Chuck shrugged. "Because it's the truth. She's okay by me. And she was a good sport at the press meet." He stepped closer to Jason. "Let her stay. She'll be gone in a few days anyway."

"But the fans. . ." Jason trailed off when he saw Gabe shaking his head. "What?"

Gabe smiled. "The fans love her. They're proud of her for scoring with three of us at once. Not jealous at all."

Jason darkened. "That's not what Inferna says."

"Sure, there are still plenty of haters, but *No Moss* loves it. Check out what Ivory Doe wrote." Gabe pointed at the screen.

Jason studied it for a few minutes then turned back to us. "Fine. But what was this shit with you and River?"

Gabe glared. "Shit, Jason? Look, the paps spotted her at our motel, and she offered to be our beard." He got up from the couch and snapped at the testy band manager. "Would you rather she outed us?"

River got up and also stepped threateningly close to Jason. He and Gabe had him boxed in. "You're the fuckhead who wanted us to stay in the closet. She helped us—you should thank her."

Jason pulled away from them and frowned at the three Fiery Boys who were banding together to defend me. He took a few noisy breaths, then turned and left the bus, muttering, "God how I hate this job." We all laughed when he was safely out the door.

After Jason left, Buck wandered into the living room. He squinted at Chuck and me. "You two can lie to Jason, but I saw you back there." Before we could straighten him out, he'd stomped back to his cubicle. It didn't matter—everything else was going well. Buck could think what he wanted.

The next city on the tour was Denver, but not until the following night. We had all day to get there, so the band packed up and left by early afternoon. I sat in the front of the living room so I could watch the world speed by.

While I stared at the road, the band kept busy with their usual pursuits. Gabe had his phone connected to his laptop and was having gleeful techno-fun. River was listening to music and drumming on the table when the mood grabbed him. Buck was hiding in his cubicle with his guitar. And Chuck was drinking tequila. Just another day on the road with the Fiery Boys.

Kira called to give me the news. "Triple score! You rule, girl." She was going to be so disappointed.

I wandered back to the bedroom so I could have some privacy. "It's not what you think."

"That's what Jo said. So what is it? I saw pictures of Chuck kissing you yesterday, and some half-dressed shots of you with River and Gabe. Now everyone figures you'll be doing Buck next."

"Oh sweet. Well here's the bad news: no sex with Chuck. The only thing that happened was those kisses at the press meet. And the chances that I'll soon be doing Buck are nil."

"Well, I'm still proud of you. So what's going on?"

I wanted to say nothing was going on, but that wouldn't do it justice. Something was definitely happening—I was forming a friendship with River and Gabe. River had opened up completely and had rekindled in me a new kind of love for him. And I liked Gabe more than I had for the past ten years.

River talked about Minneapolis, where he and Gabe lived together, outside of the city. Many of his relatives lived nearby. He loved the farm and couldn't wait to get back there. He even made me promise to come visit them after the tour ended.

Gabe also opened up and talked to me even more than before. He showed me new pages he was posting on the Fiery Boys website, suggested new features for my phone, and raved about the latest band equipment. Everything in his world was totally digital, mega, ultra, and nano. Or something like that. But we were talking quite a bit—he even asked about my friends and family. I had really connected with River and Gabe.

But I had to tell Kira something, and the truth couldn't be revealed. "It's. . . complicated." Yeah, that about covered it. "I'll tell you all about it someday, but I can't yet."

"Wow! Mystery and suspense. Well, at least you're having fun."

"Yes, I finally am."

"Can you tell me one thing, though? Did you really get drunk, pour tubs of whipped cream and chocolate sauce on each other, then have a three-way with River and Gabe?"

I laughed so hard I nearly fell off the bed. "Sorry, that never happened. But there *is* a story there, and I promise to tell it one day."

"Awesome." Kira was enraptured, even though she didn't know a thing. But she did know the Internet buzz. And that was something I wanted to hear. Gabe had looked at some sites, but Kira might have seen different ones.

I forced myself to ask, although I wasn't sure I wanted to hear the answer. "Do the fans hate me for this?"

"Not really. Most people are happy you got some. In fact, we'd be pretty annoyed if the winner didn't get at least one little romp."

Ouch. That seemed to be my destiny: not even one little romp. See? I knew I wouldn't be having sex with any of them.

"What about Inferna?" Jason had already confirmed that the slutty fan-girl was unhappy, but I was curious to know the details.

"Oh, just the usual. Now that you're a grade-A slut, she has proof that you must die."

"*I'm* a slut? Has she looked in the mirror lately?"

Kira laughed. "I know. Oh, and also, Inferna is protesting the very air you breathe and refuses to go to any Fiery Boys concerts while you're backstage."

I wondered why I hadn't seen her for a few days. "That's downright considerate of her."

"Yep. But watch out! She's rebranded her site to focus on you. Her tagline is now, 'The site for Fiery Boys fans who hate Annalisa.' And she's becoming more and more incoherent. Long nonsensical screeds on why she should have won that contest instead of you. Her latest argument is that you're an evil witch who has the Fiery Boys under a magical spell." Kira paused. "Can you teach me how to do that?"

I giggled. "I don't have that particular power, but wow can I tell stories. Wait for them."

"No problem. Besides, I have to go. I'll keep you posted on the outside world."

"Thanks, Kira." We hung up.

I had been sitting on Chuck's orgy bed in the back of the bus. The bed was unmade, a jumble of sheets, blankets, and pillows. As I stared more closely, I noticed a discolored patch on a sheet. That was enough—I got up from the bed. It had always surprised me that nobody slept in this spacious and comfortable bedroom, but I now understood the reason. Chuck came by every day and made a mess of the place. Nobody wanted to sleep here, not even him. This was just his sex pad—such a waste.

I returned to the living room for more of my romp-free week on the Fiery Boys tour bus.

Twenty-One

We pulled into Denver during the last rays of sunlight, and Chuck wandered over to the waiting fans for his special kind of entertainment. The rest of us went to the arena so Gabe could check out the space. Buck wandered through the seats while River, Gabe, and I went up on the stage. As we returned to the bus, Vaughan pulled Buck aside. "There's someone waiting for you."

Buck arched an eyebrow and folded his arms. "Who?"

"She says she's your wife. Jason told me to let her in, but I thought you should know." Buck dropped his head and groaned, clearly unhappy to see Danielle. This was the woman who broke his heart and was widely believed to have killed the band. And although I doubted she was wholly responsible for the band's demise, I still wasn't her biggest fan.

Then I realized something—I actually wanted to meet her. After all, I was here on the bus with the Fiery Boys, and Danielle was an essential element of this band. I might not be going home with any sexual conquests in my pocket, but I was collecting some incredible stories. Why not meet Danielle?

Reluctant to push myself into her face too quickly, I let the others board, then I waited a few minutes before climbing up. Danielle sat at the living room table next to Gabe, chatting and passing a joint between them. She looked exactly as she had ten years ago, cute and trim, with a full head of curly blonde hair. Chuck, River, and Buck were gone, probably hiding in their cubicles. I wondered if bad-tempered Buck had said anything to her.

When she saw me, Danielle smiled. "So you're the contest winner." She gave me an appraising once-over, nodding with what seemed like approval. Then she patted the seat next to her, so I sat down. "Are you enjoying tour hell?" I figured she should know.

Gabe sent the joint back to her, and she took a puff before offering to it me. Although I'd avoided getting high with Gabe up to this point, nothing was the same anymore. A little extra fun wouldn't be so bad. So I took a drag and got high with the closeted guitarist and the reclusive bass player's wife. Yeah, that sounded about right.

Danielle leaned close and whispered, "Heard you fucked Chuck." She gave me a throaty laugh, and I couldn't help but join in.

"Would you believe me if I told you that I haven't?"

Gabe finished the joint and left its remains in the ashtray. He leaned back with his eyes closed. Either he was more blissed out than normal, or, more likely, he was enjoying eavesdropping on this conversation. Danielle leaned closer to me and smiled. "According to the web, you got Chuck's name tattooed on your breast."

This time, I really laughed. "Let me guess—you've been reading Inferna's site. That woman is full of lies. Sorry, no tattoo, no sex with Chuck, and definitely not in love." I turned to face her. "Did they used to say that about you? Did they report that you had 'Buck' tattooed on your breast?"

"No, but if I'd gotten such a tattoo, it wouldn't have said 'Buck.' Hell, that's not even his name. I call him Charlie, like his family does. All his friends called him Chuck back in high school. Of course, Lord Jason made him change that."

Everyone knew that Buck and Chuck were both named Charles. I'd always assumed that Buck had taken that name for artistic reasons. But now I could see that, like so much else in this band, it all came down to Jason's dictatorial control. As I suspected, Danielle was definitely worth meeting.

Curious to know more, I waded carefully into the sea of Buck. "Has he always been so closed-off and angry?"

She tightened her mouth. "He wasn't back then. I think it's mostly my fault these days. Divorce is touchy business. I feel bad about it."

"Do you miss him?"

"No more than I have for the last seven or eight years." I was sad that she and Buck hadn't been close. It had to be hard being with a famous rocker.

I nodded. "I'm sorry to hear that. I don't know how you handled all the abuse. I've been roasted alive, and it's been less than a week. How did you put up with it for years?"

"I didn't. I couldn't stand it. It didn't bother me that Charlie spent so much time writing music and practicing. But the parties were nauseating. Drunk half-dressed women everywhere. And every one of them hated me for taking away their precious Buck. The male fans wouldn't get close either, since I was taken. If it weren't for Gabe, I wouldn't have had anyone to talk to back then. I'm telling you, I was a band widow. I spent most of my time either on the road and hating it, or home and lonely. It sucked."

"So what brings you to the tour bus?"

She shrugged. "I travel a lot these days, and I was in Denver to meet with a client. Thought I'd check up on the boy. He might be pissed at me, but I don't hate him anymore. It's time for both of us to move on with our lives, so I came to wish him well. We'll be officially divorced soon, you know. So go ahead and have sex with him if you want."

I bolted to attention so hard I thought my head would snap off. Danielle was full of surprises, including the ridiculous notion that I was going to bag her soon-to-be ex husband. I laughed and stared at her with wide-open eyes. "Yeah, that'll be the day."

Now it was Danielle's turn to be surprised. "Wait! You two haven't hooked up?"

"Hell no! He stays far away from me."

Danielle squinted at me for a few seconds then got up and wandered toward the back of the bus. "Charlie? Where are you?"

Buck poked his head out of his cubicle and growled at her. "What do you want?"

She stared at him for a few seconds, then shrugged. "Oh never mind. Have a good show tomorrow." She gave him a wave of her hand, then turned away. When she got back to the living room, she blew a kiss to Gabe, and they waved at each other. Then she gave me a hug. "Nice to meet you. Can you do me a favor?"

"Uh, sure."

She pulled an envelope from her purse and handed it to me. "Give this to Charlie." Before I could protest that I was the last person on this bus to deliver anything to Buck, she had climbed down the steps and left.

I headed toward Buck's cubicle to deliver the letter and get it over with, but I heard him muttering and cursing at Danielle. Now was not a good time, and I was a little looped from the pot so I didn't want to confront him. I stashed the letter in my cubicle and went back to the living room.

Sitting with Gabe, I decided to learn more of Danielle's story. I knew he'd tell me the truth. "So did she have any part in the band's break up?"

"No." Gabe shook his head. "The band died because it had a narrow demographic. We were known as the rocking sixteen year olds, young and full of energy. We quickly became the latest teen heartthrob band, especially among other sixteen year olds." He gave me a tight grin. "Like you."

Gabe took a long breath. "But for some reason, we *only* connected with teenagers. Older people couldn't care less about us. That's why we died. We didn't have broad-enough appeal."

"That makes sense, but what about Danielle?"

"The Buck and Danielle story had little to do with our breakup. We didn't care about his love life. But she did break his heart. She couldn't handle all the negative media attention—who could? It ruined her, and she took him down with it."

"Good thing I'm leaving soon."

"Good for you. Sad for me—I'll miss you. River likes you, too. And Buck. . ." Gabe looked up and shook his head. "He's actually going to miss you, too."

Somehow, I doubted that.

Day Six

Twenty-Two

The band had already set up yesterday for tonight's show, so there was nothing left to do today. River and Gabe wanted to go up into the Rocky Mountains for a little sightseeing. River loved the outdoors, and I figured Gabe just wanted to get higher. Buck and Chuck were interested too, which surprised me because I thought Chuck would prefer to power through another bed full of groupies.

I was definitely fine with the idea of getting away from the arena and the insistent pressure of fans. It seemed like a welcome diversion. So they decided to enlist Big Tim to drive us on the tour bus, out of the city and up into the mountains. Naturally, Jason loved the idea of our tour bus rolling through the countryside, advertising the band.

We got on the road, and Gabe lit up a joint. Chuck took a few shots of tequila, and the rest of us went for some beer and soda.

At one point, just before the second round of drinks hit the table, Buck changed into a ratty Fiery Boys T-shirt with a picture of Chuck on it. I regarded the singer's face with some level of curiosity. "Since when are you a fan of Chuck's?"

Buck grinned. "This is my beer-drinking shirt. Watch. . ." He set the bottles on the table and opened them, using the shirt to twist off the caps. Each time he opened another bottle, the shirt tore a little more. Chuck's picture was starting to look like the victim in a horror movie. I have to admit I appreciated each new rip, because it let me see more and more of Buck's fine body. He might be difficult, but he was phenomenally hot.

I had a fresh bottle of beer in my hand and was about to propose a toast to the band when the bus suddenly slowed down and pulled to the side of the road. Gabe got up to talk to Big Tim, then came back and collapsed on the sofa. "Bad news. The engine's overheated, and we're stuck for a while. Big Tim's calling for service."

I got up from my seat, excited by the thought of a broken engine. To me, they'd always been interesting puzzles, fun to solve. And this engine was even more interesting because it was sure to be huge. I'd never worked on a bus.

Big Tim was outside, so I left the bus to go find him. I was wearing a casual outfit today, blue jeans and a black T-shirt. I used to dress like this ten years ago when Zed and I would work on engines. Except that the shirt I wore then was my work shirt, so it was already stained with grease and oil. Now I had on clean clothes, and I was ready to check out this new toy. I found Big Tim at the back of the bus.

"Hey, Annalisa." He nodded toward the steam issuing from the grill. "Overheated."

I pointed to the colorful liquid pooling on the ground. "Spewing coolant."

"Yeah, let's take a look. The mechanic will figure it out for sure." He popped open a panel, exposing a large, hot engine. We stepped back to admire the enormity of it.

Buck wandered out to join us. Big Tim nodded at him then turned back to the engine and sighed. "Gotta open the radiator and let it cool. But I need a rag—that sucker's hot." He started to go back to the bus, but Buck stopped him.

"Here, use my shirt. It's garbage, anyway." He peeled off the torn Fiery Boys T-shirt and tossed it to Big Tim, happy to send Chuck's image to its final resting place.

I'd already been admiring Buck's pumped body, but with the shirt off, I let myself indulge. His muscles looked more than fine in the sunlight. A little of my teenage love for him started to return, and for a brief moment, I forgot about the angry and withdrawn bass player I'd known all week.

Big Tim bunched up the shirt and reached into the steaming engine to loosen the radiator cap. Then, with a yelp, he leapt back as much more steam billowed out. "Gotta let this sucker cool off for a while." He offered the shirt back to Buck but it was filthy now, so Buck waved it away. Big Tim dropped it on the ground and wandered off.

Alone with Buck, I sneaked one last look at his superfine body then turned to face the engine. I didn't need to get him started again. The steam vented for a while, and soon I could see the massive motor. "Wonder why it overheated?" I picked up Buck's T-shirt so I could poke around.

He squinted at me. "You know what you're doing?"

"A little." I shrugged. "I've worked on plenty of car engines. Don't forget that I sell them for a living." I stepped back and wiped sweat from my forehead. "I'll tell you one thing. All the engines on the showroom floor are much cleaner than your tour bus." Even Zed's old cars had cleaner engines than this monstrosity.

I turned to Buck and took a stab at conversation with Mr. Grumpy-head. "What about you? Know anything about engines?"

"Some." Buck swayed his head from side to side. "Could be a coolant leak. We'll find out when they fill it up."

I nodded toward the coolant on the ground. "If it's a leak, it can't be too bad or else there'd be nothing left to spill out. Must be something else." I approached the engine and poked around some more, gingerly guiding my hand around hot engine parts. I checked the oil level, but it wasn't low and looked relatively clean. The hoses looked good, too. I'd have checked the thermostat if it wasn't still too hot to touch. Besides, there wasn't much I could do without a decent toolkit.

The shirt caught on something and tore even more—it was definitely garbage now. I pulled it free and tossed it away. Then I stepped back to admire this huge machine. With the steam gone now, I could see it clearly. Belts and hoses and wires ran everywhere, filthy and hot.

But as I stared at the engine, I noticed something unusual. The belts. In a car engine, you can't see all of them because they're always tucked into the hood. But here on the bus, I could see every belt as it wound back and forth. And one of them was sagging. Where it should have run in a rigidly straight line, I noticed a tiny amount of curvature.

"Look at this. . ." I reached in to wiggle the slack belt. "Here's the problem."

Buck nodded. "Loose fan belt." He tugged on the belt, then his eyes narrowed on me. "Nice work. You do know engines. You're really good."

Ooh, a compliment! I didn't think he was capable of that. "You know, that's the nicest thing you've said to me." I gave him a smirk.

"Fuck that!" He propped his fists on his hips. "I've been nice to you. I got the audience to like you."

"Okay, that *was* nice. But you've been withdrawn and testy all week." It started to spill out of me now. Six days of angry Buck, brooding, picking fights, getting drunk, and hiding in his cubicle. It was push-back time, so I let him have it.

"I know you didn't want me to be on tour with the band, but I'm here. So why couldn't you just *get over it*?" I may have yelled that last part.

I could not figure out Buck. Did he like me or did he hate me? I wanted to grab him and shake him and demand that he explain himself, because whatever was going on inside his head was making me feel bad. I'd be leaving the tour soon, so it was long past time to figure this out.

But what could I do that would pierce Buck's walls and show him how I felt? The answer came instantly. With a satisfying laugh, I wiped my greasy hand on his too-perfect chest, leaving a shiny black streak. Hah! Take that!

"Oh, nice." Buck looked down with a grin. Then he reached his own dirty hand out and wiped a line of grime across my cheek. I guess I should have expected something like that.

"You bastard." I lunged for his grinning face to give him another swipe, but he caught my wrists. His smug smile dared me to escape, so I struggled against his grip with my greasy fingers wiggling at him. Of course, he held me easily, which made him smile even more. Damn him! We remained in this standoff for a long time, staring hard at each other.

Finally, after taking a deep breath, Buck loosened his grip. This freed me to resume the battle, so I reached for his face, ready to paint him with more black grease. As my hands landed on his face, his hands grabbed mine. The battle was on.

Then I noticed something unusual. Buck's hands were on my face, but they weren't smearing soot. Instead, they were relaxed and gentle and held my face tenderly. Also, he looked different. His usual anger had washed away, leaving him looking serious and calm.

His look also had a new aspect to it. A wisp of a smile that I had seen a long time ago on the old Buck, the one whose poster hung above my bed. I didn't understand it then and I didn't understand it now. But I'd always liked it.

None of this made sense. I kept waiting for him to grumble about something, but he never said a word. His bright blue eyes practically devoured me, and if I didn't know better, I'd have said he was about to give me a kiss.

So it shouldn't have been such a shock when he did.

Twenty-Three

Buck's kiss came out of nowhere, or at least from someplace I didn't expect. Sure, I'd often kissed him in my fantasies, but that was ten years ago. And those fantasies had been put to rest this week, time and again, as he ignored me and angrily brooded. So that kiss seemed completely wrong.

But the kiss was also very right. Firm and warm, his lips woke up a teenage part of me that was happy and excited. I took a second to regroup and focus on what was going on. I mean, this was Buck Morris—the stunningly handsome bass player of the Fiery Boys—kissing me with a passion I'd only dreamt of. Holy hell!

Anger washed out of me leaving only desire. Explanations could wait until later, when the kiss was over and common sense was once again established. For now, Buck was kissing me, and it felt wonderful. I let go of his face so I could throw my arms around his broad shoulders and hold him tight.

Buck deepened the kiss, and he started to caress my cheek, my face, my neck. He licked an invitation across my puckered lips, which I eagerly accepted.

When our tongues first touched, we paused to let the tender feeling linger, savoring this step toward intimacy. Slowly, we moved against each other, exploring the terrain, finding our way. Buck settled his hand on the back of my head and pulled me closer. Another hand went down my back, pulling my body to his. I relaxed into his exquisitely powerful grip.

The seemingly infinite kiss finally ended. Buck pulled back from my mouth and exhaled, "God, Annalisa." I tried to reply but he dove back in for another kiss.

Big Tim came around to the back of the bus, noticed us, and quickly withdrew. We pulled away from each other but continued to stare while I spoke breathlessly. "I thought you hated me."

"Never! I've wanted you so much that it's been making me crazy."

"Wait. . . what?" Was he so shy that he was afraid to make a move?

"I've had my eye on you all week—haven't you noticed?"

"Yeah, but you were usually frowning."

"That was me being frustrated. I tried to ignore you, to keep away or drown myself in beer. But it didn't work—you just kept growing on me. Then just now, when you dove into that engine and figured out what was wrong, I completely lost it. I'm sorry, Annalisa, but I can't hide this anymore."

"Why are you sorry?"

He shook his head. "You deserve more than meaningless sex on the tour bus."

"Hey! Don't feel bad. If you'd like to have meaningless sex, I'm all for it." I grinned. "With you, that is."

Buck grinned back. Then his face fell, and he pounded his fist on the side of the bus. "Also, I'm tangled up in this damned divorce. My lawyers warned me to stay away from other women until it's final." He tightened his mouth. "Danielle was unfaithful, so she got a modest settlement. But if her lawyers find out I'm with other women, they'll rip me apart."

His explanation made sense. He wanted me but was being held back because of his divorce, his disdain for rock-and-roll hookups, and his respect for me. No wonder he was always upset. Now it was all coming out in a tidal wave of emotion and need. "When is your divorce final?"

Buck laughed darkly. "Not until next week, and you'll be gone." He pulled me close for another kiss.

I didn't want to stop his kisses—they were incredibly good—but if he was concerned about his divorce, then I figured we should be more discrete. I pulled my lips only a millimeter away. "So maybe we shouldn't stand here by the side of the road and kiss."

He laughed and pulled back. "There are all sorts of reasons why we shouldn't stand here and kiss. I still don't want to lead you on. You're not a groupie, and you don't deserve to be treated like one. Rock-and-roll romances never work out well, and when I'm involved in them, things get even worse. I don't want people to start in on you like they did to Danielle, accusing you of destroying the band."

"Is that why you voted against me?"

Buck stared with a furrowed brow. "I didn't vote against you. I was the one who lobbied hard for you to be chosen."

"Wait. You wanted me to be chosen? Chuck said I was the first choice of three of the band members. So who was the one who didn't want me?" Suddenly, I suspected that the outlier would be Chuck, himself.

Buck let out a single laugh. "Chuck thought you weren't pretty enough. But he seduced you anyway. Asshole does everything he can to stick it to me, even if it means taking you to bed. He knew I was into you, but he didn't care." He growled, "That fucker robs me of everything he can. Why does every Fiery Boys fan love him?"

"I don't love Chuck. Never did. You and River were my favorites, even ten years ago. And now that I know that he and Gabe are an item, that makes you my absolute favorite." I grinned. "Especially if you're going to kiss me like that."

"So why did you screw Chuck? I know you're both denying it, but I heard you two in the bedroom."

"It didn't happen, Buck. I swear. I've had more sex with River and Gabe."

Buck rolled his eyes. "Don't be ridiculous. I know you didn't have sex with River and Gabe."

"Yeah, well that's only partly true." I told him the whole story of my strange night of almost-sex, from Chuck's epic fail to River and Gabe's rescue. Buck thought it was immensely funny.

I ran my greasy fingers through his silky brown hair. The two of us were already a mess, and grease was the least of our concerns right now. Buck wrapped his hand around my neck, his thumb stroking my cheek. "Damn, Annalisa. You're so beautiful. Even better looking than that photo. And tough, too—so wonderfully intense—a real firecracker." He wrapped his arms around my shoulders and gave me a quick but promising kiss.

"I'm beautiful?" I didn't want to argue the point, but it wasn't something I heard much.

"Damn straight. You've got a pretty face, dark, intense eyes, an irresistible mouth, and stunning black hair. And your smile is killer, as that photo made clear. I also happen to like legs, which you've got miles of. So yeah, you're beautiful. Don't let the haters tell you otherwise." He kissed me again, then he took my hand to quickly lead me back to the bus. We stopped long enough to explain the fan belt problem to Big Tim then ran for the door.

It had taken me nearly all week, but now I'd unraveled the band. I had the last piece of the puzzle figured out. I understood River and Gabe's love, and Chuck's limitations in that department. And now I understood Buck, a sweet man locked in a bitter divorce, wary of the road and concerned about my feelings and reputation, all while fighting a hard crush.

We raced up the steps of the bus and chased each other down the aisle. River and Gabe broke out in applause as we passed by. Even Chuck cracked a smile. Finally, I was going to live that fiery life.

Buck stopped in the bathroom to wash the grime off himself and toss a towel to me. Then he practically kicked down the bedroom door, and we disappeared inside.

Safe in the bedroom, Buck pushed me against the wall, his forearms on either side of my face so he could dive in for a lingering kiss. His bare torso smelled of soap and man and engine grease, a combination that made me dizzy with arousal. I kissed him hard as he crushed me to his body.

I decided I was overdressed and started to peel off my T-shirt, but Buck stopped me. "Not yet. Let me savor you."

He kissed me again and again, letting his lips and tongue explore. He even took a side trip down my throat, then returned to claim my mouth in another epic kiss. While our tongues danced, his hands caressed every part of me, leaving me buzzing from his exciting touch.

At one point, we eyed the bed, clearly needing to lay there soon. But it was rumpled and gross, so neither of us wanted to do that. Engine grease was one thing, but the emissions from Chuck's sex machine were definitely another. With a grunt of disapproval, Buck let go of me, stripped the sheets away, and quickly spread out a clean one. Then he grabbed me and we fell onto it, kissing some more.

Buck continued to lavish careful attention on me. Completely the opposite of Chuck, he was tender and considerate in his devotion, observing me and figuring out what pleased me. His hands explored all over—from my head to my toes and everywhere in between—caressing, grabbing, and occasionally removing another item of clothing. I responded with just as much enthusiasm, enjoying the view as I wrapped my arms and legs around his incredible body.

I could feel the heat coming from him, spilling out of his hot breath and throbbing in his powerful chest. Every touch of his fingers seemed to sear and sizzle across my body. This boy was on fire.

In return, I went wild. My first orgasm came solely from his hand. His fingers played me hard, a driving beat that thumped in my head right up to the moment that all conscious thought disappeared, leaving me spent and desperate for more.

Then he got undressed and revealed a feast, no a *bounty*, for my eyes. I had seen my share of male equipment, and Buck's was superb. More than superb, actually, it verged on excessive. Above average in length, he was as long as any I'd ever seen. But what made my head spin was the thickness of it, a monster that was both terrifying and wonderfully compelling. Buck looked like an exaggerated sex toy, a larger-than-actual-size scale model of a human male. I felt my breath catch in my throat merely from touching it and letting it press against me.

Buck knew he was too much for most women, so he took his time building me up. He brought me to a climax two more times using his deft hands and skilled tongue, refusing to enter me until he felt I was ready. When he finally did, I nearly came again, just from the feeling of fullness and firmness, the feeling of relief, the exquisite sensation of his intoxicating body.

He pounded me hard with the desperation of a soldier back from war, each of us clutching and kissing, biting and sucking, consuming and making love with frenzied desire. Our climaxes shook the bus and echoed off the walls, leaving us relaxed and happy. We snuggled together with ragged breath, submerged in deep pools of pleasure.

Laying in bed, I pinched myself to be sure I was awake. Buck and I had made love! And he was incredible. Perhaps the best lover I'd ever had. Fiery and thrilling, he was everything I'd ever dreamed he would be and more. Hiding inside of me was a sixteen-year-old girl jumping for joy.

The irony of it all nearly made me laugh. By this point in the week, I was certain that it wouldn't happen. I'd put the fantasy of any Fiery Boys intimacy completely out of my mind. But now it was all I could think about. I wanted to leap from the bed and dance naked down the tour bus aisle.

No doubt about it, I had graduated from contest winner to full-fledged groupie.

Twenty-Four

Buck and I laid together on the bed, curled up in each other's arms. We heard a mechanic arrive to repair the bus, and we gave a little cheer when the engine started up. The moment was perfect, and I wrapped myself in his body, deliriously happy. We cuddled and talked all afternoon as the bus rolled through the mountains, letting our unquenchable need rouse us back into action as often as possible.

At one point, the bus pulled over for a scenic view, so we stumbled out of the bedroom to do some halfhearted sightseeing. As we exited the bus, Chuck gave me a wink, and River gave Buck a slap on the shoulder. Gabe just stood there in a stoned stupor with a smile on his face. The view from this high up in the mountains was truly spectacular, but I couldn't seem to focus on it. I guess I was too preoccupied with a different view.

Our afternoon delight ended when the bus came back into the city. Buck and I showered and got dressed, ready to return to whatever passed for normal on a tour bus. Unfortunately, normal behavior included too much screaming from dozens of excited fans.

When faced with all those fans, Buck, River, and Gabe typically stayed safely inside the security fence. Only Chuck liked to go out there so he could stroke his ego and other body parts. But today, Buck paced back and forth in the living room, energized. "I feel like a rock star for the first time in years. Don't be mad at me, but I want to go out there."

Such a considerate man. He was concerned enough with my feelings that he actually apologized for seeking some fan love. I smiled and hugged him. "I'm not mad. In fact, I want you to go out there. You've been such a recluse, I wondered if you could even do 'rock star.'" One side of my smile curled into a grin. "Show me what you've got." I pushed him to the bus door, and he stepped out.

As soon as Buck left the enclosure, dozens of women surrounded him. Jealousy wasn't part of our equation yet. In fact, I was proud to see him getting some of the attention he deserved.

Chuck came up behind me. "I want some of that, too. Let me out."

But I didn't want to let him out. I wanted to see Buck get something without Chuck horning-in, just this once. My fiery life had burned brightly, why couldn't his? I turned around and squared my shoulders. "Let him have his fun, Chuck."

"Aw, Annalisa. You're ruining it for me. He's going to bring them back onto the bus and then I won't be able to use the bedroom." He jostled me. "Come on, move."

Wow! Was Chuck so clueless that he thought Buck would instantly jump some groupies after finally bedding me? It's not that I thought I was better than they were or had any kind of lock on this man. I understood how it worked—we had no commitments. But I knew Buck was sensitive enough that he wouldn't do something so rude. In another two days when I was gone, sure. But not today.

I held my ground. "Wait your turn for once in your life, Chuck." He groused but went back to sit at the living room table.

I kept my eyes on Buck. He looked happier than he'd been all week, signing autographs and talking to the fans. Women hugged and even kissed him, but he didn't kiss them back. I was proud of him.

After a few minutes of hormonal groupies, Buck returned to the bus. Two women managed to slip through the fence and ran onto the bus with him, but he turned and waved them off. One of them started to leave, but the other had a better idea. She peeled off her skimpy clothes and stood naked. "Come on!" she called to her friend. "We said we'd do this." Buoyed by her friend's forwardness, the other woman also got undressed. All of us stared as two blonde beauties molded themselves to Buck's body.

"Hey!" Chuck called out to them. "You don't want him. He can only handle one of you at a time. Take me—I'm built for parties."

"Yeah," Buck agreed. "Go have fun with party boy."

The women turned from Buck to Chuck, then back again. "We'd do you in a heartbeat, Buck. Are you sure?"

Buck sat down next to me at the living room table and wrapped an arm around my shoulder. "I'm sure." My heart thumped so hard that I covered it with my hands to keep it safe.

Easily diverted, the women giggled at each other and raced after Chuck. One of them aimed her phone at us as she went by, capturing Buck as he nibbled on my ear. I knew that picture would go far.

Snuggled next to Buck in the living room, I let my hand caress his beautiful sculpted face. "See, there are plenty of women who prefer you over Chuck. Not just me." Buck grinned and gave me a squeeze.

I felt a change come over him. He blew out a long breath and pulled away, slumping down on the sofa. "Fuck him! He takes everything he can. Even women." He pointed at me. "Watch your ass, he's going to want you even more now."

I reached out and took his hand. "Do you seriously think I'd abandon you for an orgy with Chuck?"

"Well. . ."

"No, Buck. Never. The differences between you two are as stark as can be. I can't imagine having any interest in Chuck now." I wrapped my arms around him and we kissed for a few minutes. "Don't ever be jealous. Especially after that earth-shattering taste of fiery life you just gave me." Buck grinned proudly, and I was happy to see him claim his well-deserved preeminence.

The first Denver show that night was glorious. After my toss with Buck, I was feeling like a supreme groupie, so decided to dress like one for my small part in the show. Jason wanted more skin and more color, so I picked lime-green short-shorts and a purple halter top. I even threw on a big necklace so it would fly about when I danced. The gossip sites were going to have something to say about this outfit.

Every song took on new meaning as I watched Buck play. I have to admit that I didn't usually watch him as much, because I was always too entranced with River. But tonight was definitely Buck's turn—I couldn't take my eyes off him.

And he was pumped. He pounded and plucked that bass while his feet kept the beat, dancing all over the stage. I also danced, harder than ever, excited by a growing desire for this very fiery boy.

I followed Chuck's advice and started "Fiery Life" dancing with him, a drumstick in my hand. During the chorus, I ran back to pound River's cymbal, then in the second verse, I danced with Gabe. He turned to face me, and we boogied together. During the third verse, I did my best to dirty dance with Buck. Even with a bass guitar around his neck, he bumped-and-grinded so hard that the audience whooped. I finished the song back at the drum kit, River and I bobbing our heads together with the rhythm.

I was in love with the Fiery Boys, and they were in love with me. Even the audience, still devoid of the toxic Inferna, loved me. Life was more than good.

After the show, Chuck beat everyone to the bedroom, even after stopping to choose four willing women. The rest of us took showers, finishing up just as Chuck was escorting his dates out the door. Now it was our turn back there. Good thing they had lots of clean sheets.

We kissed desperately, neither of us wanting to face the approaching end of my stay. But the clock was ticking, and we both felt it. Buck pulled back. "I'm going to miss you."

"You finally beat Chuck to the girl."

He grinned. "Not just any girl. The one I wanted." Even if it was a line, it was a perfect one. I sank myself into his strong arms.

Curious to understand the rivalry between them, I probed a little. "You said that he's stolen things from you. What else have you lost?"

Buck threw his head back and stared at the ceiling, an annoyed look on his face. "Well, for starts, he stole my name."

Everyone knew that Buck used to call himself Chuck. Danielle had told me that Jason made him change it. But now it seemed that Chuck had something to do with it, too.

"He took the name Chuck away from you?"

"Yep. When the band formed, Jason insisted that we all have different names. Chuck decided he was the first one, the A-Chuck as he called himself. Then he called me the B-Chuck as a joke. Of course, everyone started calling me B-Chuck, which was just stupid. So I changed it to Buck. It's okay, but it's not really me."

"Well, I think it's you. It would be weird to think of you as Chuck."

"Yeah, I don't want people to call me that anymore."

I weighed my options carefully before speaking the next sentence—I didn't want to spoil a good thing. "I noticed that Danielle calls you Charlie. Do you like that name?"

"Just call me Buck, Annalisa." He worked his mouth and took a deep breath. "I hate to be weird about her, but I've got to ask you not to talk too much about what we're doing. It's. . ."

I waved a hand. "I understand, Buck. You can't be with anyone until your divorce is final. I can handle that. And by the way, she left something for you yesterday." I laughed nervously. "I sort of forgot to give it to you. You didn't seem like you were in the mood at the time, hiding in your cubicle and grumbling about her. Then I kind of forgot about it." I retrieved the letter from my cubicle.

Buck looked at the unmarked envelope with a creased brow, then tore it open. As he read the papers inside, his face suddenly exploded in a supernova of delight. "Holy shit, do you know what this is?"

I shook my head. "No idea."

"It's my divorce! She signed the papers early. She'd had until next week to do this, but. . ." He narrowed his eyes. "What did she say when she gave you this?"

"Nothing. She just asked me to give it to you. Oh, and she gave me permission to have sex with you, which I found pretty strange at the time."

Buck grinned. "Gabe must have told her. He knew I had a crush on you."

Gabe knew about Buck's crush, too? Another band secret. I wondered when this had started, given that Buck had been avoiding me all week. "How long have you had a thing for me?"

"I liked you the instant I saw your picture. It showed a real sense of humor. Even River and Gabe agreed you'd be perfect. Then after you won, I learned about you and saw more pictures. That's when I knew I was interested."

He gave me a proud smile. Then he stared at the letter and started to laugh. Buck was the happiest I'd ever seen him, and I could understand why.

"Annalisa, this is wonderful. It means you don't have to keep this a secret. It means I can tell everyone about you. It means. . ." He lunged at me and kissed me hard, which covered everything else that it meant.

That night, we challenged each other in erotic battle, drugged on our need to push each other's libidinous limits. Buck moved hot against me, and I burned back with just as much energy. We explored each other intimately, desperate to learn every inch, every avenue of pleasure.

I had never imagined myself with a man so incredibly handsome and mind-numbingly sexy. In our post-coital moments, he would hold me tight, his body wrapped around mine. He even played guitar for me and sang tender love songs, including some new ones that he was still working on. I sang along with the familiar tunes, and he harmonized with me. These were moments I would never forget. Nestled comfortably in his solid body, I was home.

Day Seven

Twenty-Five

After a night of Buck's savage devotion, we slept late and spent most of the afternoon in the bedroom. Savoring every moment we had left, I craved his body as if it was my last meal and pretended not to count the remaining hours until I had to fly back home.

Buck wanted to know more about me, about my fan girl days, about Zed. He had read some things about me after I'd won the contest, but like a sensible person, he distrusted what he saw on the web. Naturally, I—a true fan girl—had read all I could about him, years ago. And as I was learning, much of that was wrong, too.

"How did you and Zed meet?"

That took me back a few years, to the start of eleventh grade. "My family had just moved to San Jose, and I was the new kid in school. I spent all my free time running around, trying to get to know people. One day I spotted Zed hiding in a corner, looking totally mysterious in his black leather jacket. He wouldn't talk to me—he wouldn't talk to anyone. A girl I knew told me that he was a troublemaker, and for some reason, that made me even more determined to get to know him. Besides, he looked like he was more troubled than troubling."

"The new kid and the outcast."

I nodded. "That was us. I found him the next day and started to talk to him. He tried to blow me off, even warned me that I should stay away from him." I grinned at Buck. "Like you did." We laughed at that.

"Anyway, it only made me more interested. So I followed him out to his car, an old Challenger with an air scoop on the hood. I started to ask him about it, but that made him even more annoyed. He got behind the wheel, ready to drive away."

"I assume you didn't let that happen."

"Not a chance! After following him all the way to his car, he wasn't getting away from me that easily. I hopped into the passenger seat and asked him for a ride."

Buck blew out an amused breath. "Nothing scares you, does it?"

"Plenty of things scare me. Inferna terrifies me. But Zed didn't, even though he tried his best. He started to talk about the car's gauges and controls, thinking he'd confuse me with technical talk. But I knew about cars, thanks to my dad. Finally, he got frustrated and drove off, thinking he'd scare me by driving fast. Of course, that didn't work, either. I loved it.

"After a few blocks, he pulled over and sneered at me. Said I was just a big talker who couldn't even drive his car, since it had a stick shift."

Buck laughed. "He didn't know you very well."

I smiled. "No, he didn't. Before our family moved to San Jose, we were in Mexico on a military base. Dad taught me to drive on the old jeeps down there, and all of them had standard transmissions. So Zed's car was no problem at all. I drove it back to school, and before we could even get out of the car, he grabbed me and kissed me." I smiled. "And that's how I got an awesome boyfriend."

Buck laughed, then he grabbed and kissed me to make it clear that I once again had an awesome boyfriend. For one more day.

He asked about my parents, so I told him about my military father and my wandering childhood. As the only child in my family, I had to follow my parents all over the world. Somewhat like being on a tour bus, it now seemed to me.

"Where are they now?"

I had to think for a few seconds. They moved so much that I sometimes forgot where they were. "They've been on a base in Okinawa, Japan since last year. They live in their own little world and rarely notice me. That's why they left me during my last year of high school."

"What do you mean?"

"In the summer after eleventh grade, my dad got relocated. We'd moved lots of times before, but this time I didn't want to go with them. We'd only been in San Jose for a year, but I had friends and a boyfriend who I didn't want to leave. Besides, I only had to make it through one more year before I'd go off to a university, so my parents agreed that I was mature enough to live on my own."

"Wow! They really let you stay behind?"

"Yep. I told them I'd be living with Kira." I gave a little laugh. "Of course, I spent most of my time with Zed. We saw each other every day, and I'd even sneak out to see him most nights. He lived in a detached garage in the back of his parents' big house. But his parents were always too busy to pay much attention to him, so they never noticed that I was there all the time."

Buck squinted. "Wait, he was a rich kid? I thought he was a bad boy motorhead."

"Well, he was both. I think his bad boy act was a reaction to being ignored as a kid. He always did things to try to get his parents' attention."

"I bet dying got their attention."

"Totally." I let out a sardonic laugh. "Too bad they didn't like what they saw. And they blamed me for ruining him. Needless to say, I had to pack up and go pretty quickly. If it weren't for Kira, I'd have had nobody."

Buck wrapped his arms around me and we squeezed each other tightly. The warmth of his strong embrace felt surprisingly good. "We have that in common: both of us were ignored as kids. My mother died when I was nine, but my father still went out on the road. If it weren't for my sister, I'd have had nobody, either." He kissed my neck, again and again, climbing slowly and steadily higher until he rounded my chin and claimed my mouth. We feasted, consuming each other with lustful fervor for hours, until nothing remained.

The afternoon sound check forced us from the bus. It took only an hour, but we stared at each other the entire time. When it ended, we ran for the bus and claimed the bedroom again before Chuck could gather a harem. We heard later that he'd thrown all the roadies off the other bus and had taken his pleasure there.

That night, when the show started, it was anything but boring. Feeling like the world's hottest groupie, I abandoned all semblance of modesty and wore one of Kira's outfits: a tight black blouse with a floral-print miniskirt. I even wore black ankle boots with four-inch heels, not that I needed the height. Now I was as tall as Chuck! The haters would have fun with that.

When it was time to play my favorite song, Chuck was positively respectful. "Tonight is a doubly-special show. First, we're in Denver!" He paused while the crowd cheered. "But also, tonight is Annalisa's final night with the band. This is your last chance to see her play drums on our next song." The fans burst into applause.

I didn't know if they were truly happy for me, or just glad that I'd soon be gone. The way I saw it, most of them were grateful that I'd finally stop monopolizing their precious Fiery Boys, partying with them and having sex with them.

By this point, word of Buck and me had also leaked, along with the picture of us making out on the sofa. At least I looked okay and the two of us seemed happy. Now, fans everywhere were vicariously thrilled with my full-fiery sweep. They were convinced that I'd scored with all four boys, which made most of the fans ecstatic, and the rest of them livid. As always, there was no middle ground.

Jason was one of the unhappy people, but my week was nearly over so he didn't bother to challenge me. And Inferna? The queen of outrage was merciless on her website.

But none of that mattered at the moment, because it was time to play my song. On my last night with the band, I was going to wail on that cymbal, dance with all of them, and enjoy myself as much as possible. I ran onto the stage, ready to rock.

River kicked off the song and the music took over. It moved me around, lifted me up, and made me completely forget who I was. I could have been back in my room, with posters of all four of them this time, only real. And the music was never this loud back then, so cranked that it actually shook my body. I drove into the cymbal with everything I had, throwing my entire soul into the task. I was no longer performing for the audience—they were gone. It was just the Fiery Boys, my friends and lovers.

When the song ended, I stepped closer to River and gave him a hug. Then I went to Gabe and Chuck, offering them the same level of tenderness. Finally I got to Buck. He got a much bigger hug and even a kiss, which drove the audience wild. I waved as I left the stage.

Standing in the wings, I was bursting with the energy of the peak moment I'd just experienced. Without even thinking, I screamed for joy, happier than I'd ever been. People near the front of the audience heard me, and I noticed some laughter mixed with their applause. It made me laugh, too.

A week on the bus had given me an indelible memory of the Fiery Boys, four very different people than I'd expected to find. Zed would have been so proud of me. He loved the band as much as I did and would have done anything to meet them. Yes, I was certainly living a fiery life.

After the show, Buck and I held hands as we walked back to the bus. We gave Chuck an hour to do the nasty in the bedroom, then it was our turn again, one last time.

I wanted to do something extra for Buck, a parting gift to cap off our short affair. "Tell me something you'd like, Buck."

He smiled and pulled me close. "You, of course."

"You can do better than that. This is our last night together. Any special stuff? Kinky outfits? Chocolate sauce and whipped cream?" We both laughed at that last idea.

"Save the chocolate for your other two Fiery Boys." He gave me a slow kiss, then leaned back. "But I do have an idea. . ." He opened a closet in the bedroom and pulled out a box. "Put on something from here. You pick."

I looked into the box. It was half full with items of women's clothing that looked like they came from an adult entertainment store. Lots of tiny bras and panties, but also some miniskirts, stockings, and tube tops. I even found a pair of super high-heeled shoes. "What is this?"

"Abandoned clothes from our groupies. Some gets thrown on stage, some gets left behind in the bedroom. Go ahead and put something on." He stood by the door wearing his best bedroom eyes. "I'll be out with the guys if you want me." He kissed me hard and deep, making my breath short with anticipation. Then he left.

Oh yes, this was going to be good. I stripped down so I could dress myself from the ground up. The first thing I noticed was a tiny black rectangle. It turned out to be the tightest, shortest, and most scandalous miniskirt I'd ever worn. The hem came down to just below the globes of my backside and barely covered me in front. I also found a lacy red bra that was so thin it was practically transparent. Who wore this stuff?

As I looked for an appropriate pair of panties, I realized two things. First, these panties hadn't been washed, so I wasn't sure I wanted to put any of them on. But more importantly, all four of the Fiery Boys had seen me naked, so why did I need panties?

Then another realization hit me. Why did I even need clothes? Sure, men love sexy outfits, but each man has different tastes. I had no idea what Buck liked, but I knew one thing: being naked would work just fine. And didn't every groupie I'd seen on the bus confirm this? Many of them stripped as soon as they came on board.

I tossed everything back in the box and stepped out of the bedroom wearing only the high heels. I could have stayed back there and called to Buck, but it felt much more exciting to go out there like this. I'd wanted to do it last night, and now I had the perfect opportunity. Watch out! Groupie on the prowl.

As I walked down the aisle of the Fiery Boys tour bus completely naked, I paused to consider the transformation I had undergone. This was not supposed to have happened—I'd told myself it wouldn't, many times. And yet, here I was, acting like a horny wannabe. I managed not to laugh at myself as I strutted toward the living room. So many other women had done this—why couldn't I?

The boys were sitting at the table, not expecting to see me like this. When I came into view, they whooped out loud, laughing and applauding my excellent choice of clothing.

I stopped in the hall and propped my hands on my hips, a classic groupie pose with a touch of haughtiness. I loved the feeling of posing like this, totally captivating all four of them. There were no other men in the world I'd do this for.

Slowly, I advanced toward the living room table, exaggerating my wiggle as I walked. My sexy Fiery Boy lover and I stared at each other with barely contained amusement and a hunger that all could see.

I came to a stop by his side and gave him my best game. "Oh, I just love the Fiery Boys!" My voice was an octave higher than normal and loaded with adulation. I even let out a full fan-girl squeal. "How can I get that big, strong rocker between my legs?" I swiveled my hips and pulled his face to my belly. The other three pounded the table and hooted.

He wrapped his arm around my waist and held me tight. "This outfit ought to do the trick." He stood up, slung me over his shoulder, and carried me back to the bedroom amid catcalls and whistles from the living room.

When the door closed, I danced for Buck, preening and slithering. He watched my act for a few seconds then pulled me into his arms. "You're so fucking hot." He tossed me on the bed and jumped in after me, like a caveman ready to mate. And let me tell you, this caveman had his big club ready.

After one quick, desperate bout, the rest of the night shifted down to a slow burn—a careful exploration full of tenderness and simmering heat. Each time we made love, I felt a sublime thrill that was simultaneously the happiest I'd ever been and the saddest. I would come down from each incredible climax to face the reality that this was our last night together.

Buck understood my tears, and he wiped them away to the best of his ability, both physically and emotionally. And he did a great job of it. Neither of us slept much—there was no time. If one of us did doze off, we would be awakened by the other's desperate thirst, their need to consume and be consumed, one last time.

We finally fell asleep in each other's arms, tangled and fully spent.

Twenty-Six

Pleasantly sore, I got up to pack. I could still feel the vibrations echoing though my body from Buck's girth, a good sensation that kept me dancing on the edge of arousal. My two nights with this man were more than I'd dreamed they could be.

But now it was over—I had to go. Big Tim was taking me to the airport soon. I wheeled my suitcase into the bedroom and pulled everything out to reorganize for the trip home. Buck stood there with his mouth turned down. "I'll miss you." He hugged me from behind, wrapping his arms around me and nipping at my ear. "I won't forget you."

"Thanks, Buck. I know I'll never forget you." The memories of this week were written in my brain with indelible ink. Four amazing people who I never expected to meet, and one incredible lover who I knew I'd never get out of my head. Yes, I'd done it all. It was time to leave.

As I repacked the suitcase, my Creative Writing class paper on "Fiery Life" caught Buck's eye. "Are you still in school?"

I'd completely forgotten about that paper. When I left home, it made sense to bring it along. I thought that since I was going to be with the Fiery Boys for a full week, I'd end up having deep philosophical conversations with Chuck about the meaning of his lyrics. It sure didn't work out that way.

I laughed and nodded toward the paper. "Can you believe I did an assignment about 'Fiery Life' and it got an A?"

Buck's hand hovered in the air. "May I read it?"

I hesitated, wondering for a moment whether I should let him see it. More than a paper about a Fiery Boys song, this was my life, raw and on display. And although Buck knew some things about Zed, this paper dug deeper. Still I had brought it along to show to my rock heroes, and that meant Buck. I nodded my assent and turned away to continue working on my suitcase.

I had everything packed up when he finished. "This is really good, Annalisa. You write well."

"Thanks, Buck." I fidgeted, a little put off by the fact that he was ignoring the story and focusing on my style.

Buck rocked from side to side, probably as uncomfortable as I was. "Did that song really help you recover from Zed's death?"

For some reason, I was suddenly embarrassed to discuss this with Buck. Was I uncomfortable because of his rivalry with Chuck, who had written the song? Or was it my own reticence to relive that awful day, eight years ago, when I'd found out that Zed was gone?

When Jo made me write that paper, she claimed it would do me good. But honestly, whenever I reread it or talked to someone about it, I didn't feel good at all. The paper had too many details, including Zed's last words before he got on that motorcycle, and the brusqueness of the police who'd treated his body like so much road-kill. On top of that, the thought of discussing the paper with Buck was particularly painful. Loss was such a strong theme in my life, that it hurt to talk about Zed, especially with someone who I was about to leave forever. All I could give him was a barely audible, "Yes."

He nodded his head and took a deep breath. "Do you really believe that the song urges us to remember the dead by living adventurous lives? That each new bold act you perform is somehow necessary?"

I stopped and stared at him. "It's that line in the third verse, 'Live and remember each death.' Ever since Zed died, I've lived my life so that I'd remember him. All the things I've done have been things he'd have done, and they keep his memory alive."

"Yes, but the line after that is 'Burn the life bright with new breath.' The new breath tells us to look forward, not back—don't live in the past. The death of a loved one reminds us how precious life is—how we have to lead fiery lives while we can. But we should do it for ourselves, not as an eternal remembrance of others. Yes. . ." He shook his fist. "Lead a fiery life. But lead your own, not Zed's."

My head hurt. Buck was challenging the way I'd lived my life for the past eight years. Why did this have to happen now, just as I was about to walk away from him?

But his point was valid, so I took a minute to think about it. "Maybe you're right. Have you ever discussed the song with Chuck?"

He rolled his eyes, and I understood that the idea of discussing things with Chuck was not something he ever did. "I haven't, but I'm sure he'd agree with me. Both of us have experienced loss of a loved one when we were young— I lost my mother and he lost his father. But as much as I miss my mother, I don't dedicate everything in my life to her. I live my own life."

I looked at him and swallowed. "Wow, Buck. I never thought of it that way." Had I been so focused on commemorating a dead man that I'd forgotten about myself? Jo had been telling me this, but here was that same message in the very song that had shaped my life. Could I have been doing it all wrong?

A silence blanketed us, heavy with the sorrow of parting. I adjusted something in my bag, just to break the tension. But nothing could do that.

"I had a great time with the band." It was a pointless platitude, but I couldn't think of anything else to say.

He held my head gently and stared with big eyes. His lips brushed over mine once, twice, then we dove into the deep end of an intense kiss. Minutes later, he pulled back. "Stay on the tour."

God, how I wanted that. "Can I? I doubt that Jason would let me."

"Let's find out. I know River and Gabe will support it." He took out his phone and dialed. "Jason, I want Annalisa to stay on tour with us." He paused and frowned at Jason's obviously negative reply. "No, the other three are for it. . . Yes, even Chuck." I watched carefully to see if that partial truth would be effective. Apparently not—Buck dropped his head. "Fine. Whatever." He hung up and scowled. "This isn't over. When the tour ends, I'm going to find you."

No! This had to end cleanly, not with some vague promise a month in the future. Goodbye means goodbye, especially from a rock star. If he gave me false hope, I'd wait all month and be crushed even worse when nothing came of it. I needed to say goodbye while the memories of my spectacular week were still fresh.

My smile was paper-thin as I shook my head. "Please don't say that. A lot can happen in a month. I was your rebound after a long marriage. But now you're free and on the road—you'll meet lots of women. Just think of me as another groupie. I'll tell you this. . ." I grinned. "I'll always think of you as my favorite rock star."

He pulled me into a hug. "Look, I can't explain this, but I need more."

More sounded good—I wanted it, too. But Jason had spoken. "Buck, don't make promises you can't keep. When I'm gone, go out there and howl in the night. Enjoy yourself and wave that mighty sword of yours. Have a great time. I had a wonderful time with you—the perfect end to the week. Even the fans liked me. . . mostly."

"The fans!" he laughed. "They're so fickle. One day they love you, the next day you're shit. I hate it, but for now, I'm stuck with it. I got out of my marriage contract, but I still have a contract with the band." He looked up at the ceiling and exhaled loudly. "You don't want me to make any promises? That's fine because I can't for the next month. But I will say this: we'll meet again, Annalisa Ricci."

"Thanks for being honest about it, Buck. I appreciate that. Maybe we will see each other again someday." We hugged one last time and gave each other a vicious kiss that left our mouths sore. Then I had to go.

I rolled my suitcase to the living room and gave warm hugs to Chuck, River, and Gabe. I even hugged Big Tim and congratulated him on winning the Annalisa pool. Before I left, River handed me a drumstick. "This is for you. A memento of your week with the band." All four of them had signed it. I rolled it in my hand, choked up with the beauty of the gesture. All of them, even Chuck, seemed sad to see me go.

Before I stepped off the bus, Buck and I made our final connection across the living room, a smile and a nod that acknowledged the magic that had occurred.

Home

Twenty-Seven

I came back home and tried to put my week with the Fiery Boys out of my mind. Of course, that was impossible to do. I didn't have a non-Fiery-Boys life to go back to—it hadn't existed for months. And after a week on the tour bus, my former life was a distant memory. Now I was a minor celebrity, the contest winner who had "scored" a grand slam. My picture was everywhere along with headlines like, "Girl Does Band," "Fiery Boys Rout," and "Contest Winner Cashes In." I may have wanted to forget my week on the bus, but nobody else on the planet was willing to do that, especially Kira and Jo.

My girlfriends plied me with questions from the moment we met for drinks on my first night back. This was our usual bar, but tonight they were decked out like I'd never seen them before. Now that I was a media sensation with paparazzi following me everywhere, they knew they had to look their best. Kira wore a sunset orange minidress that clung to her body like plastic wrap. Jo's tight little black dress started at the top of her breasts and ended at the top of her thighs. Even I dressed up tonight, in white frilly shorts over black tights with a white sweater and scarf. Modest but edgy, just what was expected of me.

When I'd spoken to Kira a few days before, I had denied the rumors linking me with Chuck, River, and Gabe. But that didn't stop her from asking again, now that Buck had been added to my list of conquests. Apparently, I had pulled off something that no other woman had ever done with the Fiery Boys. I felt like a cheater, but in a small way, I had earned it, too.

"So dish," Jo instructed. "Start with Chuck."

"You saw those press photos. They were posed. The most we did is to get naked, which seems to happen pretty often on the bus." I was not going to tell them about our dismal attempt to hook up.

Kira sucked in a sharp breath. "Oh my God! Have you seen them all naked?"

No sense in denying it. "Yes."

Jo pressed on, exploring every possibility. "And have all of them seen *you* naked?"

I shrugged and nodded my head. My friends were delighted.

Kira gave me a serious look. "But no sex with Chuck?"

"No. And I didn't have sex with River or Gabe, either." I stopped and thought about it, then corrected myself. "Actually, I *did* have sex with River and Gabe, but then again, I didn't." I couldn't resist a grin.

My cryptic comment didn't help much. Jo straightened and went into therapist mode, observing and silently considering my case. Kira darkened. "Explain."

I shook my head. "You know that River was always my favorite. Well, I love him now, more than ever. He's a great guy, and so is Gabe. But that's all I'm going to say about them." My words did nothing to defuse the rumors, but I was having fun helping River and Gabe protect their womanizing reputations.

Jo smiled. "I'm proud of you." She narrowed her eyes. "But isn't a gallon of chocolate an awful big mess?"

A gallon! I belted out a laugh. "Whoa, that's a huge exaggeration." This rumor had a life of its own.

"Well, whatever." Jo shrugged, clearly satisfied that I had used an appropriate amount of chocolate.

Kira leaned forward. "Now tell us about Buck. He was your favorite, too. Is he still?"

I blushed. "Yes. He's the best." As I thought about him, I sighed and swayed from side to side. Soon my whole body was flush with the heat of our recent nights.

Jo noticed me and smiled. "Oho! Something *did* happen with Buck. It's written all over your face."

"Uh. . ." I hadn't considered what I would say about this. I didn't want to brag, so I tried to downplay it. "We had a few makeout sessions."

Kira laughed. "Liar!" She turned to Jo. "I believe our girl here actually got it on with Buck."

"Okay, okay!" I hung my head, unable to hide the truth any longer. "We did. It was. . ." I couldn't see a reason to deny the intensity of my feelings. "It was *incredible*." My girlfriends exploded with excitement and plied me with questions, none of which got answered.

"No more about Buck. Besides, I've had my moment with a rock star and now it's over. I'm not going to live in the past." I folded my arms. "Let's talk about something else." I needed to move beyond this or else I'd be stuck dreaming about Buck for the rest of my life.

Kira nodded. "Okay. No more about Buck." My friends smiled to show that they understood everything, and I didn't doubt for a second that they did. We spent the rest of the evening chatting about unimportant things: work, families, even current events. It was a nice reprieve from a week with the Fiery Boys.

Twenty-Eight

Ten days after leaving the tour, I was finally getting back to something that resembled normal. The most bizarre outcome of my week on tour was that my overblown sluttiness had made me more popular than the Fiery Boys' music. The thought that I'd scored with all four of them had touched a nerve, and the press was making the most of it. My story drew new attention to the Fiery Boys, which increased ticket sales for the remaining concerts. Yes, *I* was making *them* famous!

The price of this insane power was that any privacy I might have had before my week on the bus was now completely gone. Strangers would ask for my autograph and pose with me for a picture. Cars would honk their horns when they saw me on the street. Paparazzi followed me more than ever. Every single thing I did got reported and analyzed to death.

One late-night talk show host devoted an entire segment to jokes about me. "Did you hear about the woman who spent a week on tour with the Fiery Boys? She had sex with all of them!" His face stretched into a lewd hubba-hubba leer, and the audience reacted appropriately. "Here's a picture of her." The television switched to my contest-winning photo, the now-famous beer-spray shot. The host wrapped up his joke. "You see, the thing is, that's not beer —it's aphrodisiac." The drummer beat out a rim shot while the audience cackled.

He went on with his routine. "Apparently she had sex with two of them at once in a bathtub full of chocolate and whipped cream. Now some company's selling a chocolate-and-whipped-cream product called Groupie Lube." He got another round of laughter from that.

"And wait!" I wanted it to end, but he seemed like he was just getting started. "Some Vegas showgirl is mad about this. She thought stuff like that *stayed* in Vegas." I turned off the television before he could do any more damage.

On the positive side, my car sales were better than they had ever been. People were coming from all over with the specific goal of buying a car from me. They would line up in the showroom, waiting for hours until I was available. And these were real buyers, not browsers—all of them bought cars. They'd driven far, waited long, and took full advantage of my attention. They weren't about to embarrass themselves by weaseling out of a purchase.

Yeah, I was selling cars like they were candy. And get this! Not only did I corner the bulk of the luxury auto sales at my dealership, I was disrupting sales throughout the entire San Francisco Bay Area.

My fellow salesmen, the gents, hated me for this. But I didn't hate them as much anymore. Sure, they were still sexist jerks, but after a week on the Fiery Boys bus, my former need to show them up was gone. Was this because my fame was now letting me sell cars without trying, or had I actually lost the need to kill it on the sales floor? One thing was certain. Buck's reinterpretation of the "Fiery Life" lyrics was making me examine all the things I'd been doing for the past eight years. Many of them were about Zed, but few were things I wanted to do purely for myself.

Which is why I decided to give something back to the gents. I didn't want to rob them of their livelihood, so whenever I finished a sale, I would wander the line of customers and spend a few minutes with anyone who was willing to deal with another salesman in exchange for some of my attention. One sale for me, three for the gents. I was that popular.

On my third day back at work, I went for a test drive with someone I shouldn't have. He ignored my driving directions and headed off somewhere else, assuring me that he knew where he was going. But I also knew where he was going, and it wasn't anywhere we should have been.

I turned to look at him closely for the first time and saw an unfocused glimmer in his eyes. Another delusional creepster. I should have known by now—I'd seen this look before. Normally, I'd have spotted it before we got in the car. But I was too caught up with being Annalisa, the fiery saleswoman. And this guy had waited two hours to see me, so I'd thought his urgency was understandable. I hadn't been paying attention, and now I had to deal with him.

I asked where he was going but he didn't answer. Then I warned him that I'd call the police if he didn't pull over, but he kept driving. All he would offer was a tight, "Can't stop till we get there."

At a traffic light, he had to stop. I grabbed my purse and the car's key fob and bolted out the door. With my pepper spray in hand, I called the dealership and explained what was happening. They said they'd track the car and alert the police.

My disturbed customer pulled over and tried to talk me into getting back in with him. Yeah, like that was going to happen. All I needed to do was keep him busy until the police arrived, so I engaged him in a pointless discussion about why what he was doing was wrong. The discussion was pointless because nothing could get through to this disturbed man.

The police arrived fairly quickly. A cruiser pulled up and two patrolmen emerged with guns drawn. They hauled off the unfortunate man, took a statement from me, then sent me back to the dealership. Of course both of the policemen knew who I was.

I went straight to Ed, the manager, and told him if he wanted me to continue working—which he obviously did—there had to be some changes. I would limit my customers by taking breaks between them. And there would be no more test drives. Let the gents do them. I wasn't riding in a car with some strange Fiery Boys fan. He agreed.

So that became my new work life. I wouldn't exactly call it normal, but sometimes there were moments when it came close. I'd make a car sale, run through the line of customers waiting for me so that the gents could have a chance, then spend a half hour sitting quietly in a spare room at the back of the building.

I was in the middle of one of those quiet moments on a Sunday afternoon. The television in the customer waiting room down the hall blared another story about the Fiery Boys and me. I pretended to ignore it, but I was sitting alone, so the only person I was kidding was myself.

The buzz was particularly strong in San Jose because the band was there tonight for a show. To promote the show, I'd even agreed to be interviewed by a local television news crew. And although I'd bought two tickets to this show way back when the tour was first announced, I'd sold them because I couldn't face the band anymore. After a half-dozen Fiery Boys performances seen from the wings and even occasionally from the stage, standing in the audience held no appeal.

I took a sip of coffee, closed my eyes, and thought of Buck. Our last two days together had been a fairytale, magical and surreal, something I would remember for the rest of my life. His exquisite passion was the best I'd ever had, a true rock star experience.

Buck hadn't called me since my week on tour, but I'd never called him, either. He did send me flowers after a few days, a gorgeous bouquet of mixed blossoms, bright and colorful. But that was it. The card that came with the flowers reiterated that he would contact me when the tour ended, but I knew it was unlikely.

This didn't sadden me as much as it might have. I understood that a rock tour bus was a strange and wondrous world that existed out on the road, but nowhere else. Buck was just another ex-boyfriend, a two-night hookup. And my memories of him brought me so much pleasure that the bittersweet aspect didn't hurt too much. For the most part, I was quite good with it. I contented myself with the fiery life we'd shared, whose glowing embers still warmed my heart.

Unfortunately, Buck left me even less satisfied with other men. If I'd set the bar too high by comparing new boyfriends with my idealized memories of Zed, then that bar was now even higher. Who could compare with Buck? Nobody. So not only was I on break from selling cars, I was also on break from dating men.

I reached for my coffee cup to take another sip, but a voice stopped me. "Excuse me, miss. Can I ask you a question?" I hated it when people chased me down during my breaks. I was about to send this man away when I realized I knew him. Standing in the room with me was Jason Bartholomew, the abrasive band manager and Fiery Boys puppet master.

I was actually pleased to see him, which only proved how badly I missed the Fiery Boys. "Hi, Jason. How's the tour going?"

He sat down next to me. "Fine, thanks. Are you coming to the show tonight?"

I flattened my lips and shook my head. "Sorry. I don't know if I can ever go to a Fiery Boys concert again. Everyone would recognize me, and I wouldn't be able to enjoy it as much. Besides, I think I've seen this particular show enough times already."

Jason fidgeted. "Uh, Annalisa. Could I convince you to come back on tour with us?"

I turned in my chair to look at this man and make sure he was real. Didn't Jason hate me, and wasn't he glad when my week was up? If he suddenly wanted me back, then something major must have shifted in the fabric of the universe.

Of course, Jason's offer thrilled me—returning to the tour would be a grand adventure. And even though there were many potential problems, that never stopped me before. How could I refuse?

But I was forming new rules for my life these days, and one of them was that I *could* refuse an adventure if I wanted to. So I examined this opportunity more closely. "I thought you were glad when I left. What's this about?"

"I'm willing to admit that I was wrong. We miss you."

"We?" What did he mean by that? River and Gabe, sure. Buck, hopefully. Chuck, maybe a little. But Jason? I doubted it.

"Okay, the boys miss you. I thought that having someone on the bus would ruin it for them. But you didn't do that. And for some reason that I can't figure out, you've become just as popular as they are. So believe it or not, I need you back on the bus. It's good for business."

That was more like the Jason I remembered—Mr. Anything-for-a-dollar. At least he was being honest, which beat the lie about how much he missed me.

"Isn't the tour almost over?"

"Two more weeks. You can come for some of the time or for the whole thing. It's up to you."

"That's an incredible offer, Jason. But I really have to think about it. I love the boys, and I've been helping with their publicity. A local network interviewed me last week. But going back on tour is a serious decision."

What I meant, but couldn't say to Jason, was that I was uncertain because of my feelings for Buck. Those last few days with him were overwhelmingly dreamy, a gossamer memory that I didn't want to ruin. How would I feel if I found him in bed with some groupie? What if he became withdrawn or angry again? It might be better if I didn't see him anymore.

Jason leaned closer. "Well, at least come to the show tonight and play drums with River. The crowd loves that. Then you can decide if you want to come back on tour." He handed me an all-access backstage pass.

I stared at the pass and took a deep breath. A backstage pass solved the problem of mingling with fans. But it opened up the problem of seeing Buck, which both thrilled me and terrified me. I guess I was going to the show tonight.

Since Jason was being so nice, I decided to test him and see if he could be nicer. And I knew exactly what I wanted: passes for Kira and Jo. "Can I have two more of these for my girlfriends?" I smiled sweetly and waved my pass in the air.

"Sure, why not?" With a smile, he reached into his pocket and tossed two more passes on the table. Someone must have done a whole-brain transplant on this man, he was that different. "You know the drill—doors open at nine, the boys come on around ten thirty. We're camped at the arena all day, so come over any time." He looked around the tiny unused office I was hiding in. "If you're not too busy selling cars, that is." He grinned at me, then got up and left.

I must have laughed for five minutes solid and danced for joy in the quiet office. For all my bravado about being done with the Fiery Boys, I couldn't deny that I was excited to see them again. To see Buck.

Twenty-Nine

I called Jo. "Hey, girl. Have you got tickets for the show tonight?" It was a rhetorical question, we both knew that.

"Oh hell yes! We got those tickets months ago—I've been counting down the days ever since. I thought Larry would want to come with me, but he told me last week that he doesn't like Fiery Boys music, so I'm going without him."

I laughed. "Larry doesn't like the Fiery Boys? How have you two stayed together?"

"Don't know. He always seemed to enjoy their music before. But he's become more of a jerk, lately. I think he's trying to break up with me and is using the concert as an excuse. Fine by me—I'm tired of him, to tell you the truth." Her laugh had a ring of sadness. "Anyway, I know you sold your tickets, but if you change your mind, I've got an extra for you."

"What about Kira? Is she going with anyone?"

"Nah. She only bought one ticket. The two of us are going together. I'll scalp Larry's ticket at the door."

"Good. Then I've got a new plan. Sell them all because we're going to the show tonight as VIPs. I happen to have, right here in my hand, three all-access backstage passes."

A scream came over the line, followed by the clattering of a phone being dropped. It took a few seconds for the muffled yell to die down and the phone to be retrieved. "Are you serious? Do we get to meet Chuck?"

"Sure. We can go there early and meet all of them before the show."

A fresh round of screaming nearly pierced my eardrum. Then Jo started to talk at twice her normal speed. "I've got to call Kira. How early can we go over there? Can we go now?"

I laughed. "I'm not off work until five. Why don't we grab a quick dinner near the arena, say at six, then go meet the band?"

"Yes! Yes! You're my best friend, ever. I'll tell Kira."

"Wait! Before you go, I want us to drive separately. I may have some unfinished business with the band, so I don't know when I'll be ready to go home."

"Go girl! Anyway, that's fine because Kira and I may engage in some business with the band too, if we get the chance. See you later." She hung up.

Before I could focus on the fact that I was going to see the Fiery Boys again, my phone rang. I didn't recognize the number and assumed it was another press inquiry about the band. Reluctantly, I answered. "This is Annalisa."

"Hey, Annalisa. It's River. I hear you're coming to the show tonight."

River, my dear friend. I felt better about coming back to see the Fiery Boys, just from hearing his voice. "Yes. I'm even bringing my two girlfriends."

"Good. Are you coming back on tour with us?"

So that's what this was about. Jason was marshaling the boys to convince me to return. "I definitely want to, but I haven't decided for sure. This is a lot to think about, River."

"Yeah, I know what you're thinking about, and he's standing right here." He laughed, and I heard the sound of a jostled phone. Buck was coming on the line, and I felt a wash of emotions. Part of me insisted that I hang up quickly. Another part of me couldn't have found the disconnect button if I tried.

THE FIERY BOYS **203**

Buck's warm voice came on the line and soothed me immediately. "Annalisa, how are you?" Deep and full of concern, his words pierced right through me, making me ache for him all over again.

"I'm. . . I'm good, Buck. Almost back to normal here." What was I, a comedian? I let out a tiny laugh at the absurdity of that statement. Normal! I was far from normal and getting farther just from hearing his voice.

But I couldn't begin to tell him how bizarre my life had become, so I inquired about his. "How are you?"

He grumbled. "Nothing's normal here. It's the same old crap. Jason really wants you to come back on tour."

If he was trying to convince me with that argument, he was failing horribly. "Jason? What about you?"

"I want it, too. I want you." He let out a held breath. "God, how I want you."

That was encouraging—he still wanted me. But I had other concerns about being back on the road. The world was finally starting to forget about me, but if I went back, the lunacy would start up again. Everyone would heap more abuse on the contest winner who wouldn't stay home. Inferna and the other haters would go ballistic.

Another problem with coming back to finish the Fiery Boys tour was that I'd be there at their final show. I already knew that they'd break up after this tour ended, so if I rode it to the end, I'd be there for the breakup. Then I would forever be associated with the Fiery Boys in a bad way, which would seriously suck. But then again, the haters would probably blame me for the breakup, regardless of what I did. I was that easy of a target.

And then there was Buck. Could I handle my feelings for him? My longing for more was tinged with the knowledge that no more would be available once the tour ended. We were merely a rock-and-roll hookup—even Buck knew it couldn't last. Breaking up with him again would hurt the most.

I struggled to explain myself. "I want you too, Buck. It's just that I've spent the last ten days telling myself that what we have is impossible. So even if I come back on tour, it just can't. . . I mean, there's no. . ." I trailed off, uncertain.

Buck grumbled. "I don't think we're impossible, Annalisa. In fact, when I'm with you, I sometimes feel like you're the *only* possibility. What's impossible is being able to predict what will happen to us, given that we've only spent two days together. So let's find out. Be with me, and we'll figure it out together. I know I'll enjoy these next two weeks more if you're here with me." He was saying all the right words, but I couldn't resist pointing out the obvious.

"Come on, Buck. I know you have to sow your wild oats after that marriage." I remembered those two naked blondes on my last day with the boys. They were hot for Buck. I really wanted him to enjoy himself on the tour, but I definitely didn't want to hear about it or even think about it.

"If you're asking whether I've been with another woman since I saw you last, then the answer is 'no.'"

That came as a shock. I was not prepared to hear that he was feeling the same longing as I was. That would only start up my teenage fantasies again, and I knew where that would lead—nowhere. I pushed back lightly. "Really? Buck Morris, the incredible bass player of the Fiery Boys, isn't getting any?"

"Oh yeah? How many guys have you been with since you went home? Don't tell me that the famous contest winner hasn't had a few offers." I could tell he was grinning on the other end of the phone line.

"Okay, none," I huffed.

"See? Why can't I wait for you—you've been waiting for me." Had I been waiting for Buck? In some sense, I had. But waiting for Buck was a fool's journey, so mostly what I'd been waiting for was my own return to sanity. A sanity that I was beginning to realize I'd lost eight years ago.

"Here's the thing, Buck. The two days we had together were perfect. I've got a memory that can last me the rest of my life. The problem with another two weeks together is not only that it will end, but also that it could ruin what we had. A part of me would like to remember us from those two days."

"I've got a wonderful memory of our time together, too. But I'm not worried about ruining it. In fact, I'd like to make it better. I may not be able to make promises at this point, especially not in the middle of this fucking tour, but if you join me, I'll know much more by the time the tour ends. You'll know more, too."

"But nothing can come of it. You live in Atlanta, and I live in San Jose."

He grunted. "Big deal. Geography isn't a problem. Just come to the show tonight, and we'll talk afterward."

"Talk?" I knew better.

Buck laughed. "Yeah, talk. That's guy-speak. It means I want to be with you so badly that I'm even willing to talk about us."

I laughed, too. He was certainly being honest, and I appreciated that. "Okay. I'll see you later. Then we'll see what sort of talking happens after the show."

I hung up and gave a loud whoop that echoed through the dealership. When I returned to the showroom floor, everyone stared and smiled. Then I worked straight through the afternoon and sold four more cars.

Thirty

Kira, Jo, and I walked up to the tour bus fence, which was already many people deep in waiting fans. The three of us were dressed for rock and roll tonight, both on the bus and in the wings. Kira wore a light-blue A-line mini dress made of eye-catchingly shiny vinyl. Jo was in black short-shorts with a tight white top. And I was right there with them, in an orange miniskirt, black ankle boots, and a long white sleeveless T-shirt that was nearly as long as the skirt.

Bigger Tim was by the fence, easy to spot at a distance, so I headed there. With Kira and Jo on my left and right, we powered through the crowd right up to him. "So you're really back, huh?" Not the warmest welcome, but whatever. At least he opened the gate.

"Thanks, Bigger Tim. I brought two friends with me." Kira and Jo flashed their backstage passes as they followed me in.

As soon as we stepped through the fence, I felt a familiar energy. The band's loudly painted bus and its more subdued companion sat in standard formation, with the equipment trucks parked to the side, dwarfed by a monstrous arena wall. I'd seen this all before. Even the people were familiar—I recognized everyone there and was friends with quite a few of them. Behind me were the angry voices of jealous fans. But in front of me was home.

As we made our way to the bus, Kira keened an excited mantra. "I can't believe it. I can't believe it."

Jo was more reserved. "I believe it." But when she reached the bus, she lost her composure. "This is *hella* awesome!" She let out a piercing howl.

I climbed up first to excited cheers from the band. All four of them were seated at the living room table. Buck looked incredible in a tight shirt that showed off his hard muscles. He got up and wrapped me in his arms, reminding me how much I enjoyed being with him. "Hey, babe. Great to see you." He dropped down for a brief but promising kiss.

I pulled away to introduce my friends. "Guys, this is Kira and Jo." I didn't figure I needed to tell them who these four men were. Buck, River, and Gabe waved to them and smiled.

As expected, Chuck got up and approached them with his usual enthusiasm. "Ladies!" He stepped between them, an arm around each, squeezing them like a serpent. They reciprocated and started ogling the handsome rocker. "How about a tour of the bus?" Kira and Jo grinned as the three of them disappeared down the hall.

Buck whispered in my ear. "Do your friends know what's about to happen to them?"

I gave him a little laugh. "That's why they're here."

He smirked. "What about you? Why are you here?"

"For this!" I threw myself at him, diving into a long, hard kiss. Oh God, it was so good. He was kissing me with as much desperation as I felt, making me wish it could last longer than two weeks. Much longer. I fell into the sweet familiarity of his arms.

The kiss ended, leaving us both in need of more. But since the bedroom already had three people in it, there wasn't much more we could do right then. So I sat with the band at the living room table and snuggled with Buck. River and Gabe told me about the rumors they'd heard since our night at the motel, exaggerating our playfulness into an orgy of epic proportions. Buck just sat there, a peaceful smile on his face.

It took Chuck, Kira, and Jo longer than usual to emerge from the bedroom, and all three of them had a post-coital glow. I was glad that my friends could share in some Fiery Boys action. They sat with us at the table for a few minutes, Kira and Jo sandwiching Chuck. "Look at us." He squeezed them with a grin. "Two lovely buns wrapped around one hundred percent beef."

Buck squinted at Chuck with a look of disgust, then got up. "Come on." He took my hand and led me toward the back of the bus. I followed without hesitation.

The bedroom was a total mess, with linens and clothing everywhere. The mattress looked like it had been used as a bouncy castle. I pulled away from Buck and sighed noisily.

He looked down at the sheets and groaned. "Fucking Chuck—such a pig." He pulled the sheets away from the bed while I scooped up pieces of clothing that had been left behind during the last ten days. We piled it all in a corner of the bedroom. Then Buck took out a set of clean sheets. "Let's do this right."

Staring desperately into each other's eyes, we managed to get the bottom sheet on without actually having to look at it. Then Buck's lips curled up on one side, and he lunged for me. We met halfway, landing on the bed in a bruising kiss of crushed lips and delving tongues. Bed making time was over.

Suddenly unable to undress fast enough, we nearly ripped our clothes off. Then we kissed while our limbs entwined and our bodies slid against each other, touching everywhere, feeling every inch. I had missed him so much.

Buck reached down between my legs to prepare me for his machine. But he didn't have to. It had been almost two weeks since we'd been together, and I was more than ready. In fact, I was quaking with excitement to be back with this breathtakingly stunning man.

I hissed in his ear. "I need you. Now, Buck." Turns out, he needed me, too. He soothed the ache that was burning in my body, and reminded me how wonderful it could be to live with the band and make love with him. Wrapped around each other, exquisite and ferocious, we soared, immersed in each other's bodies.

At one point, in a moment of stillness between our carnal bouts as I stared into his shimmering blue eyes, I felt something. A shift. A jolt. As if a magician's wand had been tapped on my head or a hypnotist's fingers had snapped. It left me feeling light and happy, ready to fly away.

In that moment, I knew that I had to come back on tour. I'd been telling myself it was over between us, but obviously I was wrong. My longing for him might never be satisfied, but there was nothing I could do about that. I wanted him, and I wanted to be with him for the rest of the tour. Our two weeks together would be incredible, even if we broke up afterwards. Because here, with this spectacular man, I felt delightfully at peace. We spent hours in wild intimacy.

When it was time for the show, Buck got dressed. I could barely move my body, so I laid there like a worn but cherished rag doll.

Somehow, I made it to the wings of the stage. Kira and Jo were twirling and leaping and shaking with excitement as they waited for the show to begin. When the Fiery Boys went on, they practically exploded, jumping up and down with each new song. I was so glad to share this experience with them.

Chuck paused before "Fiery Life" to introduce the song. "Hey there, San Jose. We've got our special guest drummer back for the next song. Turns out she's a local girl from right here in your city." A rumble started in the audience and soon coalesced into the Annalisa chant. It had been a while, so it surprised me that this still happened.

Kira and Jo had heard about this phenomenon. They'd seen the videos and read the reports. But being on stage while thousands of fans chanted my name seemed to catch them by surprise. Kira stared with huge eyes, but Jo just giggled. "You weren't kidding about how the audiences like you."

Even Chuck had a hard time speaking over the crowd's insistence. He finally stopped trying. "Come on out here, Annalisa."

I walked out on stage, and the house erupted in applause. After a little bow to the audience, I gave Buck a hug and stood by him, ready to dance. The band tore into the song with as much enthusiasm as I could remember, and I lost myself in the energy, dancing with all of them and pounding my cymbal. When it ended, I spent the rest of the show in the wings, floating a few inches above the floor.

All too soon, the show was over and the boys left the stage for the last time. I expected them to immediately run the fan gauntlet and then hide on the bus. Instead, they stopped and surrounded me, with Kira and Jo watching.

Buck spoke first. "Come back on tour with us."

I had already decided to do that. Being with Buck again had convinced me. Then, seeing the show again and going on stage had cemented my resolve.

But I also knew that two more weeks on the bus would have its difficulties, so I brought up my concerns. "The haters are going to tear me apart, you know. I do want to come back, but I'm a little sad to return to this celebrity insanity you guys live in."

Gabe laughed. "Yes, it's insane. But your fame is tied to us now. There'll be no peace for you until we finish this tour, whether you're with us or not. So you might as well spend it with friends." He glanced at Buck. "And lovers." Strangely enough, he was completely right. I hadn't found any real peace in my ten days at home.

Chuck grinned at me. "Chip's right, you know. Buck wants you, and you want him. How much simpler can it be?" Even Chuck knew what was best for me.

"I'll tell you what." River folded his arms and stepped back. "Take your time. Let us know in the morning." He winked as he walked away. Chuck and Gabe agreed with that and also wandered off. Buck just smiled.

We left the arena to face a good-size crowd of cheering fans. The boys went into the fray to give their best while Kira, Jo, and I stayed to the side. We finally broke free and headed to the bus.

As we were about to climb on board, Chuck pulled me aside. "Hang on, I need to talk to you." He waved Kira and Jo onto the bus. When everyone else had boarded, he led me to the back of the bus and found a dark area that the arena lights didn't reach. It looked to me like Chuck was up to his old tricks.

I turned to him with a smirk. "What's this all about, Chuck? I hope you don't expect me to join my girlfriends and have a four-way with you."

"Oh, stop it. I know we didn't start off well, but you've got Buck now. I won't try to steal you away."

"That might surprise Buck. He thinks you're out to steal anything you can."

He straightened up. "I know I've been a bastard. But right now I'm giving back. This is something important that got taken from him a long time ago. Something that I want to give to him, and to you. I'm not supposed to tell you this, but I don't care anymore. This is a secret, Annalisa."

The look on his face was more serious than I'd ever seen. I nodded at him and waited for another Fiery Boys secret. Lately, I'd collected quite a few.

He looked around to make sure nobody was listening, then he leaned closer. "I know that you love our song, 'Fiery Life.'" He narrowed his eyes and took a half step back. "I didn't write that song. Buck did."

My mouth fell open so far that you could have driven the tour bus through it. I stared at Chuck for a long time. "So how did your name get on it?"

"That was Jason's doing. When he assembled the band, way back, he had definite ideas about our personalities. I was brash and loud, River was bald and tough, Gabe was Zen—"

I corrected him. "*Horny* and Zen."

He shook his head. "It didn't start that way. The horny part got added because he kept finding women for me." Of course.

"And Buck was simple. I'm telling you, Jason had everything figured out. And it didn't wash with his plan that Buck would write an intense song about life and death. So he decided to put my name on it. It sucks, but we have to do what he tells us." He leaned close to me. "Don't let Jason find out I told you this."

"Did Buck write other songs?"

"Hell, yes. Look how many he wrote on our latest album! The guy's prolific." He listed a few other songs that Buck had written.

I stood there, stunned. Buck wrote "Fiery Life." No wonder he spoke with such authority about the meaning of the lyrics. If he wasn't already my favorite Fiery Boy after the way he handled my body, now he certainly was for the way he handled my emotions.

I looked up at Chuck. "Why are you telling me this?"

"Because I'm tired of being the bad guy. Buck's right; I've taken too much from him, and it's time to fix that. You have to come back on tour with us. I like you, Annalisa. River and Gabe think you're great. And Buck obviously has a major crush on you. I'm getting tired of his moping around, so come back and make him happy."

Chuck walked away, then stopped at the bus door. "Think about it. We could have some really great times in the next two weeks. And for once, I'm not talking about you and me in bed." He grinned, then climbed on board.

Buck wrote my song! This was definitely a message, demanding that I get my fiery life back on track. I needed to return to the tour and be with Buck, because only a fool would miss out on this amazing adventure.

I ran to the bus, thrilled to have another two weeks of fiery living.

Thirty-One

Super excited, I scampered up the steps of the bus. Gabe and Buck were at the living room table, waiting for their turn to shower. But Kira, Jo, and Chuck were gone. I peered down the aisle. "Are my friends back there with Chuck?"

Gabe grinned. "Surprised the hell out of us. That's two in a row for those three."

"Well, good for them." I sat down and faced Buck with a loving smile. "I've decided for sure—I'm coming back on tour."

Buck pounded the table, and we hugged. "That's great news."

I held out a hand to stop him and Gabe from breaking out the champagne. "But I'd like to make a request."

I was with friends here, so I took the opportunity to use whatever influence I had. "I think we should take turns sleeping in the bedroom. Buck and I get it half the nights, you and River the other half. Chuck gets the days and, of course, right after the shows. Then he's done." I grinned. "He never spends the night with anyone, anyway, so let him stay in his own cubicle. The rest of us need some space."

Everyone liked this idea, especially Gabe. "Makes sense. Besides, River and I have been talking about coming out when the tour ends. It wouldn't be the worst thing if someone saw us."

I shook my head. "Have you really stayed in the closet because of the band?"

Gabe shrugged. "We've lived quietly up in Minnesota, so we didn't mind too much. But things have changed a lot, so it's time to open up."

River returned from the shower and joined us at the table, a small white towel around his muscular body. I growled at him, which made us both laugh. Soon, Gabe left for his turn.

I gave Buck a devilish smile. "I've got an idea. Why don't you come over to my place for a shower? You're in *my* town now, so why not spend the night? I live alone, and it's not far."

River whistled. "That would be a first. A Fiery Boy going to a groupie's place."

Buck scowled at him. "She's not a groupie."

"Sure she is. She's the best groupie we've ever had." He waved at us with the back of his hand. "Go! Get the hell out of here you two." We didn't need any more encouragement.

Buck and I drove in silence for a few minutes. Finally, he spoke up. "What made you finally decide to come back on tour, Annalisa?"

"Chuck. He told me a secret that you wouldn't admit. Turns out he's not the songwriter I thought he was. He told me that *you* wrote 'Fiery Life,' and a bunch of others. 'Sizzling Love' was yours, too." I still couldn't believe that he'd written so much music. "Your songs are the most beautiful."

Buck looked like he'd been slapped. "Why would Chuck tell you that? Jason could fry his ass for letting that slip."

"I won't tell anyone—I'm pretty good about keeping band secrets." I laughed lightly. "I know enough about you four to write a huge exposé."

"Yeah, you probably could." He nodded at me, then he slowly grinned. "You know, you're a pretty good writer.

Maybe you *should* write about us. I liked your piece on 'Fiery Life.'"

"But I missed the point of the song."

"No, you got the point." He laid a hand on my shoulder. "It's about moving on after a death. In my case, my mother's. In your case, your lover's. I wrote sparse and general lyrics so people could find their own meaning. You did that." He leaned over to kiss me on the cheek.

I tingled all over. Now that I knew he had written "Fiery Life," I felt like we could discuss it some more. "You know, Buck, I've been thinking about that song since we talked about it. I may have gotten my priorities wrong all this time."

"What *are* your priorities?"

"Well, my priorities are definitely on hold for the next two weeks. But after that, I really need to stop dedicating my life to Zed's memory. You've thawed an eight-year-old layer of ice that I built around my heart. Thanks to you, I'm going to live for myself from now on."

Buck's grin stretched clear across his face. "I'm glad to hear that, Annalisa."

I brought up the subject that we both needed to discuss. "So speaking about the next two weeks. . ."

"Yes, I promised to talk about it, so let me tell you what I'm thinking." Buck sat up straight. "I have some pretty strong feelings for you, Annalisa, but I hardly know you. And you're right: this whole thing has 'rebound' written all over it. That doesn't have to be a problem, but we need to know each other better before I can make any commitments."

"Of course. That's totally fair."

"Also, I have a real problem mixing commitment with rock-and-roll. Together, it's a destructive force that ruined

Danielle and me. I was young back then but now I know better: marrying her was wrong. And I don't see anyone else on the road who knows how to make it work, either. Talia Dare's marriage broke up because she was always touring." He shook his head. "Fame corrupts relationships, and traveling makes it harder. Also, I don't want to be another person who abandons you—you've had enough of that. So I can't even begin to think about the future while we're still on tour."

I understood. Buck had plenty of issues that he needed to handle. I accepted that whatever we had would only last until the end of the tour. "So," I smirked. "No falling in love allowed."

Buck rolled his eyes. "Love! What does that even mean? Look at how groupies scream their love for us." He scowled. "They're not in love—they barely know the meaning of the word."

He paused for a second, then went on. "I have a suggestion. Let's not think about the future until this tour is over. I'll be done with the Fiery Boys then, and I'll be able to figure out my life more clearly. You will, too, and we'll know each other much better. So until then, let's not make plans —let's just have fun. Get to know each other better. If we ask no questions, we'll hear no lies. Then if we aren't ready for more in two weeks, it'll be easier to walk away. What do you think?"

How could I argue with his good sense? I'd been in love with Buck for ten years, but as he pointed out, it wasn't really love. Now I would get to experience an entirely different Buck. Anything could happen.

"It sounds like a good idea, Buck. I've been afraid to be with you again because the two days we had were so perfect. But if we just kick back and enjoy ourselves, it will add to that memory." I offered him my hand. "You have yourself a deal." Buck gave me a relieved smile and shook my hand.

The next few minutes went by silently as we got closer to my home. Then Buck turned to face me. "I still think you should write on the band's website. 'Notes from the Road,' or something like that. Get Gabe to post it."

"Really? You'd let me write about the band?"

"Hell yeah. Folks would love to read your stuff." He shook his head. "Can't tell any secrets, though."

"Are we a secret?"

"No." He grinned. "We're an item."

"Good. Then I accept." We drove on.

I could see Buck processing, his mouth working, eyes squinting. "I still can't believe Chuck told you about my songs."

"He told me he feels bad about the things he's taken from you and wants to make peace. He may be horny and clueless, but he's not evil."

"You don't know the half of it. He's taken lots of things from me." Buck's entire face seemed to darken.

There was more? How could Chuck have done so much damage? "Do you want to talk about it?"

Buck looked down and exhaled noisily. "Here's one that you know all about. He took my pride by constantly calling me dumb. Jason's original image of the bass player was someone 'slow and spare with words,' not dumb. But *Chuck*," he spat it out. "Couldn't stop himself from making jokes. How I'm thick, moronic, an idiot."

"Couldn't you get Jason to make him stop?"

He pursed his lips and shook his head. "Tried that. Problem was, the Buck-is-stupid concept took hold. Jason kept telling me 'it tests well.' So I became the dumb one, thanks to Chuck. Just another reason why I hate having to be with him."

Poor Buck. He was the band's whipping boy, the dumb one who married the band-killing groupie. Everything was his fault. I reached out to take his hand, giving it a squeeze.

"If it's any consolation, I never thought of you as stupid. I watched you closely back then and listened to everything you said. 'Spare' is certainly right—you hardly spoke at all. But I never heard anything dumb. So for me, anyway, 'spare with words' fits you perfectly. Although you became much more chatty once we got to know each other better."

Buck laughed. "I was always talkative. If you want someone who hardly speaks, meet my father. Anyway, I liked the idea of being spare with words back then. That way, when I got interviewed, I wouldn't have to say much. It suited me fine to be ignored—I hate the attention. And I hardly ever talk to the audience."

"You talked to the audience plenty in Minneapolis when you convinced them to like me."

"I had to. Chuck had thrown you to the wolves." Buck's eyes sparkled as he grinned at me. "I had to fix it."

"And you did it so skillfully. I was amazed by how you manipulated the fans. See? I knew you weren't stupid." I gave him a subtle grin.

"I've done plenty of stupid things." Buck let out a groan. "One of the stupidest things I ever did was to join the Fiery Boys."

"No, Buck. I think it was the best thing you ever did. I'd never have met you otherwise." I thought about Buck's reputation as a fool and let out a laugh. He was anything but. "Back in high school I used to get in arguments with my friends about you. I was the one who defended your intelligence, and they would tell me I was wrong. So thank you for being smart and proving me right." Both of us smiled at that, then we finished the trip in relaxed silence.

I finally pulled into my driveway. "We're here." We got out and I led him to the door. My house was small, amid many other tiny suburban homes. Just a simple granite-colored building with a red Spanish tile roof. The little lawn out front had a few shrubs by the living room window.

"Is this all yours?"

"Well, mine and the bank's. I've done pretty well selling cars, so I bought this a few years ago. Just a little two-bedroom place, but it's perfect for me. Jo lives next door. That's how we met."

I led him inside and gallantly sent him to take a shower. Then I stood in the living room and had an epiphany. Buck Morris—my rock-and-roll dreamboat—was here! Taking a shower in my little home. The incredible improbability of this made my head light.

They really should have advertised the contest differently. They should have stated that the winner would get the Fiery Boy of her choice to come to her home and have wild sex with her. Because that's what the contest had become.

And speaking of wild sex, I was tired of waiting for this gorgeous man to get clean, so I went and joined him. Hey! He'd been gone at least thirty seconds, which was way too long.

The bathroom hadn't had time to steam up, so I had a clear view of his breathtaking body, flexing under the water as he lathered himself. As expected, he was more than happy to clean my body, too. We got soapy and slippery and the room steamed-up even faster.

We tried every part of the shower, starting under the showerhead, continuing on to the other walls, and finishing in the middle, suspended in his arms, my legs wrapped around him. Hot, hot, hot! Right up to the moment that we ran out of hot water.

Before the night was up, we also made love in my bedroom, the living room, and the garage. In the garage, we did it in the back of my car, which made me thankful that I'd opted for the leather seats.

I would forever associate these places with what we did there. Buck had marked me in a way I doubted I'd ever get over. Now he was marking my house, too, like an animal leaving a scent in new territory.

The morning light was breaking when we finally fell asleep.

On The Road Again

Thirty-Two

The band did a second show in San Jose on Monday, which gave us another day to play. Buck was genuinely happy to follow me to my favorite restaurants and shops and to meet my friends. He even came to the dealership and charmed the gents, telling tall tales of vehicular foolishness.

Everywhere we went, fans spotted us. Everywhere! I thought I could avoid cameras by taking him hiking up on Mount Hamilton. But of course, we got recognized by other hikers who whipped out their phones as soon as they saw us.

Through it all, Buck was relaxed and charming. The man who hated touring and loathed desperate groupies was completely out there today. I stood in awe as he gave every fan his full attention: smiling, chatting, signing things, and posing for pictures. Even when the occasional insulting comment was made about his marriage or his I.Q., he weathered it without flinching. He just laughed and shook his head.

Buck also made sure that everyone said hi to me. Some fans snickered at the fact that the contest winner was dating one of the band members, but they were friendly about it. And nobody was upset to see me back with the band— many of them didn't even know I'd left. I guess once you're a contest winner, you never lose the title.

Buck's easy acceptance of his celebrity made me feel much better about mine. Whereas I used to be annoyed by it, I now found it thrilling because I had Buck by my side.

Not only did he divert attention away from me, he also gave me some credibility. Now I was more than a contest winner, I was with one of the Fiery Boys. It made me realize how much I needed to return to the tour.

The next gig wasn't until Wednesday in Los Angeles, so we continued to stay in San Jose for most of Tuesday. I spent the day doing various preparations to put my life on hold again. Then we left that night, and I was back on the road. Just the Fiery Boys and me, living together on the big black-and-red tour bus.

It dawned on me that my life was wonderful beyond belief. In the one week I had spent with these four famous men, I had grown to know them intimately. Even Chuck, with his endless whoring, had become my friend. And I'd fallen hard for Buck, the sensuous songwriter. For the next two weeks, my fiery life would burn with a phosphorescent intensity.

We arrived in Los Angeles so early Wednesday morning that the traffic hadn't had time to grind to a complete halt. The busses and trucks formed their usual encampment outside the arena like a wagon train in the wild West, huddled to protect against bandits.

Since Buck had been staying with me in San Jose, River and Gabe had been in the bedroom for the past two nights. But now that I was back on the bus, it was our turn. On the way to Los Angeles, Buck welcomed me back on tour in his oh-so-sexy, hard rock way. The bus's bedroom, filled with magical memories from those first two nights with Buck, became even more wondrous.

At one point, I did some modeling from the groupie-wear box. With Buck's guidance, I found the perfect ensemble. I could tell it was perfect by the way he slowly peeled it off of me and then ferociously ravished my body. I definitely needed to keep that outfit handy, along with a few other pieces that he responded well to. We played dress-up, and then down again, for most of the night.

I stretched in the late morning sun, sated by yet another bout of early-morning randiness, this time an erotic wake-up call. Buck laid on the bed like a hibernating bear, though he opened one eye long enough to give me a little smile.

Suddenly energized, I hopped out of bed. "Let's go out and see L.A." I felt the usual pull to seek adventure, and Los Angeles was full of possibilities. Also, I was hungry for something better than the usual tour-bus fare.

Buck grunted in derision. "Fuck L.A. Let's stay here."

"Oh, come on, Buck. We've been here since last night. Let's do something else. Besides, you're wearing me out—I need a break." Too much of Buck was certainly a good thing, but I had to admit I was a little sore.

He rumbled with amusement, then rolled onto his side. "You can go. I don't want to."

I furrowed my brow. "You're just going to sit on the bus until the show tonight? Come on, let's get out of here for a few hours."

"No. I told you, go by yourself if you want." He was serious.

"Is there a reason you don't want to go out?"

Buck's face grew tight. "I hate Los Angeles. Phony, backstabbing assholes. Annoying paparazzi."

Whoa, he had a serious dislike of the city. We were doing two shows here, so it didn't seem like he'd be leaving the tour bus tomorrow, either. I gave it one last shot. "Come on, Buck! Paparazzi are everywhere, and every city you visit is full of phony sycophants. Why take it out on L.A.?"

But my pushing only drove him further away. He tensed up. "I'm not doing this, Annalisa, so let it go. We'll go out when we get to Vegas."

I laughed. "That doesn't make sense. There are just as many phony people and paparazzi in Las Vegas, perhaps more."

"You're right. Just let me hate L.A., and don't make me talk about it. We agreed to ask no questions, to simply have fun for two weeks. So go, have fun."

He wouldn't budge, and neither would I. His refusal to go out frustrated me because it made him seem like one of my unadventurous boyfriends. At least he wasn't being clingy—he was fine with me going out on my own. And anyway, he was right. We were allowed to do whatever we wanted during these next two weeks—he didn't have to be with me every minute of the day. We could do things by ourselves if it suited us. Besides, who knew what would happen? We might even break up *before* the tour ended. So the need to see Los Angeles together was pretty unimportant.

I smiled at him. "Okay, we don't have to talk about it. I'm going out." I got dressed in a plain gray hoodie, black leggings, and tan ankle boots. With a pair of dark sunglasses, my urban camouflage was complete. Then I gave Buck a kiss and left the bus.

As I walked off, I worried about Buck. Something bad must have happened in Los Angeles to trigger such animosity. I'd wondered if the angry Buck would reemerge, and here he was. Only this time he was angry at Los Angeles. Not what I expected.

I decided to call Jo. As a psychologist who understood these sort of things, she might have some advice.

"Annalisa!" She bubbled across the line. "I never got to thank you for introducing Kira and me to Chuck."

I laughed briefly. "I'm glad I did something right."

Jo picked up on my state instantly. "What's wrong? You and Buck? Don't tell me the honeymoon's over already."

"It's not that bad. But he doesn't want to go out in Los Angeles. Just wants to stay in the bus all day."

"Is he insisting you stay with him?"

"No, he doesn't care if I go out by myself. I'm on my way now. But he hates Los Angeles and wont say why."

"He's allowed to hate L.A. He may not even understand it himself. Take the long view, girl. You're on tour with the Fiery Boys, your favorite band ever. And you're having great sex with Buck, who you've wanted ever since high school. So don't worry if he won't play tourist with you in L.A."

I took a deep breath. "You're right. Seems pretty foolish when you put it that way. I don't know what's wrong with me."

Jo laughed. "I know what's wrong. You're in love with him."

Was I? I'd accepted that the future was irrelevant, that these two weeks were all that mattered. But perhaps I was deluding myself. I'd brought Buck back to my home when the band was in San Jose and the two of us had "played house," acting like a couple and running around town together. It felt incredibly good, which made me think things that I shouldn't have. So even though I'd promised I wouldn't go there, a part of me still wanted a future with Buck.

Jo was right. I was starting to get a little too possessive. Even, dare I say it, clingy. This from the woman who never let a man do that to her.

"Love!" My laugh had a tinge of sadness. "We talked about that, and he pointed out that fan love isn't real love. He's right, of course. But when I'm with him, I feel so happy." I let out a loud breath. "I'm an idiot."

"It's okay. I'm an idiot, too. About Chuck."

Oh no! Was Jo in love with Chuck? That would be much worse than my hangups over Buck. I might have expected this sort of reaction from Kira, but Jo was a counselor. I'd assumed she would know better. Maybe I shouldn't have set them up, after all.

"Surely you don't think anything can happen there. He forgets women as soon as he meets them." Crude but honest —Jo could handle it.

"Well, he hasn't forgotten me. We've been texting and calling each other for the past three days. Something's going on, I'll say that."

"What! You're falling for Chuck?" That would be a terrible thing to do. And here I'd called *her* for advice.

Jo blew out a derisive grunt. "Of course I'm not falling for him. And he's not in love with me, either. He had a four-way last night with three other women."

I was glad to hear her say this, because I didn't want to be the one to tell her. But I was completely stunned that he discussed this sort of thing with Jo. "So, what *is* going on between you two?"

"I'm sure it's nothing. All I'm saying is that I understand how easily you can fall in love with those boys. They're larger than life, and we've idolized them for too long. So just forgive yourself. Give Buck some room. There's still plenty of time to get to know him better, so enjoy it." I was grateful for friends like Jo.

I headed to the fence, ready to go out and see the city. But before I got there, Jason stopped me. I really wasn't in the mood for his particular brand of crap, so I propped my hands on my hips, silently wishing he'd go away. But crap was on the menu today.

"Going somewhere?" Did he really think his pretend smiles weren't obvious to everyone?

"Thought I'd see the city." I started toward the fence but he held up his hand.

"Wait! Make sure you tell everyone to come to the show." Yeah, right. He wanted me to go out there and rub my contest-winning status in everyone's face. No, thank you.

"I'm trying *not* to be recognized, Jason."

"No, no! Take that hoodie off and *get* recognized." He reached into his pocket and handed me an envelope. "Here are some tickets. Give them away, tell everyone to come to the shows."

This guy was such a user. I would not be his shill. "No." I pushed the tickets back.

"Come on. You've got to help the band. We need more buzz, which you're good at doing. We also need to fill the arena, so go ahead, give away some tickets. Anybody who recognizes you is enough of a fan to deserve a pair."

He barked orders into his phone. "Annalisa's going out. I need a driver and some eyes." He ended the call with a smile. "It's all arranged." Then he handed me the envelope of tickets and walked away.

The man had an uncanny capacity to sour any activity. Now he wanted my day in Los Angeles to be a full-bore publicity stunt. No wonder Buck didn't want to go out.

I decided to see Los Angeles my way: privately. And although I could have dumped the tickets in the trash, I hung on to them just in case. After all, someone was certain to recognize me, so it would be nice to hand out a ticket or two.

With Vaughan shadowing me, I felt safe but not helicoptered. The man really disappeared when he was watching you. I went to Santa Monica and wandered along the beach and the promenade. Then I took a Hollywood stars tour. I'd never done that before, and in truth, it had never appealed to me. But now that I was something of a star, I suddenly wanted to see it from the fan's point of view.

And was it ever a disappointment! All the adulation my fellow star-hunters lavished on their idols made me sad, because I understood what it was like for those poor actors, stalked by entire busses full of fans. Half the people on the tour recognized me, too, so I managed to give away all of the tickets. Then, because I wasn't an actress, they lost interest in me and returned their focus to every fence and shrub, hoping to spot a real star.

When I returned to the bus, a strange sensation settled over me. The sensation of just wanting to spend a quiet day with Buck. The Hollywood stars tour had been a sorry thing to do, and I would have had much more fun if I'd stuck around today with this sexy rocker.

Yes, I was changing, thanks to Buck. The need to always do something exciting was definitely under evaluation. Did I have to lead a fiery life at every opportunity? Half of the things I drove myself to do weren't very fiery at all, so why was I doing them? Certainly not for Zed—I understood that now. I could see that the person who mattered the most in my life was me. Funny how that could be a revelation.

Zed never asked me to dedicate my life to his memory. Like Buck, he wanted me to live life for myself. So I needed to do that, starting now. One thing was certain: when the tour ended in two weeks and I said goodbye to Buck, I was going to be indelibly transformed by him. Zed had changed me profoundly, but Buck's effect might be even greater.

Thirty-Three

Notes from the Road: Things you Didn't Know About the Fiery Boys

by *Annalisa Ricci*

I've been a huge Fiery Boys fan since they hit the scene ten years ago. I watched all their interview videos and read everything I could find about them. But I still learned some new things during my week on the bus. So now I'm going to share what I learned and tell you things I bet you didn't know about them.

But before I do, I need to clear some very polluted air. Everywhere I look, people are saying that I hooked up with each of them in a single week. That is a huge exaggeration.

After living with the Fiery Boys on the tour bus, I got to be very close to them. And I *did* have sex during that week, but with just one of them. I swear on everything I find holy that I never hooked-up with the other three Fiery Boys. Never.

So who was my one conquest? Read on.

Let's start with most people's favorite Fiery Boy: Chuck. Was he my favorite Fiery Boy, now or ten years ago? No, that honor goes to River. And I did not hook-up with Chuck. So you can forget those pictures of us kissing at the press meet —that's as far as we got.

But I'll tell you who Chuck *has* been having sex with: Inferna.

Who's Inferna? Please! She's just the world's most perfect Fiery Boys fan. Surgically enhanced with hair dyed bright red, she wears killer boots and a skimpy flame-themed corset at the shows. She's impossible to miss, all dressed up like some kind of male fantasy cosplay girl.

All four Fiery Boys notice her during shows. Even women stare. Bigger Tim, the band's head of security, eyes her constantly. And you can be certain he's not doing it because he thinks she's a security risk.

But who is she, really? Inferna is a Las Vegas showgirl who runs a Fiery Boys fan site that specializes in hating me and telling lies. I don't hate her, and I won't tell lies about her. Instead, I'll tell you a story that Chuck told me.

Six years ago, Chuck moved to Las Vegas and started doing his one-man tribute show. One night, after finishing a show, he passed by the entrance to a burlesque revue. The doorman recognized him and offered him free admission if he sat up front. Chuck recognized a cheap ploy to leverage his fame and generate buzz about the show, but he didn't care. He's a sucker for showgirls, so he went in.

As instructed, Chuck took a table near the stage. Two women in sequins were singing a song, badly. But he appreciated their outfits, so he ordered a drink and dug-in for a while.

Then the song ended and a beautiful vision took the stage. The way Chuck describes it, he was struck dumb by this woman, unable to tear his eyes away for her entire act. Chuck had met Inferna.

Of course, she didn't use that name back then. Six years ago, she called herself Gypsy. And Gypsy stole his heart.

Chuck waited for her to finish her act, then he found her backstage. They've been on-and-off lovers ever since. She even follows the tour, comes to the shows, and visits the tour bus for more of her man. I wouldn't dare come between them. Now if I could only get her to stop hating me so much. . .

Next let's talk about River, who I've admitted was my favorite Fiery Boy. Is he the one I had sex with? No. But wait —I hear you say—what about the rumors of me and River and Gabe in a motel in Kansas City? Yes, we did spend the night together. The tour bus can get pretty claustrophobic at times, and we needed to get away. But we did not go there to have a three-way.

Most people know that River has a secret lover who lives near him in Minnesota. They've been together for years now, but River knows better than to give out names or be seen in public. He saw what happened to Buck and Danielle and he doesn't want a repeat of that. But since the paparazzi love to take pictures, and since the three of us were together in a motel, we decided to punk them and pretend to be lovers. Crazy, right?

Now here's something you didn't know about River. He's a serious drum collector. Some rockers collect guitars— Alejandro is famous for his collection. But River's drum collection is even bigger. Back in Minnesota, he fixed up the acoustics in a big barn so he could fill it with all kinds of drums. He goes there for hours each day to pound away. For him, it's a form of meditation, and he says he feels great when he's done.

He's even got a huge Japanese Oodaiko drum that takes up one entire corner of the barn. When he plays it, people hear it for miles. And this drum costs as much as any rare guitar—it took twenty years to make. Yes, River loves his drums, but he didn't make love to me.

So if I didn't have sex with River, then it should come as no surprise that I didn't have sex with Gabe, either. Sure, I spent that night in a motel with him. Big deal. I spent the other six nights on a tour bus with him, which is much tighter quarters.

But let me tell you something about Gabe. First of all, he's a pretty intense computer nerd. He builds his own guitar pedals, manages the band's website, and loves to tinker. You should see him after he's been to the pro shop of a music store. It's like Christmas every time.

The other thing to know about Gabe is that he smokes a lot of weed, and always performs high. That's why he closes his eyes when he's on stage. He likes to focus on the music.

The day before I arrived on the tour bus, Gabe was sitting in the living room, testing out a new electronics toy. Unfortunately, he was a little too stoned, and he wired it wrong, sending it way too much power. One of the chips on the board burst into flames, tore itself free, and shot straight up into the air. In less than a second, it had lodged itself in the bus's ceiling.

It's still there, which is why people on the tour have given him a new nickname: Chip. He doesn't like that name, but he's certainly earned it.

Finally, let's talk about Buck. I've denied any sexual activity with the others, so clearly this is the one I've gotten intimate with. Buck was always my second favorite Fiery Boy back in high school. I'm proud to tell you that he's now my number one, panty-wetting, all-time favorite. He doesn't open up much—it took nearly the entire week before he could admit he liked me. But once he did, it all spilled out. And then, before I knew it, we had found something amazing and tender and wild.

Please don't get jealous, all you fans who adore Buck. My time with him is limited. And after the breakup of his marriage, this Fiery Boy is nowhere near ready for commitment. But he's finally free to enjoy himself on the road, so I'm happy to offer him some rebound therapy.

Also, I have a very interesting thing to tell you about Buck. He is *not* dumb. That's a joke that Chuck started and still keeps on telling. But nothing could be further from the truth.

Buck is a serious musician who works hard. Just look at the latest album that the Fiery Boys released before this tour. Most of the songs were written by Charles Morris, which true fans know is Buck's real name. And not only does Buck write many of the Fiery Boys songs, he also sells songs to other artists. He's even written music for three movies. One of them, "Seattle Story" was nominated for a Best Original Score Oscar three years ago. This is not the work of a dumb man.

Which brings us to the present moment. As you know, I lived on the tour bus for a week and then went home to my regular life. Unfortunately, like an astronaut who's been to the moon, it was hard to find anything close to a regular life after I'd lived through such a momentous experience. So I came back to the bus to finish the reunion tour with the band.

I was stunned when I got asked back on tour. And particularly stunned when I found out who asked for me: you did. You chanted my name at concerts and demanded to see me on stage. You spoke well of me, even when stories of depraved activities filled the media. I love you, and all I can say is, thank you.

Also, I now have a job on the bus: writing these notes. A little something for Fiery Boys fans everywhere. So here I am, sitting up late at night, writing this article. When I'm done, I'll climb into my cubicle and get some sleep. Yes, alone in my cubicle on the tour bus. They're built for only one.

Finally, let me have a word with those of you who are not happy to see me back on the tour bus. Yes, I know who you are. I read your blogs (though I sometimes wonder why). Some of you hate me so much that you'd sooner see me crushed under the tour bus tires. You think I'm stealing hearts and destroying the band.

Well, you're wrong. I'd sooner lay under those tires voluntarily than break up the Fiery Boys. I love them and their music, and I would be horrified if I ruined their sound. So I'm giving you my promise right now that if there's ever a choice between my happiness and the band's, I'm out of here. Even sex with Buck isn't worth it if it creates trouble with the band.

So if you're a hater, all I ask is that you take a calming breath before spewing your response to this post. Then consider whether there's something else you could be doing besides making up lies about me.

Ciao. Love to you all (yes, even the haters).

- Annalisa.

Thirty-Four

Last night was River and Gabe's turn in the bedroom, so Buck and I spent a lot of time heavy petting. We wrapped ourselves in a blanket and got naked on the living room floor, generating enough steam heat to power the bus. Then we crashed together in Buck's cubicle.

This morning, I was already back in the living room when Buck came out. He smiled, then plopped down next to me. "I decided to go out in Los Angeles with you today. Figured I could handle it if I set it up myself. So I've picked out a place I want to take you."

I nodded slowly, impressed with his attempt to deal with the dreaded city. "Thank you. Where are we going?"

He grinned. "I have a treat for you. I know you like motorcycles and cars, so I thought I'd take you car racing."

Wow. That sounded like fun. How thoughtful. "We're going to watch some car races?"

"No, no. We're going to *race* some *cars*. Los Angeles Speedway lets you drive real race cars on the track when it's not a race day. They do it back home, too, at the Atlanta Motor Speedway. I like to go there sometimes when I need to drive super fast. Clears the head. I bet you'll like it." He grinned. "Today, we get to race each other."

Whoa! This was going to be *incredibly* fun. Buck didn't know that I'd raced cars with Zed back in high school. "Uh, Buck. I need to tell you something."

"Don't worry. You don't need to have any racing experience."

I laughed. "Yeah, that's what I needed to tell you. I *have* racing experience—lots of it. With Zed. Never on a track, though. We used to do drag racing."

Buck beamed at me. "Excellent. I worried that this wouldn't be your idea of a fun date, but clearly I was wrong."

We drove to the track and met the race instructor. He recognized us as soon as we arrived. "Hey, I heard about you two. Is this serious?"

I didn't want people to get any big ideas, so I shrugged. "Doubtful. We're just rocking it till the tour ends." With a frown, Buck shook his head in agreement.

The instructor quickly changed the subject and told us about the vehicles. He also showed us the uniforms we'd be wearing. The helmets had radios so we could communicate with him and with each other. Finally, we went out to the cars.

These were much more impressive than Zed's old dragster, that's for sure. It brought back nostalgia for my high school days. I wondered if they'd let me blast Fiery Boys songs while I drove.

We sat in the cars to get used to them while the instructor explained the controls. Then he let us take a practice lap so we could get even more comfortable. I studied each section of the track, paying close attention to the banking on the corners. This was a professional track, so it was banked beautifully. I'd be able to take these turns like lightning.

Finally, we got to race. I was determined to beat Buck, and I was pretty sure I could. He'd never raced this track before, so neither of us had an advantage. But I'd probably spent more time racing than he had. Did he know about fast braking, quick shifting, and tight corners? Did he know to start accelerating early in a turn so he could get up to speed faster on the straightaway? I'd learned that one the hard way many years ago.

We lined up to race. When the light turned green, I floored it and shot down to the end of the straightaway in barely any time. This was a spectacular vehicle which could take corners easily. I came out of it way ahead of Buck on the next straight section. Hah!

I held my lead for the rest of the lap, but then Buck managed to pass me on a straightaway. I'd gotten cocky and wasn't watching as he sneaked past me—now he was ahead.

Buck kept the lead for the second lap. But I had no intention of letting that stand. On the third lap, I saw my opportunity as we exited a turn. Buck's car swung wide so I cut him off on the inside, gaining the lead. I whooped into my radio as I pulled ahead.

Now all I had to do was stay there for one more lap and I'd win the race. That meant trying to focus on the car, not on what Buck was saying. He was trying to distract me with talk about how he wanted me to dance naked on stage when they played "Fiery Life." He thought he'd throw me off with dirty talk. Unfortunately for Buck, he was more affected by his suggestive comments than I was. I tuned him out and easily stayed ahead of him, winning the race.

When we got out of our cars, Buck ran up to hug me. As he approached, I noticed a flash of something familiar in his look. He had that famous shadow smile again, faintly written all over his face. The same smile from my high school poster and from the first time he kissed me. It seemed so delicate that I held my breath, afraid it would blow away if I exhaled.

Even though it was unlikely I'd learn anything, I had to ask. I grabbed my phone and searched for "Buck Morris." In no time I found the classic poster with the familiar almost-smile, the same look that was on his face now.

"Remember this picture? I had it on my wall." He glanced at my phone with a nod. "What were you smiling about?"

He laughed. "Danielle was there that day, making all sorts of lewd remarks while they took my picture."

"So that's your horny look? I see it on your face now."

"You do? Well, I guess that's because watching you drive like that makes me hot. I can't wait to get your engine going." He crushed me in a kiss that went on and on, making me start to dissolve. Good thing he hadn't done that before the race.

We got back to the arena as the band prepared to do their second Los Angeles show. I joined them for the various amusement aids that would fuel their performance, including alcohol, marijuana, and in Chuck's case, two willing groupies. I still didn't understand how they could function when drunk, drugged, and drained, but it did seem to make them loud and noisy without causing any noticeable damage to their ability to play.

That night, Inferna was in the audience, along with her aggressive lackeys. I hung back in the wings to avoid riling her up with my presence. I even asked the boys if I could stay backstage and skip my part during "Fiery Life." But they told me I needed to stand up to her. They may have been right, but I still didn't want to face that woman.

As I feared, Inferna and her succubi screamed like furies when I was introduced. And although Chuck wanted me to start off dancing with him, I felt safer standing next to Buck while I waited for the song to start. The good news was that I could hardly see her against the bright lights. And as soon as the song started, I couldn't hear her, either.

So I relaxed and enjoyed being part of the Fiery Boys, once again.

But Inferna wasn't going to go away. After the show, she and her crew were waiting by the stage door. Bigger Tim was also there, which made me feel safer. But my confidence was eroded when I saw the two of them trading looks. I'd seen this before from him, I understood that she got looks like that from most men. But when he squeezed her hand, I was surprised. And when she responded with a peck to his cheek, I nearly fell over.

Inferna and Bigger Tim? I wondered if she'd seduced him because he was the head of Fiery Boys security. She'd certainly be able to get special treatment that way. Inferna moved away quickly after their little interaction, acting cool to him. But Bigger Tim seemed smitten and kept watching her with a smile on his face. Suddenly I didn't feel any safer.

Inferna and her underlings quickly surrounded us. Buck and I held on tight, and River and Gabe flanked us. I was lucky to have three Fiery Boys on my side. Even though Inferna had many supporters, including the head of security, I felt protected.

Chuck, bless his horny little soul, sauntered up to the demon groupie. "Hey babe, looking hot."

"Hot for you, Chuck. Can we come on the bus?"

He nodded toward me. "Annalisa's back with us. You have to leave her alone."

"Why? You don't give two shits about her. Hell, she won't even put out for you." She shook her head with a snarl. "Look at her, hiding behind those fuckers. Disgusting! Don't tell me you're falling for that little tramp."

I laughed. Me, little? I was taller than she was, but in those towering heels, she might have had me beat. And tramp? She had to be kidding.

I took a step toward her to prove I didn't need to hide behind anyone. "That must make you a *big* tramp, Inferna."

I couldn't resist the stab. Besides, my guess was that she was proud of it.

All four of the Fiery Boys laughed, but Inferna was obviously not amused. She spit at me, and even though I stepped back, it landed on my shoe. The woman was all kinds of crazy!

Inferna turned to Chuck with a pout. "That bitch is going to be the death of the band. Now you don't even want me anymore."

He pulled her to his side. "You're my favorite drug, babe. But no cat fights, understand? Just you and me and. . ." He paused to survey the bevy of willing women, hopping excitedly like game-show contestants trying to get picked. "Oh, let's see, four. . . no *five* more." He turned back to Inferna with a leer. "You choose."

Chuck and six women. Astonishing—how did he do it? I watched as Inferna nominated five of her friends, then all of them headed to the bus. The remaining groupies eyed River, Gabe, Buck, and me, but we soon convinced them that the party was over.

The four of us leaned against the outside of the bus, afraid to go back in. I laughed nervously about seeing Inferna again, then shook my head. "She'll never stop hating me."

Buck agreed. "Sorry, Annalisa. You don't need her shit."

No, but I knew it was coming. I couldn't avoid it when I was the only woman who got to live on the Fiery Boys tour bus. Inferna would kill for what I had. She sure seemed like she'd kill me.

I took a deep breath. "It's all right. I knew what I was doing when I came back on tour."

He pulled me into a fierce hug, and then he kissed me, helping me to forget the world of hate out there. Buck's groping grew more intense, and I clung to him just as hard. We hadn't been to bed since our little spat about Los Angeles yesterday, so I wondered how he'd be at makeup sex. I'd bet the earth would move.

But we couldn't do that right now because Inferna was in there with Chuck and five other women. That made six women who hated me. Besides the usual six-girls-and-a-boy activities they were engaging in, they were probably also spewing vicious lies about me. Their hatred was creepy.

I pulled away from Buck. "You're going to think I'm silly, but I don't want to sleep in that bedroom tonight. I feel like Inferna's cursing it."

"You never want to go back in there again?"

I shook my head. "No, I just need to let it clear a little." I shrugged. "Sorry."

"Don't apologize, I understand. Let's go to a motel. River and Gabe will be happy to have the bedroom again."

We talked some more as we waited for the bus to be habitable. Huddled with three of the Fiery Boys as my close companions, I realized how much better I had it than Inferna. She had to share just one Fiery Boy with five other women.

I nodded toward the bus. "Is six at once a record for Chuck?"

River laughed. "No, but his telling them to respect you certainly is. You should be honored." He was right: Chuck was being very nice to me lately, telling me band secrets and trying to welcome me back. I *was* honored.

Thirty-Five

After the second show in Los Angeles on Thursday, the band made a quick run to Las Vegas for a gig on Friday night. Vegas understood celebrity and knew how to host performers—we parked in an underground facility reserved exclusively for touring entertainers. Down there, we were safe from the sun, the heat, and the fans. Who needed fresh air?

Buck and I took an afternoon jaunt to a few casinos. I wore a white dress with a bateau neck and long flowing sleeves. Buck complimented me by wearing his favorite color: black. Black slacks, a black shirt, and a thin black tie. The two of us got plenty of attention.

Buck was once again comfortable with the fans, and both of us ended up talking to quite a few of them. I was pleased to see that his L.A. phobia was indeed only for that city.

At one casino, we watched a house band play some tunes on a small stage, then we went to a lounge near the gaming floor to have a drink. Buck offered a toast to the contest that had brought us together. I toasted Jo, who had spotted the quirkiness of my beer-spray photo and forced me to submit it. Without that, I would never have met this awesome musician. No doubt, we had many unusual things to toast.

We were about to order another drink when a male Fiery Boys fan spotted us. He seemed drunk as he wobbled toward our table. "Hey, hey! It's Buck and the contest girl.

Can I have your autograph?" He looked around for something to sign and finally grabbed a matchbook from the table.

Buck smiled at the man. "Sure. What's your name?"

"I'm Harry." While Buck signed the matchbook, Harry eyed me with what looked like distaste. "You marrying this one?"

Buck sighed and handed the matchbook back. "Not likely." It stung a little to hear him say that, but he was right, of course. We were just having fun for two weeks, nothing more.

At least Buck enjoyed our time together. He sank into his chair, leaned toward me, and took my hand. I settled against him, relaxing as much as anyone could in a noisy casino. We waited for Harry to get the message and leave us alone.

Unfortunately, like so many fans that I'd encountered, Harry missed the message completely. "How about I join you for a drink?" Buck and I shared a look of disappointment. Had we done something to make this man think he'd been invited, or did he plan on joining us from the start? Pushy fans came in all genders.

Buck dissuaded the man with a gentle rebuff. "Sorry, Harry, but we'd like to be alone now. Enjoy your autograph."

The rebuff was apparently too subtle. Harry shrugged and sat down at our table. I felt Buck's hand tense on mine, and he sat up straight. Another difficult fan.

Harry scooted his chair next to Buck and handed his phone to me. "Hey, honey. Be a doll and take some pictures." Honey? Doll? Was this guy a roaring twenties mobster?

Buck was a little on edge, but since he managed to keep from getting angry, I decided to do my part, too. I reached to take Harry's phone, figuring he'd leave once I snapped a picture for him. Easy. By this point, I was used to abusive fans who treated me like trash. All part of the package deal.

But Buck was far less sanguine about the situation. Before I could take the phone, he snapped it from Harry's grasp and handed it back. "Sorry, Harry. We're done now. Please leave us alone." Buck spoke calmly, but I could hear a deeper register in his voice with a threatening edge. A thin cloud of anger now hovered above him.

Harry noticed none of this. "Oh come on. She's just a rebound after your divorce." Buck opened his mouth to speak, but nothing came out for a few seconds. Harry was right, so what could Buck possibly say?

The tirade continued from our annoying fan. "You can't seriously want to spend time with this cheap. . . this worthless. . ." He waved his hand toward me, struggling to find an appropriate put-down. Finally he snorted and finished his thought. "She doesn't give a good goddamn about you! She'll ruin the band just like that crazy woman you married."

Wow, that was rough—Harry was a classic hater. But he must have hit a raw nerve, because Buck shot to his feet, fists clenched and nostrils flaring like a bull about to charge. He was surprisingly angry.

Buck had weathered insults easily back in San Jose. But Harry was spewing hatred at Inferna's level, which was clearly too much. He spoke with controlled rage. "Get up, you little shit."

Harry might have been a shit, but he wasn't little. In fact, he was about the same size as Buck. He stood up unsteadily, giving us a leering grin once he was on his feet. Buck didn't seem at all put off by Harry's size. I could tell he was ready to demolish the man, whatever the cost. So to keep this from turning ugly, I also got to my feet in a show of support.

"So?" Harry curled one side of his mouth. "I'm up. Now what?"

Buck kept his voice under control, allowing only a light rumble of fury into his words. "You insulted Annalisa. Apologize and get out."

Harry snorted. "It's not me. Everyone is saying it. Check the web sometime, why don't you? Jeez. Touchy."

"I'll give you touchy." Buck leaned close, intentionally getting into Harry's space. His soft words carried a subdued menace. "Apologize. Now!"

The first punch caught Buck by surprise. Harry connected to the stomach, and Buck let out a grunt. But when the second swing came, Buck was ready and stepped out of the way.

Harry flashed a smile of victory—round one was his. He raised his fists, readying himself for Buck's reply. But Buck didn't retaliate—I could tell he was weighing his options. The press would like nothing better than to get pictures of a famous rocker pummeling a fan—Buck didn't need that sort of publicity.

But I could do whatever I wanted—my reputation was already toast. And Harry wasn't expecting anything from me at all. So I decided to make use of my kickboxing skills. Before Harry could start up again, I swiveled around and landed a neat roundhouse kick, right to his gut.

I'd never had a chance to really use that kick outside of class, so I'd always done it lightly. But today I really gave it to him, swinging my body hard to power the kick. Face it, I was annoyed, so I put enough force behind it to cover his insults and his punch, as well as Inferna's hate, and all of the lies I wished I could kick off of the Internet. It felt good.

Harry doubled over but stayed standing on unsteady feet, looking up at me with obvious surprise. Buck was also surprised, and his eyes flared briefly. Then, with a light smile, he swung an upper cut punch to Harry's jaw. That straightened him up again, and he wobbled for a second before groaning and collapsing into his chair, all curled up. He wouldn't be bothering us anymore.

Security closed in on us, waiting for further trouble, but Buck just nodded at Harry's sprawled-out body. "He needs his rest. We're leaving." He grabbed the signed matchbook, and we escaped from the casino.

Sitting in the back of a cab, we watched the bright Vegas lights roll by. Buck wrapped his arm around me. "Where did you learn to fight like that?"

"I've been taking kickboxing classes for years. Never had a chance to really use it, though." I turned to face him. "Where did *you* learn to fight? Those were some pretty nice moves on your part." The guy was a musician—I didn't expect him to be so tough.

Buck started to laugh. "I also did kickboxing for a while. Danielle was into it, so we took classes together. Never got good at kicks, but I learned to use my fists." He pulled me into a tight hug. "We make a good team. From now on, you kick 'em and I'll punch 'em." He grinned broadly.

I definitely liked the idea of being a team with Buck. "Can we take on the haters? I'd give anything to pound them into dust, especially Inferna." Too bad the world didn't work that way. We hugged and kissed as the cab rolled on.

Harry had taught me something tonight. No, I didn't learn that some of the fans were jerks—I already knew that. What I learned was that those jerks really believed that I'd ruin the Fiery Boys. And the haters weren't just a narrow clique of Inferna followers; they were everywhere. We rode back to the busses without saying anything more.

Vegas was Inferna's hometown, so naturally she was at the show that night. I stayed farther back in the wings and did my best to ignore her screams when I came out to play on "Fiery Life." When I danced with Chuck for one of the verses, Inferna's harpies threw plastic knives onto the stage. I'm sure they wished they could have thrown real ones.

The show ended, and Chuck entertained some number of women that I couldn't be bothered to count. I was content to notice that Inferna wasn't among them. We waited elsewhere until they'd vacated the bus.

Tonight was our turn in the bedroom, and I was no longer afraid to go there. Still, we had to start slowly and get reacquainted. We had to change the sheets, both real and proverbial. After the annoying interaction in the casino and another dose of Inferna's venom at the show, I wasn't instantly in the mood.

Buck understood, so we snuggled for a while. He played guitar for me and sang another of his haunting love songs. I sat behind him so I could lean on his shoulder, wrap my arms around his waist, and kiss his neck. I felt his arms flexing as he played the song, a rhythmic beat to his musculature that made me warm inside.

Buck finished his song, and we were about to curl up together when I noticed a new addition to the bedroom. An Inferna doll. That's right, a plush toy dressed like the notorious fan girl, mostly naked with little patches of red sewn on in strategic places. Leave it to her to give Chuck a personalized gift.

Buck noticed it, too, and laughed. "You gotta love the tour bus."

I got off the bed to examine the doll up close. Someone had put a lot of effort into making it look like Inferna. "She must have left this when she stormed the bus last night."

"Yeah, I bet Chuck likes it."

But I didn't care if Chuck liked it. I did not want this evil Tiki doll in the bedroom, watching Buck and me. "Can I throw it out?"

"Toss it in the groupie box." That made sense. I stuffed the doll deep under a pile of panties. Then I pulled out a little skirt that Buck had appreciated earlier, ready to use it to clear away thoughts of casino fights and evil dolls.

Buck got up and took the skirt away from me. "Forget that. Come back to bed."

His offer was exactly what I needed. What both of us needed. Our kisses started off lightly, but they soon grew much more intense. Buck was getting good at playing my body, learning my most erogenous areas, and bringing me to a climax as many times as he could. I did my best to make sure his peaks were just the way he liked them, too. I must have been doing something right, because he howled his approval every time.

Thirty-Six

Notes from the Road: How the Fiery Boys got Picked

by *Annalisa Ricci*

Today I'm going to delve into the back story of each of the Fiery Boys and tell you how they got to be in the band.

Let's start with Chuck. As some of you may know, Chuck lost his father at an early age. His mother remarried, and his new stepfather was less than welcoming. So to escape his home life, Chuck spent more and more time at school. He joined every after-school activity as a way to stay out longer, but his favorite activity was theater.

Before long, Chuck was acting, singing, and dancing in every school production—he really loved to perform. Soon he had a reputation outside of his school which got noticed by the Fiery Boys recruiters. And after they auditioned him, they knew they'd found their lead singer. He really is the perfect front man, with plenty of looks and talent. Someday, I expect to see him in a movie, but for now, he's all Fiery Boy.

Next, let's talk about Gabe. He comes from a wealthy neighborhood near Detroit, where he still has his home. As a child, he excelled in math and loved to play piano. When he became a teenager, his math interest turned into a love of computers, and his piano interest turned into a love of guitars. Gabe played in local bands all through middle school, with the dream of being in a successful band.

When the Fiery Boys were being formed, Gabe had an advantage. His father was a lawyer for a Motown label, and he knew the people who were putting the band together. So Gabe's feelings were very conflicted when his dad convinced the recruiter to give his son an audition. This isn't to say that Gabe shouldn't have been in the band, only that he was in the right place at the right time. I understand that—my contest-winning status was also a stroke of luck.

Still, it took Gabe a few years to get over the sense that he shouldn't have been picked. I think it helped when he realized that he was just as skillful a musician as the others. He really is. Even Alejandro, who jammed with the Fiery Boys when they were in Seattle, had a great session with Gabe, and the two of them did an incredible guitar duo during an extended version of "Sizzling Love." Alejandro even asked to buy Gabe's first guitar so he could add it to his collection. Gabe was honored by the request, but he didn't want to give up the original instrument that had launched his fame, so he declined the offer.

River is another natural musician. He has loved to drum since he was a little boy. Starting at age nine, he competed in tribal drumming contests. At age fifteen, he shaved his head for a competition so he'd look like a fierce warrior. When he won the contest, it caught the attention of a talent scout who was forming the Fiery Boys. And when the scout found out that River could also do rock-and-roll drumming, the man was sold. The audition was a mere formality.

River was very happy to be part of the Fiery Boys. But his family was less impressed. His father was actually upset that his son had abandoned tribal drumming for—as he put it—insignificant pop bunk. River still laughs when he tells that story, because his father completely changed his tune when he realized how well pop bunk pays.

Of course, the shaved head became his defining look, and they asked him to keep it that way. But for the past eight years, with the band dormant, River has been able to let his hair grow. Unfortunately for him, he had to shave it again for this tour. I'm sure he'll grow it back as soon as he can.

Finally, here is Buck's story. Buck comes from Atlanta, where he grew up surrounded by music. Most of you have heard of the famous rocker, Wyatt Morris from the seventies acid-rock band, Momo Plate. That band was as popular to my parents' generation as the Fiery Boys were to mine. Well, Wyatt Morris is Buck's father, something that most true Fiery Boys fans already know.

This makes Buck second-generation rock-and-roll royalty. But he never wanted to be a famous rocker like his dad. When he first auditioned for the band, he thought it was going to be a local group, just something that would play around Atlanta. But as soon as he got to the audition, he knew it was different. They were talking about making CDs and videos, even going on tour. He nearly walked out right then, because Buck knows all about what the media can do to a popular musician, and he doesn't like it.

But the recruiters loved him and they worked on both him and Danielle, trying to convince him to join the band. In the end, he agreed. But he never imagined how popular the band would get. He still doesn't like it very much, and he had to be talked into joining this reunion tour. Personally, I'm glad he did.

So now you know how the Fiery Boys came to be. I'll have more insider info next time.

Ciao. Love to you all.

- Annalisa.

Thirty-Seven

The tour ripped across the southwest, playing Phoenix on Saturday and Albuquerque on Sunday. The days went by too quickly, filled with these four men and their incredible shows. I felt closer to Buck every day, from the way he played his guitar, to the way he played my body; from the way he treated me with respect, and never let a fan insult me, to the way we enjoyed being together every second of the day.

Much to my delight, Inferna didn't attend any of the shows after Las Vegas. I wondered if she'd stayed home and given up following us. The more rational part of me doubted that very much.

When the Albuquerque show ended and everyone had had a chance to shower or get their sweat licked off, Jason stomped angrily onto the bus. "You!" He pointed at me with a shaking hand. "How could you give Inferna pictures from the bus? Her website is a fucking horror show!"

He had to be kidding if he thought I'd give anything to that woman. "You're wrong, Jason. I stay as far from Inferna as I can. We don't play nicely together." I wanted to punctuate that last line with a laugh, but Jason seemed so angry that I decided not to. Still, I smiled at my little joke to indicate the magnitude of the understatement I had made.

"I swear, Annalisa. . ." He gritted his teeth. "I don't care how much the boys like you. I'm going to throw your ass off the bus for this." He nodded to Gabe. "Go on, bring up Inferna's site."

What was Jason's problem? Throwing me off the bus for something on Inferna's site seemed ludicrous. Besides, Jason was the one who wanted me back on tour. What an ass.

I studied him as he faced the big television screen. He seemed eager to show everyone the latest slander. At one point, he glanced around the living room but wouldn't make eye contact with me. Then he turned back to the screen and waited for the evil site to load.

Why did Jason hate me so much? I knew it began with his dislike of the contest. He didn't want a groupie riding on the bus, and after seeing some of the groupies out there, I couldn't blame him. But he knew me better by now, so he should have known I'd never do anything to hurt the Fiery Boys.

Inferna's site loaded on the huge living room screen. The tagline was different now. Instead of hatred toward me, it now claimed to be "The site for fans who once loved the Fiery Boys but now hate them for letting us down." The introductory paragraph explained that Inferna had a new mission, which she headlined in big bold type: Fuck the Fiery Boys. She went on and on about this, claiming that she'd soon expose them for the fuckers they are. She dropped f-bombs as if she was competing with a boatload of sailors. No wonder Jason was upset.

Gabe muttered, "Wow," and continued to scroll down the page. The boys were clearly nervous, but I have to admit that I was slightly relieved by this turn of events. Inferna usually targeted me, but now it was the boys she hated. Finally, her website wasn't devoted to Annalisa Ricci.

Wait, scratch that. As more of her page scrolled into view, I realized that my sense of relief was premature. The first thing that appeared after her Fuck-the-Fiery-Boys manifesto was a picture of me, up close and fish-eyed like a fun-house mirror. My nose was bigger than ever, and my eyes seemed beady as I stared at the camera. The shot was taken in the tour bus bedroom—behind me, Buck was lounging on the bed.

My first thought was that this was a selfie. But I hadn't taken a picture of myself back there. I would never do something like that. And what a crappy picture, too!

What was it with all the crappy pictures of me? I started my whole Fiery Boys tour because of an embarrassing shot of myself losing a mouthful of beer. Every picture the paparazzi took of me after that was a candid shot that was far from complimentary. Now this one made me look like a cartoon character. Not that I expected a beauty shot from Inferna, but still! The Internet was not my friend.

If this hideous picture of me wasn't rude enough, the text that went with it was worse. It claimed to be written by me! In it, "I" explained how I loathed the Fiery Boys so much that I'd joined Inferna's hate-filled campaign. My ghostwritten words went on to explain that I was sending these pictures and videos to my good friend Inferna, so she could post them on her site.

My good friend Inferna? In her dreams.

Gabe scrolled to the next picture, which was labeled, "Fuck the Fiery Boys #1." All of us had to avert our eyes—this shot was definitely not safe for work. It showed Chuck and six other women, including Inferna, all naked and arranged in an erotic chain of flesh on flesh.

Chuck studied the screen with a grin. "Nice picture." He pointed at the caption beneath it. "Says here you took this, Annalisa. I don't remember you being there."

"That's because *I wasn't!*" Wow! Chuck had bedded so many women that he couldn't even remember whether someone he knew well had ever been one of them.

Jason ignored my plea of innocence and snarled at me. "Oh yeah? Then explain this video." He pointed to a thumbnail and directed Gabe to play it.

Chuck was at it with Inferna's vassals. Amid the sounds of panting and sighing, Inferna's voice could be heard. "Here, Annalisa. You hold the camera. I'm going in." After some jiggling of the frame, Inferna appeared and joined the orgy. She stripped off her corset and turned back to the camera. "You can come in, too. Just set the camera down over there." She pointed offscreen, then frowned and raised her voice. "No, don't turn it off, just. . ." But the video ended, leaving the blame squarely on my shoulders.

Talk about a punch to the gut! If you believed Inferna's sham of a video, she and I were good friends who gang-banged Chuck all the time.

Jason propped his fists on his hips and stared at me. "I thought I could trust you. Now you're doing shit like this? I never thought you'd stoop this low." He took a step closer to me. "You're killing the band!"

Chuck dropped his head with a groan. "Now I get it. I remember being surprised when she mentioned your name that night. She was making it up for this video." He turned to Jason. "It's a fake. Annalisa wasn't there, and she's still never had sex with me." Jason stopped and squinted at Chuck, obviously confused to hear the horny rocker continue to deny our sexual liaisons.

Chuck broke into a big smile. "And anyway, aren't sex tapes great publicity? With all these women surrounding me, what fan girl could doubt that she might be next? This won't affect us at all."

"Yeah? Well you haven't read the rest of this yet. She claims that Annalisa will soon be sending her another 'Fuck the Fiery Boys' video, the juiciest ever. She's going to post it on her website after the second Dallas show on Wednesday." He glared at me. "Are you saying that this isn't you, either?"

A chorus of "No" rang out from me and all four Fiery Boys. Jason stepped back and stared at us with a confused furrow in his brow. After a few seconds, his face softened. "All right, fine! Never mind." He turned and left the bus.

All of us were able to relax again, and we stood silently for a few seconds. I might have been spared from Jason's wrath, but the boys were in deeper trouble than ever.

Chuck gave us a curious squint. "I don't get why Inferna's so upset. She doesn't even want me anymore."

We all turned to look at him, and River cocked his head. "She doesn't want you anymore?" None of the boys believed that. But I did, because I knew who Inferna *did* want. Bigger Tim. Was she pulling back from Chuck because she really preferred the big security chief? Or was she playing both of them?

Chuck explained. "Well, for the last month or so, whenever she's been with me, she sends the other girls in but never comes to me herself. She won't even let me grab for her. She just gets her kicks from watching me with other girls. It's like she's mad at me."

River narrowed his eyes. "Did you do something to make her mad?"

"Hey! It's not me! Maybe she's pissed because she lost her job." That caught our attention.

River sat up straight. "When did that happen?"

"Just before the tour, when she dyed her hair bright red. Her boss didn't like it. I think he used it as an excuse to let her go."

It all made sense. I was beginning to understand Inferna. She could handle being the hapless showgirl in a casual relationship with the once-famous lead singer of the Fiery Boys. But when she lost her job at the same time that he got his fame back, it had to hurt. So she ditched Chuck for the security chief. This gave her access and power over the band.

I ventured an explanation. "I know she's jealous of me. But maybe she's also jealous of you, Chuck. And I think Bigger Tim has a thing with her, so watch out."

Chuck rolled his eyes. "Bigger Tim and Inferna? That's ridiculous."

I was about to tell them what I had seen in Los Angeles, but Gabe cut me off. "I'll tell you what I think," he grinned. "I think she's selling shares. My guess is that these women are paying for a piece of you, Chuck." Gabe's hand swept the air as he boomed out the scenario. "*Inferna Tours.* Full access to the Fiery Boys. The basic package gets you to the front of the audience to dance. The deluxe package includes a trip to the tour bus for sex with Chuck." He offered a pat on Chuck's shoulder. "She's got paying customers!"

Chuck slumped his shoulder away from Gabe's patronizing pats. "Whatever," He grumbled. "But I have to say, I don't remember anyone taking a video that night."

Buck agreed. "Yeah, what's up with that picture of us in the bedroom? How did that happen?" He gave me a puzzled look.

Gabe blew out a laugh. "Everything's a camera these days. Maybe she left one behind." He scrolled back to the fish-eyed picture of me. "Looks like it was taken from the dresser."

Suddenly I knew what was going on. Two days ago, when we went to bed in Las Vegas, I noticed the Inferna doll on the dresser. I remembered staring at it closely before shoving it in the groupie-wear box. I'd bet anything that the doll had a camera in it.

The realization must have hit Buck at the same time because we turned to each other and said in unison, "The Inferna doll!"

The others knew what we were talking about. River laughed quietly. "I noticed that thing, too. It showed up when we were in L.A. Haven't seen it lately."

"That's because I couldn't stand it and buried it in your box of abandoned panties."

River grinned. "Perfect place for it."

I went to the bedroom and found the doll, still hidden under the mountain of unmentionables. Squeezing it, I felt hard lumps inside. Just as I expected.

With the doll face down on the table, I poked around in the back. The seam opened easily and I pulled out a small circuit board and a battery. Now we knew how Inferna was getting her videos.

I leaned over and whispered to the doll, "Fuck you, Inferna." Then I disconnected the battery. The appeal of having the last word was too great to resist.

Gabe took the doll and pulled it apart. Nobody was surprised when he found a camera lens, hidden in the crotch. Who knew that the hole down there was more than just a suggestive touch?

I realized that Inferna had hoped to have a 'Fuck the Fiery Boys' video of Buck, but I'd foiled her plans by spotting the doll. She'd certainly be mad about that, which naturally made me happier.

Gabe continued to examine the circuit board for a few seconds, then set the doll down. "It has a radio, too. My guess is that it connected to the bus's network and sent video back to her."

As soon as the words were out of his mouth, Gabe's eyes widened and he gasped, a hand to his mouth. "Oh shit!" He turned to River with a numb stare. "You know what this means, Riv. We have a problem."

River nodded, his face blank. "Yep. The second 'Fuck the Fiery Boys' video will be us. We're going to get outed in Dallas."

He was right. I'd noticed that doll before Buck and I had spent the night in the bedroom, but River and Gabe had been there the night before, in full view of the doll's crotch. What a rude way to be outed.

Thirty-Eight

We had an off night after Albuquerque, which gave us plenty of time to get to Dallas. Too bad nobody was in the mood to enjoy the time off. With the threat of Inferna hanging over the second show, who could relax?

River and Gabe suggested that they out themselves ahead of Inferna's revelation, but Jason wouldn't hear of it. He argued that adding a second media event would only generate more bad press, and that they couldn't be sure what Inferna planned to do. The boys pointed out that they *were* sure what Inferna planned to do, but Jason wouldn't budge. In the end, Gabe prepared a statement from him and River admitting their decade-old love, but he agreed not to post it until they got outed by Inferna.

Chuck called our nemesis to try to stop the impending storm, but she wasn't interested in talking. All she did was scream about me and moan about how I would bring down the band. Really? She was much more of a threat than I was.

Of course, Inferna did have a point: I *was* a problem. For her. Besides being the reviled contest winner, I was the one who spotted her doll camera, hid it, then later destroyed it. Take that, Inferna!

We got to Dallas in the evening and sat on the bus in a near-catatonic state. There were already a few women waiting for us, so Chuck brought them back for a necessary diversion. The rest of us camped by the living room table, ignoring them. You'd be surprised at the sounds you can learn to tune out.

The next day, the band set up and did a sound check as if everything was normal. And the first Dallas show that night *was* normal. The audience couldn't tell that the boys were in less than top form, and they cheered mightily. They even chanted my name, which was nice. But nicest of all was that Inferna didn't come to the show. I knew we wouldn't be so lucky on the second night.

On the day of the second Dallas show, Jason arranged a full schedule for the boys, with interviews and even a photo shoot. By occupying every free moment until the show, he kept them distracted from the promised bombshell. The boys knew what Jason was doing, but they were grateful to keep busy and try to forget Inferna's threat.

As expected, she came to the show with her usual retinue of hangers-on. Jason had instructed the stage crew carefully and everyone knew what to do. After the second encore song, when the boys usually left the stage for the last time, something different happened. The curtains closed.

Separated from the audience, we took out our phones and checked Inferna's website. Sure enough, a new blog post was available. And sadly enough, River and Gabe were outed. This new post, "Fuck the Fiery Boys #2," had a video of them in bed. Thankfully the scene was cut off by the edge of the dresser, so only their upper bodies were visible. Still, it was enough for people to understand what was going on.

With a few taps of his phone, Gabe released the prepared statement. Then he opened his arms to hug his lover. "We're out, River."

River hesitated nervously, then laughed and hugged Gabe. "I've gotten used to acting straight in public." After ten years of secrecy, their paranoia needed time to heal.

We peeked through the curtains to watch the crowd. Every one of them knew this was coming, and they were glued to their phones. Instead of leaving the arena, they stood there staring at the video. The murmuring of the audience, which usually had a post-concert dullness after so much volume, was suddenly quite loud. And Inferna was the center of attention.

River turned away. "Come on, Gabe. Let's get out of here. Maybe rent a car and drive to the next gig in Houston."

Jason stopped them. "No. Go back to the bus first. Now that her video is out, we need to talk about it. And no fans tonight—follow me." We took the long way out, to a far corner of the arena. The door opened right next to a waiting car that took us directly to the bus.

When we got there, Jason and the boys boarded the bus. I was about to follow, but my phone rang. It was Kira. I decided to talk to her outside so the boys could work this out in private.

As I wandered around to the back of the bus, Kira jumped right into the breaking news. "River and Gabe are gay?"

"Yeah. Inferna hid a camera on the tour bus and spied on everyone."

"Did you know about them?"

"Of course I knew." I told her the real story of my famous chocolate and whipped cream adventure.

"So you lied in order to give them macho cred."

"Yeah. Worked for a while. But I think River and Gabe are glad to be out. They were going to do it after the end of the tour, anyway, so Inferna didn't change that much. But posting that video was totally obnoxious. Rock-and-roll fame really sucks."

"Uh, listen Annalisa. The band's doing two shows in Atlanta, right?"

"Yeah, on Saturday and Sunday."

"Well, I'm flying out this weekend to catch those shows. Guess I'll see you there."

"Really? You're flying across the country just to see the Fiery Boys again?"

She giggled. "I got a personal invitation from a special man."

"Wait! Chuck asked you to come to Atlanta? Is Jo coming, too?"

Kira murmured a laugh. "Get this! Jo is not coming with me, but she'll be there."

I laughed. "Good one. I suppose I deserve an answer like that after all the secrets I've kept from you. There's probably a story behind this." There had to be. First Chuck was texting and calling Jo every day, which was very unusual. Now he'd invited Kira to fly out, which was even more unusual. My girlfriends were up to something.

Kira confirmed my suspicion. "Big story on its way, but I can't talk about it yet. Besides, I gotta go, so I'll see you in Atlanta." She hung up.

Atlanta was going to be our last big tour stop. Two shows followed by a free day, so we'd be in town for three nights. A luxury in the world of touring.

Atlanta was also interesting because it was Buck's home town, where he'd been living before the tour and where his family still lived. I'd shown him my city; would he show me his? Introduce me to his friends? I doubted he would take me to meet his family. After all, the tour was over in a week, and the two of us probably would be, too.

I headed toward the bus, but Vaughan stopped me. "They're in there, discussing that video. Give them a few minutes."

I nodded. "Okay. Where are you going?"

"I'm on patrol. Just doing my rounds."

He started to walk, and I followed him. "Mind if I join you?" I'd had a soft spot for Vaughan since the day I won the contest. Shorter than me, he was built like a rock. Or should I say a boulder. But what I liked about him was his smile, an enigmatic mix of amusement and omniscience. I was curious to find out what his job was like.

"Sure. Come along if you like. I just move around and watch things. You'll think it's boring."

I kept by his side. "Do you find it boring?"

"Sometimes. In the dead of night when I'm on patrol, I read. Right now, there's enough going on that I stay focused." I followed Vaughan as he looped around the busses and trucks and everything else inside the fence. He stopped at one point in the shadow of a bus.

I teased him. "On break?"

"Just waiting here for a while. I'll do another loop soon."

"Do you always work outside? You did that when you were guarding me at my home. And you were the one who tailed me when I was out in Los Angeles."

"I like it outside. Lots of security guys prefer to be indoors, but I'd rather be outside. Easier to move about and stay hidden."

"What about during shows? Are you never inside the arenas?"

Vaughan shrugged. "Mostly not. Bigger Tim knows I like it out here so he usually has me working the busses and trucks. Besides, each arena has its own security, so they usually handle the shows." He turned to me. "Speaking of the shows, I hear your girlfriend's coming to Atlanta."

My face must have lit up enough to illuminate even this dark corner, because Vaughan laughed. I'd just found out about Kira's visit minutes ago, so how come Vaughan already knew it? The girl was definitely up to something. "How did you hear that?"

"It's what I do." An insufficient answer, but he didn't seem inclined to elaborate.

At the sound of the bus door opening, Vaughan became much less casual. He nodded to me and walked to a place where he could see everyone.

Jason and Chuck got off the bus, one headed to the arena, the other to the fans waiting by the fence. I climbed up the steps and found Buck at the living room table. "What's happening?" I slid in next to him.

"Nothing much. River and Gabe are out, and Jason doesn't care if we talk about it. I think they're secretly glad Inferna did that—they seem pretty happy. But we're not allowed to comment about Inferna's video." He shrugged, and we stared silently at each other for a few seconds, letting our smiles grow.

We both noticed the sound at the same time, that familiar pattern of women's voices, clattering heels, and Chuck's boasting, all growing louder as they approached the bus. I grinned. "Sounds like three."

Buck shook his head. "Four." He was right. The living room suddenly filled with four women's flashy outfits and bodies. Chuck wove himself around them as they moved toward the bedroom. When the door closed, the familiar sounds of a muted orgy began to play. Buck laughed, then groaned. "I can't wait for this tour to be over."

Part of me agreed—the Fiery Boys suffered all sorts of abuse from their fans, and touring only made it worse. But the other part of me didn't ever want the tour to end. I savored every day with the band, especially with Buck.

Besides, it would all end soon enough. The last concert was just a week away, after which I'd be heading home again. I needed to take this one day at a time, because if I dwelled on the end of the tour, it would only make me sad.

Suddenly, Buck had his arms around me, and he pulled me into a hug. "By the way," he whispered in my ear. "Thank you for noticing that Inferna doll and hiding it. You saved us from being the stars of Fuck the Fiery Boys #3." He kissed me deeply, crushing me to his side. I threw my arms and legs around him so I could take his smoking hot mouth for a ride. We hadn't much time left together, so it was important to savor each moment.

River and Gabe came through the living room during one of our soul-tingling kisses, and we pulled back to talk to them. They were very excited to be going to a gay club for the first time as an out couple. After they left, we heard the sounds of Chuck's orgy wrapping up, so we sat back on the sofa and waited for the women to leave.

I attempted some small talk. "Guess what? I just found out that Kira's flying out to Atlanta this weekend." Given Buck's surprised look, I knew he hadn't heard about this. "Got any favorite places to recommend?"

"Dahlia's is great for brunch." He turned on the sofa bench so his body was facing me. "By the way, I'm going to visit my family while we're in Atlanta. I hope you don't mind."

Of course he was going to visit them. It didn't matter. Kira was coming out, so I could spend time with her while Buck was with his family. "Why should I mind?"

"Because I want you to come with me."

What? This man was full of surprises. Why would he want me to meet his parents when we were about to part ways a few days later? With all discussion of our future officially banned, I was operating under the assumption that our relationship was temporary. But perhaps he had a different idea. I took his hand and held him tight. "I'd be honored to meet your family."

Buck laughed. "You mean you'd be honored to meet my famous fucking father." He sneered the alliteration.

That was awkward. I was trying to express my happiness at the intimacy of meeting his family, but he thought I was only interested in meeting his legendary dad. I couldn't deny an interest in Wyatt Morris. His music was still popular—even I had a few of his songs in my playlists. Of course, in my book, the Fiery Boys were leagues ahead of Momo Plate.

"I'm more honored to know *you*, Buck. You're my famous fucking friend." I grinned.

Buck allowed a tiny smile. "Thanks, I guess. The truth is, I never wanted to be like my dad. But I grew up in a house full of music, so I suppose it was inevitable. I could play a half-dozen instruments before I was ten." He shook his head darkly. "But believe me, Annalisa, I'm nothing like him."

I could tell there were some bad feelings here. "So you want me to help you get through a dreaded family visit?"

Buck shrugged. "That's part of it." He brightened. "Also, my sister lives in Atlanta and said she'd come by. I *do* like to see her. You'll like her, too."

This sounded like a strange family visit. But I was up for it. Why not? I had nothing to lose—this was all going to be over soon. "All right, Buck. When are we visiting your family?"

"Saturday. First day we get there. You should meet Kira on Sunday."

We might not have a life beyond the tour, but this Atlanta stop was going to be intense.

Thirty-Nine

The fallout from River and Gabe wasn't nearly as bad as they feared. The media made a huge deal about it, but the next day a Hollywood starlet got drunk and drove her car into a perfume store window. Suddenly nobody cared that two of the Fiery Boys were in love with each other.

Naturally, this made Inferna even angrier. Her website hammered the so-called news over and over, even publishing a transcript of River and Gabe's bedtime banter. The boys were pretty tame in bed, so the transcript elicited hardly a blip of reaction.

After Dallas, the Fiery Boys played Houston on Thursday and were now in New Orleans, ready to start the weekend with a big July Fourth extravaganza. Between the excitement of the holiday, the impending end of the tour five days from now, and the relief of having survived Inferna's latest wrath, everyone was in pretty good spirits. But I worried about that woman, especially if she had Bigger Tim in her pocket. I knew there'd be more trouble, and I was right.

We were sitting on the bus in a mid-afternoon alcohol and marijuana break when we heard a loud car horn. Chuck got up to look out the door, and I followed behind him.

Outside, a long limousine was parked by our bus. It had somehow managed to get inside the security fence without anyone stopping it. This had to be important.

Some roadies came over to look inside, but the windows were tinted, and the front windshield was covered with a sunshade. I didn't see Vaughan or Bigger Tim or any other security people, but I knew they were out there.

Chuck stepped off the bus so he could peer into the limo. Then he danced a little and preened for his presumed fans, inviting them to come out and play. River, Gabe, Buck, and I watched from the safety of the bus.

All at once, the doors of the limousine flew open and a flash-mob of bikini-clad women slithered out. And I do mean slithered. Chuck tried to catch a few of them, but they moved so fast that they easily avoided him.

The women ran around the limousine in a blur of activity as more of them poured out. One of them held her phone in the air, recording everything. The last to leave the limousine was Inferna, also in a bikini. She shouted something and all of the women turned at once to head toward the bus. I felt a shiver run up my spine when I saw a sea of unfriendly faces suddenly staring at me. We were under a coordinated attack.

The first bikini-clad foot soldier ran up the steps of the bus before we could stop her. Another followed quickly, and the bus began to fill with women. The boys tried to slow their advance, but they kept slithering by, taking over the driver's seat and blocking the exit. The four of us stepped to the back of the living room for safety, but honestly, there was nowhere to hide.

The last to board the bus was Inferna. Once she arrived, the action began in earnest. One woman closed the bus door, locking Chuck out. The rest of them surrounded us. Four women gathered around me, grabbing at me and pushing me toward the back of the bus. Buck tried to rescue me, but he had his own retinue of women surrounding him, keeping us apart. He even got rough with one of them, knocking her to the floor. But they kept swarming us and moving me toward the bedroom, with Buck still out of reach. These women were a carefully-drilled strike team.

River and Gabe also tried to help, but the mob pushed them away from us toward the front of the bus. I heard the bus door open and then close, but I couldn't tell what was going on up there, because I was too busy trying to resist Inferna's army. Unfortunately, I was failing. My heart pounded as the women pushed us on. What did they plan to do? Would I become a rock-and-roll casualty?

When we passed the kitchen, I saw Inferna pick up the biggest knife that we had. Now I knew I was about to be sacrificed, and a cold sweat wrapped itself around my body. Panicked, I fought these women even harder. But my march toward the bedroom continued. Why hadn't Vaughan shown up? Where was security?

The women pushed me through the bedroom door and swept me to the side, still surrounding me. Then Buck entered the room, followed by a larger group of women. With surprising precision, they pushed him past me, farther into the room and onto the bed. At the same time, they pushed me out into the hall and closed the door. I found myself standing alone outside the bedroom, while Buck was locked in there with Inferna and her band of banshees.

So that was her plan. She didn't want to kill me, just use me as bait for Buck. And now she had him. Could this be her next Fuck The Fiery Boys video? I pounded on the locked door, begging her to leave him alone.

The women sounded like a troop of howler monkeys, and Buck's voice was even louder, shouting obscenities and bellowing with anger. Soon, the bus started to shake from their antics. Whatever they were doing in there, I doubted it was sexual.

Suddenly, the door opened and Inferna stepped out, naked, with the knife in her hand. Buck was still occupied back there—I noticed a sea of women climbing over him. And all of them were naked now, even him. But I didn't have time to study the scene in the bedroom because I had a more pressing problem to deal with.

"Time to die, bitch." With her face curled in a nasty leer, Inferna raised the knife and aimed it at me. Not good.

I ran down the hall as fast as I could. Behind me, I heard the whoosh of steel slicing through the air.

I ran into the kitchen for something to use in my defense. I wished I had my pepper spray, but it was in my suitcase, stashed under the bus. Another knife wouldn't help me; Inferna had the biggest one, and all the others were no match for it. So I went for a frying pan, the largest and heaviest hunk of metal I could find. I'd have preferred a crowbar, but the pan would have to do. I raised it up to defend myself.

But Inferna was no longer chasing me. She'd stopped to stare at my cubicle. "Fuck you for sleeping right above Chuck." She started to swing the knife at my curtain, slashing it over and over, shredding it and ripping it away.

Where the hell was Vaughan? I looked toward the living room and noticed for the first time that I was completely alone on the bus. They'd locked everyone else out, even River and Gabe. I had to get to the front and open the door.

Holding the pan with two hands, I started to leave the kitchen. Inferna was in the hall, still preoccupied with my tattered cubicle curtain. I tried to sneak past her, but she turned and swung the knife. I raised the pan just in time as the clang of metal echoed through the bus. She cackled and raised the blade again.

Furious with this insane woman, I decided to fight her. I took a step back into the kitchen to get away from her blade. Then, with the frying pan in one hand, I swung my foot, hoping to knock the knife from her grip. Unfortunately, the kitchen was small, which limited my movement, and the heavy frying pan threw me off. I connected with her arm, but she held onto the knife and swung it at my leg, barely missing me. So much for my kickboxing skills.

And my troubles were just beginning. In my attempt to avoid getting slashed, I had pulled back quickly, which caused me to lose my balance and fall to the floor. Now I was in serious trouble.

Trapped by Inferna, I scooted to the far corner of the kitchen with my pan ready. She stared demoniacally at me while she rotated the knife blade from side, savoring her advantage. I didn't mind her posturing—any time she spent admiring the knife was time she wasn't spending trying to kill me. It gave me a chance to get to my feet. I also grabbed an empty tequila bottle from the box on the floor, just in case.

Inferna gave me a haughty smirk. I expected another attack, but apparently she was done with me for the moment. She turned toward the bedroom and shouted, "Let's go, girls!" The women in the bedroom started to run out. I noticed a few of them limping and some of them had bloody noses. Buck had not been a gentleman—good for him.

Inferna lost interest in me as the women filed out of the bus. I remained ready to do battle with my frying pan and bottle, but I really didn't want to engage her again. Hopefully, she'd leave too.

But Inferna never did what I hoped she would. Without warning, she raised the knife and prepared to lunge at me again. I stepped back with my pan raised in defense, but suddenly she was gone. In a blur of activity, Buck had plowed into her and knocked her away from the entrance to the kitchen. The two of them were now fighting.

"You whore!" Gripping Inferna's wrist, Buck smashed her hand against the wall, trying to make her let go of the knife. Like a rabid animal, she clawed him with her free hand and kicked him hard. It looked like it hurt, but Buck refused to let go.

I dropped my weapons so I could grab Inferna's free hand and pull her away from Buck. With her arms spread out against the wall, she stopped struggling. "Ooh, Buck." She cooed like a little girl. "I like it when you get rough. Is this how you and the contest bitch do it?" She looked at me with beady eyes. "Does he slam you against the wall when he fucks you?"

"Shut up!" Buck roared as he violently rammed her hand into the wall. She cried out and dropped the knife, which Buck quickly grabbed. "Get out!" He released her wrist, so did I, too.

Holding her injured hand carefully, Inferna ran away from us to the front of the bus. The last member of her posse was still there, holding her phone up high to capture everything. Inferna turned back to us with an angry scowl. "The next time I see you, bitch, you die. In fact. . ." She pointed to Buck. "I'm taking all of you down." She turned and ran off the bus. Her assistant gave the camera one final sweep of the scene, then she also left.

The bus was suddenly very quiet. We walked to the door in stunned shock as we watched the limousine peel away. "Buck, are you okay?" I threw my arms around my naked hero to hug him tight. He hugged me back, and we snuggled for a few seconds, both still breathing hard from the shock of this attack. Finally, he pulled away to get cleaned up and dressed.

River, Gabe, and Chuck came back on board, followed by Vaughan. "Are you two all right?" I could tell he felt bad that he hadn't been there to help.

Now dressed, Buck returned to us. "We're fine. But that obnoxious schemer filmed everything while they stripped me and writhed all over. Looks like she's got her last 'Fuck the Fiery Boys' video." I didn't doubt that some artful editing could do wonders to that footage.

Buck snarled at Chuck and pushed him against the wall, as angry as he'd ever been at his bandmate. "If you even think about bringing that bitch back on the bus, I'll kick her ass *and yours.*" Then he turned to Vaughan. "And where were you?"

Vaughan tightened his mouth. "I got assigned to the arena today, so I was inside."

Of course. I knew what had happened—everything made sense. This was Bigger Tim's doing. Inferna was using him for access to the band, so he had cleared the way for her invasion by hiding Vaughan inside the arena.

I ran off the bus to find the oversized security chief. "This is your fault!"

Bigger Tim's eyes flashed for a second before resuming their hooded disguise. "I don't know what you're talking about."

I knew I was right. "You miserable son of a bitch. I just got attacked and Buck nearly got raped. All because you can't keep your hands off of Inferna."

Buck and the other band members showed up at that point. He squinted at the security chief. "You and Inferna?"

"Hey!" Bigger Tim protested, "She said she wanted to bring some friends to the bus. It wasn't such a big deal."

"Not such a big deal!" I shoved him hard. "That woman tried to kill me just now, *with a knife*."

River leaned harder on the big man. "You're fucking her?"

Bigger Tim held up his hands in defense. "We're in love!" Although I believed that Bigger Tim was in love, I doubted seriously that Inferna felt the same way. Poor deluded man.

"You stupid idiot!" Buck shook his head. "She doesn't love you. She's just manipulating you."

"No, I swear. We're in love. Why do you think she doesn't screw Chuck anymore?"

Chuck darkened. "In that case," he shoved the big security man and pushed him back a step. "Take her away and leave us alone. I don't want to see either of you anymore."

Bigger Tim rolled his eyes. "You're not my boss, and nobody can tell Inferna what to do."

Jason had joined us by that point. "So let me get this straight." He poked Bigger Tim in the chest. "You traded access to the Fiery Boys for a few flings in the sack with Inferna?" He didn't wait for an answer. "Well, *I am* your boss, and you're fired."

Bigger Tim dropped his head. "I thought I was helping. She promised all sorts of great publicity for the band. And she's planning to visit Chuck one more time at the end of the tour. Something big that she's been preparing for weeks."

Gabe tilted his head. "Exactly what does she plan to do?"

Bigger Tim shrugged. "Beats me. She never tells me anything about her plans. But I've learned one thing about her. When she decides to do something, nobody can stop her."

Jason stepped closer to his former head of security. "No more threats. Get your stuff and get out." He turned to Vaughan. "Congratulations. You're head of security now. I want four more guards for the D.C. show." Vaughan nodded and walked away.

Buck turned to me. "You mentioned that they were together last week. How did you know?" The four Fiery Boys surrounded me and waited for an explanation. Jason waited too. Even Vaughan's smiling face appeared—the wily security man was also curious.

I stared at them, amazed. "Really? I was the only one who knew they were getting it on? Are you telling me that not a single other person on either bus knew? Because I saw them holding hands and even kissing when we were in Los Angeles. In public! So I figured everyone knew." I shrugged. "I guess I caught their only slip-up."

Jason frowned. "You should have told us."

"I did! Nobody believed me. They thought I was making a joke. I just never imagined he'd put us all in danger. And really, their personal lives were none of my business. Don't forget, I'm the keeper of secrets around here."

"You did fine." Buck hugged me. "You did better than fine. Thank you for figuring this out." He showed his appreciation with a long, slow kiss.

Atlanta

Forty

Late Friday night the tour loaded up and headed to Atlanta, an important stop. We would be there for three days, plenty of time for shows, fun with Kira, and a visit to Buck's family. All good things, I told myself. But I still felt a little melancholy.

The tour was nearly over, which meant that my time with Buck wouldn't last much longer. When we were together, we had a great time. But if anyone asked him whether we were serious, he would darken and say, "No comment." This wasn't a positive sign, but I could handle it. What choice did I have?

I was also understandably upset about Inferna. Getting slapped was bad enough, but she'd actually swung a knife at me yesterday and promised death to us all. No wonder I was feeling a little down.

Buck and I managed to find a few moments of passion last night. Moments that lifted us into a private place of personal joy where nothing else mattered, not Inferna, not the haters, not even the end of the tour and our final separation. His lust was perfect, and we rose to exquisite sexual peaks, then slowly drifted down, drained and sated. We fell asleep wrapped-up in each other's arms and legs, secure for the rest of the night. My world might be chaotic, but when I was with Buck, everything was right.

In the morning, we awoke and snuggled in the bedroom, safe in the cocoon of our bodies. But soon enough, the new day's light brought all of my concerns with it. Buck could tell, and he gave me a squeeze. "My family's not that bad."

"I'm not worried about your family. They can't be any worse than a bus full Inferna and her toadies." We laughed at that.

Buck wrapped me in his arms. "Sucks, doesn't it? Touring is like being an animal in a traveling zoo. But let's power through the last few days and enjoy ourselves. I'm actually excited to be back here and show you around." He was right—Atlanta would be fun. And even if it hurt like hell to say goodbye to this incredible man, I knew it was worth it.

I thought about the one upside of Inferna's hate and gave Buck another laugh. "I'll tell you this much. You think Chuck took everything from you, but now you two are even on one score. Both of you will soon have Fuck-the-Fiery-Boys sex tapes."

Buck allowed an amused grunt, then shook his head. "Chuck's still way ahead of me."

"Come on, Buck! You have to get beyond that. So what if he took your name? People know all about that, and they don't care. Personally, I like 'Buck' better than 'Chuck.' And if he took your pride by calling you dumb, then you simply have to show the world that it's not true. As for those songs with his name on them, people will know someday that you wrote them. And then they'll know you're definitely not dumb. So let it go. Chuck can't do any real damage to you."

Buck darkened. "He already did."

"There's more? What else has he taken?"

We laid there in silence as Buck hissed a few breaths through his teeth. Finally he looked at me and admitted it. "He took my wife."

I saw the pain on his face and I understood. Chuck, that wanton whore, had seduced Danielle. Probably broke up Buck's marriage, destroyed the band, and drove a permanent stake into any friendship the two of them might have had. "Oh God, Buck. I'm so sorry."

"Happened in Los Angeles at some trendy fucking party."

Suddenly, his dislike of that city made sense. "So that's why you hate L.A."

I wanted to soothe him, but I couldn't find the words. What could I say that would give him hope when we were just days away from parting?

We finally got ourselves up, dressed, and caffeinated. As we were about to go out, Kira called. That lifted my spirits. "Hey girl! Are you in town?"

"Yep. Got in late last night."

"Excellent! I'm afraid I'm busy today. Buck and I are going to visit his family soon, but I'll be back later, and we can go to the show. Also, tomorrow is wide open, so we can hang out more then."

"Actually, I've got a lot to do today, too, including a dinner with an electronics distributor. So I'll have to meet you at the show tonight. But I'm free tomorrow, so we'll play then."

"Perfect. See you later."

Buck got a car, and we drove to meet his family. Nervous about my Internet reputation, I'd dressed in jeans and a white short sleeve blouse. Just a simple girl from California.

Buck's family lived an hour south of the city, down a private road in the middle of wide-open farmland. Safe from prying eyes, they had a giant Colonial-revival-style house, complete with tall columns and beautiful brickwork —all the grandeur of an old plantation. Of course, the fancy sports cars parked out front spoiled the illusion. I expected to see a horse and carriage.

But the sports cars still fit in with the home's impressiveness. They spoke of a new kind of majesty, from the world of rock and roll. This was the home of Buck's famous rocker father, Wyatt Morris. Even Buck's stepmother, Octavia, was a musician: a concert violinist. I was more than a little dazzled to be meeting them.

Buck's older sister, Fiona, lived nearby, so she'd arranged to be there and greeted us at the door. "Quick, get inside before anyone notices." She ushered us up to her old room.

When we were settled, she gave me a huge hug. "Annalisa, I love your blog. It's so much more interesting than Inferna's one-track bullshit. But wow. . ." She rolled her eyes at Buck. "Have you seen yourself, Charlie? Her latest video makes you look like a total slut."

He shook his head. "Haven't seen it yet, but we knew it was coming." He told her about Inferna's siege of the bus.

Fiona laughed. "I'll tell you one thing—it's good you're not with Danielle anymore. This would have made her head explode. Annalisa's a pretty good sport to put up with this." Fiona gave him a smirk. "You definitely need to see this video, although maybe Annalisa shouldn't."

I laughed. "Hey, I was there when it happened. I can't wait to see the Hollywood version."

Buck frowned and shook his head. "Yeah, the person who shouldn't be seeing this is my sister. But it's too late now, so go ahead—play it."

She started the video on her phone. "Don't worry, you're not very exposed. But I counted ten women in bed with you. My husband is jealous." She grinned.

The video, "Fuck the Fiery Boys #3," claimed to be the biggest Buck orgy yet, another reputed contribution from Inferna's best friend and partner in crime, me. Inferna had done a skillful job of editing the footage, making Buck appear to be rolling enthusiastically in a sea of primordial heat. Unlike the other two videos she had posted, this one didn't include any actual sex, because there wasn't any. Also, there were very few shots of Buck's face because we knew he wasn't smiling.

The most surprising thing was his voice. In the video, Buck spoke seductively, encouraging the women to do increasingly lewd activities. But the voice wasn't his.

"Fuck! They dubbed me. I never said those things." Fiona and I knew he was right because we were familiar with his voice. But most fans wouldn't be able to tell.

So for the most part, the video accomplished its goal. Inferna had her sex tape. Now she had video of all four Fiery Boys in flagrante. The woman was shameless.

When the video ended, Fiona giggled. "Congratulations, Charlie. Dad will be proud of you. First you joined a band, and now you've seduced a harem."

I was confused. "Your dad will *like* that orgy video?"

"Sure," Fiona explained. "The old fucker did plenty of that in his day."

My mouth fell open. It was one thing for Buck to refer to his father as a fucker, but when Fiona did it, too, I had to wonder. "Do both of you hate your father?"

Fiona started to answer, but Buck cut her off. "No, don't."

"She doesn't know? Come on, Charlie, tell her. She can take it."

Buck got up and started to pace, a worried look on his face. But Fiona was unperturbed. "Fine. *I'll* tell her." She turned to me. "Dad's wandering dick killed mom." Buck groaned, but he didn't stop his sister.

I sat straight in my chair. I knew about Buck's mother, who had been killed in a car crash after being chased by paparazzi. It was a classic Princess Diana ending, and the press had made much of the similarities. But I didn't see how his father factored into it. I waited for more details.

Fiona went on. "Mom always hated Dad's fame. Pretty much the same way Danielle hated Charlie's." She cocked her head at Buck and he shrugged his assent. "But what she really hated was Dad's playing around. He kept bedding groupies. One day it all became too much for her, and she drove off in a rage. The press knew about this and wanted to get her reaction, so they followed. You know the rest."

I understood so much more now. Growing up with a famous father definitely shaped how Buck felt about fame. And I could see how Danielle's affair had affected his feelings about fidelity. But now I saw how these patterns kept repeating in his life. Fame and infidelity were a poison cocktail for Buck.

I got up to take Buck's hand. "That's so sad. But you can't run from your own fame just because of your dad. You are *not* him. You're a good man, and you've lived your life right. Have faith in yourself, Buck. Maybe someday you'll be able to forgive him."

Fiona's eyes widened, then she got up to face her brother. "She's right. I've forgiven him, now it's your turn. He *did* change his ways after Mom died. He married Octavia and actually settled down. And he stopped touring—he actually raised us."

"He tried." Buck huffed his opinion about that.

"He did okay, Charlie. I think you're still mad because your own fame brought up all those issues for you." She squinted at him. "You gotta get out of that band, bro. You've got someone nice here, so settle down, relax."

Seriously? I doubted we'd be settling down and relaxing. More like breaking up and never seeing each other again. It surprised me that Fiona thought we were such a serious couple. But she'd just met me, so her predictions were understandably inaccurate.

I let out a sad laugh. "You may be presuming too much. I don't expect us to make it past the end of this tour."

Buck fidgeted uncomfortably. "Hey, my divorce just came through, you know. Give me a few seconds to regroup before I settle down again." He was right, of course. Settling down was not on the agenda.

Fiona narrowed her eyes and stared at the two of us. "Take all the time you want. Just. Don't. Fuck. It. Up." She poked him in the chest between each word, driving her point home. "Go visit her when the tour's over, you big fool."

Buck groaned. "Enough talk. Let's do this parent thing already." We went downstairs to meet Buck's infamous father.

The first person we met was Buck's stepmother, Octavia. She was easy to find, because she was practicing violin in her music room. Buck followed the sound and led us in. She stood there in a navy floral pattern dress, long and silky with fluttering open sleeves. She was so focused on playing that she didn't even notice us for a while.

When she finally saw us, she stopped playing and ran to give Buck a hug. Thin and lithe, she moved with grace. "Charlie! I heard you're in town for a concert." Then she noticed me and seemed surprised. "You brought someone home." She took my hands. "Hello."

"Hello, Ms. Morris. Nice to meet you. I'm Annalisa Ricci."

"Welcome, Annalisa." She gave me a hug and led us down the hall. Part way down, she pounded on a door and shouted through it. "Wyatt! Charlie's home. Get out here."

The door opened, and there stood Wyatt Morris, the iconic lead guitarist of the acid rock group, Momo Plate. His face was craggy but his smile was the same one I'd seen countless times. I felt charged up by the thrill of meeting this man, but for Buck's sake, I kept it hidden.

Buck and his father hugged rather stiffly. Then Wyatt arched an eyebrow and gave me a so-who-are-you look. I wanted to introduce myself but was so stunned by this rock deity and his piercing stare that I couldn't find my tongue.

Buck's stepmother saved me. "This is Annalisa, Charlie's girlfriend." Wow, *girlfriend*. It sounded so simple when she put it that way. Gone were the modifiers that usually accompanied my name these days. Modifiers like cheating, lying, skank, CWILF, and band-destroying-contest-winner. I almost laughed when I realized how deeply I'd been inhaling those Internet fumes.

Wyatt nodded at me then turned back to Buck—he still hadn't said a word. When he finally opened his mouth, he was brief and to the point. "Enjoying fame?" He curled his lip into a sneer that spoke volumes about his disdain for celebrity.

Buck rolled his eyes. "You know I don't. And get this." He winked at Fiona and me. "Someone faked a sex tape of me with ten women."

His father furrowed his brow. "They had to fake it?" I did laugh at that. Buck was right. The only thing his father was upset about was the fact that Buck hadn't made a real sex tape.

Buck grumbled loudly. "You never had to."

Wyatt nodded curtly. "Made my own."

Octavia frowned at her husband. "That's enough reminiscing from you." Then she turned to Buck. "If you hate touring so much, why did you go back on the road?"

"The other three begged me to do it. I couldn't let River and Gabe down."

Octavia nodded. "Are you still writing music?"

"Yeah. That's the good thing about the tour. I got ten new songs produced."

Buck's sister added, "Using *your* name, this time."

He grinned. "That was part of the deal: nobody takes my songs this time around."

Octavia's eyes danced between Buck and me. "But other than that, I guess nothing good has happened." She gave Buck a sly smile.

Buck looked down at me with his own little smile and wrapped an arm around my shoulder. "Annalisa happened. That's also good."

Good. Yeah, we were good. Personally, I thought we were much better than good, but that's because I was having the time of my life living on the Fiery Boys tour bus with an all-access pass to my favorite rocker. But I understood. Just because he was the best lover I'd ever had, didn't mean that the reverse was true.

Wyatt had had enough chitchat by this point, so he turned to go back into his study, leaving us with a simple, "Bye." That suited Fiona and especially Buck. I could feel a lightness overtake him just from having his father leave.

We talked with Buck's stepmother and sister for another hour, then we left. As soon as we got in the car, Buck let out a long deep breath and sank into the seat, finally relaxed.

Forty-One

We left the Morris family home and got back on the road. After a few miles, Buck started to fidget. He looked like he wanted to say something, and he kept working his mouth, unable to speak. With a final breath, he glanced my way.

"My sister's right, I do want to visit you in San Jose after the tour ends. How would you feel about that?"

I felt ecstatic, almost light-headed. He actually wanted to keep seeing me! I sucked in a breath and smiled. "I'd feel wonderful. How would you feel if I visited you?"

"Wait. You want more?" Buck turned his head to stare at me for a few seconds before turning back to the road. "I thought you were done with me when the tour ended."

I stiffened. "Why would you think that?"

Buck grunted a half-laugh. "Because every time a discussion even touches on our future together, you always say that we're going to break up soon."

"Oh my God, Buck! That's just me trying to defend my heart from the sadness of ending this. We agreed to enjoy our rock-and-roll fling and not think about the future, so I prepared myself for the worst outcome. But believe me, I don't want to say goodbye to you!"

I dropped my head, nervous about what I was about to say. "I've fallen in love with you, Buck. And not just fan love, either. I really do love you. The last thing I want to do is to say goodbye when the tour ends."

He slapped a hand to his forehead. "Okay, I'm stupid. Here I am, wondering how we can keep seeing each other and worrying that you don't want me. And there you are, acting tough about us and talking about breaking up because you're worried that I don't want you."

"Well what do you know," I snickered. "Who would have thought that communication could be a good idea? And here we agreed not to discuss our future because we thought it would ruin things."

He chuckled and pulled the car to the side of the road. "Maybe we should talk."

I gave him a grin. "I think that's what we're doing. So tell me, what do you want to do when the tour ends?"

"I want you, Annalisa. More than I expected. You make the music so much sweeter—we *have* to keep seeing each other." He shook his head and took a deep breath. "I wish I could be more specific, but I'm not sure what to do. I know this is a rebound, so I'm afraid to jump into anything serious or permanent. I'm not about to move to San Jose, and I don't think it would be wise for you to move to Atlanta. But I've *got* to have more. So I think—at least at first—that we should work this as a long-distance relationship and keep seeing each other when we can."

I was stunned. This was so much more than I expected from him. I realized it would be difficult—Buck needed to process his divorce. And long-distance relationships rarely worked. I'd known too many people who broke up after trying to live apart.

But what could I do? Sure, I could move to Atlanta. I could probably even find a job selling cars there. But then what? It would put too much pressure on Buck, and that might be just as bad.

"I guess that makes sense. I understand that we can't suddenly make huge commitments after we've known each other for only two weeks. I also understand that these two weeks on tour are not how life would be for us. We'll have to start over in some sense. So I'm willing to fly to Atlanta to see you. It would certainly be better than never seeing you again."

We threw ourselves into a hug, then kissed each other with a newfound enthusiasm that demanded more. The thrill of being able to keep seeing each other had us both excited, and we needed to get back to the bus. Buck pulled away and got back onto the road, driving as quickly as he could to the arena.

I thought about my life, and realized it had been a spectacular journey. I'd started as a high school military brat with no real home and a bad-boy lover. A lover who'd burned so brightly that his memory still filled my head, all these years later. But now I had a much better lover. A man whose fire was just as hot and had branded me in so many ways. Not just in bed, but with his music, too. Could it last?

When we got back to the bus, Gabe was busy analyzing Buck's orgy video. He'd spotted a number of editing flaws, but he doubted his analysis would convince anyone that it was a fake.

Chuck and River were there too, as well as Jason, all of them trying to figure out how to respond to this latest attack. They were also worried about Inferna's promised end-of-tour stunt. Unfortunately, the best response seemed to be silence. Everything else the band did only served to make things worse.

Then I got an idea—a crazy idea, a scandalous idea. It involved the unprecedented notion of telling the truth. "I have a suggestion that none of you are going to like." They stopped talking and turned to me. "Why don't we co-opt Inferna by posting our own revelations? Real things about the band that we've never admitted before. You know, fight fire with fire. Or should I say, fight fire with Fiery Boys. We can shovel dirt, too."

Gabe finished tapping on his tablet and leaned back. "Such as. . ."

I smiled at him. "Such as the fact that you pimp for Chuck. Little things that you guys have never revealed before. If we give the fans some real truth, maybe they'll stop believing the bull that Inferna is slinging."

Gabe grinned at me. "Are you going to reveal something about yourself, too? Might make your article even more believable."

Why not? Gabe was right. Admitting my own secrets would help me sell this as an honest story, and honesty was something that was hard to find on the web these days.

I spent some time with River, Gabe, and Chuck, trying to figure out which of their dirty little secrets I could publish. Buck wasn't consulted: I already knew what I would write about him. Then I wrote and rewrote my blog entry so it had just the right tone to outdo Inferna's "Fuck the Fiery Boys" videos and win back the fans' trust.

At least I hoped so.

Forty-Two

Notes from the Road: Band Secrets

by *Annalisa Ricci*

Hey, Fiery Boys fans! It's been a wild ride lately, full of lies and half-truths. For example, Inferna (who has hated me since I won the tour contest) now claims to be my friend. I'll tell you one thing for sure: Inferna and I are *not* friends, and I have never sent any pictures or videos to her. Yes, she's making it all up. If you think I'm on her side in attacking the Fiery Boys, think again. The attacks are all hers.

Sometimes the truth is hard to spot. So today, I'm going to do some serious truth-telling to show you that I'm not out to trick anyone. And after weeks on the tour bus, you know I've got the inside dirt. So kick back, because I'm dishing out a full plate of honesty today. Here come some brand new tidbits about every one of the Fiery Boys.

Who should I start with first? How about River and Gabe? Most of you already know a big secret about them, but I have others. So before I get to my secrets, let's discuss that one you've been hearing so much about. Is it true—you ask—that River and Gabe are gay?

That's an easy one to answer: yes. Not only that, but they've been living together for the past ten years. They're one of the closest couples I know, and I couldn't be happier for them. And here's some breaking news for you: they've decided to get married when the tour ends. So get over it already.

You might ask why they stayed in the closet all this time. But if you think about it, that's a foolish question. River and Gabe were just fifteen-year-old high school kids when the band was being formed. They were barely aware of their own sexuality when they got swept into the rock-and-roll machine. As they discovered each other and fell in love, they were forced to keep it quiet. The band's manager wouldn't let them come out, so the secrecy became a habit. Let's face it: we've made great progress in gay rights lately, but our rock gods are still expected to be straight and horny.

So the good news is: River and Gabe are gay, and they're finally able to be out and proud. But that's not a secret. And I promised you secrets, didn't I? So here they come.

I'll start with Gabe, the horny guitarist. You already know that he's not horny for female groupies. And since he's been in a committed relationship for years, he's not horny for male groupies, either. So how come everyone calls him horny?

It started nine years ago, when the band was at the peak of its popularity. Back then, the boys couldn't cross a street without attracting a willing woman to their side. Chuck was more than happy to pick-up whomever he could, but Gabe was less thrilled because he had to constantly make up stories about why he wasn't interested.

One evening, when Chuck had had too much tequila and Gabe had smoked more than his share of marijuana, the two of them were discussing this very issue. Gabe was unhappy about the women who flocked to him, and Chuck was unhappy that he didn't have enough of them. The solution seemed obvious, at least to these drug-addled rockers. Gabe would send the women to Chuck.

The next night, he tried that out, asking a groupie if she'd mind joining others who were with Chuck. He didn't even have to make up excuses for himself—all that mattered was that Chuck was having an orgy, and all were welcome. It worked great.

Everyone was happy with this new arrangement. Chuck got more women, Gabe got fewer, and he didn't have to make up any lies. The paparazzi loved it, too, and took endless photos of Gabe with a different woman each time. These photos spread quickly, and Gabe got labeled the horny band member. But it's simply not true.

And what about River? I've always had a soft spot for this Fiery Boy, and that hasn't changed much—I still get weak when I see him. Just because he'll never feel the same way about me doesn't change a thing, because it's always been a mere fantasy. Gay or not, he's smoking hot, and he still pounds those drums in ways that make my head light.

So here's River's little secret: he doesn't drink. Never did. There's alcoholism in his family, so he's never even wanted a drink. He does have an occasional toke with Gabe, but most of the time he's straight and sober.

Some of you longtime Fiery Boys fans will find this strange, given that River did all those beer ads, years ago, where he flashed two bottles at once. They made him do it, and he hated it. Sorry, beer company. You chose the wrong spokesman.

Now before I move on to reveal secrets about Chuck and Buck, let me pause to tell you a secret about myself. I know what you're thinking: who cares? This blog is about the Fiery Boys, so how dare I pretend to be as important as they are. Well, I'm not, and that's part of my secret.

When the band first announced the contest to pick someone to spend a week on the tour bus, all of us thought we were entering a beauty competition. But here's the dirty little secret: it wasn't about looks. In fact, the band manager rejected anyone who seemed too pretty or too sexy, which was most of them. The twisted logic behind this reasoning was that any contest winner with too much going on would alienate the fans. Whereas a winner who seemed ordinary and not too sexy would be seen by most people as merely lucky. Of the fifteen thousand pictures that got submitted, only one thousand survived this cut. Yes, it's true, I was pretty far down the list.

So if you looked at me and thought that you should have been chosen because you're way prettier than I am, then you were right. And that's why you didn't get chosen. But if you looked at me and thought that you were just as pretty and only lost the contest because of stiff competition, then you were also right.

How do I feel about the fact that I won the contest because I'm ordinary? It wasn't the high point of my stay with the band, I can tell you that! But somehow, this ugly duckling has managed to have a great time with the Fiery Boys. So perhaps there's a lesson here about beauty.

Okay, enough about me. Let's talk about Chuck. What can I say about him that would be a secret? That he has sex with multiple women at once? That's no secret. We've been hearing about that for years. And those of you who've visited the tour bus can state with certainty that it's true.

So what's Chuck's secret? He *needs* that many women to get off. That's right: put Chuck in a room with one woman, no matter how good looking, and he's just not interested. This Fiery Boy is built for rock and roll. So if any of you are planning a romp in the sack with Chuck, bring a friend.

Now finally, a secret about Buck. I'm going to reveal something that I shouldn't, a secret that could get me thrown off the tour bus. But I don't care anymore, and the tour's nearly over. So here it goes.

If you look through the first three Fiery Boys albums that they released years ago, and count the number of songs that each of them wrote, you'll find that Chuck, Gabe, and Buck each wrote eight songs. River wrote two of them. Well guess what? That's a lie. Sure, River did write those two songs, and two of the songs attributed to Gabe are actually his. But Chuck never wrote a single Fiery Boys song. The remaining 22 songs were all written by Buck, including my favorite, 'Fiery Life.' And their latest album shows more of his talent, with 10 out of 12 songs written by him.

Once again, this is proof that Buck is not dumb. He's actually one of the most intelligent men I know. And he writes some of the most beautiful music I've ever heard.

So that's the truth about the Fiery Boys. Next time Inferna starts up with her random statements of dubious veracity, please remember that the Internet is full of lies, and once they're out there, they multiply and spread like a bad rash. Don't be fooled.

Ciao. Love to you all.

- Annalisa.

Forty-Three

Kira had been in Atlanta all day on Saturday, but we didn't get to see each other until an hour before the show that night. The boys were already in the arena, getting ready for the show, so we sat alone in the bus and quickly caught up on the last two weeks. Then we went backstage to watch the final preparations.

Kira wore a tan miniskirt with a tight fire-red tank top. She got plenty of attention back stage, but it took a while before the one she really wanted to notice her, did. Chuck wrapped his arms around her and pulled her into a hug. "I'm glad you made it. Can't wait till later." He gave her one last squeeze then went back to prepare for the show, leaving Kira dazed and grinning.

I was impressed. Chuck seemed very happy to see her. He'd invited her to come to Atlanta, had gotten her a backstage pass, and even arranged for Vaughan to watch her. I had never seen him go to so much effort for a single woman. Perhaps she *should* have won the contest.

"Chuck seems quite taken with you."

"I know! I can't believe it, myself." She hopped up and down.

"You said Jo would be here. Is she coming after the show?"

Kira gave me an enigmatic smile. "Jo's still in San Jose." My face must have shown my confusion because Kira burst into laughter. "I'll tell you more about it tomorrow."

"Crazy!" I wanted more details but the show was starting and Kira wasn't divulging anything. Talk could wait.

The Fiery Boys burned hot at the first Atlanta show, and we had a great time dancing in the wings. When it was over, Chuck made good on his earlier promise. He grabbed Kira's hand on his way off the stage, then he lead her away. I wanted to follow them and check for more women, but Buck had other plans.

He led me down a few hallways that took us to a garage. Sitting there was a car with its doors wide open. "Hop in. I've seen your place. Now you're going to see mine."

We got in the car and drove up a ramp to the exit. Vaughan was waiting outside the garage door, ready to help us escape by clearing a path through the post-concert crowd.

"Very nice, Buck. A total rock-star maneuver, having a getaway car." He didn't often flex his fame muscles, but I could tell he was enjoying this.

"It's my turn to host you, so I thought I'd show some class." He wagged his eyebrows in mock sophistication.

Buck's condo was in a high-rise section of downtown, up on the twentieth floor, with views of the busy city. He had a small recording studio as well as a serious collection of guitars and other instruments. We hid out at his place and spent the night enjoying rare privacy. Buck even played a few songs for me, switching instruments after each one. He was a capable musician who played bass in the band, was skilled at lead guitar, and even claimed to be able to play drums, although not as well as River.

He could also sing pretty well, and we sang together as he played. At one point, after I'd belted out a hard-rocking Fiery Boys song and my throat was raw, he gave me some singing tips. He showed me how to sing from my chest, not my head, so that I could get the energy out without hurting my throat. He even claimed that I was a pretty good singer, which, coming from him, was quite a compliment.

That night, when we made love, Buck seemed happier than I'd ever seen him. I was delighted to see him that way, and even more delighted to know that this wouldn't be the last time I'd be here with him. We slept peacefully.

On Sunday we had a full day to ourselves since the band was playing a second show that night. Kira was still in town and we needed more time to talk, so I arranged to meet her for brunch at Dahlia's, Buck's favorite.

She was sitting outside at a sidewalk table when I arrived, wearing pink shorts, a black-and-white striped men's shirt, and little red booties. I raised the red quotient by wearing a red tailored jacket over my jeans and black top. We got quite a bit of attention.

I would have preferred to sit inside, away from curious eyes, but Kira was already there so I didn't make a fuss. Instead, I positioned myself with my back to the street, my hair up under a baseball cap, and my sunglasses on. I was getting good at this.

We ordered mimosas and started to scan the menu. I was still confused about what was up with her and Chuck, so I took the direct approach. "So did you and Chuck have group sex with other women last night?"

"No," she smiled. "Just the two of us."

Chuck alone in bed with Kira? I may have been impressed with how he was acting toward her before, but now I was blown off the map. Who was this person who claimed to be the lead singer of the Fiery Boys?

Kira must have noticed the shock on my face, because she started to laugh. "Yes, I read your blog where you said he couldn't make it with just one woman at a time. But last night, he proved you wrong."

Oh great! Not only was I the plain-looking contest winner, the girl so ordinary that Fiery Boys fans everywhere looked at my picture when they needed to feel better about themselves, but I was also so homely that Chuck couldn't find a drop of enthusiasm for me. He probably made up that excuse about needing multiple women so it wouldn't hurt my feelings. But all he needed was a hottie like Kira.

I groaned. "I feel like a fool."

"No, you were right about him having sexual problems. You just didn't figure out his particular kink."

I arched an eyebrow. "Okay, what would that be?"

Kira smirked. "He's a voyeur. He gets off on watching. Jo noticed it when the two of us were with him in San Jose. Apparently she sees lots of sexually challenged men in her practice, so she's good at spotting these things. She noticed that he was always with one of us on the bed while he watched the other one put on a show for him."

"I put on a show for him. Didn't work."

"Of course not. He couldn't pretend he was sneaking peeks when it was just you. That's why he needs multiple women."

"But last night. . ." I awaited an explanation.

Kira gave me a crooked grin. "It was Jo's idea. She made a racy voyeur video. It's set outside, looking in through a window, watching a woman get undressed. It starts with little glimpses and then builds up more and more as the video goes on. And get this! Jo filmed herself. She claims she did it so he could have a virtual three-way with familiar people. Personally, I think she did it to give him a little something to remember her by."

I laughed at that. "So he watched Jo on video while he had sex with you?"

"Yep. It worked great. The video has a powerful finish, and after that, Chuck's ready for anything. Even sex with just me. We watched it a few times last night and got it on every time."

Well that explained the mystery of Jo, how she was here and yet wasn't. She was here on video only. And her virtual presence was all Chuck needed to make it with Kira. I squinted at her. "Are you okay with this?"

"Sure, Annalisa. I'm not marrying the boy, just enjoying a toss in the sack. If he were some jerk I'd met in a bar, it *would* be kind of creepy. But this is Chuck Van Dorn, for crying out loud, the lead singer of the Fiery Boys! For sex with Chuck, I'll play a porno."

Oh, Chuck! The only Fiery Boy who hadn't grown up and was still really a boy. I was impressed that Jo had figured him out. And I was happy that Kira got to have another romp without having any unrealistic expectations.

As the waitress brought our brunch, Kira's phone rang. She frowned, answered it, and spoke quietly. When she hung up, she dropped her head. "Damn! I've got to go. I forgot about an appointment I made yesterday with another stupid electronics store." She got up and put some money on the table. "I'm sorry, Annalisa, but this is important. I'll see you later." She finished her mimosa, took one bite of her lunch, and left.

Forty-Four

I was pretty annoyed to be alone on a sidewalk in Atlanta, exposed to the world while I ate my brunch. I looked around to see if anyone was watching me and caught a few broken stares, people turning away too late to avoid being caught. If I didn't want to see pictures of food being stuffed in my mouth, I had to get out of there.

I was about to signal the waitress to ask if I could move inside when there was a commotion at the edge of the dining area. Everyone had turned to look down the sidewalk at someone more important than me. Or so I thought.

But the excitement had *everything* to do with me—the person heading my way was Buck's ex-wife, Danielle. She'd been friendly enough when I'd met her in Denver, but now that Buck and I were lovers, I worried she'd be much less happy. Being on tour was certainly complicated.

I should have considered the possibility that I might run into her in Atlanta. After all, she and Buck used to live here together. So it was no surprise that his favorite brunch place was also hers. Now, the fact that she was heading my way would make people think we were meeting intentionally. I was stuck.

As Danielle got closer, people shouted questions at her. "Are you going to see the show tonight?"

"How do you feel about the Fiery Boys now that you're not married to Buck?"

"Are you meeting Annalisa at Dahlia's?"

Danielle had been ignoring the questions until that one. She stopped and frowned, obviously confused. Then she spotted me and gave me a wry grin.

She walked to my table and stood there in her brown shorts, black halter top, and open floral print shirt. "Hi, Annalisa." She pointed at Kira's barely touched meal. "Are you here with someone?"

I shook my head with a little laugh. "Something came up and my girlfriend had to run. Hungry?"

Danielle looked at Kira's brunch. "Not for that, but let's pretend. Come on." She picked up Kira's plate and walked quickly into the restaurant. I grabbed my plate and followed. It looked like we were having a Buck's women get-together, after all.

She led me through the restaurant to a small unoccupied room that was probably used for private parties. As we sat down, Danielle offered me a friendly smile. "I see you found a good restaurant, I bet Charlie mentioned it." I laughed and nodded.

Then her smile turned into a mischievous grin. "And speaking of Charlie, I should also congratulate you on finding a good man." She wiggled around in her seat, wagging her eyebrows in case I didn't get the innuendo. She wrapped up with a statement that we both knew to be true. "Charlie's hot." Charlie, Buck. Whoever he was, I couldn't disagree.

But I wasn't ready to pursue this line of discussion with Danielle. Was she going to tell me his favorite positions? Would we compare orgasms? Talk about Buck's unusual size? I simply didn't feel that close to her.

I nodded once to acknowledge our shared interest, and she took that as a sign to continue the investigation. "So, are you two serious?"

We were more serious today than we'd been yesterday, but the future was still unknown. I didn't want to pretend that it was anything more, so I gave her the only truth I knew. "We're just dating. It's too soon to call it serious. When the tour ends, I'll be back in San Jose, so we'll have to fly back and forth to see each other. Hard to say how that will go."

She nodded. "Having a good time?"

There was no point trying to hide it. "The best!" A smile took over my face.

She smiled back. "Then good luck. I'll tell you one thing about Charlie. He likes stability—it's something I couldn't give him."

I decided I liked this woman. The last time we met, she'd signed the divorce papers early, giving Buck complete freedom to be with me. Now here she was, continuing to encourage the relationship. I figured this would be a good time to find out more about Buck.

"What was he like back in high school, before the band?"

Her expression seemed wistful. "He was even cuter than he is now. But he was just as big and strong." She took a long breath. "Oh God, I fell so hard for him. He was hot, played music, and even had a famous musician dad. I've always had a soft spot for musicians, but I never considered what a pain it would be for him to be so well-known." She scrunched her mouth.

Danielle might not be hungry, but I was, especially after the active nights I'd been spending with Buck. I took a few bites then dove in for more dirt.

"But you married him two years after all the fame started, so you must have known what you were getting into."

"We were just high school kids, pretending to be all grown up and in love. And I was an idiot, not very mature." She flopped back in her chair.

"You can't blame yourself."

"Oh, I don't know." She took a sip of water. "We were still riding that high when we decided to get married. Then once the engagement was public, nothing could stop it. And a few months after that, the band started to lose popularity, so everyone blamed me. Jason knew it wasn't my fault, but he didn't want me to be seen with the boys anymore. It was easier all around if I wasn't in every photo, so I started spending more time alone, away from the band." She closed her mouth and bit down on her lips, seemingly holding her tongue while thinking about what to say next.

After a few seconds, she blew out her breath and went on. "Truthfully, I was angry and alone too much of the time. I went to a party one night and met a famous musician. He knew who I was, of course, and we started to talk. He was gorgeous and horny, and he fell for me easily. I really couldn't resist him, either. We both knew it was a one-night stand—musicians are like that. But it fed my wounded ego, so I started to do it more often." She laughed. "Rockers are such easy lays." She drifted off, lost in thoughts about her former life as a rock-and-roll seductress.

I tried to be sympathetic. "The scandal rags loved to make stuff up about you."

She shook her head. "No. They didn't make up much. I was a mess. In fact, the rags missed half the stuff I did. You have no idea."

"So what did they miss, if I may ask?"

Danielle stared at me for a few seconds, probably considering what to say. Finally, she nodded and went on. "I had sex with Chuck." She looked away, shielding herself from my potentially violent response.

But I already knew this. Buck had told me about the many things Chuck had stolen from him, one of them being her. I could imagine the entire scene as Chuck pursued Danielle with his endless sexual badgering, not letting up until she caved, in a moment of weakness. I could also see him having sex with her and some other groupies without a moment's thought for Buck's feelings. What a shame.

I felt like I understood Danielle's plight, so I offered some support. "Well, I can't deny that Chuck's appealing—even I was tempted. But it was wrong of him to seduce you."

Danielle laughed sadly. "He didn't seduce me, Annalisa. In fact, he tried to stop me. He knew how bad it would be for the two of us to do anything."

I must have had a shocked look on my face because she started to giggle. "Surprised? Chuck's a good man. Somewhat depraved, but so were all the other rockers I was chasing. He tried to push me away, so I lied to him. I told him that Charlie and I were on the outs, and that it was all right."

I stammered. "When did this happen?"

"Years ago."

"So maybe you *did* break up the band."

"No, the band was already terminally ill by then. It died of natural causes."

"But after the band was dead, couldn't you and Buck get back together?"

She sighed. "You don't get it. I didn't want to. Chuck and I weren't a one-night stand. I actually fell for him the first time we met, back when the band was starting. But I was with Charlie then so I didn't do anything about it."

She toyed with the food on her plate then went on. "It was a few years before I found out that he had his eye on me, too. And by then, things sucked so badly with the band that I went for it. Chuck and I have been occasional lovers for years now. I made sure that my work schedule took me to Vegas as much as possible, and we hook up every time. Things between us only stopped when the divorce got going and my infidelity became an issue."

"What about Chuck's multi-woman thing?" I doubted that Danielle knew about his voyeurism. His sexual issues were only now being understood.

"Yeah, I had to work around that. The first few times we did it, I was just part of his orgies, along for the ride. But even that was a major thrill, so I couldn't resist. Sometimes I brought a friend with me. It's easy to find women who want a piece of Chuck, you know. I even shared him with that Vegas showgirl a few times. One way or another, we made it work. I always made the other women promise to keep my secret. They were usually trying to keep secrets, too, so it wasn't a problem."

"What was Inferna like back then?" The woman was a complete wreck now and was still plotting something for the last show. Had she always been like that?

"Inferna!" Danielle giggled. "Love that name. Much better than Gypsy or even Mary. Too bad she's a mess. I see lots of hate coming from her, which wasn't there before. But other than that, I don't think she's changed much. Just a showgirl with big breasts and bigger insecurities." She thought for a few seconds with pursed lips. "She never liked sharing me with Chuck. He tended to favor me over her, and I know she resented it."

Danielle stopped and stared at me. "I don't know why I'm telling you this. I guess I thought you needed to know the truth."

"Thank you. I appreciate it." More than ever, I was the keeper of the secrets.

I wondered if Buck knew the extent of Chuck and Danielle's affair. I doubted that he knew Chuck had tried to stop it, and that the affair was mostly Danielle's fault. Buck seemed to hate Chuck more than he hated Danielle, but perhaps he had it wrong.

"Buck thinks Chuck stole you away. Does he know you were the instigator?"

Danielle tightened her mouth. "Maybe?"

"Or maybe not?"

She deflated into her chair. "Or maybe not."

"Now that you two are divorced, don't you think it's time he found out the truth?"

"What good would that do?"

"It would heal his relationship with Chuck. The last time we met, you told me that you and Buck needed to move on with your lives. This will help him do that." I took out my phone. "Call him, Danielle. Tell him."

"Please don't make me do that."

"If you don't tell him, I will. You're tough—you can do this. Tell him I forced you."

"Can I text him instead?"

"No. You should really do it in person, but a phone call will have to do." I set my phone down in front of her with Buck's number on the screen. "Please?"

She stared at it for a few seconds. Then she picked it up and tapped the call button.

Forty-Five

After the Atlanta shows, we had a free day before moving on, so we stayed in town until the afternoon, lazily packing up. The roadies were so numb to the routine that they could do it in their sleep, and most of them seemed to be doing just that. Of course, the true numbing factor was the impending end of the tour. Only two shows remained: Charlotte tomorrow and then Washington, DC on Wednesday. And everyone knew Inferna was going to make trouble at that final show.

We'd spent Sunday night at Buck's place again where I basked in his good cheer and his delight at being home. As I'd hoped, Danielle's revelation gave him quite a boost. He even had a heart-to-heart with Chuck about it.

Buck showed his appreciation by devoting himself to my pleasure many times that night, taking his own pleasure only after I insisted. I had to demand that he take me, ravish me, and find release in my body. And did he ever! That man had a monster lurking inside.

We returned to the bus Monday afternoon, ready for another city. The plan was to head out in the early evening for a quick hop to Charlotte, leaving plenty of time to setup for the show on Tuesday.

As soon as we approached the bus, Vaughan pulled me aside and handed me a bulging envelope. "This is from Kira." I'd seen her at the show again last night, but she'd flown home early this morning. What had she left for me?

I stared at the bodyguard as I took the envelope. As usual, his smiling face revealed nothing. "When did you see Kira?"

"Pretty much all weekend." His grin made it seem that he'd done more than just protect her.

I still didn't understand why Kira needed a bodyguard. None of the other groupies who came on the bus were in any danger—why was she special? Chuck must really think highly of her if he'd asked Vaughan to keep her safe. I thanked Vaughan and followed Buck onto the bus to examine the envelope.

River, Gabe, and Chuck were sitting by the living room table. I stopped there and tore open the envelope, which contained a letter and a flash drive. As I read the letter, my mouth fell farther and farther open until all I could do was scream and jump like a child.

Buck stepped closer to me, and the others looked up. Everyone wanted to hear the news. They were going to love this.

I waved the letter in the air. "It's from Kira. It turns out she did quite a few things here this weekend, not just spend time with you, Chuck." In her letter, she even mentioned that their relationship had cooled slightly, and that they had only been to bed on the first night. She also admitted that she had never visited any electronics stores when she was here.

Chuck was obviously aware of Kira's true activities because he sat there with a knowing smirk. But the other Fiery Boys stared at me and waited for more information. I took a few seconds to laugh before explaining. "She joined Inferna's groupies."

Buck curled his lip. "So she was playing us?"

"No! That's the thing. She was playing Inferna. She did it to infiltrate the clique. And guess what she found?" I waved the flash drive in the air and smiled at Buck. "It's the original video from the attack on you. Kira says it will totally embarrass Inferna and show everyone what a pathetic manipulator she is."

"Let's take a look." Gabe took the drive and plugged it in. Soon we were watching a very different video than the one Inferna had posted. The original soundtrack was there, with Buck angrily shouting the whole time. And from the moment they had stripped his clothes away, it was evident that he was anything but interested as he fought off Inferna's naked army.

Instead of an erotic porno of Buck and a bevy of groupies, this video came across as more of a joke. Each time he swore and pushed a groupie away, all of us laughed harder. At the end of the video, we applauded Buck's performance. Of course, occasional snippets were easily identifiable as the footage Inferna had used, but in the broader context, it told a completely different story.

I smiled at Gabe. "I think we need to use this to expose Inferna. Let's present this along with her version, then I'll write it up for the website." I glanced at Buck to see if he minded, but he was smiling and nodding his head.

Gabe grinned. "Good idea. I'm on it."

While Gabe worked, I called Kira. She had just landed back home. "Stellar work getting that video, girl!"

"Thanks. Let me tell you, Inferna's crazy."

"I know! Were you scared?"

"Not at first. I went to a local meet-up of her devotees in San Jose. These women were mostly Fiery Boys fans, with a lot of hate for you thrown into the mix. I had to grit my teeth through that part.

"But when I came to Atlanta, the Inferna group was so stoked to be getting a visit from their leader that they'd become a little nuts themselves. They were practicing anti-Fiery Boys chants and making big shows of destroying CDs."

"Wow. Intense."

"Believe me, it got even worse when Inferna finally showed up. She's scary, and I worried that they'd figure out who I was. Good thing Vaughan was hiding nearby—that made me feel safe. He's. . . well he's kind of awesome." She giggled.

"What's that supposed to mean?"

"Oh, nothing." Her voice had a casual tone, which made me even more suspicious. "Anyway, Inferna. . . wow. She was really pissed when she found out that the contest wasn't about beauty. Now she hates the Fiery Boys more than ever. And she's drinking pretty heavily, too."

"That's so sad. How did you find that video?"

"One of the women there had been in the bedroom with Buck, and she showed us the original. I stole a copy from her computer when she wasn't looking." Kira paused. "And another thing. Inferna's got the strangest collection of electronic gadgets I've ever seen."

"I guess that makes sense since she made that camera doll to spy on the boys."

"No, Annalisa. I sell electronics, and I'm familiar with the latest surveillance toys. The stuff she's got with her is not simply spy gear. It's strange. I spotted some little metal things with wires coming out of them. Thought they were capacitors at first—we sell them at the store. But when I examined them, they didn't have the usual markings, so I have no idea what they were. I wanted to take a picture of them but Inferna spotted me and I had to move away."

"I owe you big time for this."

"Thanks. Oh wait, get this. . ."

"There's more?"

Kira laughed. "There's always more with Inferna. She's working on a new corset for herself."

That worried me. "But the tour ends in two days. And the boys banned her, so when is she going to wear it?" Deep down, I knew the answer to that question: she'd wear it when she arrived for her final promised appearance. Something was brewing, and Inferna was definitely planning to make trouble.

"Who knows? I was telling Jo about this. She thinks Inferna's having some sort of breakdown. So if you do something with that video I sent you, watch yourself. Inferna is diabolical."

"Yeah, I got that part."

Forty-Six

Notes from the Road: The Biggest Hater

by *Annalisa Ricci*

In case you didn't know, the Internet is full of haters. Some of them are reading this right now, eager to find something they can use to rip me a new one. It's not hard; I understand that. The press writes about me constantly, and I've been posting insider dirt about the Fiery Boys and even myself. I'm an easy target. Good thing I have a sense of humor.

But today, I'm leaving my sense of humor at home so I can turn things around. Today, *I'll* be the one doing the hating. I'm after you, Inferna.

For those of you who don't know, her latest trick was to sneak a camera into the tour bus bedroom, hidden inside a plush Inferna doll that even had a miniature corset and boots. I nearly burst out laughing when I saw it. Did you see that picture she posted of me staring into the lens? That's me, looking at the doll and marveling at the extent of this woman's narcissism.

And what happened after that picture was taken? I'll tell you. I stuffed the doll into a box so I wouldn't have to look at it when I made love to Buck. Yes, we made love. I'm willing to admit that, but I'm not willing to let you watch.

Then, because Inferna couldn't get a real video of Buck having sex, she had to make one up. That's right. The video she posted of him in a room full of naked women is a fake. It looks like they're going at it like rabbits, but he's actually fighting them off because she ambushed him.

I can prove it because I have the original video right here, thanks to one of Inferna's devotees who couldn't stand the lies anymore. Play it and see for yourself what really happened, how Inferna's video was made with careful editing and even dubbing of Buck's voice.

Pathetic.

But enough hate. It's making me sick.

So to all you fans of my blog, I'm sorry for not having any fun tidbits about the Fiery Boys today. Maybe next time.

Ciao. Love to you all.

- Annalisa.

P.S. Inferna, if you're still reading this, I have a personal request, just between you and me. . .

Can you dial it back, please? Your hate is thoroughly annoying. The first time we met, you slapped me across the face and screamed at me to die. Not a good first impression. When you stormed the bus to attack Buck and make that video, you actually tried to kill me with a knife. If Buck hadn't stopped you, I might be dead now.

Perhaps I shouldn't be so surprised, given that your website has been demanding my death for months. Still, you've got some serious anger issues.

Look, I get it. You're jealous because I won the tour contest. You thought you would be the one they picked, but as we both know, they didn't pick you because you're too damn hot. The way you look screams sex clear across the arena. Yet another area in which you should dial it back.

And now you've turned your hatred on the Fiery Boys, too. You're sore because you got banned from the bus. Banned for making that video raid on Buck. And banned for outing River and Gabe. They're glad to finally be out, by the way, but it was supposed to be their choice, not yours.

So, to paraphrase your own website, which calls for my death on a daily basis, maybe it's finally time for *you* to die. Or at least give me a damn break.

The Last Show

Forty-Seven

Our arrival in Washington DC was filled with tension. Inferna was going to do something tonight, and everyone was worried. None of the boys spoke about it, perhaps hoping that silence would solve the problem. But I could see them moving a bit more carefully and looking around more often. Even I was nervous. I kept thinking about her hatred, her pure venom, and the gleam in her eye when she swung that knife at me.

Another layer of tension that hung in the air was the end of the tour. After tonight, we'd all go our separate ways, making my relationship with Buck more complicated. We had grown so close these past few weeks, and I was too much in love with him. Yet I still wasn't convinced we'd survive as a couple once we weren't living together.

Jason gathered the boys around the living room table. Standing there in front of them, I could tell he enjoyed playing the boss one last time. He waited until everyone was seated, even me.

"This is the end of the tour, boys. We all go home tomorrow. The question is: what next? Are you going to make more music together or not?"

"Not." Buck raised his hand. River and Gabe raised their hands, too.

Chuck kept his hand down, but he didn't seem to mind being outvoted. He sank down in his chair with a tight-mouthed look of concentration. "So we're done," he grumbled. "I'm not surprised. Should I tell the fans tonight?"

Jason shrugged. "I don't care. And by the way. . ." He gave everyone a nasty smile. "I happen to agree. As your manager, I also say, 'Not.'"

Gabe belted out a laugh. "Well, thank you. But why? You were the one who wanted us to get back together."

"Because your tour was not a success. You started with a good buzz, but it didn't last. Annalisa actually helped the band around mid-tour, and her 'Notes from the Road' blog got quite a following. But Inferna ruined it with her 'Fuck the Fiery Boys' videos. That cost you the most. Here at the end of the tour, when you should be peaking, you're nowhere. Your videos aren't getting enough views, and your songs aren't selling. So in summary. . ." He took a step toward us. "The four of you are pains in my ass, and you're losing money. After tonight, I quit." With a smile, Jason bowed to them and left the bus.

"Best news yet." As expected, Buck seemed completely happy. "The band is finally broken up. And Annalisa didn't do it, Inferna did." He winked at me.

I doubted it would be that easy. No matter how the band died, my presence at the funeral would be reason enough for the haters. But it was nice to have someone else to blame.

The boys did their best to unwind for the next hour, and were ready to rock when Jason called for the last sound check. My blue-eyed lover and I walked to the arena with our arms around each other, strolling slowly like we were taking a Sunday walk in the park. We got there last, and he stopped me for a searing kiss, long and hard and wrapped in a unbelievably-fine body. Then he grinned and walked off to the stage, leaving me tingling all over.

The sound check went on longer than usual because the boys were having fun playing. Nothing mattered anymore, because this time they were playing for the pure enjoyment of it. They rehearsed every song in the show, lingering over them and savoring each note.

That night, the show was the most energetic I'd seen. For my last time on stage, I wore a black miniskirt and a white T-shirt with huge red lips on it. Let the haters say what they wanted; I didn't care anymore.

Gabe took an extended guitar solo during many of the songs and River howled as he thrashed the drums. Chuck was all over the place, from writhing on the floor to crowd surfing. Even Buck was more animated than usual, joining Chuck at his microphone and singing harmony for a few songs. The fans shouted their delight.

We stumbled out of the stage door, high on this peak moment. Life was good, and all of us were feeling it. I should have known it couldn't last.

Vaughan ran up to us with his arms outstretched, stopping us. "I have to warn you, Inferna's waiting at the bus. She had a backstage pass and disguised herself. One of the new guards didn't recognize her and let her in." Everyone knew where she got that pass: from Bigger Tim.

Buck scowled. "She's on the bus?"

Vaughan shook his head. "Bus is locked. She's waiting just outside it."

Chuck seemed mildly interested. "Alone?"

"Just her and a bottle of vodka. She's pretty far gone."

Buck grit his teeth. "Get rid of her."

"Yeah, about that." Vaughan frowned. "It's going to be hard because she chained herself to the bus. That woman's a wildcat, and I don't want to have to mess with her if I can avoid it. I could call the cops, but I know how Jason likes to take care of these things without too much publicity. So I figured it would be easier to let you boys deal."

All of us stopped at that news, shooting concerned looks at each other. Chuck let out a nervous laugh. "Well then, let's see what she's up to." He squinted at Vaughan. "And get Jason."

We left the stadium and went into the parking lot. Inferna stood by the bus and waved at us when we came out. "Hi, boys!" She spoke with treacly sweetness, completely out of character.

I barely recognized her—she looked so sedate. Her hair wasn't red anymore, it was black. And she wasn't wearing boots, just white sneakers. All she had on was a long white T-shirt that doubled as a skirt and went all the way to her knees. Printed on the shirt was the name of a Fiery Boys song: "Painted Flames." The only thing out of place was the chain around her ankle that ran under the bus.

Then I realized that something else was out of place. That song title—it had to have been picked for a reason. I froze and gripped Buck's arm, making him stop, too.

"Painted Flames" was a song about a super fast car with flames painted on it, much like our tour bus. Well, minus the super fast part. But the thing about the song that worried me was the ending, where the car crashes and burns, turning painted flames into real ones. Inferna had something in mind—she was too much of a Fiery Boys fan to choose that song title lightly.

Jason arrived and furrowed his brow. "What the fuck is she doing now?" Nobody knew the answer to that, so the boys huddled together.

Annoyed to have lost her status as the center of attention, Inferna dropped the sweetness act and snarled at us. "Hey, you fuckers!" She took a swig from the vodka bottle. "Get your asses over here." Ah, yes. Now I recognized her.

Chuck and Jason obeyed and started to head her way. I held back, having no interest in being near her for any number of reasons. Buck stayed with me, as did River and Gabe.

I had to admit my fears. "Buck, I don't like what's on her T-shirt."

He nodded. "Think she's going to set the bus on fire?"

"I don't put anything past her. She did try to stab me, so I think I'm allowed to worry a little."

Buck ran ahead a few steps and grabbed Chuck, stopping him with a warning. "Don't get any closer." He and Jason stopped, about thirty feet away from the bus. River, Gabe, and I were farther back, so Buck slowly rejoined us.

Chuck called out. "Hey, Inferna. What's up?" I heard the tension in his voice and could tell he was forcing himself to act casual.

Inferna slipped back into the sweetness act. "Waiting for you, Chuck." She crooked her finger with a smile.

Chuck smiled back and stayed where he was. "No corset tonight?"

"Oh yeah! Check it out." She pulled the T-shirt from her head and revealed her new corset, red with vertical black lines. Obviously the one that Kira had mentioned. This corset didn't attempt to cover her above or below, so she stood there, essentially naked.

All of the men, even River and Gabe, stared at her amazing Vegas body. But not me. I was staring at her corset —it worried me.

The vertical black lines looked too straight and too fat, as if something long and inflexible were stuffed in there. In my mind, where extreme thoughts continued to take root, I wondered if those were sticks of dynamite. How else could she make that song title real? And what about that wire I saw coming out of the bottom of her corset? Inferna's outfit was very wrong.

I latched onto Buck's arm. "We have to get away, Buck. You'll probably think I'm being paranoid, but I think she's going to blow up the bus."

River and Gabe laughed. Buck smiled at me. "Don't be silly."

"I'll be as silly as I like!" I called out to the others. "Chuck, Jason! Get back here." I started to move farther back, as did Buck, River, and Gabe. Jason also joined us, but Chuck stood where he was, entranced by the fan girl from hell. I tried once more to get through to him. "Chuck, get back here. She's insane."

But Chuck wouldn't budge. "Yeah! Insanely sexy." The man was such a tool. He turned back to Inferna and continued to chat her up. "Nice corset! Looking foxy tonight."

Inferna slurred, "You've got no idea. Come over here and give me a hug."

That was too sinister for me. My fantasy head was spinning all sorts of scenarios. "Don't, Chuck. She's going to do something bad. I think she's wearing a bomb." We kept backing away.

Chuck looked confused. He squinted at Inferna. "Is that right, babe?" Obviously, he couldn't see her corset because of all the other parts it wasn't covering, so he had to ask.

"It's just a hot little corset, Chuck. Get your ass over here and you can check it out."

Chuck turned back to us with a smile. "See? She just wants some fun. I say why not."

The poor man really was ruled by his libido. "She's chained to the bus, Chuck. Don't you think that's weird? She wants to kill you."

Inferna snarled, "Lying bitch! I would never hurt him." She tried on the sweetness act again. "Come on, baby. Just give me a hug. After that, I promise I'll go away and never bother you again."

My spine tingled as all of us started to retreat in earnest. Soon we were much farther away than Chuck was, all the way back to the doors of the arena. But he was still blissfully ignorant of any danger.

I continued my tug of war. "Don't do it, Chuck."

She laughed. "Do it, Chuck! One last fuck before the tour ends. For old time's sake." She reached behind her and pulled out a small box that had more wire coming from it. "I have a special surprise for you." Now I knew she was going to blow herself up.

Buck finally understood when he saw the box. "Shit, you're right." He shouted at Chuck. "Get your butt back here, idiot! She's wrapped in dynamite." He also hissed at Vaughan. "Get everyone else the hell out of here." Too many groupies were gathered at the security fence.

Chuck folded his arms and turned back to look at all of us, now quite far away. "What's the matter with you people? That's just the corset design." He turned back to Inferna and took a step closer.

I screamed at him to stop. "Please, Chuck. Come back here. She's going to blow you up."

Inferna cackled and tipped the vodka bottle straight up, draining it down her throat. "*Fuck you*, Annalisa." She hurled the empty bottle at us.

Her aim was miserable. The bottle soared over Chuck's head and smashed on the ground, far from where we were standing. Inferna giggled. "Come on, Chuck. Last chance for a piece of me." She slithered at him and squeezed her breasts. Chuck fell under her spell and took another step.

"No!" I practically cried out, "Don't get closer. Please, I'm begging you!"

Chuck turned toward me again and huffed. "Jeez, Annalisa. You're such a nag." He narrowed his eyes and stared at us. River, Gabe, Buck, and even Jason were beckoning him over, too. He scrunched his mouth and stomped his foot. "Okay, okay!" He started to head our way.

With nobody left under her spell, Inferna threw her head back and keened loudly, wailing into the darkness.

Then she made good on her fiery name and lit up the night sky.

The explosion was the loudest thing I'd ever heard, and I'd been to plenty of hard rock concerts. Buck and I held tight as the hot air blew over us. But Chuck got hit much harder, and I saw him fall down.

The bus's painted flames had become real.

Forty-Eight

We camped by Chuck's hospital bed for days, staring at his unconscious and heavily bandaged body. The most fiery of the Fiery Boys had been so badly burned that it took two operations to get him back together. The doctors still didn't know the full extent of the damage.

We visited in teams, Buck and me, then River and Gabe. He laid there as we talked to him and to each other, wondering how much of what we said was getting through. I read news articles to him about his favorite subject: himself. Stories like "Fiery Front Man," "Suicide Fan Scorches Singer," and "Exploding Groupie." He was universally praised and honored for surviving the deadly fan girl. I told him that when he got better, he'd be even more famous. I tried to be upbeat and energetic.

But inside, I was wracked with guilt over Chuck's condition. I chastised myself for not being more convincing, for not getting him to turn away sooner, for each step closer to her that I let him get. If he'd been a few feet farther away, he'd be awake by now, on his way to recovery. Or if I'd forced him to pay attention to the corset instead of her naked body, Chuck might have believed me and run away. It was all my fault that he was laying in this hospital. So even though he was unconscious, I told him that he better wake up or else I'd never forgive myself.

And while I was wallowing in guilt, I also felt a bad about Inferna. Not too bad, of course, but still. . . My latest blog entry had lashed into her and even suggested that she should die. Then she did. So although my comments about her never approached the level of vitriol that hers did about me, I still wondered if I was somehow responsible for her suicide.

Buck tried to make me feel better by pointing out that I was not to blame for either of these people. If I'd never said anything to Chuck, if I hadn't tried to stop him at all, he'd be dead now. So I'd actually helped. And as far as Inferna went, we knew she was planning her final exit gesture long before I wrote my hateful blog entry, so her death wasn't my fault, either. But I still felt bad about this whole mess.

On the third day, while Buck and I were there, Chuck woke with a groan. "Shit, I'm thirsty." I'd never heard such beautiful words.

We gave him a drink and rang for the nurse, ecstatic to have him back. Buck patted him lightly. "Hey dude. You survived. Which is more than we can say for Inferna."

Chuck looked up with sad eyes. "Why?"

"She was crazy, man. The police found more dynamite at her place in Vegas."

Chuck groaned again. "Mary wasn't crazy. She was my friend. And lover." He tried to move in the bed and winced. "She should have told me what was going on."

"No, it was too late for that. Her roommate told the cops she'd never met any woman who drank so much. Truth is, Inferna was an alcoholic on a bender. Total clusterfuck."

A nurse came in and fussed for a while, so Buck and I went outside to wait. I leaned against him, and we relaxed into each other. Chuck was going to be okay, which relieved me. But I still felt awful about it. "What a terrible way to end the tour."

I could feel the vibration in Buck's chest as he sighed. "Yeah. He's pretty messed up."

"All because of a deranged fan. It's scary, Buck. This band stuff is nuts."

"See? That's why I was worried. I didn't want to expose you to this insanity."

I laughed. "You didn't want to expose me to this insanity? I've endured nothing but, since the day Chuck read my name on TV. Good thing I like adventure, because this tour's been full of it. But now that it's over, I'm looking forward to something normal." I took a breath. "I need to get back home. We should figure out a schedule for visiting each other."

Buck gave me a powerful hug, and we stood there for a minute, luxuriating in each other's arms. Then he pulled away and took my hand. "Come with me."

He led me down to a small garden that the hospital provided for patients and visitors. We sat on a bench and he pulled me into a long, raw kiss. Soon we were fiercely entwined in each other.

Buck pulled back and took a breath. "How are you feeling about us?"

"Oh, Buck, how can you even ask? You're the most amazing man I've ever met. Smart, talented, strong, and sexy. You've even helped me get my life together. You always make me happy." I paused for a second, then went to the heart of the matter. "I'm totally in love with you, so I feel great about us. But what about you?"

Buck nodded. "I'm still positive, although I've had a change of heart recently. Three days ago, I was planning on telling you that I was falling in love with you. I was going to suggest that we get together every other weekend, take long vacations, stuff like that. I didn't know how we'd make it work, but I needed to try."

Love! He was falling in love. A jolt of pure lightning lit up my body, making me feel like I was glowing.

"This is awkward." He took a long breath. "Um, like I said, I've changed my mind. I'm not falling in love with you anymore."

I frowned, but he shot me a grin. "That's because I'm already there. After these last few days, I'm deeply and desperately in love with you." I sucked in a breath and stared at him.

Buck pulled me closer. "You're the finest woman I know, Annalisa. Capable and considerate, beautiful and sexy, even clever and perceptive. You see things that others don't, like Bigger Tim with Inferna, that camera doll, and especially the dynamite. You repaired my relationship with Chuck, and I bet you could help me deal with my father. Look at how you even repaired the bus!" We both laughed.

He cupped my face with his hands and his smile deepened. "You're the woman whose picture I picked for the contest, the prettiest and most interesting of all. And God, do I ever crave your body!" He gave me a brief but hot kiss.

"Then, being here in this hospital and talking with you for the past few days has made me realize what a good friend you are. Loyal to Chuck and a comfort to all of us. You had a unique opportunity to get to know the four of us as people, and you did it so well that now we all count you as a good friend. I even feel better about my fame when I'm with you. In this totally phony world we live in, that's truly incredible."

He took a long breath, his eyes never leaving mine. "I know it's fast. We're still getting to know each other, and I've just gotten divorced. But I don't care anymore—I'm too much in love with you. If we broke up because we lived thousands of miles apart and only saw each other every other week, I'd kick myself for the rest of my life. So I've changed my mind about the long-distance romance." He paused, then spoke more slowly. "I want to be with you, Annalisa. Now, and forever."

The air blew out of my lungs so hard that there wasn't anything left for words. All that came out was a thin squeak. "Forever?"

Buck nodded. "Marry me, Annalisa."

I think my heart stopped right there and the universe slammed to a halt. A silence descended on me, and all I could see or hear was Buck, smiling warmly at me, our breaths heavy with anticipation. After what felt like an eon had passed, I finally blurted out, "Oh my God."

Buck's smile grew wide as he handed me a small box. I took it with shaking hands and flipped open the lid. The stone was a sparkling emerald surrounded by diamonds in an intricate white gold setting. Undoubtedly the most beautiful ring I'd ever seen.

"It's amazing, Buck." He took the ring and slipped it on my finger.

I stared at my hand for a few seconds, then I threw my arms around him and we hugged. I couldn't have been more euphoric.

Buck laughed. "Is that a 'yes'?"

"Yes! This is definitely me, saying 'yes.'"

"We still have to work out where we're going to live. I kind of like San Jose." Such a wonderful man, he was even willing to move for me.

But I was willing to move for him, too. "Well I kind of like Atlanta." Hey, I'd move to Tierra del Fuego to spend my life with Buck. We stared at each other with broad smiles, then we dove into another kiss, fierce and joyous, each of us relieved to have found so much happiness.

Buck stood up and pulled me to my feet. "Come on, let's tell Chuck. He needs some good news."

As we approached his room, River and Gabe were waiting in the hall. Gabe shook his head. "Can't go in now. They're checking him out." The four of us retired to a waiting area.

As soon as we sat down, River pointed to my hand. "Do you two have something to tell us?"

Buck slapped him on the back. "You're not the only ones getting married. We are, too." We got big hugs from both of them.

Gabe narrowed his eyes. "Where are you going to live?"

I shrugged. "We haven't worked that one out yet. Atlanta, San Jose, or somewhere in between."

Buck grinned. "I say somewhere in between. Let's start over in a whole new place."

River and Gabe smiled at each other, then nodded. Gabe turned back to us. "I have a suggestion."

Epilogue

I came down to the kitchen in my plaid flannel pajamas to find River already there, sipping coffee and staring out the window at the snowy fields. This was my first winter here, and I loved the broad white landscapes, especially when I got to watch them from a warm house.

River's hair had grown back since the tour, so I couldn't resist the urge to run my fingers through it. He chuckled and gave me a hug, then he went over to the coffee maker and poured a cup for me. We sat there for a few minutes watching water drip from icicles as they melted in the morning sunlight. A deer wandered by.

Gabe came in with a sack of sticky buns from a local bakery. He grabbed a plate from the cupboard and set them out. The three of us dug in.

Halfway through his breakfast, Gabe looked at me. "When are you going to wake sleepy head?"

Buck stepped into the kitchen, rubbing his eyes. "Sleepy head is awake." He sat down, took a pastry with one hand, and wrapped his other around my waist to pull me into a good-morning hug. We exchanged a tender but promising kiss.

I truly had it all. Three months after the tour ended in flames, Buck and I got married. We combined our nuptials with River and Gabe's, and had a secret double wedding ceremony up on Mount Hamilton near San Jose. Quickly assembled and carefully guarded, the event managed to evade the paparazzi. Then the four of us retreated to our new home.

River and Gabe's farm outside of Minneapolis had one hundred acres of land, two huge houses, and an assortment of barns, stables, and sheds. Gabe had suggested that they subdivide the property and sell half of it to Buck and me, including one of the houses.

The idea instantly appealed to all of us. Buck and I loved River and Gabe, so we weren't worried about living out in the country with them. After all, we'd lived together on the tour bus, which was much tighter quarters than these two big homes, a quarter mile away from each other.

Also, the location made sense. It was halfway between San Jose and Atlanta. And it was near Minneapolis, the city where Buck first stood up for me and taught the audience to chant my name. It seemed like the perfect place to live.

Interestingly, although we had much more room on our Minnesota farm than we did on the tour bus, the isolation of the countryside brought us closer together than we expected. With the nearest village a few miles down the road and Minneapolis an hour away, it was often just the four of us. River and Gabe came over for breakfast every day and we usually cooked dinner together. It wasn't uncommon for me to come down in the morning to find one or both of them already sitting in my kitchen.

But we weren't bored out there—we kept very busy. Gabe started playing with digital music, programming filters and effects to make ever-stranger sounds. He even released a Fiery Boys app that became fairly popular. He converted one of the small sheds into a server room and loaded it with racks of computers. I called it the beehive, because that's what it felt like when I went inside, buzzing with complexity and hidden activity.

River still loved his barn full of drums, and he spent hours there every day, meditating and drumming. He also started writing his own drum pieces. Every month, he hosted a drumming circle there, which became surprisingly popular among the locals.

Buck moved his recording equipment from Atlanta and took over another barn. He soundproofed the walls, then he redesigned the interior to have a control room, various recording spaces, and a lounge. Of course, he fell in love with the place and started spending every day there, writing and recording music. More and more of his songs got picked up by other bands, and he was negotiating with another movie to do the score. I was happy that he could write and play while enjoying the seclusion he craved.

With three of the Fiery Boys living so close to each other, they also found opportunities to play together. They jammed on occasional evenings and got a gig at a local bar, just for fun. Buck and I sang vocals.

In order to keep our playing out of the public eye, we never announced when we would appear, so that no one could count on seeing us. We played when we played, and the folks in town were good with that.

I got a job selling luxury cars in Minneapolis. The commute was pretty far, so I only went in a few times a week. But I loved it, and so did the dealership. After all, in addition to being an experienced saleswoman, I now had a minor level of fame as the woman who rode on the Fiery Boys bus up to the very end.

I also kept writing the Fiery Boys blog, commenting on the incredible trip that the band had undertaken and reporting on other bands that came through Minneapolis. A local newspaper even asked me to review music for them. Given my level of notoriety, the column quickly grew in popularity, and before I knew it, I had become a syndicated music critic. I didn't even need a diploma—the fame from the tour gave me all the credibility I needed.

Yes, the Fiery Boys were once again famous. In the six months since the spectacular explosion of the tour bus and Chuck's nearly fatal incident, the band had become phenomenally popular. "Painted Flames" was a hit everywhere, often accompanied by a video of the burning bus. It's a sorry comment on our society that the story of Inferna's suicide brought her and the band much wider recognition. Jason couldn't have bought publicity like that if he'd tried.

With the band hot, once again, Jason wanted to organize another tour. But it was too late. That bus had already departed, even for Chuck.

And speaking of Chuck, he recovered nicely and found a new hardcore band called Royal Arse. They were much less popular, but were about to do a big music festival with Alejandro and Talia Dare, two famous rock and roll heartthrobs. Imagine all those sexy singers on the same bill! Chuck was primed to take his new band into the big time, and I had no doubt he could do it. He even stopped by to visit us whenever he swung through Minneapolis.

But there was something else about Chuck that really surprised me: he settled down and got a steady girlfriend. One of my girlfriends, in fact. No, not Kira. Chuck fell for Jo! It happened like this. . .

After Chuck got out of the hospital, he contacted Jo to get a copy of the voyeur video she had made. His had been destroyed with the bus, but he really liked it and wanted it back.

Jo arrived in person to deliver the goods, and she used the video to seduce Chuck. This made her only the second woman to ever have sex alone with him. He found it exciting to see the same woman in a video and in real life, and he asked her to stay with him for a while and help him with his sexual issues. So Jo took the "job."

Things between them were cool at first. Chuck kept having orgies, and Jo treated him with as much professional distance as she could stand. She was diligent and patient while they worked on his issues. But over time, he realized that he enjoyed the orgies less and less, especially when Jo made more videos for their boudoir. So, much to Chuck's surprise, he and Jo started to have a relationship. They didn't live together, but they visited each other pretty often. And the last time I saw Chuck, he admitted that he didn't want anyone else. I guess it took a couples therapist to make this happen.

And Kira may not have landed the rocker of her dreams, but she did find someone from the band. Vaughan. I suppose I might have seen that coming if I'd been paying attention. The two of them had been flirting since that first night when I'd won the contest. He'd also been her bodyguard when she'd infiltrated Inferna's organization, and she'd spent her second night in Atlanta with him. So that weekend had yet another good outcome.

Something about the smiling bodyguard appealed to Kira, and he was just as smitten. He showed up at her electronics store the week after the tour ended and he never stopped guarding her body.

And me? I couldn't have asked for anything more. I got to be a music writer. I got to live with the three best Fiery Boys. And I got to marry the gorgeous and talented Buck Morris. The perfect combination of sexy lover, rock-and-roll hero, and best friend forever.

Fiery Boys

2014 Tour Schedule

Sun	Mon	Tue	Wed	Thu	Fri	Sat
					May 30 Boston	May 31 New York City
June 1 New York City	June 2 Pittsburgh	June 3	June 4 Detroit	June 5 Chicago	June 6 Chicago	June 7 Minne-apolis
June 8 Kansas City	June 9	June 10 Denver	June 11 Denver	June 12	June 13 Salt Lake City	June 14 Boise
June 15 Seattle	June 16 Seattle	June 17	June 18 Portland	June 19	June 20 San Francisco	June 21 San Francisco
June 22 San Jose	June 23 San Jose	June 24	June 25 Los Angeles	June 26 Los Angeles	June 27 Las Vegas	June 28 Phoenix
June 29 Albu-querque	June 30	July 1 Dallas	July 2 Dallas	July 3 Houston	July 4 New Orleans	July 5 Atlanta
July 6 Atlanta	July 7	July 8 Charlotte	July 9 DC			

About the Author

After completing my *Westerley* trilogy, I didn't have to think very hard about what to write about next: rock and roll! It was an obvious choice, because I was once the lead singer of a California garage band. Of course, the things that happen in this book never happened to me, but it was fun to pretend.

After a lifetime of reading general fiction, I discovered romance at age 59 and fell in love with it. Now I fill my time reading and writing romance novels.

Life in Northern California is full of surprises, including my novels. I have been happily married for over thirty years, and we have raised two wonderful children. I honestly wouldn't trade places with anyone else, living or dead, real or imagined.